The Devil's Harvest

by
Don Wright

For Joe & Jona Burke
my Classic niece & her
perfect husband.

Best Wishes

Don Wright

Joe, remember Cry of the wild goose &
He did it his way.

New Way Publishing   Lancaster, OH

Chapter One

The long black Chrysler raced through the pre-dawn darkness, its wiper blades fighting the rain from the windshield. A tall man slouched behind the wheel, effortlessly guiding the car through the night. As he negotiated a sharp curve, his headlights picked up the faint glow of tail-lights rushing towards him.

A small foreign car was stalled in the middle of the road, apparently having been drowned out by the water that had overflowed the shallow ditch alongside the highway. In less than a second, his sharp, black eyes took in the scene before him, and he made his decision.

Without checking his speed, he swung the heavy car to the left and jammed the accelerator to the floor. The tires slipped on the soft berm, causing the car to fishtail back and forth as he plowed through the water standing in the road. The driver of the foreign car failed to get his window up in time to avoid being soaked by the screen of water that had been thrown up by the speeding Chrysler. The victim cursed savagely, not at the passing car, but at himself for buying the overgrown bug that had left him stranded.

Inside the new 1959 sedan, the driver breathed a sigh of relief. From the seat beside him, he took a pack of cigarettes, flipped one out and stuck it between his lips, showing for a second the perfect white teeth that were seldom seen. There had been little in this man's life to make him smile. He opened the vent glass and instantly the water began to dance up and down it.

As he heeded the oncoming stop sign, he snapped his lighter, touched the flame to the cigarette and inhaled deeply. When he turned left, his headlights reflected off the waters of the Ohio River. The car again picked up speed as it followed the highway alongside the river.

The rough clothes he wore seemed out of place on the luxurious upholstery of the car. He was dressed in black boots and faded Levi's. A western-type shirt with turquoise snaps completed the ensemble. This manner of dress would not have distinguished him from the other

1

inhabitants of the area where he was going, except for the snub-nosed Colt .45 revolver that rode easily under his left arm. It was held there by a soft leather holster and harness that had been designed exclusively for him. The .45 was no fancy-dan gun, but a stopper.

Ahead, a flashing arrow caught his attention, and he glanced at his gas gauge. Finding it almost "Empty," he swung into the truck stop. A face appeared at the driver's window and asked, "Fill it up, sir?"

"Yes, high test, please."

As the attendant went about filling the car, the driver stepped out, noting the musty smell of the river. Walking to the rear of the car he said, "I'll grab a quick coffee if the car won't be in your way."

It'll be fine right where it is. We have plenty of room," the attendant answered, wiping rain from his face. He was about to comment about the nasty night, but the man was already walking away.

Inside the restaurant pretty, young Irma Butler was serving breakfast to an assortment of truck drivers and construction workers. She strutted back and forth behind the counter, well aware of the thoughts the men were entertaining concerning her full figure.

In a booth near the front door, a tobacco warehouse bully and his married girlfriend were arguing about her flirting with the owner of the Bay Horse Bar earlier that evening. Irma was considering calling the manager to evict them when a tall, well-built man walked in out of the rain. The black hair, which grew to a widow's peak on his forehead, glistened with rain drops. He took a seat at the counter, pulled a napkin from the holder and wiped his face with it. Irma moved quickly to serve him, the argument in the booth temporarily forgotten.

Like all romantically inclined young women, she hoped that sometime a man would walk through that door with whom she could fall in love. She hoped he would be such a man as this one. As she stopped before him, he looked up into her eyes, and she joined the many women who had been fascinated by the mysterious world behind the face of Clay Barron.

"Black coffee, please," he said. His deep voice was pleasant to her ears.

She brought the coffee and asked, "Anything else? The doughnuts are fresh."

"Thank you, no," was the quiet answer.

"Bad night out." Irma attempted to engage him in light chatter. He merely nodded as he poured water into his coffee to cool it more quickly.

"He's in a hurry. Too bad," Irma thought to herself as she moved away. She would have liked for it to have been this one.

The man who had been arguing with his girlfriend had gone to the men's room, leaving her alone in the booth. When he disappeared through the door, she quickly left the booth and moved to the stool beside Clay.

"Mister," she asked hurriedly, "are you going down the road to Aberdeen?"

"You're wasting your time; I'm in a hurry," he answered as he drained his coffee cup.

Her voice took on the bleating tone of a sheep. "You've got me wrong, Mister. That fella' I'm with won't take me home and my husband is due to get off work in Maysville at seven o'clock. I just gotta' get home."

As Clay stood up he answered, "Sorry, I can't help you. Why don't you take a cab?"

"I don't have any money," she whined.

"I don't know what to tell you," he answered sarcastically. "You should have considered these problems before you went out screwin' around."

When Irma walked up to take Clay's money, she gave the woman a hateful look. Her boss didn't want those waterfront floozies hustling the customers who stopped here.

As she started toward the register to get Clay's change, Irma heard the woman's boyfriend give a harsh bellow, and as she turned around, she saw him swing a huge fist at the stranger. Irma had been brought up around the river, and fights were nothing new to her, but the grace and ease with which the stranger blocked the blow, and the almost gentle chop he delivered to the bully's Adam's apple with the cutting edge of his right hand, was a new way of fighting to her. The boyfriend was left hanging over the counter, his mouth working like a fish out of water. As the stranger walked back into the rain from whence he had come, Irma instinctively knew she would never see him again, and for this she was sad.

On the highway once again, Clay steered the car through Aberdeen and onto the bridge that crossed over into Kentucky.

As the speeding Chrysler's tires sang across the bridge, Clay's mind sped with them. It had been thirteen years since a heartbroken, vengeance-swearing boy had fled from those fog-shrouded mountains on the other side of the river.

When the car reached the end of the bridge, Clay veered east and pressed down on the accelerator. The big car responded and leapt ahead. As the Chrysler ate up the road, the face of the driver became fierce and sullen; the mouth had drawn up to a cruel, thin line. The fever for revenge burned out all other thoughts. It had taken years to get the charges against him dropped, and now he begrudged the time it took the surging automobile to get him to his destination.

Clay's thoughts drifted all the way back to the beginning for the reason of his being here on this lonely road tonight. He shook his head to clear his mind of the picture of his father lying dead in the mud of the school yard with Silas Hook standing over him with a gun. His thoughts continued on to the trial. These were the memories that brought a taste of bile to his mouth and the lust for blood to his heart.

*   *   *

Clay had been only fifteen years old when he sat beside Sheriff Billy Sutton when the county prosecutor tried Silas Hook for the killing of his father, Brack Barron. On the first day of the trial, Silas had swaggered in with a lawyer from Grayson and had stopped to chat with several spectators in the courtroom. When the proceedings got under way, the Grayson lawyer incessantly objected to the prosecutor's bumbling presentation of evidence in the case. It became immediately apparent that the prosecutor was badly outclassed.

When the Grayson lawyer presented his defense, he tore at the Barrons unmercifully. He pictured them as all killers and described in detail the vicious temper of Brack. He told the jury that if Silas hadn't shot him first, Brack Barron would have killed one of the Hooks with the knife he was wielding.

Although he was young and had never seen a trial before, Clay could tell things were going right for Silas Hook. He was going to go free.

Clay had sat stone still throughout the trial, except when he had been called on to testify. When he tried to relate the facts of the fight as they happened, he became enraged and confused by the constant harassment of the experienced defense attorney.

As Clay's anger reached the point of hysteria, the judge ordered him from the stand, and the prosecutor never called him again.

As the trial continued, Clay's distraught young mind began to form a plan that was soon to become a reality.

All eyes were on Silas as he stood up to receive the verdict. A murmur ran through the crowd as the foreman intoned, "Not Guilty."

A jubilant Silas Hook shook the hand of his lawyer, a smile of triumph spreading over his face.

Clay's hand had darted down, then up, with the swiftness of a striking copperhead. When it came up, it held the sheriff's gun. As he squeezed the trigger, the sheriff grabbed his arm. The bullet, meant for the space between Silas' eyes, struck him instead in the lower face, tearing out a chunk of cheekbone and ripping a long gash through his neck. He squealed like a stuck hog and floundered to the floor, where he tried to crawl behind the judge's bench.

Still hanging onto Clay's arm, the sheriff was fighting for his life. He knew that if he turned the gun loose, Clay would certainly kill Silas and anyone else who got in his way. Over and through the tables and chairs they fought. The sheriff was trying to take the gun, and Clay was trying to force it down to shoot him loose.

The spectators were standing aghast, watching the death struggle between the sheriff and the boy. The sheriff felt the gun begin to slip in his hand. In seconds, the straining boy would have the barrel pointing at his chest. From the look of wildness on Clay's face, the sheriff knew he was looking death straight in the eye.

"Help me, somebody!" the sheriff shouted.

Broken out of their trance by his commanding voice, several men sprang forward, wrestled Clay to the floor and took the gun from him, after which the sheriff handcuffed his hands behind his back.

With the help of a husky farmer, the sheriff began to half drag Clay from the court room. As they passed Silas, still on his knees, blood flowing through the fingers that held his shattered face, Clay screamed at him, "The next time I won't miss. I'll make the Little Sandy run red with your goddamn Hook blood."

Once inside the jail cell, the sheriff had stormed at Clay, "Now ya done it. I thought ya had more sense'n ta pull some trick like that."

He turned to the young farmer and said, "I gotta' git back over 'ta the court house fer a bit. I'll git back as soon as I kin. Don' let nobody in 'til I do git back."

Clay lay for a long time on the bunk, his rage still churning in his stomach. He felt like he was going to vomit. After what seemed an eternity, but was only a short period of time, the sheriff returned to the jail, opened the cell, crossed to Clay and unlocked his handcuffs. Clay sat up on the bunk as a commotion took place at the front door. His great-uncle, "Big Pap" Keaton, shoved the farmer aside with little effort and entered the jail, followed by Clay's great-aunt, Sarah."

"Come on, Clay, we's goin' home," bellowed Big Pap.

"Newt, now, listen ta me," the sheriff said. "Judge Holbrook has ordered Clay held for a hearin' at 10:00 o'clock tomorry mornin'. Don' do nothin' ta make it worse."

"He's only a boy. I won' have 'im in jail," roared Big Pap.

"Let's all simmer down now an' try ta figger some way ta make th' judge see that Clay didn' know whut he wuz doin' taday," reasoned the sheriff, trying to keep Big Pap under control.

"Pap, take me outta here now," pleaded Clay. "I wanna kill that son-of-a-bitch."

"Clay. Clay. Listen ta me, Boy," the sheriff begged. "I know how much ya loved yer paw. I know some day ya'll kill Silas, but not now—yer too young. Don' fight me, Boy. I wanna help ya. Clay, I'm yer friend; I allers wanna be. Don' make it so's I cain't help ya outta this."

"Are ta takin' me outta here or not, Big Pappy?" Clay's angry voice fairly spit the question.

Big Pap looked from the sheriff's set face to Clay and said, "Let's try it Billy's way first."

Clay turned his back to them and stared at the wall as the sheriff, with more soft words, convinced Big Pap to go home and return at 10:00 the next day.

At the appointed time the next morning, Clay stood between the sheriff and Big Pap in front of Judge Holbrook.

"Son, you're under age and first thing I am going to do is declare you a ward of the court," began the judge. "The next thing I am going to do is sentence you to the Boys' Reformatory. The length of your sentence depends on you. Give me your word that you will make no attempt to harm Silas Hook, and I'll make it a year. If you don't, I'll see that you stay there until you are twenty-one years old."

Looking into Clay's eyes, the judge asked, "Do I have your word?"

"No."

The black eyes glittered in a young face twisted by hate.

"Nobody—not nobody on God's green earth'll keep me from killin' 'im. You go on an' lock me up, an' that makes you standin' aside him, and you'll die with 'im when I git out."

The judge's face was white with controlled anger as he quietly answered, "I have tried to make allowances for your loss and confusion, but I find you incorrigible. It is as much for your protection as that of society that I sentence you to the Boys' Reformatory until the age of twenty-one, or until I'm convinced that you are no longer a menace to yourself or any other citizen."

Later, back at the jail, Big Pap was raging. Now it was Clay who calmed him and wiped away Aunt Sarah's tears.

"Ya understan', don' ya?" he asked them. "You know I couldn' promise what he wanted, evin if it wuz thirty years they gave me."

"I understand ya, Son. I shoulda busted ya outta here yesterday," Big Pap mumbled as he turned to go.

The crowd of idle curiosity seekers gathered outside the building fell back silently, leaving a path open to the stalking giant with a cloudy face. No one wanted to chance his wrath by questioning him about the happenings inside. Without looking back, Big Pap and Sarah continued walking toward their home on the side of Rainbow Mountain.

Clay was pacing in his cell when a reporter for a Cincinnati newspaper came in.

"The sheriff said it was alright for me to talk to you," he stated.

"Whadda ya want?" Clay asked, sullenly.

"My newspaper," the man explained, "has authorized me to give you $1,000.00 for your exclusive story on the killing of your father, and your sentence to the reformatory."

"No," answered Clay.

"But Son," the reporter argued, "$1,000 would come in handy when you get out."

"Mister," Clay hissed, as he grasped the bars with both hands, "any story I give you today wouldn' have no endin'. Some day when I'm a man, I'll come back here. Then I'll give ya a story that I promise you will have an endin'."

The venom fairly poured from his twisted mouth, and the uncontrollable rage danced and darted from his black eyes.

Larry Stein had interviewed many bad men, even in the death house. Never before had he felt the hair rise on the back of his neck as he did now. For nothing on earth would he trade places with Silas Hook.

That night, Clay's sleep was broken by the rasping sound of metal on metal. Grabbing a chair, he stood up on it at the rear window of his cell and looked into the sardonic face of Big Pap. He was standing on the back of his horse, his mighty arms forcing the hack saw through the steel bars at unbelievable speed. When the opening was big enough for Clay's body, he wriggled through and swung to the ground. Big Pap dropped nimbly into the saddle and guided the horse towards the hills, Clay running beside him.

A figure sitting in the shadows of a doorway across the street from the jail smiled as he took out the Bull Durham and rolled a cigarette. Smoking contentedly, the sheriff continued his nightly rounds.

That night, before he fled the mountains, Clay Barron had sworn eternal vengeance against the entire Hook clan.

* * *

As the memories of the past swirled through Clay's mind, the night began to slip behind the hills and the dawn of the new day came. Now, he was traveling into the bowels of the hill country. The highway followed the valley floor, bordered on each side by mountains of timber, but he was unconscious of the beauty around him.

With the passage of time, the car began to climb, winding its way around and around the mountain, continually going up. When he reached the top, he encountered a Y in the road. The highway to the left ran down into Wolf Creek. The road to the right took its curving way around the Brown Ridge. He swung right and slowed the speed of the car as the tires began to squeal on the sharp curves. Many a drunk or wild driver had taken his last ride off one of the cliffs on Brown Ridge. As he reached the end of the ridge, the road went straight down. Now he could see the town below.

As the long black hood tilted downward, he muttered to himself, "Sons-of-bitches. I'm no kid on this trip."

The town was built on the side of two hills with a small river separating them. It looked somewhat bigger now than the last time he had seen it. The sign ahead read "Hookville."

Clay Barron drove slowly into the small town. His black eyes missed nothing as they flashed from one side of the street to the other.

"Not much change," he thought. "Same stores with the same names on the front."

When he reached the center of town, he pulled to the curb and parked. At the bottom of the hill was the bridge that spanned the Little Sandy. On his right was the courthouse. Beside it stood the same little jail. The bars had been welded and repaired so many times there was no pattern to them anymore. Hill men had never liked being closed in, and the broken and repaired bars told the story of those who had chosen not to remain. He had been one of those who had fled.

On his left was a clean-looking restaurant. Beside it stood a movie theater. That was new.

Clay realized he hadn't eaten for hours and decided that this would be as good a time as any. He reached into the backseat and got his raincoat and slipped it on as he stepped out of the car. It was still misting.

He breathed deeply. Nowhere did the air smell so clean as here in the mountains. Turning, he strode across the street and entered the restaurant.

Larry Stein came into the Cincinnati newspaper office as usual that morning. His ulcer hurt, and he was miserable.

"This business is going to hell," he thought. "There's just nothing going on."

On his desk was a telegram. He opened it absently, but his mind snapped taut as he read:

ENDING OF THE STORY I PROMISED YOU NOW GOING TO PRESS
                                    /s/ Clay Barron

"Teddy," he bellowed at the startled office boy. "Go to the morgue and get me my file on the Barron and Hook feud."

Chapter Two

"Time shore does seem ta slip away as a person gits older," thought Billy Sutton as he tore another leaf from his calendar.

"Spring is here agin, an' these ol' bones shore can tell it."

He walked across the room and stood looking out the window of his office that was located on the second floor of the courthouse. He was proud of the sign on the window that read 'Billy Sutton, County Sheriff.'

He was a man of small stature and slight build. His gaunt face was topped by a head almost void of hair. Glasses now covered the once piercing blue eyes. Although thin and small, he feared no man. For years, through his sheer courage, he had demanded and received the respect of some of the most dangerous men who ever lived in one of Kentucky's toughest counties.

Three sheriffs in succession had died violent deaths before he took office. Hoot Oliver, who lived on the Little Brushy, had killed a man when he refused to marry his youngest daughter, who was in a family way. Joe Bob Black, sheriff at that time, had gone to arrest Hoot. Hoot was hiding in the cellar of his home. When Joe Bob found him there, Hoot shot and killed him.

Joe Bob's older brother, Clifford, succeeded in getting himself appointed sheriff in order to make it legal for him to go after Hoot. He had no intention of arresting him; he only wanted to kill him. After hunting him through the hills for two days, Clifford found him, only to meet the same fate as his brother.

For some time after that, the county was without a sheriff. Then a Texan, who had made a big name as a tough game warden, heard about the sheriff-killing county in the backwoods that was so violent they couldn't get anyone to take the job. He packed his guns, put on his cowboy boots, big Stetson hat and headed for Hookville. After his arrival, he had no trouble securing the office of high sheriff.

The next day he went after Hoot, and when he didn't return that night, some of the men went to look for him the next day. They found him dead. No one ever knew whether Hoot killed him, or whether it had just been someone who didn't like the idea of a sheriff who wore a Stetson and cowboy boots.

Billy Sutton had been a logger most of his life, and was well known as the best mule man in the area. He had long nursed the ambition to be sheriff, but never had the nerve to put his name on the ballot. His wife, Elviney, wasn't too happy when he told her he was going to apply for the job. Like all mountain women, however, she relented when she realized it was what her husband really wanted.

Hoot Oliver had become so cocky he even ventured into town now, knowing there were two murder warrants and one suspicion of murder filed against him. He enjoyed the notoriety and the way people whispered when he passed.

When a mountain man wears his bib overalls buttoned at the sides, it usually means he's just another hard-working farmer. When the sides are left unbuttoned, its often not for ventilation, but for quick access to the gun being carried on a belt around the waist and hidden by the bib.

After being sworn in, Billy Sutton walked from the courthouse in search of Hoot, who he had heard was in town. He found him on the street in front of Hutchinson's store. Knowing that he was on trial before the whole town, Billy wasted no time. His future as a law man depended on how he handled this situation.

"Hoot," he called, "you're under arrest for murder."

The tough old wart hog gave Billy a broken-toothed grin and reached beneath the bib of his overalls for his gun. In the ensuing gun battle, the new sheriff was shot twice before his job was thirty minutes old, but old Hoot lay dying in the strret.

"Allers knowed ya was a fiesty leetle bastard," muttered Hoot, as he coughed and blew blood bubbles through his lips.

"Don' sweat this, huh, Billy? I never wanted ta kick off frum bein' sick abed nohow."

The grizzled old killer noted the gathering crowd as he said, "Shore is a heap o' people lookin' at me."

He attempted to raise a hand in farewell to the onlookers, but it fluttered and fell back. The old man's head rolled to one side and Hoot Oliver died, but a sheriff was born.

Billy would be sixty-five before fall. He was known all over the county as a fair man.

"Word good as gold," everyone said.

This was to be his last term. For twenty-four years he had served as sheriff. No sheriff had a right to live that long in this county. His one failure in office had been in trying to call an end to the Barron and Hook feud.

As he looked out the window, a big black car pulled alongside the curb and stopped. He leaned forward, trying to see the driver.

"Never seen thet car aroun' here afore," he thought.

The car door opened and a man stepped out, pulling on a raincoat. Billy strained his eyes to see the man better. The man turned and walked across the street. There was no mistaking it now. The man's stalking, light-footed stride and slightly rolling shoulders—it was like seeing the walking ghost of Brack Barron. That had to be Clay.

"Elviney. Quick. Look out th' winder," he exclaimed as his wife came up beside him.

"Look thar. See thet man goin' into Upton's Cafe? Clay Barron—thet's who thet feller is. Shore as hell's apoppin', thet boy's come home."

He continued, "I wuz certain he'd come home sooner or later when they fetched thet big tombstone and put it in Brack's grave a few years back. I knowed fer certin it waren' goin' ta be long when I got them papers from Frankfort last week droppin' them ol' charges agin' 'im."

As Elviney watched Clay cross the street, she felt the age-old dread that comes to every woman when she knows her man is in danger. The killings would start all over again, and Billy would be in the middle.

Unaware of her thoughts, Billy went on. "Clay's bin payin' th' taxes on that damn mountain of his fer all these years. I nivver could find out whar th' money come frum. It was allers th' same; a check from some lawyer in a way-off town. It's finally come, Elviney. Thet boy allers had so much of Devil John apoppin' outta 'im thet no power short of death kin stop 'im now."

Elviney Sutton was a plain little woman whose care and attention to the county prisoners was well known. No man had ever sawed through the bars of the jail because he was underfed.

Her face showed concern as she turned to her husband and asked, "Billy, why cain't he jest let it be? Why do all of 'em have ta be alike? Too much pride. That's what's allers bin th' trouble with the Barrons," she answered herself.

The sheriff reached for his gun belt on the desk and strapped it around his thin middle.

I'm gonna go over an' chat with th' boy," he said. "Mebbe I kin git this thing stopped afore it starts. No, I cain't stop it, but ennyhow I orta do ma job an' try."

Elviney moved closer and touched him on the arm as she cautioned, "Be awful careful, Billy. He ain' gonna' be th' same little feller thet used ta foller ya all over town. Recollect how he turned on ya after th' jury let Silas loose? He'd a kilt ya fer certin thet day ta git at 'im."

"Clay wasn't hisself thet day," Billy answered. "I jest happen't ta stand between 'im and 'im gittin' ta Silas, thet's all. Thet boy and I wuz awful close. He'd never do me a hurt apurpose."

"Man alive," Billy reminisced, "thet boy shore wuz somethin' thet day. It was like grabbin' aholt of a young panther. I'll wager he's a tom-cat's kitten now."

When Clay entered the restaurant, there were only six people there. He didn't know any of them. He chose a table at the far end of the room, removed his coat, tossed it over the back of a chair and sat down.

Alongside the rear wall was a large aquarium with many brightly colored fish drifting aimlessly about. Anytime Clay saw something caged, he had a suppressed desire to free it.

"Nothing in the world," he thought, "should be the confined pet of anyone. Why should the life of any creature be denied its own personal happiness and pleasure of living, even for man?"

The waitress was telling about her big night in Ironton the Saturday night before. Clay thought to himself, "I'll bet she's leaving out the best part."

When she finished her story, she sauntered over to take his order, patting her hair in place with both hands. He ordered a bacon and tomato sandwich, promising himself to look for hairs before he ate it.

"Why the hell do waitresses have to put their hands on their heads before they serve the food?" he wondered.

The sandwich and coffee came, and he ate in silence. All eyes in the room were on him. Not many strangers came through here, and no one seemed to recognize him yet.

A lanky youth in overalls and a work shirt shuffled up to the juke-box and dropped in a dime. A hillbilly singer wailed a broken-hearted lament. When the record finished, everyone went back to staring at Clay.

The restaurant door opened, and through it walked a short, thin man who seemed to be off balance from the weight of the .45 on his hip. This was no strange face to Clay; it had only aged a bit. Clay could see the uneasiness on his old friend's face.

As the sheriff approached the table, Clay stood up and held out his hand.

"Uncle Billy," he said, "I sure am glad to see you."

Billy Sutton took the offered hand in both of his and squeezed it hard and long.

"Little Clay Barron," he smiled. "All growed up, ain't ya? I tol' Elviney a bit ago whin I seen ya walk acrost th' street, thar goes a Barron. Ain't no one else walks like the Barrons. Welcome home, Clay."

"Thanks, Uncle Billy."

"I knowed you'd be a droppin' by soon. I jest got word up from Frankfort that them charges agin ya had been dropped. How'ja git thet done?" questioned Billy.

"Money, Uncle Billy, money," answered Clay quietly.

"Myrtle, fetch me a cuppa coffee with a leetle dab a cream, an' fill up Clay's cup again," Billy called to the waitress.

She hurried to comply, for Billy Sutton was a man of importance around here.

When the sheriff had seated himself, he sipped his coffee in silence for a long moment. He then looked up into the hard, cold eyes across the table and asked, "Ya gonna be aroun' here fer a spell, Clay?"

The younger man attempted to change the subject by asking, "How is Aunt Elviney?"

"Fine, Clay. She's shore alookin' forward ta seein' ya. Why don'cha bunk in with us? Thar's plenty a rooms."

"Thanks, Uncle Billy. I'll stop and see her soon. I'm in kind of a hurry to get on up to the mountain. I want to go to the graveyard before dark."

Now the lids drooped ever so slightly over the cold black eyes; the lips curled up from the corner of his mouth in an unconscious snarl. He fought to control himself, as he always had to when the thought of his father's being in a grave came to him. The blood pumped into his face until the veins stood out on his forehead.

The sheriff's eyes dropped to Clay's hands. They were balled into fists, clenched so tightly that they caused the muscles in his neck to stand out in ridges. This man was, at this moment, a killer. In his mind now was the picture of Silas Hook dying before his gun. It was warm inside the restaurant, but Billy Sutton shivered.

Clay saw the sheriff observing his hands, so he slowly unclenched them, and his whole body once again relaxed.

Clay smiled at Billy and said, "I really must be going. It's a long walk, and I want to take my time and enjoy it. By the way, will my car be all right where it is until I get back? I'll leave the keys with you."

The sheriff saw that Clay smiled only with his mouth; the smile never reached the rest of his features. Here was a man holding inside himself a hate that had been festering for years. Unlike the other Barrons, he had learned to control himself. This man had come home worldly and intelligent. This made him doubly dangerous.

Billy could see in his face that he wanted to rip and tear with his bare hands. This man had come home to kill. It would be useless to try to dissuade him, but Billy Sutton understood. Had he been blessed with a son, he would have wanted him to be no different.

"Shore, Clay, leave th' car right thar' whar' it's at. I'll keep a watch on it fer ya. Them thar' roads up the mountain is one thing that ain't changed none since ya bin gone. They's just as bad as ever," Billy told him.

"That's good," Clay answered. "No roads means few visitors, and that's how I want it. That doesn't mean you, Uncle Billy. You can come to Rainbow Mountain and be welcome anytime."

"I know that, Clay, and I thank ya. Th' friendship I had with ya when ya wuz a kid is still one of my most thought-of posessions. I shore do hope ta continue on with it now."

"Uncle Billy, I always have and always will consider you one of my best friends," Clay answered him.

Turning to the waitress, Clay asked, "Could I have a box of Dutch Masters?"

"Shore thing, Mister," she said, her dirty teeth showing in a grin as she handed him the cigars.

He pushed the box across the table saying, "A peace offering for trying to shoot you that time in front of the whole county."

"Home twenty minutes an' yore already a tryin' ta bribe th' law. Jest like a Barron," the sheriff laughed.

After they finished their coffee, Clay put on his raincoat and he and the sheriff stepped back into the street and crossed to Clay's car. It had stopped raining, so Clay removed his coat and opened the trunk and put it inside.

The trunk was full of luggage and a long, plaid garment bag that was bulging with clothes. It was apparent to the sheriff that Clay had come home to stay.

Holding out the keys to the sheriff, Clay said, "I'll be back in a couple of days, Uncle Billy. Use the car if you want to."

The sheriff took the keys, saying, "Thanks, but I've got a jeep th' county bought fer me ta use. I'd never be able to figger out a fancy machine like this'n, anyhow."

Clay turned to go, but Billy caught him by the arm and turned him around so that he could watch his face.

"Clay," he said, "you allers meant an awful lot ta me; kinda' like th' kid I never got. Whut I'm gonna say now I wan' ya ta fully understan'. I'll put up with no more killin' in this here county. Things aroun' here has changed, too. Th' ol' days is gone. I ain't had no trouble with th' Hooks since yer pa died."

"You said that wrong, Uncle Billy." Clay's voice was almost a whisper. "The proper word is 'murdered.'"

"That wasn't whut th' Court an' jury come to, Clay. You wuz thar— they said 'self-defense.' Thar' waren't nothin' ya could do then, and ain't nothin' ta be done now ta change that. Why don' ya pay a visit ta yer mountain an' go back to wherever ya bin? You cain't do yer pa no good now. Don' mess up yer life, Clay," Billy pleaded.

"You're wrong again," said Clay. "This isn't something that's been dead for years. It's been alive in me for thirteen years. I've thought of and prepared for nothing else. I've learned well; I know the law of 'self-defense.' I have in Lexington now on retainer the finest trial lawyer in the state of Kentucky. In a Lexington bank is enough money to pay for a dozen trials. Don't worry about it, Uncle Billy, they will all be 'self-defense.'"

As Clay turned to walk away, the sheriff called after him.

"Think about whut I've said, Clay. Look in thet damn Barron grave-yard of you'rn an' you tell me if'n ya think it's worth it."

Chapter Three

The street sloped sharply down hill from the courthouse to the bridge. Clay felt the weight of many eyes on him as he went striding along. In a few hours, his return would be the talk of the county. He knew these people well. Their gossip alone would eventually force a fight, from pride, if nothing else. Sooner or later, one of the Hooks would come for him, and that one would be the first to die.

When Clay reached the bridge, he walked to the middle and stood leaning on the iron railing, peering nostalgically into the clear waters of the Little Sandy River. The river wound its way around the hill at the end of the bridge, and flowed through twin rows of green willows to the falls directly under the bridge.

Here it swirled and foamed over the slate rock before being once more quieted and cleared by the deep pool beyond. It seemed so long ago that he had swum and fished in these waters with his father.

At this moment, Clay felt gratitude for the richness that had once been his life here in the hills, yet a haunting loneliness of spirit assailed him as he contemplated his future.

"Don't worry, Old River," he whispered. "I haven't forgotten my promise to you."

His eyes lifted to the old grist mill that sat on the left bank. It was deserted now, and sparrows were flying in and out of the broken windows. The front of the mill sat level with the street, while the back was built on heavy timbers set in the ground. To make the floor level inside, a space about five feet high had been left under the mill. The horse weeds grew seven feet high along the back of the mill in the summer, making a perfect camouflage for the poker game that took place there every Sunday afternoon.

As Clay thought back to the poker games, he walked further along the bridge until he could see up the hill beyond the mill.

"Yes, there it is," he thought. "The same house. The smokehouse is gone, though. I wonder if she still lives there."

His mind lingered on that day in the past.

* * *

Clay's father, Brack Barron, was best described as a paradox. He had lived by the same code of behavior that had ruled the lives of the Barron family for generations, but he never asked, nor even expected, any other individual to live the same way. By the standards of most people, he was a hard man, but to some persons of a more dove-type nature, he even appeared cruel.

Only Clay knew the full extent of the tenderness and understanding his father possessed. He was extremely affectionate, and through his words and actions, Clay was never in doubt of his complete love. He could read a book, tell a story or bind a stubbed toe as sensitively as any mother.

Most Kentuckians find it difficult to speak of or demonstrate love, but Brack had never felt less a man because of the kisses he bestowed on his son's cheek.

The rearing of Clay had always been foremost in Brack's mind. His methods were not the same as those brought over by the Puritan fathers, but for the most part they were effective.

As a child, Clay had been frightened of thunder and lightning. Many times he had sought the strong arms and soft, reassuring voice of his father during a storm. On one such night, Brack had led Clay, who was nearly petrified with fear, into the woods during a violent electrical storm. As they stumbled over the dark, rain-drenched hills, the thunder rolled and the lightning flashed its jagged arrows through the sky.

"See, Clay," Brack had shouted, "thar's nothin' ta be afeard of."

At that moment, Brack had stumbled over a clump of green ferns and fell headfirst into the leaf-filled hollow below, where he rolled over on his back and started to laugh hilariously. Clay had begun to laugh, too, as he jumped over the edge of the hollow and rolled down on top of his father. As they lay there beneath the trees, whose leaves had given up holding the rain, Clay's fears of the storm had been washed away.

Brack continued, "As I wuz about ta say afore our slide, ya know better'n anybody thet when it comes ta religion, I ain't much count, but if'n thar is a God an' He should want somethin' like me up thar with 'im, I hope he puts me in charge of the thunderin' and lightnin' detail. Man, wouldn' thet be a real feelin' ta stand on the highest cloud in heavin an' throw thunder and lightnin' with both hands?"

Brack had wanted Clay to be a man, and he never let his affection interfere with discipline. There would be no coddled or spoiled Barron. Above the mantle had been a long, slender willow branch which had been brought up from the river below.

When Clay was naughty, as all boys invariably are, he would receive what Brack chose to call his "willow switch tea." The dose of tea seldom had to be given twice for the same offense.

Brack seldom drank, but when he did, anything went. He would gamble with anyone on anything. He boasted that he could whip anyone in the county. Some men had questioned this, but only once.

Clay had always remained inconspicuously in the background when his father was drinking. If he passed out, Clay would enlist the assistance of someone not so drunk to help him load him on their horse. Clay would then take him home. Brack had always told him, "When I'm drunk, you'll hav' ta be master of our mountain."

Clay would never forget that Sunday evening when everyone was drinking and gambling. His father had been lucky and was winning most of the money. Due to lack of funds, everyone had now dropped out except Brack and Ezra Fultz.

Ezra was a big, slow-witted, twenty-four-year-old coal truck driver with a compulsion to gamble and drink whiskey. He lived across the street on the hill in front of the mill. More than once his fifteen-year-old wife, Hallie May, had hounded him out of the game. Later, he could be heard thrashing her for making a fool of him in front of the other men.

Brack and Ezra were bumping heads, and Clay could see that Ezra was about out of money. During the next hand, Brack again poured it on. Clay had thought at that time that he was trying to run Ezra out to finish the game. Clay recalled wondering why his father was acting so intoxicated when he had drunk nowhere near his capacity.

On the last raise, Ezra had run out of money and couldn't call, even though he had a good hand. With what was showing, he had the pot won. He tried to borrow money, but had no luck, as the others were all too drunk or too broke to pay any attention to him. He wanted to put his horse up for the last call, but Brack wouldn't go for it.

"Thet stump-suckin' horse of you'rn would eat up our barn in two months, Ezra. Him I can do without. 'Course, ya do have somethin' I've kinda' had my eye on."

"Whaz zat?"

Ezra's face was dripping with perspiration now. He had to call that hand. That was why he was in this situation; he had to always see the last card.

Clay became tense as he watched his father shift his position so that he faced Ezra, with his feet planted in a manner to enable him to move freely in either direction. Knowing his father so well, Clay sensed the change in him that went unnoticed by the others.

"Why did he take that defensive position?" Clay wondered.

"Hallie May," Brack answered, never taking his eyes from Ezra's face.

"What 'bout Hallie May?" Ezra croaked hoarsely, half rising from his seat.

"Thet's th' bet. Th' pot agin' a night with yore Hallie May."

"Hell, no," Ezra shouted. "She's ma wife. I'll . . ." Then he stopped.

"Why not?" his whiskey-fogged brain reasoned.

"This here is one pot I'm gonna win, anyhow. It'll go a long spell ta gittin' me even. Barron's tryin' ta run me outta th' game so's he kin buy th' pot. Now he's tryin' ta git me ta make a bet he knows I cain't make so's ta make a fool outta me. This here's one bluff I'm gonna ram down 'is throat. Hope he chokes on it."

Ezra smiled knowingly, "Hit's a deal. Tarn over yer cards."

Clay remembered how his father's black eyes glittered in concentration on Ezra's face as he turned up his cards.

Ezra's breath whistled between his teeth like air escaping from a balloon. He stood up, bumping his head on the floor of the mill. He didn't seem to notice. He turned and stumbled around the side of the mill toward the street leading up to his house.

Brack shouted after him, "I'll be thar' 'bout 7:30!"

Clay remembered how his father had taken him uptown then for a meal. By this time, most of the town knew of the bet. Everyone was wondering if Brack would try to collect, and what would happen if he did. Clay, too, had wondered what his father had intended to do.

At 7:30 they finished their meal, and Brack stood up.

"Come on, Clay, it ain't polite to keep a lady awaitin'."

"Ya goin' through with it, Paw?" Clay asked, wide-eyed.

"'Course, Son. Let this be a lesson to ya. Don' never gamble nothin' thet means somethin' to ya. Money is the only thing thet should be gambled with. It ain't got no value."

Clay walked with his father down the main thoroughfare and turned left on the street that ran alongside the mill. There were people watching the horseshoe game taking place in front of the mill. They pretended not to notice Clay and his father as they came down the street.

Clay had turned as if to join the spectators at the horseshoe game when his father said, "No, Clay, you come along with me."

Without a word, Clay followed his father up the path toward Ezra's house. Brack ignored the men staring after them. As they approached the porch, Ezra came through the door. In his hand was a long wooden-handled butcher knife.

Thet's as fur as yore a'comin', Brack," he warned.

"Ya git on outta here. Ya know I was only funnin' when I made thet bet."

"Ya made a bet, Ezra. I don' wanna' have ta kill ya ta collect it," said Brack, as he started around the porch to where the steps were.

Ezra leaped off the porch toward him. Brack reached up on the edge of the porch and grabbed a stick of wood from the pile there. As Ezra slashed at his face, Brack swung to the right and smashed Ezra across the arm as he went by. The knife went spinning to the ground.

Before Ezra could get his balance, Brack kicked his feet out from under him. He held down the ranting Ezra, as sobbing curses of frustration escaped him. Brack had him lying face down on the ground with his left arm twisted up in the middle of his back.

When he stopped struggling, Brack lifted him to his feet, shoved him into the smokehouse, slammed the door shut and shot the heavy steel bolt home.

The smokehouse was made out of thick heavy logs sealed with blue clay that had hardened like concrete. There were no windows. Ezra made several lunges against the door, but it held. He was done.

Holding his broken arm, he crawled over to a corner and curled up in a ball as if he had a stomachache, and whimpered like a pup that had been taken from his mother's milk.

Brack said, "Ya wait out here, Clay."

Clay sat on the edge of the porch with his legs dangling down, ignoring the raucous laughter of the group in front of the mill.

He could hear the murmur of voices coming from inside. Sex was nothing new to Clay. He had observed animals in the act for as long as he could remember. Lately, he found his mind dwelling on the subject. More and more he found himself daydreaming about girls.

His father had brought women to their mountain for years. One time he had peeked through a keyhole and watched Brack and Les Pritchard's wife, Flora, as they heaved and strained against each other on the bed.

He recalled how Flora's breath had come in loud snorting gasps as she flung herself up to meet the down-rushing body of his father. By the time she reached her climax, she was squealing almost as loud as that little bay mare of Eldon Grissom's had the week before when he held her head while a mammouth jack mounted her. His father's arched body, in the heat of passion, had somehow reminded him of the jack.

Brack had been in there for ten minutes. He could still hear voices inside. He had never thought of his father as being much of a talker.

He remembered how Hallie May looked as she walked around in her tight sweaters and skirts. His mind imagined all kinds of scenes about to start inside.

He was so deep in his own thoughts that he was startled into jumping off the porch when he heard his father's footsteps behind him.

"Wha' ja say, Paw?" Clay asked.

"Well, Son, it jest occurred to me awhile back thet I bin neglectin' one of the mos' 'portant parts of yer bringin' up. Ya bin aroun' these hills too long not to know some things, but in this here game knowed as love and life, it's the experience that counts."

"I suckered thet Ezra inta this little deal 'cause from whut I heerd this Hallie May is one hot little piece. I don' want no dead-ass cow gittin' aholt of ya the first time. It don' make no sense that a little patch of hair 'atween a woman's legs will make friends kill each other and even kings git down from thar throne, but thet's whut it duz to a man."

"So's th' only defense is to be so good thet the little patches come a lookin' fer ya 'stead of makin' a fool outta ya. Half the wimmin a man gits in this life is through his reputation. Git a reputation as a luvver and wimmin will crawl over each other ta git ta ya. Today, Son, yore ol' daddy is startin' yer reputation. How fer ya kin go with it from here depends on what's 'atween yer legs and how ya use it. I changed yer diapers long enuff ta know thet ya got th' equipment."

"Everythin' is all fixed up with Hallie May. Ya go on inside. I'll sit out here on th' porch fer a spell an' then mos' likely go on home. Be shore an' tell Hallie May not ta let Ezra outta th' smokehouse in th' mornin' 'til ya git a good head start ta home."

As Clay walked up the steps on the porch and crossed to the door, he hesitated. Brack, seeing Clay pause, continued, "Looky thar' at thet buncha dum' bastards down thar' agawkin'. They'd give thar left nut ta trade places with ya. Allers remember, Son, thet it's them with guts thet gits, an' them without guts gits got."

Clay's left eye closed in a wink at his father. He squared his shoulders, stepped inside and closed the door.

Brack took out his pipe, filled it with tobacco and struck a kitchen match on his pants leg before drawing the smoke deep into his lungs.

"Hit's shore agonna do ma ol' heart good ta see thet boy aruttin' through these ol' mountains," he mused to himself. "Guess ma reputation with the wimmin won' be of no hindrance ta 'im."

By the time he had finished his pipe, the spectators and horseshoe pitchers had drifted away below. As he walked down the path to the street, he paused by the door of the smokehouse. The whimpering inside disgusted him. He spit over his shoulder and walked on.

Chapter Four

Hallie May Fultz had been born on Middle Fork. She was the fourth child of eleven born to Rufus and Nellie Balls. She was fourteen-years-old when she first began planning to escape from home. In her pretty, round face was the bloom of youth.

Her eyes were blue above a pert little nose and a full, slightly pouting mouth. Her hair was cut in bangs and fell down on her shoulders, where it lay in a thick red mass. Unlike most redheads, she had no freckles anywhere on her body.

Her hips were beginning to flare out on each side of a flat stomach. Even the cheap print of her shapeless one-piece dress could no longer hide the swell of her budding breasts. As short as she was, someday she would get squatty and fat, but now looking at the graceful curves of her young body, no man thought of tomorrow. Each man was devising his own plans for today.

As long as she could remember, they had lived in a big old ramshackle building that her grandfather, Tom Begley, had built one summer. This occurred after a hellfire and damnation preacher had been through there and described to him what the Devil had in mind for him if he didn't repent his sins and follow the word of the Lord.

After being saved, Tom Begley had decided to go further than just repenting his many sins. He decided to build a church. Since there was no preacher on Middle Fork, he guessed that was just the way of the Lord letting him know that he had the calling.

Up and down Middle Fork he went, haranguing his neighbors about their ungodliness. He offered to cleanse them of all their sins—past, present and future, if they showed up every Sunday with tools and supplies to help build his new church.

The women of Middle Fork were his staunchest supporters. Each Sunday a group of red-eyed men and shining-eyed women met on the banks of the creek that ran down Middle Fork into the Little Sandy River. Beneath the big sycamore tree that stood in what was going to the churchyard, they sang hymns and listened as Tom Begley blessed them and the work they were doing for the Lord.

After the services, as the men set about the building of the church, Tom would walk among them, patting them on the back. He spurred them on with many a "God bless you, Brother," and "the Lord be with you, Sister."

It never occurred to him to do any work. After all, he had donated the ground that was his eighth of the old homeplace where the church would be located. Anyway, a man of God should have time for prayer. He would cross the creek at the shallow part that ran over the slate rocks. He had placed large stones there to walk across on. By stepping on the stones, he kept his feet dry. It wouldn't seem right for a preacher to be walking around with his shoes making a squishing sound.

On the other side of the creek, a stone cliff hung out twenty feet or more from the face of the hill. Here Tom had built an altar. He would go up there to pray every Sunday afternoon, being careful to stay in the sight of the working congregation below.

"This is the coolest place on Middle Fork," he had said to himself many times.

When the church was finished, Tom had immediately organized a revival. He was going to save the residents of the Middle Fork area, whether they liked it or not. Every night by the light of the kerosene lanterns he preached. Back and forth in front of the huge crowd he charged, his voice starting out at almost a scream, then dying down to barely a whisper as he ran out of breath. He seemed to begrudge the time it took to take another breath before returning to his attack on the Devil.

One night he became so self-possessed that he climbed up on the pulpit, stood shaking his fists and shouted a challenge to the Devil, daring him to enter the church and fight him for the souls of the men and women there.

Resembling a giant bird of prey, Tom stood poised on the pulpit for a moment in silence before leaping down and walking around the room. Talking in a loud, hoarse whisper, he said, "He's here in the room with us now. I can feel his evil presence."

A woman on the left side toward the front began shouting, "Praise the Lord." Others joined in. An old man of eighty stood up and began speaking in unknown tongues. He stood in a trance with his face upturned and his eyes closed, speaking in a language never heard by anyone in the room before.

The words sounded like, "Come see ya, come see ya, come see ya." The congregation believed he was talking directly with God. When he came out of the trance he would remember nothing; they never did.

That night Preacher Begley brought twenty-seven sheep into the fold.

As Tom Begley's fame spread through the hills, he was called on for revivals in other communities. He was always glad to go, as there was usually a donation for the revival preacher. On Middle Fork the most he could hope for was that someone would invite him home for a chicken dinner on Sunday.

On one of these trips he met Cora, Hallie's grandmother. She had a fairly good singing voice and played the guitar passably well. After a quick courtship, in which he convinced her that the match was made in heaven, they married. Cora traveled with him, playing and singing, until Hallie's mother, Nellie, was born.

After the birth of Nellie, Cora became ill, forcing their return to Middle Fork. Finding himself with no income, Tom rented a farm and tried to put out a tobacco crop. His flock thought it was all right for them to raise tobacco, but for their preacher to work in the tobacco field all week and raise hell about smoking on Sunday wasn't right.

As time went by, the once avid followers began to drift away.

Tom just didn't have the spark anymore. After a hard week's work in the fields, conducting the Sunday services had become a chore of which he was quickly tiring. One Sunday Tom failed to appear at the church, and no one came by his house to see why.

Arriving at the church the following Sunday, he found himself the only one there. He ambled around the room aimlessly, trying to recapture his lost spirit. Failing to do so, he decided to ride over to Hookville to play some poker. He had always loved to play poker before he had been saved. He might even get drunk.

After his backsliding, Tom found few people willing to help him. After the tobacco crop had been sold, he was asked to move. He had no choice but to move into the church that had been built on his property.

Hallie's mother, Nellie, lived in the church house with Tom and Cora until she married Rufus Balls. The newlyweds had made their home at a nearby logging camp where Rufus was employed. Preferring to spend time in bed with his new bride instead of working, Rufus was summarily discharged, which forced them to move in with her parents. They all lived together until Tom and Cora's deaths. Now Rufus and Nellie were rearing their family in the same church house in which she had grown up.

As long as Hallie could remember, the only partitioning in the room had been blankets strung on the wire. In the far right corner of the house was her father and mother's bed. The rest of the family slept on pallets on the floor.

The mattresses were made of bed ticking stuffed with corn shucks. All the quilts were made by piecing together rags and feed sacks with cotton sewn in the middle. They slept jammed together four or more to a pallet.

There always seemed to be two or three of the younger children who continually wet the bed. Here, to bathe more than once a week was unheard of. To add to the stench, Rufus had a big white enamel pot he kept beneath his bed in case of a bowel or bladder movement at night. Everyone used it, and by morning it would be brimming full. The lid had been lost long ago.

When Hallie woke up each morning, the odor would be almost unbearable. She always got up as soon as she awoke and took out the pot, often becoming nauseous on the way. She would then take a cake of homemade lye soap and go to the creek and scrub herself vigorously.

The worst times were when her father would go to Hookville and come home drunk. On these occasions he invariably made love to her mother. As Hallie lay in the dark listening to the mating of her parents, she would fervently hope that her mother wouldn't get caught again. Hardly a year went by that she wasn't either suckling one or carrying one. There were times that she had done both.

Hallie May thought constantly of running away. Each time she planned to leave, the sight of her mother screaming at the kids to help with the work always stopped her. Her mother needed her most of all, since she was the oldest girl. Then something happened that made her see how unimportant she really was to them. From now on she would look out only for Hallie May. She knew with certainty now that no one else would.

Her father, Rufus, had discovered a vein of coal running through the hill behind the old church house. He opened a mine there and dug just enough coal to sell for the essentials of existence. He had always thought of himself as capable of running a large mining crew and making big money. Since he had no cash with which to hire men, he convinced his youngest brother, Harry, To come to live with him and work in the mine.

Rufus had said that the mine was too much for him to operate alone. Actually, he hoped to get most of the work done by Harry. He had said for a long time that if he had more time for managing and figuring he could really put that mine on a paying basis.

When Ballard Balls named his youngest son Harry, he thought it was a great idea. So did all his other drunken cronies.

"Anything for a laugh," old Ballard always said.

Twenty years of hearing snickers every time someone mentioned his name had made Harry bitter and cruel. Bad luck seemed to have teamed up with his father to make his a miserable life.

He had been badly burned when he was a baby learning to walk. Left unattended in the house, he had fallen against a red hot coal stove, resulting in one side of his face and neck being a mass of scars. One ear was turned in flat against his head and the scalp above the same ear was bald halfway up his head.

Harry had never been with a woman. Even had he been handsome, what girl would have wanted to be known as "Mrs. Harry Balls?"

An example of Harry's cruelty showed up shortly after he came to live with his brother, Rufus. Rufus used an old mule named Barney to sled the coal off the hill from the mine down to where it could be loaded on a truck. Always before a good, steady worker, well broken to a man's voice, Barney one day ran away with a sled of coal and tore up the sled. When Rufus finally got him calmed down, he found that Barney's penis opening had been stopped up with blue clay, which prevented him from urinating.

Rufus ranted and raved so much trying to find out who was responsible for this act that one of the smaller boys, fearing a beating himself, confessed that he saw Harry do it. Rufus then laughed it off.

"Boys will be boys," he told Nellie. "No use upsettin' Harry by raisin' a big stink 'bout a little thing like thet."

"Besides," he reasoned to himself, "thet Harry shore kin dig hell outta thet coal."

One day sometime later Rufus went to Hookville to get some blasting powder for the mine. He needed it only because he had hidden the other powder from Harry to give himself an excuse for going. Before he left, he told Nellie to send Harry's dinner up to the mine by one of the children.

"No use havin' 'im waste good workin' time arunnin' up 'n down the hill," he explained.

As noon approached, Nellie fixed a bucket of buttermilk with corn pone crumbled in it for Harry's lunch. She called to Hallie May and told her to take it up to the mine to him.

Hallie May had been tending the fire under the big kettle down by the creek. They boiled their clothes in it before scrubbing them on a board. The big kettle was also used for rendering lard during hog-killing time. In addition, Nellie also made all her own soap in it. Before leaving the creek, Hallie stoked the fire around the kettle.

On her way to the house she paused to watch, without disapproval, one of her little brothers who had attached a long piece of thread to a captured June bug's leg. He tossed the bug in the air, and as it attempted to fly away, he held to the end of the thread, forcing it to fly in a buzzing circle above his head. When it became too exhausted to fly any longer, it fell to the ground and tried to crawl away. In a childish rage, her brother jumped on it with his bare feet.

She continued on to the house for the bucket before heading up the hill toward the mine. The road, cut out of the side of the hill, was dry at this time of year. Halfway up she looked down and below her she could see the tin roof of the house throwing off heat waves as the sun beat down. Her mother was bent over the tub now, scrubbing clothes on a scrub board.

"What a life she's alivin'," thought Hallie as she turned to climb the last half of the hill to the mine.

The dark mouth of the mine was at the end of the road. To one side the rocks, slate and all kinds of rubble from the mine had been thrown down the side of the hill until it had stacked up level with the road. A set of steel rails like those used on the railroad ran from about thirty feet outside the mine back to where they were digging the coal. They had an old railroad handcar with wooden racks built on the sides to haul the coal out of the mine.

They would pull the car back to where they were digging coal by hand, and as they dug the coal they would throw the big hunks in the car until they got it full. They would then wrestle it outside and unload it on the waiting sled. When the sled was full, Rufus would bring old Barney up and pull the sled down to where the truck came to load it.

As they had blasted further into the mountain, they hit a vein of water. They had dug a ditch alongside the rails that carried out most of the water from the mine, but there was always some that crept down the roof and made a steady dripping sound as it fell to the mine floor.

Hallie May stopped inside the mine entrance and allowed her eyes to adjust to the darkness ahead.

"Harry, can you hear me?" she shouted.

When there was no answer, she followed the rails further on back into the mine. She got the same feeling each time she came here. Maybe the roof would fall down behind her. Her father never did anything right.

"Whut if'n the beams holdin' th' ceilin' should give out?" she thought.

She looked behind her. The entrance showed only faintly in the distance now. Before her was a curve in the mine and beyond it was a wall of blackness. She stopped and stood still, holding her breath. She could hear the dripping of water and in the distance the sound of Harry's pick striking the coal.

"Harry," she shouted again. "Kin ya hear me?"

The sound of the pick stopped. Coming toward her presently was Harry. As the flame caught the draft from the entrance, the carbide light hooked to his miner's cap cast eerie shadows along the walls of the mine.

"I brung yer dinner, Harry," said Hallie, as he reached her.

Ain't Rufus got back frum town yit?" asked Harry, as he reached for the bucket of milk and pone.

"He hadn' when I lef' th' house," answered Hallie, as she turned to leave.

"Wait up a minute, Hallie," Harry said as he reached out and caught her by the arm.

"I wanna show ya the new vein we foun'. It's off'n the main shaft and dry. We got a big room dug out in thar' now. Shore'll be a heap better aworkin' in thar this comin' winter than in thet wet damp shaft we wuz diggin' in last winter."

The light from the dancing flame made Harry's face even more hideous. Hallie wanted to pull away and run back out into the sunlight. She hated this place, and Harry frightened her the way he was looking at her. As she began to pull away, she remembered how angry her father became when anyone upset Harry.

"Guess it won' hurt none to take a few minutes ta see it," she answered. "I'm none too anxious ta git back to thet hot sun and washin' nohow."

Harry followed the rails deeper into the mountain, holding on to Hallie's hand. He knew the mine so well he could go in and out without using a light, and never bump against any of the outcroppings of rock that reached out towards the rails. He turned to his right, into a cave-like cavern. They had dug out a big room there. There was a lantern hanging on a peg driven into the wall. His pick and shovel lay where he had dropped them when Hallie had called him.

He set the corn pone and milk down on a ledge without releasing Hallie's hand, and thought to himself, "Now's as good a time as I'll git. Rufus is gone and he don' never get back 'til late of a night when he goes to town. He won' wan' me ta leave, 'cause he's too damn lazy ta work. Thar' won' be little, if'n anythin' said 'bout it later. Nellie kin go ta hell. If'n she sez anythin', I'll tell Rufus 'bout thet time when I wuz afishin' down the crick and seen Elmer Ferguson slip into th' barn."

Harry remembered how he had watched out of idle curiosity until he saw Nellie come out of the house with her egg basket, heading for the barn. He had given them plenty of time, and then walked in on them. He often laughed when he recalled how Elmer looked running out of the barn, jerking at his bib overalls.

Nellie had set up in the hay and asked, "Ya gonna tell Rufus, Harry?"

"No, don' think so, Nellie," Harry had leered. "Seems ta me if'n yore gonna give it away, might jist as well keep it in th' family."

From then on he held a heavy hand over Nellie. He had only to look at her and she would make it available to him some way. Sometimes he would catch her in the kitchen when no one else was around, bend her over the table and breed her like a dog. It gave him a welcome sense of power to drive her to take all kinds of chances to satisfy him.

Several times at night he had crept across the room and woke her as she lay sleeping beside Rufus. Motioning her out of bed, he would crawl to the pile of dirty clothes that lay behind the side door and there, in the same room with her sleeping husband and children, would force her to his will.

No, I ain' gonna have no trouble with Nellie or Rufus. Thet leaves only Hallie."

As Harry pulled her towards him, Hallie sensed then what he was trying to do. She fought with teeth and nails, as they struggled violently across the room. As her nails tore at his scarred face, the hat with the carbide light fell from his head and landed on its side, causing the flame to sputter out. The only light now came from the lantern hanging on the wall.

Hallie got loose once and made a dash for his pick. As her hands closed on the handle, he caught her from behind and twisted it away from her while he held her pressed against the rock wall. She pulled at his arm with both hands, trying to get her breath, as his left arm began to tighten around her neck. He reached around with his right hand and began to roughly squeeze and kneed her breast. With her air supply cut off, Hallie began to weaken and could no longer stop him from pushing her to the dirty floor of the mine.

She screamed painfully as he entered her. Her fighting and terror-stricken cries only served in driving Harry to assaulting her more viciously. The screams stopped as she slipped into unconsciousness. The only sounds in the mine were Harry's snorting, rasping breathing and the scraping of his boots on the mine floor as they fought for a toehold to help him lunge deeper.

When he had spent himself, he stood up and leaned against the mine wall, still breathing heavily as he looked down at her. There was no remorse in his look.

She lay on the mud and coal slack floor of the mine, her dress still bunched up around her waist. As Hallie regained consciousness, she began to sob uncontrollably.

"Git up!" Harry commanded, unmoved. "I'll take ya back outside."

When Hallie made no move to get up, Harry reached down and jerked her to her feet. Not stopping to pick up his fallen light, he dragged her, stumbling and sobbing, through the dark mine until they reached the sunlight.

She made no effort to pull away as he continued to hold on to her saying, "Don' ya go tellin' nobody 'bout this. If'n ya do, I'll say yore alyin' and Rufus'll give ya a terrible whoppin'."

When he let go of her, she stumbled away and began running down the hill. She was unaware of the torn and dirty condition of her dress, or the blood running down her legs.

As she came into the yard she ran to her mother, who was hanging clothes on the line. Nellie turned when she heard her sobbing, and caught her before she fell.

"Whut in th' world happen't, Hallie, honey?" she inquired anxiously.

As Hallie sobbed out her story, Nellie stroked her matted hair as she tried to comfort her. As the crying subsided, Nellie took a wet towel, and raising her dress, began washing the blood and dirt from her daughter's legs. As the blood continued to trickle down the inside of her thighs from the broken maidenhead, her mother said, "Better strap a rag aroun' yerself. I gotta git ya cleaned up afore yer paw gits home. Put on yer other dress, too," she added.

"Whut do ya think Paw'll do whin ya tell 'im about this?" Hallie asked.

We won' never know, Hallie. I ain' gonna tell 'im, and ya hadn' better, neither," she answered.

"Harry's a big help to yer paw. Cain't change things now. Whut's dun is dun an' thar ain' no sense in worrin' 'bout it. Ya jist keep outta Harry's reach from here on. If ya git caught, I'll see Harry stans' by ya, uncle or no uncle."

Seeing the broken look on her face, Nellie told Hallie, "Honey, ya gotta git yer cherry broke sometime. Why, Baby, I don' think I wuz a day over eleven or twelve when I had ma first tumble in the hay. You 'member thet hucksterin' feller thet used ta come through here?"

She started to tell Hallie about it, but Hallie had already turned around and was walking away.

Chapter Five

After that day in the mine, Harry never touched Hallie again. She carried a paring knife with her at all times.

"If'n thet bastard ever takes aholt a' me agin, I'll kill 'im," she promised herself.

Harry seemed to know what she was thinking. He confined himself to leering at her. It was sickening to Hallie the way her mother always catered to Harry, even after knowing what he had done to her. This bothered her less as time went on, as she became more absorbed in planning how to get out of Middle Fork.

Hallie May had little chance to meet anyone from anywhere except Middle Fork. From her observance of the way the women of Middle Fork lived their lives, she knew she wanted no part of that. Her only means of escape from this environment in which she was trapped would have to be a man. She would marry a man who would take her out of here.

After her fifteenth birthday the following spring, she decided the best bet for her was Ezra Fultz.

"He's kinda thick 'atween th' ears, an' not much to look on, but leastways he's gotta job," she calculated.

Ezra was employed by a trucking firm as a driver who hauled coal from the mine operated by Hallie's father. The number of men who were employed in this area was limited. Another point in his favor was that he lived in Hookville, which could be a springboard to anywhere.

It took little effort to capture Ezra's interest. Each time he came for a load of coal, she would loiter near the truck while they were loading it. Ezra's ego soared as he answered her questions concerning the large towns to which he hauled coal.

Occasionally she would remain in the house when he came. Peeking through the curtains, she noted the disappointment on his face when searching eyes failed to find her. She was unaware that she was instinctively playing one of the oldest games of time, as she planned to deliver the coup de grâce.

Ezra drove the International truck up Middle Fork as fast as he could hold it on the road. Usually, he was a careful driver who made a habit of picking up anyone walking along the road. Today, he roared by everyone he passed without seeing them. He scattered guinea hens and chickens in every direction as he passed Lucille's Store. As he pulled into the coal yard, he could see Harry waiting for him beside the sled.

"I ain't never had no likin' fer thet surly bastard since I've known 'im. Shore is galdin' th' way he looks on Hallie May," Ezra thought as he pulled the truck to a stop.

He got out of the truck and took a quick look around, but saw no sign of her again today. It had been a week since he had seen her.

Ezra said to Harry as he started toward the house, "I'll be righ' back and hep' ya ta git loaded up soons' I git a drink of water."

Harry smirked, not bothering to answer.

As Ezra approached the open door he could see Hallie inside churning butter. Her breasts moved up and down in rhythm with her arms as she pushed the paddle into the milk. Ezra could feel the sweat running down the middle of his back as he watched her.

"How's 'bout a drinka water, Hallie?" he called through the doorway. She stopped churning and went to the water bucket that sat on the table, removed the dipper from it, and joined Ezra outside.

Might jist as well draw some fresh," she said. "Thet in th' bucket is too warm ta drink."

Ezra followed her to the well. There was something more than the heat bothering him, anyway—a different kind of heat. She lowered the bucket tied to a rope that ran through a pulley down into the well.

She had to lean over the well box and swing the rope back and forth to get the bucket to sink into the water. As she pulled on the rope and the bucket began its way up toward the squeaking pulley, her buttocks came up hard and tight against her dress. Ezra could hardly keep his hands off her. He snapped out of his erotic daydream in time to reach down and catch the bucket and set it out on the well cover.

Ezra filled the dipper and handed it to Hallie. She drank and refilled it and passed it back to him. He drank three dippers full of water, but they did nothing to squelch the flame that was burning inside him.

"Ezra, kin I ride down to Lucille's Store with ya?" Hallie asked, as Ezra handed her the dipper. "I gotta git some sodie an' sich fer supper."

This was more than Ezra could have hoped for. At least now he would have her alone, away from the all-knowing looks of Harry.

"Shore, Hallie, be glad ta haul ya down ta the store," he answered. "Won't take no time ta git thet coal loaded. I'll git to it righ' now."

Hallie watched out the window as Ezra and Harry loaded the truck. Ezra was throwing coal on the truck faster than she had ever seen him before. Harry suspected there was something going on about which he didn't know. He was loafing, letting Ezra do most of the work. Ezra was so absorbed in his own plans that he didn't even notice.

When the truck was loaded, Hallie walked out and got into it. She sat far over toward the middle. She took pleasure from the dark, glowering looks Harry was sending in her direction.

Ezra drove down Middle Fork slowly; he wanted this to last as long as possible. When the truck began to lug down on a small rise, Ezra shifted to a lower gear and let his hand fall to Hallie's leg that was beneath the stick shift. She made no attempt to remove his hand. He shot a quick look at her, and she smiled coyly back at him. As he drove on, his fingers began to tighten on her knee. She made no objection as his hand moved toward her thigh beneath the thin spring dress.

Ezra's mind was becoming so scrambled that he could hardly keep the truck on the road. The feel of the warm, rounded flesh of Hallie's leg beneath his fingers was driving him mad. His maleness had been aroused to the throbbing point.

"Much more a' this," he thought, "'an I'll hav'ta stop farther down th' crick an' dump some a' this rusty load."

Just ahead was the last big hill they had to ascend before reaching Lucille's Store and Post Office. Ezra had been trying to think of some way to keep Hallie with him a little longer. Pulling the truck to the side of the road, he explained to Hallie, "I allers hav'ta let th' truck cool off here afore makin' this hill with a load."

If she knew he was lying, she made no indication. He flipped off the ignition, and turned to Hallie, trying to pull her toward him.

"Not here," she protested, as she pushed him away. "Somebody might see us an' go tell Paw."

"Le's take a walk up that thar branch, Hallie. Ain' nobody up thar to see nothin'," Ezra coaxed as he opened the door and lifted her from the truck. Hallie allowed him to lead her across the road to the wire gate that crossed the footpath, which was a shortcut from Middle Fork across the hill to Bruin on the other side.

Ezra yanked up the loose barbed wire of the gate. Hallie crawled under then waited for Ezra to straddle over the top. Having seen men do this all her life, she wondered if anybody ever got his nuts caught in the wire.

"Th' way hogs squeal when they gits theirs cut out, I guess a man'd really put on a hoedown if'n he got his caught in the barbed wire," she thought to herself.

She hoped this wouldn't happen to Ezra just now. That wasn't part of her plan.

Ezra led her up the path until the scrub brush and trees hid them from the road. A shallow hollow ran to the left of the path. He pulled her after him, as he thrashed through the paw-paw bushes that grew alongside it. He stopped beneath a big walnut tree that grew on the side of the hill, with its roots running through the green ferns that abounded on the side of the hollow. On the upper side of the tree, a moss carpet covered the level ground, which was protected from the sun's rays by the heavy foliage of the trees.

Ezra dropped to the velvety green carpet and extended his arms to Hallie. He pulled her down beside him and kissed her fervently. She returned his frantic kisses, pressing her resilient young body to his. Ezra could hardly believe this was happening to him. No girl as pretty as Hallie had ever given him the time of day.

He had been with a few women before, but no one compared to her. As Ezra fumbled at her dress, Hallie sat up and pulled it quickly over her head. She wore nothing beneath it. She lay down lazily, naked on the green moss before him, watching him frenzily remove his clothes.

As he lunged down on top of her, she had a moment's misgiving, remembering the pain in the mine. Forcing herself to relax, she began to explore this new thing that was happening to her. As Ezra's passion rose to a peak, hers soared with his. His subsided; hers didn't. He lay there breathing in gasps, trying to hurry the oxygen back into his lungs.

"There must be something more," Hallie thought. She wanted to continue. She pulled at Ezra, but he was unable to help her. She continued to undulate her hips, pushing her buttocks deeper into the moss.

They quickly returned to the truck without exchanging conversation. There is nothing for a man to say when he has failed to satisfy a woman.

"You go on an' I'll walk th' rest of th' way," Hallie told Ezra. "Best a buncha' people don' see us together now."

Ezra was quick to take advantage of the opportunity to get away. He would never feel like a man around this girl again.

Hallie watched the truck until it was out of sight, then turned around and headed home. Soda she didn't need. She had gone the first mile on her way out of Middle Fork.

Hallie waited for "the curse." It came right on time. Now she would have a month before they would find out that she had lied. Her father, Rufus, looked at her in disbelief when she told him she was going to have a baby. It hadn't occurred to him that she was grown up enough for anything like this.

"Did'ja tell him yet, Hallie?" he asked.

I'm afeared to, Paw," Hallie puckered up, as if to cry.

"By God, I'm not," Rufus shouted heatedly. "He's agonna marry up with ya—thet's jist whut thet son abitch's gonna do. Nex' time he comes fer a load a coal, we're gonna have an understandin' right quick. Ain't nobody gonna go a triflin' with any a my girls and leave me their young'uns ta fetch up."

He'd scare the hell out of Ezra Fultz. He remembered how scared he had been when old Tom Begley had come after him for the same reason.

Ezra and Hallie May were married and moved into a three-room house up behind the old grist mill in Hookville. It wasn't much of a house, but to Hallie it was a mansion, compared to what she was used to.

Each morning after she had fixed Ezra's breakfast and he had left for work, she would go up town and browse through the stores. At night Ezra would come home dirty and tired. Sometimes he would want to make love. She looked forward to these times, but always there was something missing.

As she continued to haunt the stores in town, the merchants began to make notice of her. One day she was in the big general store owned by Walter Hutchinson when it was closing time. She was so absorbed in looking at a pretty yellow sundress that she was unaware that Walter had closed and locked the front door.

She glanced up in surprise as he stopped in front of her and asked, "Would'ja like ta have thet yeller dress, Hallie?"

"Oh, I jist luv it," she answered, holding it up to her body. "Course, I ain't got no money. I jist like ta tetch purty things."

"What would ja say if'n I tol' ya thet ya could have thet outfit fer free?" Walter asked.

"Oh, Mr. Hutchinson, I'd know fer shore you wuz only funnin' me," she answered.

"No, I mean it," he asserted. "Let's me an' you go back thar in th' storeroom fer a spell and when we come back out, I promise I'll wrap it up fer ya and ya kin take it home with ya!"

Now Hallie understood what he wanted. This ugly little man with a chew of tobacco in his cheek wanted to lay with her. She looked at the dress again. She just had to have it. What if he was ugly? It seemed that she was always getting mixed up with ugly men—even married ones.

As she started to walk toward the storeroom, he was breathing right down her neck. Inside the back room he led her to one side where the new mattresses were stored. Pulling one off the pile, he wrestled it into the aisle and clutched at her, all in one motion.

Hallie May lay back on the mattress and pulled up her dress, baring her young loveliness to the lecherous eyes of the aged storekeeper. She had never liked those bloomers that some city women wore.

"Oh, my God. Oh, my God," old man Hutchinson kept repeating as he stared down at her. He knelt beside her and ran his gnarled hand over her flat stomach and rounded hips. Hallie May was becoming excited now. She began to slither and move back and forth on the mattress.

"Whut's he waitin' fer?" she wondered, as she lay with her eyes closed.

She could hear him grunting and straining his arthritic body out of his trousers, as he wheezed his way over her bare stomach.

He clambered up crying, "Oh, no. Oh, no. Damn. Damn. I couldn't wait."

Hallie opened her eyes and looked up at him, trying not to laugh. He looked so ridiculous standing there on the mattress with his pants down around his ankles, his manhood shriveling to nothing before her eyes. She could no longer restrain her laughter when he began gagging and choking.

For the first time in thirty years, Walter Hutchinson had swallowed his tobacco cud.

As time went by, Hallie found it easy to trade what she had for what she wanted. She found a difference in men. Some were tender and sweet; others selfish and cruel. The one thing they all had in common so far was that none had been able to tame the tiger in her that ran wild each time she slept with a new man.

Chapter Six

It was Sunday afternoon and Hallie May had sat watching the men coming and going around the old mill all day. Ezra was down there with them. As afternoon wore on toward evening, she grew impatient.

"I oughta go down thar and git 'im," she thought as she paced back and forth in front of the window.

She was discouraged from doing this, as she recalled the last time she had gone down after him. When they reached home, Ezra had taken off his belt and had given her a terrible beating with it. As she watched, she saw Ezra come out from under the mill and head for the house. From the way he walked, she could tell that he had lost again. He looked even more beat than usual.

"I'll bet that stupid ass ain't even got enuff money lef' ta take me over ta Morehead to the pitcher show tanight," she thought dejectedly.

He hadn't even cleared the doorway until she started harrassing him.

Ya dirty son-of-a-bitch," she screamed shrilly. "If'n ya think I'm agonna sit here Sunday after Sunday whilst yore under thet ol' mill throwin' away our money, ya got 'tother think acomin'. Ya promised I'd git three dollars fer myself outta this check. Whar is it?"

He staggered in and collapsed into a chair. If he had heard a word she had been saying, he gave no indication. Hallie crossed the room and stopped in front of his chair.

"Whut's happen't to ya? Might's jist as well tell me now."

She could tell that he was drunk, but there was something else this time. Ezra sat in a dazed stupor as he confessed to his wife what he had done.

"Ya did thet ta me?" she shrilled. "Ya low-down bastard! I'm apackin' up an' movin out righ' now. I've had other offers, an' I'm atakin one of 'em."

"Honey, please," Ezra pleaded, as he followed her into the bedroom.

"I wuz so shore I wouldn' lose. I didn' really mean nothin' by it. I wuz only kiddin' anyhow. Brack'll see thet when I 'splain it to 'im. You wait an' see—everythin'll be alright."

"Alright, yore ass, ya big ugly, dum' son-of-a-bitch," she raved on. "If ya think I'm spreadin' ma legs jist ta git ya off'n th' hook on a bet with Brack Barron, ya better think again."

"Brack'll understan' when I tell 'im how things is," muttered Ezra, without much conviction.

Hallie paced around the room, muttering to herself and calling her husband every vile name that came to her mind. In the years she had lived in these hills, she had heard and remembered many. As her rage subsided, a plan to hurt Ezra came to her mind.

"Well, ya made th' debt," she said. "If'n I have ta pay fer yore drinkin' and gamblin', I guess it won' kill me."

She walked over to the mirror and stretched up on her toes and threw back her shoulders, causing her ample breasts to stand forth boldly. Running her hands down over her hips and thighs as if to smooth her skirt, she taunted him.

"I might even like it. Hear tell this Brack Barron is a real stud of a man. Might be worth it ta git with a' real man fer a change. I've had enuff a' yer kind."

Ezra spun her around and slapped her across the face, knocking her to the bed.

She raised up laughing at him, "I wonder if'n ya'll slap Brack Barron like thet when he comes ta bed down your wife?"

Ezra whirled away and ran to the kitchen, where he picked up a butcher knife. He hurried back to the living room and pulled a chair to the window, where he could watch the street, and sat down.

"Ill kill 'im if'n he shows up," he kept mumbling to himself.

In the bedroom Hallie began to feel an exciting expectation creep over her.

"Thet Brack's some good-lookin' piece of man. Not like them store-minders I've been messin' with. He looks big and hard all the way through."

She felt her skin tingle as she had the added thought, "At least I hope part a' him kin stay hard."

She heard Ezra catch his breath as she walked into the front room behind him.

"Thar' he comes. He's even got 'is kid with 'im. I'm gonna go out an' tell 'im ta leave. He better had," Ezra gritted.

"Ya stay inside and keep th' door bolted," he commanded as he stepped out into the porch. Ezra seemed to be nearly sober now.

Hallie ignored him and went to the window and watched Brack and Clay walk into the yard.

"Thet Clay's gonna' be the spittin' image of his paw," she thought.

Although Clay was fifteen, the same age as she was, she thought of him as a kid.

As she listened to the exchange of words and watched the ensuing fight in the front yard, she found it sexually stimulating. All those people down by the mill knew they were fighting over her. Everyone in town would hear about it tomorrow. She could just picture the way peoples' heads would turn when she walked by. Now they would all know her and know that she was worth fighting for.

It came as no surprise to her to see the Barrons locking her husband in the smokehouse.

She backed away from the window as she heard Brack's footsteps on the porch. As he came into the house she stood up in the middle of the room. She had her feet placed like the models did in the Sears Roebuck catalogue. She wanted to show off her body to its best advantage. This Brack was going to find that she wasn't going to be easy. Her body trembled in spite of herself as she thought of losing.

When Brack closed the door behind him, she warned, "You keep away from me. I don' give a damn whut Ezra bet ya, I ain' beddin' down with nobody I don' want to. Anyways, I'm leavin' thet puke soon's I git 'nuff bus fare outta here. So go kill 'im 'cause he cain't pay off. See if'n I care."

Brack stood smiling at Hallie. "So you want ta leave ol' Ezra, huh?" he asked. "Well, thet makes things some easier."

Reaching into his pocket he said, "I got here in my hand thirty-seven dollars I won maself in thet poker game taday."

He held out his hand with the money in it. "This should take ya a fer piece."

"Whut do ya think I am—some whore or somethin'?" shot back Hallie heatedly.

Now she was really becoming angry. She had wanted to bring Brack to his knees by making him beg to make love to her. Instead, he was offering her money.

"Thet's not whut I think a'tall, Hallie May," he was quick to answer. "It jist seems a faster way a' you gittin' whut you want—which is outta here—an' me gittin' whut I want, too. I'd only consider it a gift to a friend fer doin' me a favor."

Hallie May tried to look seductive as she answered, "Since ya put it thet way, come on back ta t'other room. Don' guess we gotta worry about Ezra any."

Brack looked at Hallie for a long moment. He thought to himself, "A man's kids don' never really appreciate th' sacrifices made fer 'em by their daddies. She shore looks like a real wild ride. Oh, hell, guess it won' kill me to miss one."

"Hallie," he said, "I'd better clear this up a little bit. It ain' me I'm askin' fer. It's fer ma boy out thar. I'm all Clay's got. His maw died when he was a baby. He's never been aroun' no wimmin much, an' I thought since you wuz more his age it would be better ta git his first frum you. Might not be as embarrassin' ta 'im as t'would if he had it first from some older woman."

Seeing an expression of uncertainty cross Hallie's face, he hurried on. "I wan' ya ta make 'im think he's the greatest thing that ivver come down th' road, even if'n he's no good 'tall. All a young man needs is confidence in hisself. Above all, if ya do this fer me, don' never tell 'im I give ya any money fer it."

"Why not?" Hallie thought as she listened to him talk. She had looked forward to a real time with a real man, but it seemed her luck ran to ugly Harrys and Ezras, and soft-bellied dry goods pushers. "Guess teachin' a kid ta diddle won' be no worse," she thought.

She held out her hand and Brack put the bills in it. As he turned to leave, he smiled and said, "Ya take good care a' my boy, now, Hallie."

Hallie could hear voices outside.

"Mebbe Brack's havin' trouble gittin' Clay ta come in. No matter. I've got th' money an' I'm akeepin' it. If'n he comes in, I'll whip one on 'im he won' never forgit. When I'm through with this kid, he'll brag fer years about Hallie May Fultz bein' th' best piece he ever got."

She walked into the bedroom and sat down before the mirror at the vanity. When she took the ornamental combs out of her long red hair, it fell to her shoulders in a mass of color. She heard the door open and then the faltering footsteps coming toward the bedroom. As he stopped in the bedroom doorway, Hallie studied his reflection in the mirror. He was larger than most men already, but his peach-fuzz cheeks marked him still a boy.

Without turning, she said, "I allers brush ma hair afore goin' ta bed. 'Ja wanna help me?"

She passed the brush over her shoulder to him. Clay stood behind her without speaking and took the brush she offered and began to pull it through the long red tresses. Her eyes met his in the mirror. His face was red with embarrassment, and his hand on the brush was shaking nervously.

Clay seemed to get control of himself as he said to her, "I don' need nobody ta go 'round gittin' wimmin fer me. I'm gonna pick out ma own. I only come in here 'cause I don' wanna hurt Paw's feelins.' He thinks he's doin' right by me. I admit that I ain' done no friggin' aroun' with any wimmin yet, but it's jist 'cause I ain' foun' none thet I wanna mess with."

He paused for a moment but when Hallie made no comment he went on.

"Jist las' week a bunch a' th' boys had ol' Effie Hiatt—ya' know her; she's th' one they call 'Effie the Coon'—down on th' crick bank. I coulda had some of thet; most a' th' fellers did, but I jist couldn' see messin' round with some dirty ol' woman thet's about half-addled jist ta say I'd had some. Paw must' heard 'bout it an' got worried over me. He don' need ta worry 'bout me. I feel everythin' I'm supposed ta when I'm 'round a woman, 'specially one whut's all built up like you."

He kept brushing her hair as he continued, "I'll stay here 'till Paw leaves an' it git's clear dark. Then I'll leave. I kin sleep th' rest a' th' night up in the cliffs an' he won' never know th' difference."

Hallie continued to hold Clay's eyes in the mirror, much as a snake charms a bird. Her lips were half parted as her hands moved slowly to the buttons of her blouse. The brush strokes stopped as she came to the last button. She then slipped the blouse off her shoulders, letting the wild flaming hair cascade down her milk-white shoulders and back. The brush remained poised in the air, now completely forgotten by Clay as he stared, trance-like, at the proud, jutting breasts in the mirror before him.

She turned and took the hair brush from him and laid it on the dresser.

"Yore so nice, Clay," she said. "I could jist kiss you. I believe I will kiss you. Have ya ivver kissed a girl afore, Clay?" she asked.

"No," he gulped.

She stood up and pulled his arms around her. She tilted her face up, and putting her hands behind his head, drew him down and pressed her lips to his. As his mouth stirred under hers, the rest of his body seemed to come alive, too. His fingers dug into the soft contours of her back as he crushed her to him.

"He's strong as a ox," she thought, as his lips moved to her neck and shoulders, leaving a streak of fire as they passed.

She moved sideways and pulled him down on the bed beside her. They lay across the bed, wrapped in each other's arms. Hallie's leg slipped between his as she moved even deeper into his embrace.

Clay pulled back and cupped her breast in his hand. He'd seen many women's breasts as they nursed their babies, but this was the first one he had ever held in his hand. Clay caressed the full resilient breasts until Hallie pulled him down so his face was burried between them.

"Do ya still wanna sleep in the cliffs tonight, Clay?" she whispered.

From the confines of the twin mounds of flesh he mumbled, "No, I wanna stay here."

Hallie knew it was time. She breathed in his ear, "if'n ya took off yore clothes and I took off mine, we'd git done twice as quick."

As they came together there in the fading light of the room, she guided his every move. Each time she had made love in the past, it had always been the man who had been the aggressor. This time she was the experienced one. As she held and fondled Clay, she did to him all the things that she had learned from other men. He learned fast, and she soon found herself following his lead.

As the full darkness of night filled the room, the only sound was the squeaking of the rusty bedsprings and the labored breathing of the pair as they reached for what was unknown to both of them.

At intervals during the night they would lie very still in each other's arms until the exploring hands of Hallie May would again awaken Clay's young blood. Time after time the bedsprings made music during the night. At last, during the early morning hours, the tiger in Hallie May was sleeping.

She smiled to herself in the dark. "All this and money, too. I should have paid Brack Barron."

As the first streaks of dawn showed in the east, she awoke with Clay's hands bringing back the night before. Once more they made love, as only the young and very virile can.

Later, completely relaxed, she drifted off to sleep again. When the sun touched her face, she awoke with a start. She sat up in bed and called out, "Clay, whar' are ya?"

He was gone.

Chapter Seven

Clyde Vansant sat in his plush office in the Hookville bank, secure in the knowledge that he was the richest and most influential man in the county. Despite this, he was unhappy. The reason for his unhappiness was his daughter, Valarie. She was discontented and he didn't know what to do or say to her. Each time he tried to find the cause of her moodiness, she gave him the same answer.

"There's nothing wrong with me that time won't take care of."

That Valarie was the most beautiful girl in the area made him swell with pride each time he looked at her. His delight in and love for her had long ago overshadowed his disappointment that she hadn't been born a boy.

His practical banker's mind summed up her assets as he observed her now sitting behind her typewriter. She sat straight in her chair, her fingers racing over the keys. Her long black hair lay against her neck and spilled down over her shoulders, curving in front to a half circle. It was soft and silky, with just a touch of natural curl. Her eyelashes were so long they looked artificial, and although the eyebrows were heavier than most women, she wore them natural.

The large blue eyes, small straight nose and tapered face led to a firm but feminine chin. It was her mouth, however, that made men stare. Her lips were full and sensuous; the upper slightly arched, the lower full and inviting. Her even teeth fairly sparkled when she smiled.

Her neck was long and slender above full breasts that threatened the fabric of her sheer white blouse. Her sheath skirt fit snugly at the waist and curved down over her hips. She had no need for a girdle. Her legs were long and gracefully formed, with ankles so slender they looked fragile. The three-inch spiked heels she wore brought her eyes to a level with most men.

These assets were in complete harmony with each other, comprising a truly beautiful girl.

He could think of nothing to list as a liability except her temper. He dismissed this quickly. Valarie didn't get angry often.

There was a strange, haunting mystery about this exquisite daughter of his. So often he had observed her staring off into space. Once, six months ago, he had heard her crying into her pillow. He had entered her room and held her in his arms until her sobbing had subsided. He had never asked for nor received an explanation for the tears that night.

Several times in the last year he had heard her get up and drive off in her convertible in the middle of the night. From the window of their home overlooking Hookville he and his wife, Izetta, had watched her pass over the bridge and disappear down Sandy Valley. At other time she would saddle her black Arabian stallion, Bones, and ride away. He never questioned where she went, although it was often dark when she returned.

"What the hell's wrong with the men around here?" Clyde wondered to himself, as he continued studying his daughter.

"Here is one of the loveliest girls that ever graced this part of the country. She has a college education, gorgeous figure and a wealthy father. What the hell more could any man want?"

Money he had never mentioned to her in conjunction with the men she dated. He wanted Valarie to marry a real man. Clyde knew he could help him make money, but he could not help him to be a man. That every male must do for himself.

Since she was sixteen he had watched them come and go. He had high hopes when she went to college, but they diminished when he visited her at Morehead State. All the men he had met there seemed to fall into two categories; the over-educated intellectuals with whom he had nothing in common, and the rah-rah boys, who were worse. After that trip he lived in fear that she would marry one or the other of that tripe. His fears were allayed, however, when she returned home after graduation to live and work.

In the ensuing months he invited to his home, on one pretext or another, all the men whom he considered eligible. None had made the least impression on her.

Valarie startled Clyde's thoughts by tearing the paper from the typewriter and throwing it into the wastebasket. She got up and walked to the window facing Main Street and stood looking out absently. Her father's face was troubled as he watched her.

"I wish I knew what's wrong with her," he thought. "She's nothing but a bundle of nerves. I'll talk to Izetta tonight. Maybe a trip to Europe this summer would be the answer."

"Papa, he's come back," she whispered softly. "I knew he would sometime. I just knew it."

Hurrying across the room toward her he asked, "Who's come back, Honey? What are you talking about?" He put his arm around her.

Clyde's eyes followed her gaze and fixed on a man talking to the sheriff behind a black car. When he turned facing the bank, Clyde sensed something familiar about him.

"Brack Barron. Couldn't be. Brack's boy, that's who it has to be. What had she said? What did she mean, 'I knew he would come back?'"

He looked at his daughter's face as she stared wistfully after Clay as he strode down the hill toward the bridge. When he had passed out of sight she turned in her father's arms and said simply, "That man is Clay Barron, Papa. I've waited for thirteen years for him to come back."

As Clyde started to speak, she pressed her fingers to his lips.

"I know a ten-year-old girl can't fall in love, but I did, Papa. He doesn't know I'm alive, but he will. I knew if I stayed here I'd have a chance to see him again."

This had all come too fast for Clyde. He walked to his desk and sat down. Looking up at his shining-eyed daughter, he realized now the source of her discontent.

"What do you know about him?" he asked. "Maybe he already has a wife."

She answered both of his questions at one time. "I don't know anything about him, and if he has a wife, I'll take him away from her."

He was shocked at the vehemence in her voice. Here was a Valarie he didn't know existed.

She continued, "You always told me if there was something in life I wanted, I wasn't to wait for someone to give it to me; I was to go out and take it. I've trying unsuccessfully for years to find out where he went. All those vacation trips I took were to run down leads Uncle Billy gave me as to his whereabouts."

Her father made no comment, so she continued, "You know his aunt and uncle, Newt and Sarah Keaton, who live on the side of Rainbow Mountain? They have been getting a check from a different lawyer each year for the last ten years, with instructions to pay the taxes on the mountain and use the remainder for themselves. I've checked out every lawyer, with the same results. None of them knew the name or address of their client."

"Is that where your Sunday rides were to?" Clyde asked.

"Yes, I visited Next and Sarah often. I didn't want him to come and be gone without my seeing him."

"Two more things, Valarie. First, are you aware of the Fultz incident? Do you know who that little hellion, Milt Fultz's father really is? Second, do you know Clay is still wanted by the law for a shooting right here in the courthouse and escaping the county jail?"

"I cried all my tears over that first question when I was a little girl, Papa. As to your second question, that thing with the law has been dropped. Uncle Billy told me that a week ago."

Clyde stood up and put his arm around her.

"Okay, Honey," he said. "If that's who you want, that's who you're gonna get. No one Barron could ever be a match for two Vansants, especially one as lovely as you, and the other as rich as me. First thing we have to worry about is keeping him alive. There's a bloody fight coming, and you know that Hook bunch are all Tush hogs."

"I'm going to stop that fight, Papa," she said with conviction. "I don't want Clay all shot up or crippled."

"I'll say one thing—he sure is a big devil. Walks cocky like Brack always did," her father teased. "Course, you know I can't ever give you to any man I can whip."

She punched him in his unsuspecting middle with a hard little fist as she broke away.

"I'll help him," she retorted. "No Vansant would stand a chance against a Barron and a Vansant."

As she headed for the door and smiled over her shoulder, "Better promote Betty Ann, Papa. I just quit."

After leaving the bank, she hurried to the courthouse and went directly to the sheriff's office.

When she opened the door, Judge Holbrook brushed past her on his way out without pausing for his usual friendly greeting. The sheriff was smiling as she entered.

"Reckon as how th' jedge is scared half ta death thet Clay's come home ta kill 'im like he done promised. If'n he don' shape up I reckon Clay won' have ta tetch 'im. He'll jest pass away from fright."

"Unlce Billy, do you really think Clay will go after the judge?"

"Naw, I'd say thet as Clay growed older he come ta understan' thet th' jedge wuz only doin' whut he was obliged ta do. I'm shore thar's no need ta fret."

"What's he like, Uncle Billy?" she asked excitedly. "Who did he ask about? Where's he going now?"

"Whoa, girl, one question at a time," he grinned. "Whut he's like I cain't rightly tell. Seems awlful bitter an' cold ta me. Don' think he's got no real interest in nobody but the Hooks. As ta whar he's agoin'—to thet mountain of his'n—whar else?"

"Where has he been all these years?" she probed.

"Cain't answer thet jest yit, but he left 'is car out yonder. It's got a Michigan license plate and I'm arunnin' it thru the motor bureau. Whin I git an answer from them folks up thar I orta know more 'bout 'im then."

"Uncle Billy, would you please get in touch with me if you think he's about to leave town?"

"Shore will, Valarie, but he said afore he left thet it'd be a coupla days afore he'd git back."

She leaned over the desk and kissed him on his bald head, leaving tell-tale lipstick marks.

"Thanks, Cupid."

She left then, her high heels clicking their way down the hall.

The sheriff shook his head. "Whut a helluva mess this is gonna be."

Dr. Jody McKee had been in the bank at the time Valarie rushed from her father's office on her way to the courthouse. She wondered, with half-interest, what Valarie had been so excited about. After making her deposit, Dr. Jody left the bank and walked toward her office, which was located in the small medical building in the first block beyond the bridge. She smiled and spoke to those she passed on her way.

When Dr. Jody's predecessor, Dr. Aaron Crow, had died two years ago, the general consensus had been that no one could take his place. He had been "One of them," having been born and reared here in Hookville. His hard drinking and philandering caused considerable unfavorable comment, but there was no question as to his medical ability.

He had entertained several eccentric notions, one of which was his refusal to have his hair cut. It was as black as the wing of the bird whose name he bore, and fell in a confused mass to his shoulders. When the end came for him, there had been many tears shed in the county besides those of the mistresses he had kept for years out on the Brown Ridge.

After running ads continuously for several months in various medical journals, the county officials finally received an inquiry from Dr. Jody McKee of Philadelphia. There had never been a woman doctor in Hookville, but since hers had been the only inquiry, she was asked reluctantly to fill the vacancy left by the death of Dr. Crow.

Upon her arrival, Dr. Jody sensed an air of skepticism in the people who lived there. This attitude, however, began to change to respect when she went into a caved-in mine in search of a trapped miner. She and the mine foreman found Jack Flannery lying unconscious on the mine floor, his right leg crushed beneath a huge boulder. Fearing a complete collapse of the mine shaft, the foreman had ordered the other miners to safety when they had been unable to remove the stone from his leg.

When they reached the trapped man, Dr. Jody, without hesitation, amputated the mangled leg and assisted in dragging him to safety. They had barely reached the outside before the mine caved in.

She paid no heed to the roaring crash behind her as she continued to administer aid to her patient. Since then, she had crawled across swollen creeks on footlogs to deliver babies and had, at times, performed operations with only the light from kerosene lamps.

The county toughs now bragged, "She kin take out a bullet slicker'n even ol' Doc Crow hisself."

To them, this was the crowning compliment. In Hookville if one couldn't say something complimentary about Dr. Jody, it was best to remain silent. A traveling salesman had learned this the hard way.

He had been lounging with a group of men on the front porch of Hutchinson's Store when he observed Dr. Jody walking across the street. She had been in a blue business suit that was failing miserably to curb the curvacious form beneath it. Not being aware of the esteem with which these people held her, he made an off-hand comment.

"Now there's what I'd like to spend my nights in Hookville with. Course, any man that'd touch that should be arrested for violating the Pure Food and Drug Act."

The salesman's face showed bewildered astonishment when Junior Flannery jumped him with a knife, slashing him several times on the hands and face. When he got away from his attacker, he fled down the street to the sanctuary of a friendly store. He heard the knife-wielder shout after him, "Don' never say no more dirty thoughts 'bout Dr. Jody, or yore gonna git yourself kilt."

The merchant had taken the salesman to the clinic for treatment, being closely followed by the sheriff. After Dr. Jody had sutured his wounds, the salesman left, shaking his head negatively when the sheriff asked him if he wanted to press charges.

When they were alone, Dr. Jody asked the sheriff, "Who did that, and what was it all about, anyway?"

"Junior Flannery's th' one whut did the cuttin', I reckin."

"That name sounds familiar. Don't I know him?" she questioned.

"I guess mebbe ya do. His paw's th' one thet ya crawled back inta th' mine and took th' leg off of."

"I wonder why he'd do a thing like this?" she asked.

"Wal, this sellin' feller seems ta a made some snide remark 'bout someone Junior's pretty fonda," he answered.

"That's still no excuse for what he did," she retorted.

"Now then, thet depends some," the sheriff said. "Course, ya could help me stop this sorta thing," he continued.

"How could I possibly help?" she queried.

"Wal, fer one thing, ya kin walk slower whin ya go uptown, an' thet way ya won' wriggle so much."

Her face flamed. "You mean this was over me?"

"I'm 'fraid hit wuz, Doc."

His eyes twinkled in amusement at her scarlet face as he closed her office door behind him.

As Jody neared the river, she saw a strange man standing there in the middle of the bridge, staring down into the swirling water. As she walked toward him, she felt a sense of uneasiness come over her.

The expression on his face was tragic, and something about him breathed danger. As she passed him, she focused her look squarely on him and experienced an almost forgotten sensation. Not since the death of her husband had thoughts such as these penetrated her invisible shield. As she continued on by him, her disgust at herself concerning these thoughts did nothing to relax the muscles that had tensed in her stomach, or remove the growing ache in her breasts.

When she reached the end of the bridge she stopped before crossing the street and glanced back. He was still standing there, but now he was surveying the old mill. She hurried across the street, not wanting to admit the disappointment she felt because he hadn't even noticed her.

Dr. Jody opened the door to her office and called, "June, come out here a second."

Her receptionist and practical nurse, June Brickley, walked out on the porch.

"What is it, Doctor?" she asked.

Jody pointed to the man on the bridge and asked, "Do you know that man, June? He has me worried. He acts like he might be going to jump off the bridge."

As she spoke he turned and began walking toward them. June stared intently at him as he crossed the street and came on.

"Oh, Lordy," she exclaimed. "He's come back, jist like he sed he'd do. Dr. Jody, thet thar's Clay Barron, the one who swore th' oath ta kill Silas Hook."

"So that's the wild boy who shot up the courthouse and broke out of jail. I've heard the men brag about that incident so often that I feel I almost know him."

"Dr. Jody, I did know 'im. I knowed 'is father, Brack, too. Him an' Clay was allers a horseplayin' aroun', more like brothers than father an' son. They used ta be always gittin' in some kind a' trouble. Why, I 'member well thet Sunday over thar' on th' hill behind the mill. . . ."

Jody interrupted, "Never mind. I've heard that story, too."

Clay was almost abreast of them now. The latent urge again tugged at Jody's body as she watched the tall, dark man with the gloomy, brooding face stride by. June waved at him, but he never noticed.

As he continued on up the street, June stated with conviction, "Thar's gonna be a bloodbath for shore."

"What do you mean by that?"

"When you've lived in these hills long as I have, you'll know thet whin a man kills 'nother man down here who's got a son thet worships him like Clay did his, if'n ya want to stay alive you'd best kill off the son, too. If'n Clay's turned out like th' rest of the Barron men, Silas Hook is nothin' more'n a walkin' dead man righ' now."

"I don't think so, June. Things have gotten better here. I can even tell a difference in the last year. There's more law here now. Besides, time heals all things. My guess is there won't be any trouble. Anyway, let's get to work. I've heard enough about both these barbaric families to last me a lifetime."

Chapter Eight

Clay turned away from the sight and memory of the little house behind the old mill and began to quickly walk across the bridge. A faint smile played at his lips as he thought, "Yes, my father was sure something else."

At the end of the bridge, the street went up hill again. His long strides carried him hurriedly to the top. The street wound its way around the top of the hill and down the other side, where it became a gravel road that ran on through the valley alongside the Little Sandy River.

When Clay stopped at the top of the hill, he could see before him the wondrous Sandy Valley, stretching green and gray in the distance. On the right-hand side of the river about halfway down the valley lived the Hooks. On the left-hand side of the river a mountain rose skyward. It was so high that Clay had to look up to see the top, even though he was on high ground now. There before him, at last, rearing its head majestically toward the clouds, was Rainbow Mountain, the place of his birth.

He felt a sense of the openness, of the vastness of the mountain. Its wildness and strangeness had so long beckoned to him. Oh, how he had yearned for the lazy, quiet days and lonely, silent nights. How he had longed to hear the thunder carried on the high winds and the rain clatter on a tin roof, to once more see the trees burdened with icicles and fresh snow glistening like diamonds as the morning sun came to claim them.

Yes, this wild, weird mountain had long ago claimed the soul of Clay Barron.

At the bottom of the hill the street became a gravel road, which had been covered with oil to keep the dust settled. There were houses on both sides of the road. As he walked along, Clay would sometimes recognize someone and lift a hand in greeting, but took no time to talk with anyone. He could sense people whispering to each other as he walked along.

It had been many years since the roar of guns had been heard in these hills and valleys. All the old battles would be re-fought around the kitchen tables tonight, and the inevitable one to come would offer them something on which to speculate in the days ahead.

On the left side of the road ahead was the three-room schoolhouse that Clay had attended. A dirt road ran to the left of the building and continued its way up Rainbow Mountain. Clay passed the road by and his feet dragged as he approached the schoolyard. The hitching rail for horses and mules was gone now. In its place sat a pair of nondescript automobiles.

Pupils up to the eighth grade attended this school with four grades to a room. The third room was used for a cafeteria. In the backyard of the school, two new toilets had been built out of cement blocks. This was the only visible improvement in the Sandy Valley school in thirteen years.

His footsteps made a crunching noise as he walked into the school yard, which was covered with cinders from the coal stoves that were used to heat the building. Woodburning stoves had been in use when Clay was a pupil here.

Directly in front of the school in the middle of the yard stood a huge walnut tree. As Clay leaned against this familiar tree, his hands clenched at his sides. He wasn't seeing the cinder yard now; he was seeing a mud yard as it was long ago.

He was seeing his father sprawled out in the mud with the life blood running out of his body. He was seeing the evil grin on old Silas Hook's face as he slammed another slug into the already dying body of Brack Barron.

He turned and stared intently down the Sandy Valley before walking to the back of the schoolhouse. He continued across the rear yard and climbed the steps that were built over the fence and took the footpath that, for longer than anybody could remember, had been used as a shortcut up Rainbow Mountain.

Inside the school, Brian Ferguson was listening to a sixth grade boy read. He looked out the window and saw a man walk into the school yard. He recognized Clay instantly. He had taught him for three years and had, in those years, been able to witness firsthand the complete, undying, unselfish love between the boy and his father.

When Clay was going to school, the system that had been used to go to the toilet was a card that had "IN" printed on one side and "OUT" on the other. One day Brian had noticed Clay sit up straight in his seat and appear to be listening for something. Pretending not to notice, Brian had heard the faint call of a bobwhite. The only difference was that this whistle had two "bobs" in it. Clay had dashed out of his seat and flipped the card "OUT" and left the room. A few minutes later Brian saw Brack cross the steps on the fence and head up the mountain.

A few days later, when Brian again heard the whistle, he walked over and turned the card to "OUT." Only one student at a time was allowed to leave the room, and with the card showing "OUT," no one else would be permitted to leave. Clay got up quietly and left the room anyway.

When he returned, Brian told him to remain after school. When school was dismissed and they were alone, Brian asked him why he had left the room without permission.

Clay answered simply, "My Paw wuz expectin' me."

"You think a lot of your father, don't you, Clay?" he asked.

"More'n anythin' in this here world. 'Enny man who hurts ma Paw dies," the boy answered.

Now as Brian saw him looking down the valley, he felt cold. He was glad he had come into these mountains to teach, but the sudden violence of these people always came as a shock to him. A man had killed this boy's father. The code of the hills said, "Now this man must die for it."

* * *

It had been a pleasant surprise to Brian that November election day thirteen years ago when Brack and Clay had ridden in double on their horse and hitched him to a rail in the school yard. Brack hadn't voted since he returned from the army. It was his conviction that he didn't want to share in the responsibility of any more 'political wars;' he just wanted to be left alone.

Brian had lectured the students on the importance of voting, and Clay had pestered Brack until he consented to vote.

As they dismounted, Brack saw Silas Hook and his four sons standing with a group of men at the side of the schoolhouse. Ignoring them, he instructed Clay to stay with their horse, as the stallion was a fighter and couldn't be left alone with other horses and mules.

After Brack had entered the schoolhouse, their horse humped himself up and excreted his body waste in the school yard.

Jubal Hook sauntered out from the group of men and commented, loud enough for Clay to hear, "Jist like a Barron horse—no manners atall."

Clay glared at him, but made no reply.

Jubal was eighteen and the light of his father's eye. He was better looking and smarter than his brothers, and although he was the youngest, he could thrash any of them. Silas laughed aloud as he watched Jubal bait Clay. He had observed Brack closely when he dismounted and was almost positive he was unarmed. The gun Silas carried in a belt under the bib of his overalls gave him confidence.

"Brack's got soft atter thet brat was borned," he thought.

All the Hooks looked alike, with the exception of Jubal. They had long, dirty-colored blonde hair and faces like possums. When he had gone to school, Silas had been called "Possum Hook." They were all stocky with thick, broad shoulders and hairy, muscular arms. Jubal was blonde, too, but his features were less pointed and his jaws broader.

Clay remained quiet and tense as Jubal walked toward him.

"I think thet whin a man's horse shits in th' school yard he orta be made ta clean it up. Whut ya say, Boy?" Jubal asked.

Clay's eyes flashed angrily, but he continued to remain silent.

"Why don' ya jist pack it out thar' ta th' road righ' now afore I lose patience with ya?" taunted Jubal.

When this failed to get a response from Clay, he jeered, "My Paw allers sed th' Barrons wuz all shit-eaters. Mebbe ya'd like best ta carry it out in yore mouth."

He moved closer to Clay saying, "Boy, yore 'bout ta find out how horse shit tastes.

Without warning Clay sprang at Jubal and landed a glancing blow to his cheek before Jubal battered him to the ground. Jubal pounced on him and they rolled and fought beneath the frightened horse's belly.

Clay's face was about a foot from the horse manure as Jubal clutched him in a strangle hold and pulled him closer and closer to the pile. Clay made no sound but fought blindly, kicking out and trying to bite the arm that encircled his throat. Clay's face was practically in the manure pile when he felt Jubal's hold on him broken, and saw Brack throw him to the side.

Clay rolled away from the hoofs of the plunging horse as Brack dived down on top of Jubal, opening a wide gap in his mouth as he knocked out half a dozen teeth with the first blow. Before he could swing again, the other Hooks piled on him.

Now it was Everett, Isom, Wilson and Jubal all fighting Brack, as Silas looked on in glee. Over and over they rolled, flailing arms and legs in all directions. There were so many Hooks they were interfering with each other, and Brack's heavy fists were beginning to take their toll.

Clay came off the ground with a big rock grasped in both hand and brought it crashing down on the head of Wilson, who made no sound as he slipped into unconsciousness. Isom hit Clay and he went down, the rock flying away from him.

Seeing Clay go down again made a mad man out of Brack. With Everett on his back, he kicked Isom in the pit of the stomach and threw Everett over his shoulder into him, and they both went sprawling to the ground.

Jubal drew a knife and swung at Brack with it. Now his army training came to his aid as Brack moved out of reach and knocked Jubal down in one motion. Brack went down on Jubal and bent back his arm until he dropped the knife. As Brack grabbed it, Jubal rolled beyond his reach. Brack turned with the knife in his hand, blood running down his face, to meet Everett and Isom as they moved back in on him. The only sound in the school yard now was the labored breathing of the fighters.

The silence was broken by the roar of a .45 pistol. Brack Barron spun around and hit the ground with his face, the knife flying from his hand. His arms reached and the fingers pulled grooves in the mud as he tried to pull himself up. The gun roared again, making his body jerk with the impact of the slug as it struck his back. His hands clutched wildly at the air, as if reaching out to pull back the life that was fleeing him. He shuddered once and then moved no more.

A horrible, unearthly scream poured from Clay's lips as he crawled and scrambled across the muddy yard to his father. The crowd stood transfixed as he lifted Brack's head from the mud and looked into the sightless eyes.

As he wiped the mud and blood from his father's face, he pleaded, "Paw, please don'. Please don' die."

Cradling Brack's head in his arms, Clay sat rocking back and forth in the mire as he continued whispering in the unhearing ear.

"Don' leave me, Paw. Please don' leave me."

Uncontrolled tears fell from Clay's cheeks onto Brack's face. Clay kept trying to wipe them away with his shirt sleeve as he sat alone in his grief. No one moved to touch or speak to him.

Sheriff Billy Sutton, having heard the gunfire, rushed from his office to the schoolhouse. He ran to where Clay sat holding his father and pried Brack from his arms. With the aid of Brian Ferguson, he gently loaded the body into the back of the pickup truck.

As he helped Clay into the back of the truck, he said to the crowd, "Y'all better still be here whin I git back."

The following two days had been pure hell for Clay. After the initial outburst, no tears had passed his eyes. The funeral arrangements had been taken care of by Big Pap and Sarah. The casket had been made by Big Pap from seasoned oak boards that he had been saving to build his own.

Clay had sat beside his father's body day and night until time for the funeral. He made no acknowledgement of the people who tried to console him. His eyes studied and his mind recorded each feature of his father's face time and time again.

At the graveyard on Rainbow Mountain a large crowd gathered, as much from curiosity as from respect. Among them was Larry Stein, the Cincinnati reporter. This latest killing in the long line of deaths brought on by the blood feud was news. The last time he had been to this infamous county was when they had buried "Devil John" Barron, and the two Hooks he had killed before he died.

Clay Barron stood dry-eyed that day, looking on the face of his father for the last time. He reached down and gathered up some of the blue clay that had been dug from the grave. He tore it into two sections, rolled one piece into a ball and dropped it into his pocket. The other he rolled into a ball and slipped it under the folded hands of his father. Clinging to the side of the casket, Clay raised his face heavenward, but the words that passed his lips were no prayer.

"Paw." The young voice came strong and steady. "I swear on my mem'ry of ya thet I'll kill ever' goddamn one of 'em. Ever' time I bust one a thar' heads with a slug, I wan' ya thar', Paw. Ya stick close ta me, now. I'll come ta ya thin, Paw. Whin th' last one's gone, I'll come ta ya. I don' wanna be nowhar' 'ceptin' with you. It ain' agonna take long, Paw. I promise."

The picture taken of Clay at that time by Larry Stein was captioned "The Promise". It was carried in all the major newspapers from coast to coast, and won him a national award.

Bending over the casket, Clay cupped his father's face in his hands and kissed the cold cheek for the last time. As he straightened up, he picked a piece of lint from the black suit of the corpse before he took one more long look, as if to forever burn in his mind the image before him. He signalled to Big Pap to nail on the cover, then walked away from the grave site so as not to see the casket committed to the earth.

* * *

Brian Ferguson had seen it all. The love. The violence. The pain. The hate. This boy, who had shown so much promise, was a man now. He would take his place on the stage of the hills. He would play his role. He would kill as the Barrons and Hooks before him had killed, without mercy or conscience. Like Devil John, he would be a star and die a legend—or a bit player who passes quickly from the stage to be forgotten.

As Clay walked away from the school, the teacher shook his head. The insanity of man never failed to boggle his mind. He knew that only God could bring down the curtain.

Chapter Nine

After crossing the school yard fence, Clay took the foot trail that lay alongside the dirt road going around and up on Rainbow Mountain. After walking some ten minutes, he reached the point where the path and the road separated. The road took a longer, more curving route around the hill, while the path went straight ahead and up.

From years of use the trail was worn bare, and the recent rainfall had left it soft and damp. The black clouds had drifted on now, allowing the sun to show its face for the first time this day.

Sometime later he came to another set of steps that had been built over the barbed wire fence that completely encircled the mountain. As Clay scraped the mud from his boots on the fence, he noticed that in their growth the trees had swallowed the wire that had been nailed to them.

Big Pap and Clay had installed the steps to prevent Clay from tearing his clothes on the wire as he passed this way to and from school when he was a boy. Years ago, his grandfather, Devil John Barron, had strung the fence around the mountain so as to leave no doubt as to his boundary lines. If there had been any questions about his property coming to where the fence was erected, no one had ever voiced them aloud. Devil John had always said, "The title says 'more or less.'" He had made sure it wasn't less.

Clay crossed the fence and was now on soil that he knew some day would belong to him. When Devil John's sister, Sarah, had married Newt Keeton, he had given them three hundred acres for a wedding present. Their line began here and ended halfway up the mountain.

Upon the death of the couple, who were childless, Clay would inherit this property, and once again a Barron would control the entire mountain.

As Clay entered the woods, he became gradually aware of the beauty around him. While dogwood, redbuds and honeysuckle turned the forest into a profusion of color. As he continued up, the air become wonderfully keen.

Over a period of time, the leaves had accumulated on the footpath, leaving it soft and spongy, and giving the effect of walking on expensive carpet. There was also a hint of decay in the air. For everything that lived, something had to die to support it. He paused beside a dead oak and watched a woodpecker boring holes in it in search of insects. Although dead, the oak was still contributing its share to the scheme of nature.

As he walked on, the path rejoined the road that was rutted from the wheels of Newt's buggy. It would be impossible for a car to get through here.

"Strange," thought Clay to himself, "that so few hours of travel could bring a man from the asphalt and cement world of an ultramodern city to this land that hadn't changed in a hundred years."

He vowed to himself that he would never let it change. He realized that only here was life real. In his soul now lived the spirit of all the Barrons before him who had lived on this mountain.

He walked between the ruts until he came to Blue Bank. He didn't know who in his family had first named it that, but it couldn't have been called anything else. He had often wondered what freak of nature had caused the bare clay bank here in the otherwise abundant woods. The blue clay clung to his boots as he followed the road.

At the edge of Blue Bank was a spring walled up by some long dead and forgotten Barron, but the fruits of his labors still gave pleasure to those remaining.

"Every man," thought Clay philosophically, "should leave something to remind the world that he had passed through. How lonely and restless must be the soul of a man who lived but contributed nothing."

*   *   *

Years ago on this very spot, a sequence of events had taken place which accounted for the Cherokee blood in Clay's veins and the slightly aquiline appearance of his features.

In the old days, the Indians had come here from miles away to dig the clay, from which they made their pottery. On one such occasion, Clay's great-great grandfather, Ott Barron, had become friendly with the powerful Cherokee Chief Flint. It was here he saw for the first time the chief's beautiful daughter, Blue Bird. Her black, mysterious, slumberous eyes had offered a silent challenge unequalled by any white woman he had ever met. As was the custom, he tried to buy her—but to no avail.

In the days that followed, while the squaws made their pottery, old Flint hunted with and came to like and respect this wild young man who lived on the high mountain. When he noticed the covert glances his daughter gave the white man when she thought she was unobserved, the chief had explained to Ott, "The daughter of Flint has been promised to the greatest of all the Cherokee braves, War Club. He's strong as a bear, quick as a panther, and fierce as a starving wolf. As long as he lives, I can give her to no other."

"I," bragged the brash young Barron, "am strong as a bull elk, quick as a striking copperhead, and fierce as a he eagle protecting his young. Fetch this big stick who calls himself "War Club" to me, that I may break him into little splinters and keep for myself the Bird of the Cherokee. Since my eyes have touched on her, I know that should she fly away from me, I would be as the turtledove that has lost his mate."

Blue Bird's heart had throbbed as he made his challenge, but she held little hope that he could best the giant War Club.

After drinking from the spring, Clay stood looking around him at the location of one of the most fierce hand-to-hand battles ever fought in these or any other hills. The story of this fight had been passed down from the lips of one Barron to another. Clay gloried in it, even now.

Flint had sent for War Club, who came immediately to accept the challenge of the white man. War Club was a mature man of thirty-two and had many scalps to his credit, both red and white; hence he asked permission to take the white man's hair when he won.

Ott's father, Jeb, and four brothers had come down from the mountain to witness the impending duel. Old Jeb agreed to War Club's request.

"If the boy's dead, he won't give a damn what happens to his hair."

Jeb Barron, advancing in years, had never known the equal of this youngest of the Barrons. Smaller in stature than his brothers he had, nevertheless, learned every trick of battle known to them, and had invented some of his own. His physical condition was such that he could run twenty miles before breakfast.

Old Jeb relished the thought of Flint's daughter being brought into his family.

"A family left go without new blood too long breeds weak," he reasoned.

The blood of Flint's, mixed with his own, would assure the Barrons of powerful and fierce fighters for many generations to come. Jeb, being a man who took advantage of every opportunity to turn a profit, walked among the Cherokees, who were avid gamblers, and covered all bets offered against his son.

The Cherokee chief had laid down the rules. It was to be a fight to the death. Weapons were to be a knife and a tomahawk for each man, and neither was to be thrown. A brave stood with a notched arrow, ordered by Flint to shoot and kill either of the contestants who broke the rules.

The battle had raged up and down the same area where Clay now stood. As the larger War Club swarmed over him, Ott had been forced to fight a defensive battle. He was soon bleeding from several wounds, as was War Club. The Cherokee brave's savage onslaught had driven Ott into the woods below the road.

They had slashed and hacked their way along the hollow that carried off the overflow from the spring. Fending off the ferocious attack of the Indian, Ott failed to see the fallen log that caused him to fall backward down into the hollow.

Thinking that at last he had his elusive enemy trapped, War Club gave a whoop of victory and dived in at Ott. The white man was like a cat; he had flipped to his feet while still falling backwards. As the Indian flew toward him, Ott's muscular arm drove the tomahawk past War Club's upraised arms and sank the blade to the handle in his forehead. Although dead in the air, the momentum of the hurtling body of War Club carried him into Ott, bowling him over and coming to rest on top of him.

There was silence along the hollow. The end had come so fast no one was sure which one had been killed. Ott shoved aside the gory body of the Indian and tried to crawl out of the hollow. A wild shout had gone up from the Barrons as they slid down to assist the victor.

Old Jeb, knowing how the Indians loved to brag about their feats in battle, began striding up and down in front of the warriors, expounding to all the bravery and courage of his young whelp, who had torn out the throat of the he-wolf.

The "purchase" of Blue Bird was conducted with much pomp and ceremony that night in the Indian camp. Ott presented to Flint a new rifle, ten skins of seed corn, and one young, well-built mare of exceptional speed.

After the feasting and marriage of Blue Bird and Ott Barron, there was no more killing between the Barrons and the red men. All the tribes knew that the high mountains came under the protection of the Cherokees, and their raiding parties were careful never to trespass on the forbidden ground.

*   *   *

Clay knelt and drank again from the spring. He knew it wouldn't take long for him to forget the chlorine water of the city.

Old Jeb Barron and the Cherokee Chief called Flint could they see Clay now striding through the woods would be proud that even civilization and the softness that comes to a people who do not know hunger and strife had failed to weaken the bloodline or curb the killer instinct established by the union of their offspring.

Everywhere Clay turned there was something to remind him of his father. He stopped now to reminisce beneath the branches of two giant beech trees that stood alone just inside Big Pap's line fence. Their spreading limbs and long roots had cut off the sun and moisture from everything beneath them, leaving a small clearing. The beeches didn't have this space all to themselves, however. A colony of ants had built a hill here, and for as long as Clay could remember they had been rushing back and forth beneath the trees.

On his tenth birthday, he had brought them a piece of the birthday cake his Aunt Sarah had baked for him and sat there watching them until they had stored it all inside. He was careful as he moved closer not to step on any of them now. They didn't seem to have fared badly during his absence. The ant hill was higher than ever. He wondered if they had missed the food he left them on his way home from school.

Looking down the mountain from the two beeches, Clay could see Gratt Waggoner's farm. The back of the house nestled against the hill and the front faced the Sandy Valley. There was no sign of life below, and he hoped nothing had happened to "Old Grumpy," as Brack had called him. Grumpy was a retired Navy man who had bought the farm 'for a song.' No one wanted to live between the Barrons and the Hooks, knowing a full scale war might break out between the two at any time.

Gratt had dealt often with war during his thirty years in the Navy, and was unconcerned with the activities of his hostile neighbors. After taking possession, he immediately erected several "No Trespassing" signs on his property.

Clay recalled the day Grumpy had caught his father and him ignoring the "No Trespassing" signs and heading for their favorite fishing hole on his land. He had escorted them, at gun point, to Hookville, where he filed charges against them for trespassing. This had been the first charge of its kind filed in that county in ten years. The fine had been three dollars or three days in jail each. Brack had paid Clay's fine, but stubbornly spent his three days in jail.

Upon his release, he had conceded to Clay, "Grumpy's got a righ' ta run us off'n his land, but I bin afishin' thar too long ta quit now. 'Pears as if'n we're agonna' haf'ta git on more friendly terms with our good neighbor by doin' somethin' extrie nice fer 'im."

Grumpy's love of race horses had prompted his purchase of an old, broken-down Thoroughbred mare. He planned to take her to Lexington to breed her to one of the sons of "Man of War." He entertained visions of a great racing stable starting from this meager beginning.

Brack was loafing in Hookville the day Grumpy was bragging about taking the mare, who was in heat, to Lexington the following day. Hearing this news, Brack rushed home and got Clay and a rope. Together they sneaked the racing mare out of Grumpy's barn that night, undetected, and led her down the valley to Leroy Butcher's mule farm. While the rest of the countryside slept peacefully, they bred the Thoroughbred mare to a jackass.

Unaware of what had transpired the preceding night, Grumpy trucked her to Lexington the following day, but it was too late. The jack had done his job well. As the months passed, when Clay and his father walked to and from Hookville, Brack would break up with laughter as he looked down the hill at the mare's swollen belly.

"Ol' Grumpy is a gonna have the fastest mule in the whole state of Kintuck," he would roar. "Cain't ya jist see it now, Clay? Thar they is, th' dancin' Thoroughbreds waitin' fer th' start of the Kentucky Derby. Thar' 'e comes now, carryin' th' Waggoner colors, th' longest-eared Thoroughbred in racin' his'try."

When the mare was ready to foal, Grumpy had gone to town for the vet. He allowed several town loafers to accompany them back to the farm to witness the birth of a champion. When the veterinarian pulled from the mare a long-eared mule colt, Grumpy could only stare in disbelief. The town bums were rolling around the barn floor, hysterical peals of laughter escaping them.

"Brack didn't like being put in jail fer trespassin', I guess," chuckled the vet.

With this, Grumpy stomped out of the barn and headed toward the house, leaving the vet to transport the wise-cracking onlookers back to town.

The next day Clay and his father crossed the fence here at the two beech trees and strolled across Grumpy's field to their favorite fishing spot. The "no trespassing" signs were gone.

A rare smile softened Clay's features as he left the two beeches and followed the road back into the woods until he reached a medium-sized hickory tree. It was here that he had killed his first squirrel when he was only eight years old. It had run across the road in front of him and jumped on the side of this tree. He hadn't been permitted to carry a loaded gun then, and Brack allowed him only one bullet.

He had told Clay, "If'n ya don' git 'em th' first shot, ya don' dasarve 'em anyhow."

Clay recalled how he had fumbled the bullet out of his pocket and into the single shot .22 Winchester. As the squirrel took off up the tree, he shot it in the back. He grabbed it by the tail and ran all the way back to Big Pap's, where Brack was waiting for him.

"Git th' skinnin' knife an' I'll help ya skin 'im," his father had beamed.

Clay had held the squirrel by the front feet while his father used the knife and pulled from the other direction. When they came to the part where the bullet had broken its back, the squirrel pulled apart.

As Clay stood holding the front half of the squirrel, Brack had said to him, "Whin ya shoot small game anywhar but in th' haid, ya allers ruin a lotta meat."

It had been a simple statement, but Clay had understood its meaning. After that, if he didn't have a clean shot at the head, he would pass it up. It was sometime before he brought home another squirrel, but when he did he carried it proudly with his finger stuck through the bullet hole in its head.

He left the road now and walked through the trees. At one time he had been like a shadow in the woods. Today, he felt strange and clumsy. Ahead, in another level shelf in the mountain, he could see the shingles on the roof of a small log house. He stopped behind the thick laurel bushes at the edge of the clearing, pushed some of them aside and peered out.

"Nothing's changed here," he thought. "Same neat cabin; same barn still braced at the back with hickory poles; same fruit trees with bee hives beneath them. There's even a scarecrow still in the garden."

On the front porch snoozing peacefully in the spring sun, an enormous man sat in a rocking chair. A full grey beard covered his chin and rested on his chest.

Clay watched the lazy rocking of the old man for several moments, then pursed his lips and gave the call of the bobwhite three times in succession. The third call had two "bobs" in it. The rocker stopped. The old man's head turned slowly in the direction of the woods. Clay remained motionless. Once again the rocker began its rhythmic movement. From Clay's lips again came the three calls.

The great bearded man's boots slammed into the floor as he heaved his ponderous bulk out of the rocker. The chair continued to rock back and forth as he strode to the edge of the porch and stood staring intently toward the woods.

"For a man like this one to grow old is a shame," Clay thought, as he once again gave the quail call. The old man was now galvanized into action. He leapt off the porch and shouted, "Sarah, come 'ere, quick."

A tall, thin, white-haired woman opened the screen door and stepped out onto the porch. Her dress came almost to the floor. In her hands she carried a sunbonnet. This was his great-aunt, Sarah; the only female love he had ever known.

"Whut is it, Newt?" she questioned, as she walked to the edge of the porch.

"It's Clay, Sarah. He's out thar in th' woods now."

Sarah walked out into the yard and stood beside her husband. She put on the sunbonnet to shield her eyes and squinted in the direction of his outstretched arm.

"I don' see nothin'," she said. "Mebbe you wuz dreamin' ya seen 'im."

"Didn't see 'im," her husband answered, "but he's out thar."

He cupped his hands to his lips and made the call the Barrons often used when they approached the house during the day. Sarah's heart leapt with joy when she heard the answer come from the woods.

Clay Barron stepped through the laurels and walked toward the old couple. They stood calmly watching him come, as if he had been gone only since yesterday instead of thirteen years. He had left them as a boy, but the figure hurrying toward them was that of a man.

When Clay was about fifteen feet from them, Newt suddenly yelled, "To the left. A Hook."

Clay's left hand jerked open the snaps of his shirt as he whirled to the left. The hills echoed with five roars that came so fast they blended together from the gun that had appeared magically in his hands. In the garden, a scarecrow's head was torn apart by the slugs from the .45.

As this last of the Barrons turned back towards him, Big Pap smiled and nodded an affirmative answer to his own thoughts.

"Yep, he's a Barron, shore 'nuff. He's even 'membered Devil John's rule of leavin' one bullet in 'is gun, evin whin practicin'."

Chapter Ten

Clay slipped the gun back into its holster and held out his arms as he reached the waiting couple. Aunt Sarah clung to him as he squeezed her thin shoulders and kissed the wrinkled cheek, wet with tears.

With one arm still around her, he turned and asked, "How have you been, Big Pappy?"

"Jist 'bout as fine as possum hair," Big Pap answered, his teeth gleaming in a smile of welcome.

Clay dropped his arm from around his aunt's shoulders and reached for Big Pap's hand. It came as he knew it would—the slow, crushing pressure on his fingers. Big Pap had tested Clay's gun; now he was testing his strength.

Clay could remember how Big Pap and Brack used to arm wrestle by the hour, but in the end Big Pap always won. Many times after a drinking spree in Hookville, Brack would stop at Big Pap's on the way home, roust him out of bed and challenge him, but never did he emerge the victor. To Clay's knowledge, Big Pap's arm had never been put down.

Big Pap felt the hand in his begin to tighten, but could detect no change of expression on Clay's face.

He thought, as he applied more pressure, "This 'ere's th' strongest hand I've had aholt of since his daddy. He's mebbe even stronger'n Brack."

The two mighty muscular arms moved up and down as each strove to outgrip the other. The two men stood locked together until Sarah broke them apart by saying, "Ya leetle boys cut out yer silly game and git on up on the porch so's we kin git acquainted agin."

Newt felt a moment's regret in this happy reunion. He wished that Devil John and Brack could see the boy. He possessed all the qualities that had been so important to them; namely, a fast gun, strong arm and quick mind.

As they walked to the porch, Sarah asked, "Whar ya bin an' whatcha bin a'doin, Clay? Whut took ya so long ta git back home?"

"I just got the charges dropped against me a short time ago," he answered. "I didn't dare try to get in touch before. If I had been found, it not only would have caused me trouble, but also the man who kept me hid all these years, and I couldn't take a chance on that."

"We oft'times wundered whar ya went thet night after ya got outta jail," she probed.

His answer came in the form of a question. "Do you remember the man whose life Grandpa saved in the army that time he won the French medal?"

"Cain't recall 'is name right off, but I know whut yer talkin' 'bout," she answered.

"Well, anyway," Clay continued, "when I was seven or eight years old Paw showed me where he kept the medal and the name and address of the soldier Grandpa rescued. He told me that if I should ever need anything and there wasn't anyone else to turn to, that I should take the medal and go to Moe Carrio and tell him who I was."

"Carrio had told Grandpa before he left France that if there was anything he ever needed to just come and ask for it. When I left Big Pap that night I went back on the hill to say good-bye to Paw, and I remembered about the medal. So that's what I did. I went to him and he took me in and I've been with him ever since. That's enough about me now. What I want to hear is what's been happening around here since I've been gone."

Big Pap settled himself again in his rocker. Clay sat on the floor with his legs dangling over the edge of the porch.

Sarah said as she opened the screen door, "I'm gonna go git my weddin' jug. I bin savin' th' last of it fer yore comin' home, Clay."

As the rocker began to creak under its heavy burden, Big Pap spoke. "Nothin' has happen't here ta amount ta nothin' since I bused ya outta jail an' they quit scourin' th' mountain lookin' fer ya. Thet Judge Holbrook tried ta git me indicted by the grand jury fer breakin' ya out, but Billy Young tol' me how he sat thar in th' doorway acrost th' street an' watched me tarn ya' loose."

"Why didn't he stop you?" Clay asked in wonder.

"He tol' me he swore an oath ta keep th' law as ta th' best of his ability, an' he din' think sendin' ya to th' pen an' makin' a killer outta ya fer shore wuz th' way ta do it. Ya owe thet man a lot, Clay. I wanted ya ta know it."

"He never said anything to me about that today when I talked to him," Clay said.

"He wouldn'," Newt answered. "He don' wan' ya ta feel beholden to 'im. Whut did he say ta ya?"

"He told me to visit my mountain and leave," Clay replied.

"Ya gonna do thet, Boy?" Big Pap queried.

"No, Big Pappy. I'm not ever going to leave." There was absolute conviction in Clay's voice.

"Don' guess ya seen none of th' Hooks on yer way in?"

Clay shook his head negatively as Big Pap continued. "They bin eatin' powerful high on th' hog since ya bin gone. Most everybody in th' country is afeard of 'em. They've took over th' whiskey makin' and sellin' in th' whole country."

"Why hasn't Uncle Billy stopped them?" Clay asked.

"He cain't," replied Big Pap. "You kin 'member how things wuz here. They's still th' same. It's an unwritten law thet th' sheriff leaves th' still raidin' to th' federals. Billy'd nivver git 'lected agin if'n he interfered with th' whiskey makin', no matter how much everybody hates them Hooks."

"Yeah, I guess I have been gone a long time," Clay mused.

"Whut's yer plans now, Son?" Big Pap inquired.

"No plans, Pappy," Clay answered. "I'll move back on the mountain. Just my being here is bound to bring trouble, and when it comes I'll take care of it."

It was an effort for Big Pap to look at Clay as he informed him, "I'm afeard ya cain't move back on th' mountain."

Clay's head jerked up, his eyes narrowing as he demanded, "Why not?"

"Someone burned down yer house th' night after ya left. Hooks, I' rikkin."

Big Pap had expected Clay to become enraged upon hearing this news, but the only sound that came from him was the dull thud of his boot hitting the wooden front of the porch as he swung his leg back and forth.

Sarah broke into both their thoughts as she came back out onto the porch, carrying an old stone jug.

"Do ya 'member this jug, Clay?" she asked as she poured a generous amount of whiskey into each of their glasses.

"Sure, I do. This was your wedding jug." He took it from her and examined it fondly.

At the time of Sarah and Big Pap's wedding, one of the local customs was a jug race. The course for a jug race was fifty yards walked off in any field. The biggest and slowest man at the wedding was handed a stone jug containing whiskey, which had been furnished by the bride and groom. The object of the race was to cross the finish line with the jug, which the winner got to keep. With the starting man having only a five yard advantage, it didn't take the other contestants long to pounce on him and take away the jug.

"That must have been some fight, huh, Pappy?" Clay asked.

"Nivver seen nothin' like it afore or since," he grinned. "Fifteen or twenty of th' biggest and meanest men in th' county fightin' for this jug. I nivver will fergit it. John Tom Gullet finally got it acrost th' marker.

He hadn' brung no present, so he give it ta Sarah fer a weddin' gift. Poor man got killed in a fight over a line tree down on th' Little Brushy not more'n a week later."

"From what I remember hearing when I was a kid, that must have been some romance you two had," laughed Clay. As he set the jug down, he observed the warm glances being exchanged by these two people he loved.

A private, knowing smile passed between the two older people and Sarah thought, "Don' seem possible it's bin so long. I kin remember how it happen't like it wuz only yesterday."

Being the sister of Devil John Barron hadn't been easy when Sarah was a young woman of courting age. An occasional longing glance at the black-haired beauty from the high mountain was all the young men of her age dared because of their fear of her brother. Then came the day that Newt Keeton was to see Sarah in Hookville and lose his heart to her even before knowing who she was.

The next Sunday found him on his way to her mountain home. He had been warned about Devil John, but Newt Keeton was a man without fear. He was dressed in a homespun suit that he didn't like, but it was the best he had and he wanted to look respectable. The suit coat was too small, and he had to keep his massive shoulders hunched up from fear that they would burst through the cloth.

When he rode into Sarah's yard, the place seemed deserted. As he dismounted, a soft voice from behind him inquired, "Whut's yer business here, Mister?"

Looking over his shoulder, Newt saw a young man holding a rifle loosely in his hands. The deep-set black eyes in an unsmiling face were carefully measuring him. This, of course, was the young man known as Devil John Barron.

Newt walked forward and held out his right hand. "I'm Newt Keeton, an' I've come acallin' on yer sister, Sarah," he answered.

Devil John ignored the outstretched hand as he asked, "Did she give ya a invite here?"

Newt's hand dropped as he said, "I ain' met 'er yit. I tried ta find a mutual friend ta interduce us, but everybody wuz afeared ta come up here. I wuz ahopin' you'd do th' honor of interducin' me ta Miss Barron."

A slight smile played for an instant on the hard mouth before he said, "Wal now, comin' up here ta my home without no invite and expectin' ta court Sarah without bein' interduced takes considerable nerve. I've allers bin a man thet respects thet in another'n, so I'm gonna let ya ride off'n this mountain all in one piece, but if'n ya ivver come back. . . ." He left the sentence hang with a slight shrug of his shoulders.

"I'll leave when an' if'n Miss Barron tells me to," Newt answered stubbornly.

Devil John's appearance changed from amusement to anger at this big, overgrown ox who dared come here to his mountain and defy him.

Devil John's voice came low and cutting as he said, "Clim' on thet horse and ride outta here, or I'll sen' ya outta here belly down on yer saddle."

Newt turned toward the horse, but he didn't mount. Instead he removed the suit coat and threw it over the saddle. Next came the ruffled shirt and stiff collar, which he carefully placed on top of the coat.

Devil John stood there watching Newt in disbelief as he thought, "This hairy monster of a man is agonna fight me."

Looking out the window, Sarah thrilled to the voice of Newt as he said to Devil John, "I come up here respectful-like ta see Miss Barron, an' if'n I hav'ta fight ya' to see her, I will. I ain' no good with a gun, an' don' evin carry one. If'n ya wanna throw me off'n this mountain, why don' ya put thet gun down an' see if'n ya kin do it man-ta-man?"

Sarah held her breath. Her brother was an unpredictable man, but she knew he would accept the challenge and would fight the only way he ever fought—to kill. For some reason she didn't want anything to happen to this big giant of a stranger.

As Devil John leaned the rifle against a tree and began to remove his shirt, Sarah hurried outside and stepped between them, confronting her brother.

"John, do you remember whut ya sed two years ago whin I tried talkin' with ya 'bout havin' gentlemen callers?" she asked.

When he failed to reply, she continued, "You sed I could have a caller enytime one had nerve 'nuff ta cum' up here. Looks ta me like this one's had 'nuff nerve. This gentlemen sez he'd like ta be interduced ta me, an' I'd be very happy ta make 'is acquaintance. If'n this is still gonna be ma home, I'd like fer you ta put yer shirt back on and do th' interducin'."

Her brother looked from her to Newt, and his shoulders again gave the expressive little shrug. Sarah knew that John would often wonder if he could have taken the bigger man, but he was to never know.

Without a word, Devil John picked up his shirt and slipped it on.

Newt was struggling into his ruffled white shirt when Sarah said, "If'n ya don' mind, leave th' collar and coat off. I hate ta see a man all choked up."

Devil John then stepped to the side of his sister and said simply, "Sarah, I would like fer ya ta make the acquaintance of Newt Keeton."

He turned and said to Newt, "Mr. Keeton, I present ma sister, Sarah."

Sarah held out her hand and watched it disappear into the big calloused hand of her caller. As they stood there looking into each other's eyes, Devil John picked up his rifle and walked away grunting, "Looks lak' thar's gonna be 'nuther man on th' mountain."

After a brief courtship, Newt and Sarah were married. Devil John had helped them build their house in the beautiful glade on the side of the mountain.

Sarah later found that she was unable to bear children, but this only bound her and her husband closer together, as Newt attempted to make up for their absence. Many years passed before Sarah was to realize the fulfillment of her mother instinct, which came through the death of Brack's wife.

Brack had married young Belinda McGoffin from Floyd County and had brought her to the mountain to keep house for him and Devil John. To Belinda and Brack a son had been born. Devil John had been beside himself with joy, and could barely keep his hands off the baby.

As the infant clung to his huge thumb, Devil John said, "This leetle tyke sticks tighter'n blue clay."

Belinda had looked up at this old man, who had been a paragon of viciousness all his life, holding her young son so tenderly and said, "That's whut we'll call 'im, then, Blue Clay Barron."

Belinda had been as headstrong and wild as Brack. Following one of their heated arguments, she had raced her horse down the mountain, not taking time to use the trail. She knew Brack would follow her, and she wanted to get to Sarah first to enlist her aid in the argument. As she ran the horse through the trees, she looked back to see if Brack was following, and never saw the low-hanging limb that broke her neck.

Sarah had held wide her arms when Brack brought her Clay, who was then nine months old. As he grew older, Clay had two homes. He would "batch" with Brack and Devil John for a few days at a time, then come back to her. If he stayed up on the mountain much more than a couple of days at a time, she would ring the big dinner bell in the front yard. When he heard it, Clay knew she was lonesome for him and he would waste no time getting down there. He had called her "Mammy" and Newt his "Big Pappy," and they both loved him as their own.

As Sarah raised her glass in a toast, she was thinking as she looked at Clay, "He's growed up ta be a man, but whut terrible hurts he's had since goin' beyond ma reach."

She longed to pull him into her arms and cry away his past, but instead she said, "Here's ta th' Barrons, both livin' an' dead."

Clay felt the sting of the liquor as it entered his stomach. It was a wonderful, yet strange feeling, for him to have a drink with these two people who were his only family.

After draining her glass, Sarah asked, "Did ya come alone, Clay?"

"Yes, I'm all alone. Why?"

"Oh, I jest wanted ta know if'n ya had a fam'ly or wuz tied ta enybody wharivver ya bin."

"No, Mammy. You and Big Pap are the only family I have or need," he answered.

"I'm glad ta hear ya say thet, Clay, but I'm athinkin' ya might change yer mind when ya see my young friend thet comes over here ever now and thin."

With little apparent interest he asked, "Oh? Just who might your young friend be?"

She replied, "Ya jist sit tight right here while I go inside an' git a pitcher of 'er. I wan' ta see if'n ya 'member who she is."

She quickly returned with a picture of a girl dressed in riding clothes standing beside a black horse.

"Do ya recollect who this is?"

Clay looked closely at the picture before answering, "No, can't say I do. Who is she?"

"Do ya 'member thet leetle skinny black-haired gal thet used ta make ya so mad follerin' ya round all th' time at school?"

"Surely you're not going to tell me this is Valarie Vansant?" he asked incredulously.

"Ain't no one else," she beamed.

"I'll be damned," he exclaimed. "From the looks of this picture she sure has grown into a gorgeous piece of woman."

"Thet picture don' do 'er justice," Newt cut in. "Clay, this girl is the mos' beautiful woman since Sarah, and one of th' finest persons I ivver knowed."

"Why are you two telling me all this?" Clay questioned.

"No use beatin' 'round th' bush," Sarah said. She'll be over here soon's she finds out yer home. Thet girl allers has bin and still is in love with ya."

"You gotta be kidding me," he scoffed.

"No, I'm not kiddin' ya," Sarah shot back. "This feelin' she's got fer ya is a mighty serious thing with 'er, an' I'm tellin' ya ahead a time 'cause I'm not 'bout ta have ya hurt 'er."

"I still don't understand your big interest in her," retorted Clay.

"I'm interested in 'er 'cause she wuz interested 'nuff in me to come'n see me almost every day last winter whin I took sick, an' also on accountta she wuz interested 'nuff in ya to pester th' sheriff nigh ta death tryin' ta git 'im ta help 'er find out whar you wuz."

"Sounds to me like the girl has been reading too many romance stories. Anyway, don't worry yourself about my hurting her. I have no intention of picking this flower of the hills you two are so bent on protecting. I want no woman jackin' with my mind until I get done what I came here to do."

Big Pap leaned forward in his chair and spoke directly to Clay. "Here's th' whole thing, Son. Me an' yer aunt thinks th' world and all a' this girl. I've lived 'round too many a' th' Barrons fer too many years an' seen 'em run through too many wimmin not ta know thet you'd be like all th' rest. As a favor ta me an' yer aunt, I'll only ask ya not ta play with th' girl if'n ya don' mean it."

"Big Pappy, when she finds out that I'm not the man on the white stud horse, she'll be all right, so let's talk about something else," Clay said, closing the subject.

As the afternoon passed and Clay sat talking to the old couple, a deep tenderness swept over him. At times they would sit for long minutes, just enjoying the silence of each other's company.

"Aunt Sarah, do you know what I would like to have?" Clay asked lazily. "I'd like to have a big chunk of that cornbread you always keep around and a glass of buttermilk."

"No sooner sed then dun," she said. "Here we bin sittin' jabberin' away an' I didn' even think thet ya might be hungry."

"Mammy, this is more a hunger of the mind than the stomach."

While she prepared his snack, Clay strolled out to the garden, pulled a handful of green onions and stripped the skins from them. Sarah was waiting with his bread and milk when he returned to the porch.

As Clay sat relishing the food he said, "Mammy, anyone who hasn't had cornbread, buttermilk and green onions just hasn't lived."

"Seein' ya sit thar apiecin' like ya used ta makes me feel awful good, Clay."

Clay smiled his appreciation at her as he set down the empty glass and walked out into the yard. He surveyed the sun that was beginning to drop in the sky, and his eyes then turned to the mountain behind the house.

"Guess I'll go on up to the top now," he said quietly.

Sarah started to tell Big Pap to go with him, but Big Pap, reading her thoughts, shook his head 'no' before she could speak.

"Yer room is jist as ya left it, Clay. Ya jist feel free ta come an' go like ya usta," said Big Pap.

With mixed emotions they watched him until he disappeared into the trees.

Chapter Eleven

Clay took the trail behind the cabin that led to the top of his mountain. The woods was still at this time before sunset. A squirrel, protected from sight by the green leaves of a hickory tree, sat quietly watching him as he passed. A giant oak had given up the fight for life and had allowed the wind to drive it to the ground, where it lay blocking the path. Clay stepped around the upturned roots and paused to look back down the footpath and saw a curious fox that had been following him glide into the underbrush.

The hill upon which he stood was rich in timber. There was a marked difference in the trees on this mountain from other trees in the surrounding area because a sawmill had never run here.

"A virgin forest today is as rare as a virgin woman," Clay thought. He was glad he had the forest.

He stood completely motionless, savoring the faint sounds that were undistinguishable when he was moving through the woods. A cool breeze caressed his brow and the quiet and solitude soothed him.

Since leaving this mountain, he had felt like a lost wanderer in a strange world. Overhead, a woodpecker began banging on a dead tree limb. With this atmosphere enveloping him, he began to sense that he was really home. The feel of the hills was coming back.

Upon reaching the top of the mountain, he emerged out of the trees and entered his paradise at the top of his world. It lay before him like a park. The long bluegrass bent gently to the ever-present breeze. The glow of the setting sun shining on the three fresh-water lakes, which were surrounded by evenly spaced maple trees, gave off streaks of blue and yellow color.

His mouth tightened as he looked to where the house and the barn had stood, and saw now only a pile of rubble. The rusty tin roof was lying on top of the rest of the debris, twisted grotesquely from the heat of the fire. Only the stone chimney still stood, stubbornly holding its head in the sky, as if waiting for Clay to come and make it once again a part of his life.

Clay pulled his narrowed eyes from the ruins of his home, and once more because the avenger. The past few hours he had spent with his aunt and uncle had somewhat removed from his mind the purpose for which he was here. That purpose came back with a vengeance, and his hate fed on the scene before him.

His feet carried him through the boot-high grass to a plot of ground that was surrounded by a morning glory- and rose-covered fence. As he walked through the gate, the tombstones shone bright in the fading light of evening. The pine trees, planted one behind each stone, stood sentinel as the sun touched them for the last time that day before slipping behind a far-off hill. As he passed among the stones, the world around him was becoming as gray as his thoughts. The wind was rising and began to moan in the trees.

Clay passed the stones until he came to the last one in the row. It read, "Brack Barron. Born July 15, 1914. Murdered November 3, 1946."

Below this was an inscription which read, *"In life I took courage from my ancestors. In death I will be avenged by my descendants."*

Clay had ordered the inscription to forever remind himself of his heritage.

The tall man dropped to both knees beside the grave. His lips began to tremble, and his thick shoulders shook with emotion. His body slipped forward until his outstretched arms encircled the mound of earth covering his father. Now, at long last, the tears came. They streamed down his cheeks in torrents. The big man sobbed as if his heart would burst.

Here, all alone on the mountaintop in the gloom of the evening, all of the loneliness, bitterness and frustrations of a boy being shoved into manhood too soon poured out of him. These were the first tears to pass his eyes since the day he held his father's lifeless body in his arms.

A hoot owl alighted in one of the pine trees, but took to the air again as it saw the unfamiliar figure lying across the grave below.

Long into the night the mountain creatures listened to the strange sounds from the man lying there. Clay became exhausted from his grief. A complete weariness overtook him, and his mind sought an escape from the torment of his thoughts. As he slipped into the luxury of a deep sleep, he felt relieved of everything except the hate. This still lay in the pit of his stomach, and like a cancerous tumor, it kept growing. He would have to remove it, or it would surely destroy him.

As the first rays of dawn pushed back the darkness of night, awakening the day dwellers and putting to sleep the night creatures, Clay stirred and came awake. His face showed streaks of dirt from the mingling of tears and soil, but his body felt relieved and relaxed. Last night he had rushed to his father as he had done when he suffered from pain as a child. He felt this morning as he always had before, after his father had comforted him.

Clay wandered through the Barron cemetery, studying the other grave markers. Most of the stones had been erected before he was born. The two headstones of his uncles, Bado and Wilder Barron, bore the same death date. He could barely remember them. Bado and Wilder had gone to a church camp meeting on the Elk Fork. On their way home they had been ambushed and killed by an unknown number of drunken Hooks, who were aided by their two cousins, Jack and Tom Rigsby. The Rigsbys later made the mistake of bragging about their part in the killings.

Clay would remember how his grandfather would stand and stare at his sons' graves and suffer his grief in silence. Sometimes, he would then check his pistol and stalk down to the valley. Often, when he returned to the mountain, there would be mourning below.

Jack Rigsby had been down on his knees getting milk out of a springhouse for his wife when Devil John stepped out of the bushes. Devil John pressed the long barrel of his pistol to Jack's head and pulled the trigger. Jack's wife collapsed in a dead faint when John kicked her husband's body into the spring. Ignoring her, Devil John turned and nonchalantly walked away.

Upon learning of his brother's death, Tom Rigsby hastened to leave the country. Devil John had been like a bloodhound on his trail. Tom's body was soon discovered hanging by the feet from a willow tree near the village of Blaine. To the weight of his body had been added five .45 slugs. During that year, two more Hooks met deaths that were never explained.

Buried next to Wilder was Devil John's wife and Clay's grandmother Lucy, and the infant daughter to whom she had tried to give life.

The next stone brought a flood of memories to Clay. This one read, "John Barron. Born March 18, 1884. Died June 14, 1937." Here was buried the remains of the vengeful killer known as Devil John Barron.

The story of this man's life could tell most of the history of the bloody Barron and Hook war. Devil John had been only an embryo in the body of his mother, Sybil, when it all began. Devil John's father, Quentin Barron, who was half-Cherokee, had gone down into the valley to court Sybil Patrick. Drew Hook, who wanted to marry her himself, had been furious. After Quentin married Sybil and took her up on the mountain to live, Drew Hook never became reconciled to it. To be beaten out by a half-breed was to him the crowning insult of his life.

Quentin and Sybil's firstborn was a daughter whom they named Sarah. Sybil was carrying her second child at the time Drew Hook shot down and killed her husband Quentin. Upon his death, she turned from a self-assured woman into a person possessed with her lust for revenge.

Later, when she overheard Quentin's brothers Lige and Feril planning to kill Drew Hook, she had demanded that they wait to see if the baby she was carrying was a boy.

"If'n hit's a boy child, it's his place ta kill Drew Hook. If'n hit's a girl, you two kin go git 'im."

Sybil's voice had been filled with malice.

When the baby boy was born, they named him John. Honoring their promise to Sybil not to kill Drew Hook if she bore a son, Lige and Feril turned their vengeance instead on Drew's brothers Leslie and Henry Hook. They succeeded in killing both Hooks in a furious gunfight, but Feril suffered wounds that caused his death the following day.

After Feril had been buried, Lige proposed marriage to Sybil.

"It ain' proper fer us'ns ta live here alone since Feril's gone," he'd said.

Knowing the love Lige held for little Sarah and John and not wanting to leave the mountain, Sybil had accepted. Lige and Sybil went to Hookville the following week to be married. When they came out of the preacher's house, they were confronted by Drew Hook and two of his brothers, W. T. and Gaston.

When the gunfight started, Lige completely ignored Drew Hook, but killed both his brothers. Drew kept pumping slugs into Lige until his gun was empty. The crowd then pressed around Lige and heard him whisper to Sybil as he died, "I saved Drew fer little John."

Sybil continued to live on the mountain with her two children. One day she walked into the post office in Hookville and mailed a letter addressed to Sam Colt. A couple of weeks later a package addressed to her arrived from the Colt Firearm Company. There was no doubt in anyone's mind what the package contained.

John was five years old when he received the gun for his birthday. It was a beautiful gun; a single action Colt .45 with a long barrel and walnut handles. It was so big the boy could hardly lift it, but he spent some time each day with the gun, learning to hold it and pointing at imaginary targets.

When he was seven, Sybil bought bullets for the gun and now he started practicing in earnest. As the years passed, more packages came from Sam Colt with replacement parts for the ones worn out by John.

Then came the day Sybil rode into Hookville, sitting stiff and unrelenting on her horse. Beside her rode seventeen-year-old John. That day Sybil brought back the monster that was to feed on the hate of the two families until his death.

As it was Circuit Court Day, a large group of men had gathered in front of the courthouse. Young John stopped at the hitching rail, dismounted and handed the reins of his horse to his mother, who remained mounted. In the crowd was Drew Hook, talking to a horse trader. Drew saw John coming toward him. He had known for years that someday he would probably have to kill this boy. He detached himself from the other men and stepped out to meet John.

"I don' wanna haf'ta kill ya, Son," Drew called. "This thing's all over an' done with far as I'm concerned."

John's teeth clicked together like the snap of a steel trap. "Yore beggin', then?" he questioned.

"No, by God, I ain' beggin'. Do and be damned."

A diabolical smiled played at John's lips as his mother's voice came from behind him.

"Shoot out both eyes, John."

Drew Hook and John Barron reached for their guns simultaneously. John's .45 spoke twice in rapid succession, and Drew Hook lay face-down, unmoving. The young boy walked forward and turned the body over with the toe of his boot. The .45 tilted up a fraction of an inch and roared again. He turned and walked back to his horse.

As he mounted, he apologized to his mother. "Thet secont shot wuz a might wide, Maw."

An old man in the crowd whispered, "He's a devil, boys."

Henceforth he came to be known as Devil John Barron.

The years that followed the killing of Drew Hook were the only peaceful years that Devil John was ever to know. He married and became the father of three sons—Bado, Wilder and Brack. His wife died trying to give birth to their fourth child.

Bitterly mourning the death of his wife, Devil John welcomed the news of the war with Germany. Realizing his need to lash out at a tangible enemy, he left his sons with his sister Sarah and enlisted in the army. When he went to war, his only friend was the .45 beneath his shirt.

The name Devil John Barron was again on the lips of the mountain people. He had won the French Croix De Guerre in the Meuese Argonne action. His citation read that he crawled two miles through enemy territory with a wounded comrade on his back.

When they were only a short distance from the safety of their own lines, they found their way blocked by an enemy machine gun crew that had an entire platoon pinned down. John left the wounded man hidden with instructions for him to wait five minutes and then call out. When the wounded man yelled out in English, the German gun crew tried to turn the machine gun to meet what they thought was a new threat, but before the crew could get organized, John's .45 was delivering its message of death.

After the war he came home and put aside his gun until his sons Bado and Wilder were cut down by the Hooks. Death stalked the mountain again as he renewed the war.

As Clay stood looking at the stone, he was remembering not the killing of Devil John Barron but rather the gentle grandfather so few people knew. This man had so loved his mountain home that he had traveled willingly halfway around the earth to fight in strange lands that it might remain unchanged. He loved nature and all her inhabitants, large and small. From him Clay had learned the names and calls of the birds that lived here. He had once even opened a beehive so Clay could see the queen bee.

Devil John taught Clay to show fear of no living thing, but taught him compassion for the helpless. Together they had climbed a tree and took from a nest a pair of starving young hawks whose mother had failed to return. Although he would kill a hawk that chased his chickens, he could not leave the little ones there to starve.

They had cared for the two baby birds until they learned to fly. The hawks came and went as they pleased until mating season, when they left and never returned. Often Clay's grandfather pointed out to him a high, circling hawk that would soon land on a tall snag and sit calmly, without fear, watching the house.

"Thar's either Jimbo or Jumbo," Devil John would smile.

Clay remembered best the affinity his grandfather held for the wild geese. It had been many years since the two of them had watched a 'V' wedge of wild geese winging through the sky heading south.

"Thar, Clay," his grandfather had said wistfully, pointing toward the geese, "iz th' only creature on this here earth that I envy. I wunder what deelights awaits them now down thar in th' south. They leave us humans here ta trudge thru th' snow and shiver our bones in th' cold while they cavort on some beautiful lake in th' sunshine. When spring comes, they pass over us agin, goin' north an' thar honkin' seems ta say ta me, 'Silly man, why ya plantin' corn? Yer life is passin' ya by. Whar ya bin taday? Whar' ya goin' tomorry? Cum with us. Fergit this world areality an' foller us into th' sky an' larn th' true meanin' a' freedom.' If thar is sich a thing as reincarnation, Clay, I shore wanna come back as a wild goose."

In the years following his grandfather's death, Clay would throw up a hand in silent greeting when he would spot a flock of wild geese as they passed overhead. Just maybe that big gander on the point of the formation—that one with the wild cry—was the spirit of someone he had once loved.

Once more, as he stood looking at the grave, Clay's mind left the pleasant memories of the past and went to the unpleasant of the present. He recalled now how they brought home the body of his grandfather, torn and bleeding from Hook bullets. Although mortally wounded, Devil John's mind had remained clear until the end. Realizing that there would be no one left to look after Clay if anything happened to Brack, Devil John made Brack promise to drop the war until Clay was old enough to take care of himself.

"Thet boy's gonna be th' King Stinger of th' Barrons," Devil John had told Brack, "an' I wanna make shore nothin' happins ta 'im. After he's growed up ya know whut's expected. You do it thin."

Brack knelt beside the dying man and gave him his promise; a promise that cost him his life when Silas Hook mistook his unwilling- ness to continue the feud as a sign of weakness.

"Clay, boy, come here," Devil John had whispered as his eyes began to lose their brilliance. "Come ta Gran'pa."

Although he was young in years, Clay understood what was about to take place. He moved to the bedside of his grandfather and slipped his arms around Devil John's neck and placed his smooth boy's cheek against the weathered, stubbly face.

Feeling Clay's tears on his cheek, Devil John spoke haltingly. "Be a man, Son. Be ennythin' in life ya wanna be, but allers be a man first."

"I will, Grandpaw," Clay sobbed. "I promise."

Devil John Barron whispered to Clay, his voice becoming more faint. Clay leaned forward and pressed his ear to his grandfather's lips to catch the last words. The great muscular shoulders that would never again carry Clay heaved and a legend was dead in his young arms.

"Whut did he say, Clay?" Brack choked.

"He sed th' wild geese wuz waitin' fer 'im," wept Clay.

Chapter Twelve

Silas Hook sat on his front porch in a once-plush easy chair that had now been reduced to a mass of broken springs and cotton stuffing protruding from the many holes in the cover. One of the rear legs had been broken from the chair and bricks had been stacked under the corner as a substitute. He paused in his idle task of picking dog hairs off the chair to reach down and pick up a half-quart Mason jar of whiskey. After two huge gulping swallows, he set the jar down beside him, wiped his mouth on his shirt sleeve and glared around toward the screen door.

"Orter be 'bout time ta eat," he growled.

Silas had been working all morning at his still. He had brought home a quart of the new "run" to test it. After drinking the fiery liquid he would decide it was too strong for selling and cut it with water. This made more whiskey, which meant more profit. This procedure never changed.

"Belle," he shouted as he heard his stomach rumble. "Ain' ya got ma vittles done yit?"

From the outhouse that was located to his right came her high-pitched answer. "Hit's on th' table awaitin'."

"Goddamn ol' sow won' even call me ta eat. She's gonna git her'n an' damn quick," he muttered as he kicked the spotted hound dog that lay curled up at his feet. He watched it crawl away on its belly. Kicking something always made Silas feel better.

When Silas entered the kitchen he saw Little Jesus, Belle's big yellow cat on the table eating out of the gravy bowl.

"Thet done it, damn ya," he shouted, as he made for the cat.

The feline was too quick for him, however. As he lunged for it, it jumped off the table and ran into another room.

Seeing that the cat had eluded him, Silas picked up the bowl of gravy, spooned the top layer off and threw it out into the back yard. He returned to the table and poured the rest of the gravy onto his plate. He then tore apart several large biscuits and after wiping them through the gravy, he stuffed them into his mouth. The hound had come around to the back door and was now busily engaged in licking the gravy from the ground. The man seemed to be competing with the dog to determine which was the noisier eater.

After satisfying his hunger, Silas poured a bowlful of milk and started through the house in search of the cat.

"Here, kitty. Here, kitty," he called. "Come 'ere, Little Jesus. Nobody gonna hurt ya, leetle pussy cat," he continued in his softest possible voice.

Finally spotting the cat under his bed, he put the milk down on the floor still calling, "Here, kitty, kitty. Come on out now, Little Jesus. Come on an' git yer milk. Ain' nobody wants ta hurt ya."

The cat's hunger finally overcame its fear, and it appeared from under the bed, sidled warily up to the bowl and began to lap up the milk. Silas moved slowly so as not to frighten him, still talking in a soothing voice. Suddenly the big hairy hand shot out and caught his wife's pet by the scruff of the neck.

"Now, by God." Silas gritted his teeth as he glared into the cat's face. "You bin struttin' 'roun here like th' Almighty I named ya fer long 'nuff. I tol' thet damn ol' woman ta keep ya outta th' house, but no—you two thinks yer people. Evin eatin' ma food. This brings us to a very simple conclusion. No Little Jesus—no cat in ma dinner."

When Belle emerged from the outhouse, Silas was on his way to the barn, swinging the cat by the scruff of the neck.

"Whut ya doin' with ma cat?" she screamed.

"Wal, now, why don' ya try figgerin' thet out?" he smirked. "Dumb as ya are it shouldn' be too hard."

"Damn you," she hissed as he entered the barn, with her trotting along behind him. "Don' ya hurt thet cat or yore gonna be sorry."

He ignored her as he picked up a burlap sack and a piece of fodder twine from the feed bin and walked back outside. He then headed for the river that was just beyond the Sandy Valley Pike that ran in front of his house.

"Don' hurt th' cat, Silas," Belle pleaded. "I'll keep 'im outta th' house. I promise he won' ivver trouble ya no more."

"I've heard all thet afore. I'm gonna make shore onct an' fer all thet he don' nivver bother me agin."

Turning deaf ears to her pleas for the cat, he crossed the highway and continued on to the river. Carrying the cat in one hand and the sack in the other, he began searching up and down the river bank for a rock.

"I'll give th' cat away, Silas," Belle promised, her voice taking on a hysterical note.

"No, ya won'. Thar's only one thing thet'll take care of a smartass cat. Course, bein' a fair man, I'm willin' ta let ya keep 'im if'n whut they sez 'bout cats havin' nine lives is true an' he comes back after I git through with 'im."

Finally finding the size rock he was seeking, he knelt and rolled it into the sack, stuffed the cat in with it and secured the top with the fodder twine. As he started to get up, Belle jumped on his back and tried to grab the sack from him. Wrestling himself loose from her he stood up, caught his balance and kicked her in the shin with his heavy brogan. Holding one leg, she hopped along the creek bank after him, screaming one vile curse after another. He swung the sack in a circular motion above his head several times in an effort to get more distance, then let go of it. It sailed out over the water and splashed into the middle of the Little Sandy and sank immediately.

After watching the last of the air bubbles float down the river, he whirled toward his wife and threatened, "Nex' time ya yell at me like a banshee I'll take th' whip ta ya 'til ya larn some respec'."

His wife made no reply, but the look she gave him left no doubt whom she would have preferred to be in the sack on the river bottom.

Silas was crossing the road on his way back to the porch and his easy chair when the sheriff's jeep pulled up alongside him.

"Howdy, Silas." The sheriff's look and tone of voice gave no indication of friendliness.

"'Lo, Sheriff. This social or bizzness?" he asked suspiciously.

"Bizzness, Silas. The Barron boy come home yisterday."

The sheriff was startled by the instantaneous, shrill, maniacal laughter that came from Belle, who had come up alongside his jeep.

Silas towered over her menacingly. "Shut yer mouth," he commanded.

"Haw! Haw! Haw! Whut ya gonna do ta me, Silas, if'n I don'? Kick me in t'other shin?" She continued to bait him. "I'll bet ya won' put 'im in no sack so easy as ya did Little Jesus. Thar's gonna be mor'n cat hair in th' Little Sandy now. Thar's gonna be Hook blood. Yore blood, ya rotten bastard! He lef' 'is mark on ya th' last time. This time he's agonna kill ya fer shore!"

Silas raised his hand to strike her, but she hopped away from him and headed for the house like a crippled chicken, her laughter trailing behind her.

"Whut's wrong with Belle?" the sheriff asked.

"Hit's ma cross ta bear," Silas answered solemnly. "She's become a mite tetched. Course, it runs in 'er fambly. I shoulda listened ta ma paw an' not married up with 'er in th' first place. He tole me she'd go crazy on me someday."

"Silas," the sheriff said coldly as he brought the conversation back to the original subject. "I come here ta tell ya th' same thing I tole Clay

Barron yisterday. Leave th' bad blood lay. I'll shoot or sen' ya ta th' pen, which ever one of ya thet starts it agin."

Silas' hand moved to the side of his face where his fingers traced the outline of the long jagged scar on his cheek and neck as he answered, "Sheriff, ya knows I'm a law-abidin' man, but if'n some hot head comes 'roun' pushin' me or mine, I got a right ta take care of maself."

"Ever' man's got th' right ta pertect hisself an' 'is family, Silas, but don' try no deal like ya did with Brack. Evin this county won' stand fer nothin' like thet agin."

"Sheriff, ya got no call ta talk ta me thetaway, but jist ta ease yore mind, ya got ma word thet if'n thet pup stays up on 'is hill whar he belongs, we'll stay down here an' everthin'll be jist hunkie dorie."

"Fair 'nuff. I'm gonna holt ya to thet, Silas," the sheriff said as he shifted the jeep into gear and drove on down the valley.

When Belle Hook entered the house, the pain from her bruised shin was forgotten in the pleasure she derived from the sheriff's news. She recalled vividly the wild-eyed boy she had watched day after day during Silas' trial for the killing of Brack Barron. During the proceedings, Clay had watched Silas much as a turkey gobbler watches a snake before pouncing on it.

All eyes in the courtroom had been on Silas when the verdict was read except hers. She was looking at Clay. As the foreman announced Silas' acquittal, she saw the hate that completely engulfed the boy. When Clay grabbed for the sheriff's gun, she whispered a silent prayer for his success. The death that hovered over Silas that day was not destined to descend, and she had been committed to her wall-less prison for all the years since.

"Dear God," she now prayed softly. "This is ma las' chance. Don' let 'im miss agin."

Belle Hook had never had a first chance in life. She had been little more than a child of thirteen when her drunken father forced her to marry Silas Hook, who was then twenty-seven. A year later when their eldest son, Isom, was a baby, Silas tired of having her father underfoot, consuming his whiskey and making a nuisance of himself, so he had him committed to an insane asylum. Belle never saw her father again.

Left alone, she had little choice but to remain with Silas and become no more than a brood animal and slave to him. As the four sons she mothered grew to be men, they gave her no more love or respect than did her husband. Sometimes she hated them almost as much as she did him.

It had been only in the last year that she had begun to fight and talk back to him. A few months ago, after slapping her across the face, Silas stood frozen in astonishment as she grabbed an iron skillet and attempted to split his skull with it. Only the quickness of Jubal grabbing her descending arm had saved him. He hadn't struck her since, until he kicked her today. She knew from the way he talked about her to other people that he was planning to send her to the same institution that he had her father.

She stood watching out the window as her husband walked back from the highway and seated himself on the porch.

"You corpse-screwin' bastard." To herself she always called him the vilest things she could imagine. "I'll live ta bury ya an' piss on yer grave. I'm gonna steal yer money, too."

Each time Silas received payment for a load of whiskey she had later observed him going to the barn. She knew that somewhere in that barn he had hid his money. During his absence from the farm she had searched the place time and again, but found nothing. She finally mustered enough courage to crawl through the high weeds that grew beside the barn and spy on him through a knothole. He had gone directly to the tramp area and took down a goose-necked hoe from the wall, with which he began to scrape the manure from the floor.

The top of a metal box soon came into view. It was buried so the top of the box was just below the level of the rest of the barn floor. Setting aside the hoe, he cleaned the remainder of the straw from the top and pulled the box out. After wiping the manure stains from his hands onto the legs of his overalls, he took a key out of his pocket and unlocked the box.

When the lid came open, she could hardly believe her eyes. The box was almost full of greenbacks. He took a packet of bills from his pocket and put them on top of the other money, relocked the box and replaced it in the hole. He put new straw on the box and then scraped fresh manure over the straw, leaving no trace of the hiding place.

"I shoulda figgered thet out," she thought, as she scurried back to the house ahead of him. "Jest like 'is warped mind ta hide 'is money in a pile a' shit."

She glanced down now at the piece of plastic she had used to replace a window pane that had been broken out. The wall, papered out of last year's newspapers, next caught her eye.

"It won' be long now, I hope," she muttered, as she observed her frizzled, mishapen image in a cracked mirror. "Jest you wait, ol' house, 'til I git my hands on 'is money. Thin we'll both git us a general overhaul."

She gathered up the staggering load of laundry, carried it outside and proceeded with her washing. Today she didn't complain to herself about having to do it on a scrub board. Everyone else in the valley had purchased a washing machine since electricity had been wired through. Silas, however, seemed to enjoy watching her struggle with the wet, heavy clothes and had refused to buy her one. Today the metal buttons of the overalls scraping on the scrub board seemed to harmonize with her happy humming.

After watching the sheriff's jeep out of sight, Silas returned to his chair on the porch. He wanted to think. Never had he fooled himself into believing that Clay would not come back. He had expected him before this.

"Shet up thet infernal noise!" He cursed his wife, who was washing clothes at the side of the house. "A man cain't even think 'round here no more."

The cackle that followed his outburst only tended to make him more angry. His mood gradually changed to pleasure as he remembered the publicity he received after he had killed Brack.

A picture of Silas had been put on the cover of a detective magazine with bold capital letters that declared, "I KILLED THE FEUDING BARRONS." The account of the story given by the city writer wasn't really the way it occurred, but his description of the feud and killings sounded better than the truth.

Silas' superego led him to accept the fictional instead of the true story as fact. Lately, the men who had once feared him were becoming openly disdainful of the aging killer. More and more often it was taking the vicious fists of his sons to keep the county at bay. Whiskey making was a profitable business in this dry county. Many men grumbled about the stranglehold the Hooks held on it, but none were foolish enough to face the whole clan to try to break it.

Silas liked to hear himself referred to as the "Gray Fox of Sandy Valley." This, undoubtedly, was brought on by his being called "Possum" Hook as a boy. The thought of carrying the name of an animal that hung by its tail and quietly awaited any fate its enemies desired to mete out to it infuriated him.

Today, sitting on his porch thinking his sly thoughts and making his devious plans, he seemed to deserve the title he preferred of "Gray Fox."

There was no doubt in Silas' mind that the sheriff would do as he promised if trouble started. He would have to arrange it so that it would come under the unwritten law of the hills, and then would automatically be immune to local prosecution.

He would have to sacrifice one of his own to get it in that position, but there was too much money buried in the barn to get squeamish in his old age. After some thought, he decided to send his second son Wilson after the Barron boy first. Wilson had been somewhat retarded since Clay had hit him in the head with the rock during the fight in which Brack had been killed.

"If'n Wilson got hisself killed, it wouldn' be as much of a loss as if it wuz one a th' other boys," Silas reasoned, "but it'd open wide th' door fer th' rest of 'em to go after Clay."

Here in the hills that was a man's right. Silas could hear himself now, pleading his case to the public. "He hits ma boy in th' haid with a rock an' makes 'im a idiot fer life an' then 'e comes back an' kills 'im."

He realized that he would get little sympathy, but more importantly there would be no interference.

"If'n Wilson should git lucky an' kill Clay, th' mos' they could do ta 'im'd be ta put 'im in th' nut house. It's common knowledge 'e ain' right. Either way, 'e'll be better off," Silas consoled himself.

Wilson's condition, over the years, had somewhat shamed Silas, but now he reasoned it must have been meant to be. Wilson had been made not responsible for his actions by the man he would now try to kill.

Silas was eager to put his plan into effect.

"Them newspapermen thet forgot all 'bout me soon after th' trial's gonna be sorry now. I might not given 'em no statement 'tall this time," he thought, knowing better. "Wonder if'n thet feller thet wuz gonna write a book 'bout me'll show up agin. If'n 'e duz, an' he don' call th' book *The Gray Fox of Sandy Valley,* I ain' agonna tell 'im nothin'."

Another reason for his haste to eliminate Clay was his wife. He had planned to have Belle committed next week, but that would have to wait. This delay galled him. He dreaded going to bed at night, fearing that she would kill him in his sleep.

Something else had been brewing for him, too. Lige Begley, his bootlegger on Dry Fork, had sold a large batch of whiskey consigned to him by the Hooks and had gambled away the money. He intended to force him to work at the still until he had paid back all the money he had lost.

Upon arriving on the Dry Fork and getting a look at Lige's sixteen-year-old daughter Ruby, Silas changed his mind. He consigned him more whiskey, knowing Lige would do as all gamblers do. He would go to the trough again to try to get even.

One can scrub a leopard all day with Ajax, but his spots will never change and neither would the compulsive gambling habit of Lige Begley. This weakness would make it easy for Silas to keep a hold on him.

During the past few months Silas had made many trips between Sandy Valley and Dry Fork. He was well aware of but not disturbed by the fact the only interest Ruby had in him was his money. He went blissfully along, accepting her body, and promising her a new convertible, a big home and a new change of clothes for every day in the year.

When these promises failed to materialize, she finally issued an ultimatum. "Take me ta Hookville ta live, or I ain' foolin' 'roun' with ya no more."

Ruby was no beauty by most standards, but her plump young body pushed back the years and brought the almost forgotten heat to Silas' loins again.

He could depend on Lige, who wanted no part of the collection tactics of the Hooks, to help him handle her.

"You keep Ruby here 'til I git my ol' lady put away or, by God, the buzzards're goin' ta have a feed," he had threatened Lige.

He knew he had to hurry before some young buck came along with a stiff horn and showed her that convertibles and clothes weren't all there was to life.

Silas looked across the valley and snarled at the mountain he hated.

"Once and fer all, goddamn ya." His mind searched for the word he wanted and found it. "Extinct—that's whut you Barrons iz gonna be!"

Chapter Thirteen

As the morning sun spread a blanket of warmth over the peace and quiet of the mountain, Clay left the graveyard. In every man's life there is a summit of feeling from which he cannot go beyond. Some men achieve this summit with a woman who equals their passion and drives them on to delights of which they never dreamed they were capable. Other men reach this pinnacle through their work. Clay Barron stood on his summit as his eyes surveyed the length and breadth of his mountain.

This place had been called Rainbow Mountain longer than anyone could remember. Almost every time there was a hard rain it would be followed by a rainbow, and often with twin rainbows. The color and the mist hanging around the arches was unbelievably beautiful.

Generations of the Barrons had soaked up the rainbow's spiritual promise and told their children that this place was truly the Barrons' pot of gold. Clay, as the others before him, was bonded to this mountain. As he walked across his land, he held wide his arms as if to embrace it. When he reached the first lake he knelt and tested the water with his hand.

"It's cold, but not too cold," he thought, as he removed his clothes. At the water's edge he placed the gun and harness on top of his clothes.

He waded into the water and swam about cautiously, making sure that no foreign objects had been thrown in the lake since he had last swum here. When he came into the shallow water alongside the bank, he stood up with his hands full of mud and sand, which he rubbed vigorously over his body. It wasn't soap, but it would get him clean. After a leisurely swim of half an hour's duration, he left the lake and got dressed.

As he continued on toward the charred wreckage that had once been his home, he walked on ground that was as level as the Sandy Valley below. In some places the bluegrass was beginning to lose its battle for existence to the crabgrass and scrub bushes. Clay reached down and broke off a blade of grass, cupped it in his hands and blew on it. The resulting shrill whistle startled a hummingbird, causing it to pause in midair to observe him before darting away.

He paused at the grape arbor that had been located in front of the house. Most of the vines had been killed by the fire, but the remaining ones grew in wild confusion around the rotting, fire-blackened board frames. Continuing on, he came to the wreckage of the house. There was no visible emotion in his face as he poked through the debris.

He presently came to the place where the stairway had led to the cellar. The cookstove had fallen into the burned-out stairway, partially blocking the entrance to the cellar. Clay took a long, heavy piece of charred timber and pried at the stove until it tumbled on down into the darkness. He took a firm grip on a smoke-blackened wood beam and swung his body down into the cellar. His feet touched the stove and he sprang lightly to the floor, where he remained still for a few seconds as his eyes adjusted to the dimness of the room.

When the first Barron had settled here, he had made his home by digging this hole in the ground and covering it first with a ceiling of heavy logs, then a layer of flat rocks, covered by two feet of blue clay. The second generation of Barrons had built a log cabin over the dugout. As the succeeding generations of Barrons had come, they had each added something to the house, but the cellar had remained the same. The thick clay and rock ceiling had saved it from the fire.

As Clay poked around the cellar, he found a beat-up old saddle, a muzzle-loading rifle, and a rusty hunting knife still hanging in the same corner where they had probably been for three-quarters of a century. On a shelf along the back wall, he found some jars of canned fruit. Selecting a jar of peaches, he took the old knife and cut the top off. After hesitantly testing them and finding them unspoiled, he ate the peaches hungrily, but they only whetted his appetite. He climbed back up on the stove, grabbed the beam overhead and swung himself out of the cellar. After a short search through the ruins of the barn, he left the mountain and headed for Big Pap's.

"Should be about time for breakfast," he thought.

Big Pap sat in the kitchen watching Sarah prepare the morning meal.

"If'n he ain' back soon, I'm agonna go up thar," she was saying. "I don' like it. Up thar all nigh' alone. Mebbe th' Hooks knows he's got back. They may've already gone up thar after 'im."

"Come on, now, Sarah," Big Pap reproved. "Clay ain' no baby no more. 'Sides, it's bin quite a spell since he wuz up thar. Jist leave 'im be alone fer awhile."

"I still don' like it nohow," she continued. "I've waited too long fer 'im ta come back ta me. If'n I 'ave ta shoot Silas Hook maself, I ain' havin' nothin' 'appenin' ta 'im now."

Hearing the chickens squawking, Big Pap looked out the window and saw Clay walking through the barnyard.

"See," he smiled, "all ya gotta do is start fixin' breakfist. Thet allers brung the Barrons off'n th' mountain."

Clay was washing his hands at the washstand beneath the cherry tree in the back yard when his aunt came to the door.

"Clay," she called. "Breakfast is nigh ready. I got hot biscuits, sorghum an' salt-cured ham. Th' gravy's jist like ya allers liked it— brown an' so thick ya kin cut it with a knife."

"Mammy, if there was another woman in the world like you, I'd take her up on the mountain and never come down again," he said as he followed her into the kitchen.

Big Pap always had a short drink of whiskey before breakfast.

"How 'bout a blood-thinner, Boy?" he asked as Clay seated himself at the table.

"No, thanks, Big Pappy. This morning I don't want to waste any space that can be used for food."

As Aunt Sarah was placing the food on the table, Clay untied her apron strings.

"Yore as big a picker as ya iver wuz," she scolded, obviously pleased that he still enjoyed teasing her.

After they had finished breakfast and were leisurely sipping on a second cup of coffee, Big Pap remarked, "Taday's Friday. We allers do our tradin' in town on Friday. Like ta come along, Clay?"

"No, I think not—just yet."

"Is thar anythin' ya'd like fer us ta git fer ya special ta eat?" Sarah asked.

"No, Mammy. As long as you keep the cornbread and biscuits coming, I won't be hard to please. You could bring my luggage back with you, if you have the buggy. It's in the trunk of my car. Uncle Billy has the keys, and he can show you which car it is."

"We'll have plenty a' room fer it. Anythin' else?" Big Pap asked.

"There is one thing I could use, and that's a shave. Do you have a razor I could borrow?" Clay questioned.

"I got a straight un yore welcome to. Nivver did like them safetys," Big Pap answered.

"I've never shaved with a straight razor before, but there's no time like the present to learn," Clay replied.

"'Afore ya start shavin' an' we leave fer town, thar's somethin' I wanna give ya," Sarah said as she left the room.

She returned presently carrying a huge pistol.

"Yer gran'pappy tol' me long afore he got kilt thet whin he wuz gone an' you become a man thet he wanted ya ta have 'is gun. Rekkin's how ya bin a man fer quite a spell now. He said thar wouldn' never be no need ta tell ya not ta dishonor it," Sarah explained.

Clay took the gun and held it fondly in his hand.

"Grandpappy's pistol," he mused. "What a story it could tell if it could only talk."

The walnut butt slapped into his palm as he drew down on an imaginary target. "The balance and feel of this gun is just fantastic. I feel as if all I would have to do is point and fire to hit anything I would shoot at. Maybe it's the long barrel."

Clay continued, almost reverently, to examine the cold steel.

"Big Pap, here's some money," Clay said, peeling a hundred dollar bill off the top of a considerable roll. "Bring me back ten boxes of forty-five slugs, and you and Mammy buy yourselves something with the change. I want to do some practicing with this gun."

From the battery-powered radio an announcer's voice had been droning on with local news, but when he started to editorialize on an item in the national scene, Clay's attention snapped to his words.

"In Junction City, Michigan, authorities are investigating the disappearance of 'Boots' Carrio, the heir apparent to the Moe Carrio syndicate. The elderly Carrio told investigators last night that his young nephew had retired from business for personal reasons, and that he had no knowledge of his whereabouts. The uneasy questions plaguing the city are, 'What personal business could take the younger Carrio away from a million dollar juke box empire?' 'With Moe Carrio in the twilight of a long career in the syndicate, who will take his place?'"

"The city is fearful of a struggle for power like the one that left a dozen or more mobsters dead when Carrio wrested the lucrative amusement and gambling machine territory from Thomas Lomatto shortly after the first World War. As always, in these things, only time will tell."

As the announcer went on to other news, Clay could feel the silence pressing down on him.

Looking Big Pap in the eye, Clay said, "Yes, what you're thinking is true. I'm 'Boots Carrio.' I got the nickname from the hobnailed boots I was wearing when I showed up there."

Big Pap's face had set in a scowl. "Th' man's a hoodlum an' a thief. Yer paw wouldn've wanted ya growin' up with a man like thet."

Agitation edged Clay's voice as he retorted, "Moe Carrio's no thief. He's a businessman in a legitimate business that most people don't understand or know anything about. Sure, he's killed, but only to protect himself or his property. What difference is there in his killing to save his life or us Barrons killing to honor our dead? The loser is buried just as deep, either way."

Seeing a slight softening in the expression on Big Pap's face, Clay continued. "When I went to Moe Carrio hungry and frightened, he took me in. He got me forged papers, identifying me as his nephew, and gave me a job. He's been using his influence in high places for years to get the charges in Frankfort dropped. He even hired private tutors to educate me so I wouldn't have to take the chance of being discovered by attending public school."

"At first, he was just paying back a debt to Grandpappy, but as time passed we became very close. He did the best he could to be a father to me, and I'll never be able to thank him enough."

"Ya plannin' ta go back ta thet whin yer business here with th' Hooks is finished?" Sarah inquired, haltingly.

"No, Mammy," Clay answered her softly. "As I said before, I'm home to stay. After I've taken care of the Hooks, I'm going to bring Moe here to live with me on the mountain. He wants to retire, and knowing that I have no interest in taking over his business, he is even now negotiating the sale of it. When he comes here, he will be made to feel welcome and wanted, as he made me feel when I needed him. Those who refuse to welcome him won't be bothered with me, either."

Big Pap shrugged. "OK, Clay. If'n ya say he's all righ', thet's good 'nuff fer us. None of us iz purfect. We'll speak 'bout it no more. Whin he comes, 'e'll be made ta feel at home."

"Now, Clay," Big Pap said, changing the subject, "if'n ya 'member how ta harness up a horse, how 'bout hookin' up th' buggy fer a tired ol' man?"

After his aunt and uncle had disappeared down the tree-lined road on their way to Hookville, Clay returned to the house and wandered aimlessly about. He picked up the weekly newspaper and tried to read, but nervousness forced it from his hands. He next went to the kitchen and took Big Pap's straight razor from the cupboard and stropped it on the black leather strap hanging there. Next, he took the tea kettle outside and filled it with water at the pump and returned to the kitchen and rekindled the fire in the iron range to heat it.

Waiting for the water to get hot, he strolled into the bedroom he had occupied as a boy and found everything just as he had left it. On the bed was no gaudy bedspread as would be found in most mountain homes, but Clay's favorite patchwork quilt. He had been helping Aunt Sarah sew together squares for this quilt when Big Pap walked in and teased him unmercifully for doing girls' work. To this day Clay still felt embarrassed at his taunting words.

On the wall beside the mirror hung his red, heart-shaped pin cushion. It was made of velvet, with a red and white crocheted border. Noticing the way he had admired it while she was making it, Sarah had given it to him when she finished it.

"I migh' not be livin' whin ya git married," she had said, "but in case I ain' I wanna leave yore wife a weddin' present ennyhow. I'd like fer ya ta keep this fer her."

This was the only feminine thing Clay had ever owned. It was somewhat faded now, but to him it was still beautiful.

On the dresser sat an iron dog almost six inches high and a foot long, which had been given to him one Christmas Eve by Big Pap. He reached down and lifted the tail and watched the fierce-looking jaws open at the same time. When he dropped the tail, the jaws clanged shut. In front of the fireplace during the winters of his youth, many bushels of walnuts had been cracked between the dog's iron jaws.

Just as he had left them, he found his clothes on hangers on a wire stretched across one corner of the room. He took down a pair of jeans and held them to his waist. He smiled wryly when he looked down and saw the bottom of the legs came only to his knees. Clay had grown and changed, but the room remained the same.

In the top left-hand drawer of the dresser he found a box of photographs that brought back memories that had been forcibly stored away for years. He could not have kept fresh all these memories and stayed away as long as he had.

He was about to replace the box of photographs when he noticed a yellowed, folded newspaper towards the rear of the drawer. He pulled the newspaper out and spread it apart.

"The Promise" blared the bold black type above an enlarged picture that he barely recognized as his own. Clay earnestly studied the long-haired youth in the picture, whose face was tilted toward the sky. It was so twisted with grief and hate that it seemed to belong to someone else. He carefully replaced the paper in the drawer. The flame of vengeance had once again been fanned in his soul.

He backed away from the mirror, his left hand flashing to the front of his shirt. He jerked suddenly and the snaps popped open and the .45 appeared in his hand. He continued to practice the draw from several positions, until the tea kettle whistled him back to the kitchen.

He removed his shirt and filled a wash basin with water from the kettle and carried it and the razor out to the washstand beneath the cherry tree. After lathering his face with soap, he looked at himself in the small mirror wedged in the fork of the tree.

"Well, here goes. At least, if I cut my throat it will be less messy out here."

After taking half a dozen strokes and watching the blood from the nicks turn his face pink as it mixed with the lather, his ears picked up the sound of a horse coming up the road behind him. As he watched over his shoulder in the mirror, a magnificent black horse came into sight, moving at a high trot. Its feet seemed to barely touch the ground. The rider posted effortlessly.

The razor in his hand remained poised in midair as the rider swung down. After tying her horse, she ran her hands over her hips and thighs, smoothing out wrinkles that weren't there.

Clay realized that he had been holding his breath, and let it slip quietly through his teeth as she moved toward him.

Chapter Fourteen

Valarie had arisen earlier than usual this morning, spurred on by her anticipation of the day ahead. She stood under the pelting water in her shower until her skin began to tingle. All the tingle, however, wasn't from the shower. Today she would see Clay again. Today, if things went as she planned, she would talk with him.

As she stood with closed eyes letting the water run over her body, she entertained the idle thought that someday she might take a shower with him. Emotions, held too long in restraint, were tugging at her now to be released. She had denied until now the call of her body to mate, because she wanted only Clay.

She was still waiting for the first time that strong arms would gently capture her, when a man's tender lips would turn hard and demanding, when her mind would go hazy and her body would become lazy as she reached the complete fulfillment of mental and physical love.

As Valarie continued floating along on the high tide of her fantasies, she imagined she could feel the arms around her now. She could feel the soft hairs of his chest moving against her bare breasts as he completely engulfed her.

Her eyes popped open suddenly, bringing her back to the disappointing reality of water running down the curved swell of her breasts and springing from her taut nipples.

She shook the daydreams from her mind as she stepped from the shower. Wearing a large soft towel wrapped around her, she went about the task of selecting the riding clothes she would wear today. She chose a white crepe blouse whose V-neckline would force down the eyes of a hard-shelled Baptist preacher. After wriggling into a pair of brown felt riding breeches, she stood before the full-length mirror observing herself from all angles, her eyes showing satifaction with the image.

She took extra care with her make-up this morning. With the clothes she was wearing, too much make-up would make her look cheap. She only wanted to feel like a hussy, not look like one.

Her long black tresses received her attention next. She brushed her hair until it shone. She reached for a ribbon, but changed her mind, deciding to let it swing loose and free about her face and shoulders.

She quickly pulled on the brown patent leather boots that hugged her slender calves, and went down stairs. When she entered the kitchen she smiled at the look of amazement on her mother's face.

"Valarie!" she exclaimed. "You're not going to the bank dressed like that?"

"Of course not, Mother," she answered gaily. "I quit that dreadful job yesterday. I just couldn't see any future there. The boss is married, you know."

"What's going on here, anyway?" Valarie's mother asked her father. He had gone back to consuming his enormous breakfast after giving Valarie an appreciative whistle.

"It's her story," he answered.

Seeing her mother's eyes turn to her questioningly, Valarie replied, "It's really very simple, Mother. Clay Barron came home yesterday and I intend taking all my time to see to it that he falls in love with me. I want to marry him."

"I see," her mother answered with understanding. "I was beginning to fear he would never come."

Valarie's father stopped eating long enough to answer, "You mean you knew about this all along, Izetta?"

"Not for sure. Just a guess. I remember how Valarie cried the day he left. She's handled that school picture of him so much she's just about worn it out."

Turning to Valarie she continued, "I just hope he's become a decent sort of man. A woman should always pick a strong man. With his background, I'm sure he will be that."

Clyde finished his breakfast and stood up, his eyes twinkling at his daughter.

"I'd saddle Bones for you, but the nasty bastard would probably try to kill me."

Valarie was an excellent horsewoman and posted to the stallion's road-covering trot with ease. The flow of the finely tuned muscles and the tender mouth made him an ideal woman's mount. The wind picked up Valarie's hair from her shoulders. The horse's arched neck and flowing mane and tail completed a picture that could not be excelled on any eastern bridle path.

She pulled the stallion to a walk, then stopped him beside the buggy when she met Big Pap and Sarah.

" 'Pon my honor, Valarie," Big Pap said, giving her a teasing leer. "Ya didn' hav' ta git all duded up like thet jest ta pay an ole briar-hopper like me a leetle visit."

"Don' pay no mind ta 'im," Sarah cut in. "I take it ya know Clay's got home."

"Yes, I saw him from the bank window yesterday. I could hardly believe it!" She leaned forward in the saddle. "He doesn't have anyone, does he, Aunt Sarah?"

"No, an' I ain' too sure you'll want 'im, either. He's changed so much. Uster be sich a nice, sweet boy. Now, I cain' tell 'tall whut he's thinkin'."

"Th' only thing thet's wrong with Sarah is thet he ain' all th' time slobberin' and gushin' 'round over 'er like he usta," broke in Big Pap. "Th' boy's all right, Valarie."

Turning to Sarah he said, "He's bin gone a long time, an' hit's only nacheral thet he'd feel a leetle strange fer a spell. After he's bin here a week er two, 'e'll be smoochin' on ya like he ain' never bin gone."

As Big Pap raised the reins and clucked to the horse, he smiled at Valarie saying, "We'll be gone quite a leetle bit, so injoy yer visit."

Valarie took a deep breath as her horse carried her along the woodland road.

"We're about there, Bones. Now what do I do? What do I say?" she wondered aloud to her mount.

All her adult experiences with men had been spent in retreat. The tactics of advance were still to be learned.

When she came into view of the house, she say Clay standing under the cherry tree shaving. He didn't turn around, but she knew he was watching her in the mirror. After dismounting she walked to a spot directly behind him where it was impossible for him to see her in the mirror.

He turned toward her then, his black eyes moving slowly, almost caressingly, over her from head to foot. The eyes said they liked what they saw. His low voice cut through the pounding in her ears.

"Hello, Val."

He had always called her Val instead of her full name when she was a kid.

She was pleasantly pleased at the controlled, almost lazy voice with which she answered him.

"Clay, it's so good to see you again. I was on my way over to see your aunt and uncle when I met them on their way to town, and they told me you were here. I decided to ride over and see if you still remember me."

She held out her hand to him, and he squeezed it firmly.

"Of course, I remember you, and after seeing you now I find that you have fulfilled all my father's predictions."

Disengaging her fingers from his, she smiled up into his face and asked, "And what did your father predict about me?"

"He said that some day you would be the most beautiful woman ever seen around here. At the risk of sounding like all the other men before me who have told you the same thing, I can only say that you're a very lovely woman."

"I remember your father," she said. "All of us young girls thought he was terribly handsome. You should be proud that you look so much like him."

With eyebrows raised slightly, she jested, "Now that we have made it through the compliments, what, if I may ask, are you trying to do to your face?"

"I was trying to shave with a straight razor," he laughed.

"I left my safety razor in town and should have left the beard on until I got it. I was to the point of surrender when you rode in."

She reached out and took the razor from him saying, "You wouldn't be much bloodier if you had used the gun on your whiskers."

He looked down self-consciously at the gun hanging under his arm, but made no explanation.

"Sit down here where I can reach you," she commanded, pushing him down on the washstand. "I've had lots of experience with one of these things."

Moving around behind him she reached over his shoulder and held his face with her left hand and with short, smooth strokes, began to finish shaving him. The soft swell of her breast pressing against the back of his head was disturbing to Clay, and he didn't want to be disturbed now.

"In case you're wondering where I acquired this valuable experience and perhaps coming to the wrong conclusion, I'll explain. My father refused to shave on Sundays, no matter what. So, after looking at his stubbly face every Sunday for years, we finally made a deal with him. Now, either my mother or I shave him every Sunday."

After finishing her task, Valarie wet one end of the towel under the pump and washed the lather and blood from his face.

"Do you have anything inside to keep these nicks from getting sore?" she asked.

"I'll look, but I doubt it," he answered. "From the looks of Big Pap, he doesn't use much aftershave."

Taking the towel from her and picking up the razor he said, "Come on in, Val. There's still some coffee on the stove."

She followed him to the door, her eyes loving him behind his back. Inside she went to the cupboard for the coffee cups as he retrieved his shirt from the back of a kitchen chair and put it on. He hadn't removed the gun.

"I'll see what I can find for the wounds now," he smiled as he left the kitchen.

After filling the two cups with steaming coffee, she sat down at the red checkered oilcloth-covered table and heard a painful "ooooooooooooh" from another room.

When Clay came back into the kitchen, still rubbing his face he said, "There wasn't any shaving lotion, so I used some of Big Pap's whiskey. It stings more outside than it does inside."

In her daydreams, Valarie had always pictured herself rescuing Clay from some menial job with no future, and through her influence, making him a success. In the few minutes they had been together, she had perceived the force of his personality. This, coupled with his dark good looks, obviously left him in need of no one.

She sensed that here was a man who would ask no woman to love him, but rather might allow one to. She felt a pang of jealousy as she looked at his hands and wondered how many women they had pulled against him. How many noses had nuzzled the soft hair at his throat?

She wasn't experienced enough to know that for a man to love many women means nothing more than that he is healthy. It's when a man has loved only one woman that it's hard for another woman to reach him.

Her voice gave no indication of her inner thoughts as she asked, "Where have you been all these years, Clay?"

"Val, some day I'll tell you the whole story, but for the present I'd rather not talk about it. Instead, why don't you tell me what's been going on around here since I left?"

The conversation that followed was of the usual type carried on between friends who hadn't met in a long time. Then, without warning, she dropped the bomb.

"I hope you don't think I'm nosing into your affairs, but what do you plan to do about the boy?"

"What do you mean?" He looked startled. "Why should I do anything about any boy?"

Valarie's face turned crimson as she started to speak, then hesitated in confusion. It was obvious that he didn't know what she was talking about. Big Pap and Sarah hadn't told him.

"Clay, forgive me! I thought you knew about him or I would never have brought it up."

"Brought up what? Val, what in the hell are you talking about?" he asked impatiently.

She bit her lower lip as she thought, "Why didn't I keep my mouth shut? Why did I think I had to solve all our problems the first time I saw him? I didn't want to be the one to tell him, but it's gone too far now."

She looked into the inquiring eyes as she searched for some proper way of telling him, and finding none, she finally blurted out, "I'm talking about your son."

He leaned back and smiled. "You really had me worried for a minute. I don't know what you're talking about, but there's one thing I'm sure of. I've never been married, and I don't have any of the other kind of children, either. Besides, I wasn't much more than a child myself when I left here."

"I'm afraid you were a little more than a child, Clay. Do you remember Hallie Fultz?"

She saw the smile slip from his face as the realization of the possibility hit him.

"No, I can't believe it. If she had a kid, it's not mine! She left here right after I . . . no, you're mistaken!"

"She left, it's true, Clay, but she came back right after you left. Ezra took her back in. She had the baby right at the time it would have figured out you were with her.

"Val, how do you know so much about all this?"

"I had it written in my diary. At the time you were with her, I had a silly schoolgirl crush on you and I cried all over the page when I wrote it. When the baby came, I looked it up and it figured out to the day."

"That still doesn't prove he's mine," Clay argued, although his voice had lost some of its conviction. "You know how promiscuous she was. He could belong to anyone."

"I had hoped so, too, Clay. It's not my place to discuss with you something as personal as this. All I'll say is, go look for yourself. I've seen him many times, and he's as much a Barron as you are."

Clay, who smoked only when he was nervous, reached for a cigarette as he asked, "What's the boy's name?"

"They call him Milt. He's had a real rough life ever since he got old enough to begin looking like you. Ezra works him like a mule and treats him worse. He ran away from home once, but the judge had him brought back."

"One day when they were delivering coal at the courthouse I saw Ezra sitting out front chewing tobacco and gossiping while he made Milt unload the truck. Milt went into the courthouse to get a drink of water and when he came back, Ezra took a belt to him in front of everyone for leaving the truck without first asking his permission. He didn't stand there and just take it, either. He fought Ezra like a wildcat until Uncle Billy broke it up. Uncle Billy told Ezra he'd take a horsewhip to him if he ever saw him beating Milt like that again. The boy knows about you, Clay. He knows who he belongs to. Do you want to know what he said to Uncle Billy?"

Clay nodded, expressionless.

"He said, 'Don' bother, Sheriff. Clay Barron'll kill 'im when 'e comes back. Us Barrons don' need no one ta take up fer us. We take care of our own.' If he isn't taken out of there, Clay, something awful is going to happen to one or the other of them."

"Where do they live now?" Clay asked quietly.

"They moved back to the Middle Fork with Hallie's mother and father in the old church house."

"Milt, that's what you said his name is, wasn't it?"

She nodded her head yes, and he continued, "I'll take care of it."

Crushing out his cigarette, Clay got up from the table and crossed over to the window. Looking up the mountain with his back still to her he began to speak.

"If my father hadn't been saddled with me, he would still be alive today. I'm not going to make the same mistake. I'm not going to let this interfere with what I came back here to do. I do thank you for telling me about him, Val. One good thing—the boy's gotten along without me for years, and he won't have any trouble surviving if I'm killed. I'll take care of the boy financially, but I just can't change my plans."

Valarie crossed the room and turned Clay around until he faced her, saying, "Clay, do you have to continue with this thing with the Hooks? Silas Hook will have his day of reckoning. You know what the Bible says about vengeance belonging to the Lord."

Standing before her now was a man different from the one with whom she had been talking earlier. She suddenly realized what Aunt Sarah had been trying to tell her about him. She felt the tower begin to topple from her dream castle as he snarled, "Silas Hook is mine! If the Lord wants His vengeance from him, He'll have to take him quick before I get to him. I wouldn't give up killing any one of the Hooks for a guarantee of the pie in the sky."

Valarie had thought of Clay as some knight of old coming home to defend the family honor, but looking into the onyx-like eyes she realized that this was no romantic fairy tale. This was for real. He planned to kill the entire family. She experienced and controlled a small shudder of revulsion as she turned away from him.

If she decided she still wanted him, she would have to hurry. She would have to blunt his vengeance with love. She would have to make him love her and want her more than he wanted to kill them.

"I must be going now, Clay," she said, as she walked to the door. "I've enjoyed so much talking to you again."

He followed her outside and said, "I'm sorry, Val, that we got on the subject we did. It won't happen again. I had no intention of spoiling your visit."

"You didn't spoil my visit, Clay. It just upsets me to think of you ending up killed, like the rest of your family."

"I have no intention of getting killed," he replied as he gave her a leg up on the stallion that was eyeing him warily.

He stepped back and looked directly into her eyes and said, "There's very little in this world you can be sure of anymore, but there is one thing of which I am sure. I want to see you again."

A long moment passed as the attraction that had started as a small seed in a girl's mind and was nurtured by girlish dreams until it came into full bloom in the bosom of a woman reached out to him.

She gathered the reins in her right hand and smiled down at him.

"I want to see you again, too, Clay. My mother and father are going to Wheeling for the weekend. Why don't I fix steaks for us tomorrow evening? That is, if you don't have other plans."

"I have no plans. I'd be delighted to come."

"Wonderful! Come about six, and we'll have a cocktail before dinner."

She suddenly leaned down and pressed her lips to his. As he reached for her, she neck-reined the stallion.

"Until later," she laughed gaily, as the horse sprang away.

Clay strolled to the wood yard and sat down on the chopping block to ponder this new turn of events in his life. The thought of a son began to warm the inside of him as he became more used to the idea. Without returning to the house he started the walk to town.

"I'll go pick up the car and go see the boy," he thought. "There will probably be those who won't be too happy to renew my acquaintance, but I could care less!"

Chapter Fifteen

Ezra Fultz guided the big coal truck into the yard alongside the house. He called to Milt, who was just coming off the hill from the mine, and told him to remove and repair the outside dual on the right side of the truck. The boy made no answer, but moved sullenly to obey.

Ezra had no jacks, so two huge stones and a broken railroad tie were used as substitutes. One end of the tie was placed on the ground, the other end on top of the stones. Milt got in and started the truck and carefully pulled it up on the tie so only the inside tire was on it. That left the outside tire suspended in the air, where it could be removed and repaired. After pulling the emergency brake and chocking the left rear wheel, he took a wrench and tried to break the lug nuts loose. Their rusty condition made it necessary for him to jump up and down on the end of the wrench to break them loose.

After instructing Milt to repair the tire, Ezra had joined the rest of the family in the shade at the front of the house.

Milt wore a pair of coveralls that was a hand-me-down from Ezra. When the legs had been cut off, they hadn't been hemmed and they now flopped around his bare feet. Sweat was running in rivulets down his face and from the stringy muscles of his young body. As he began to beat the lock ring off, he glanced at the group relaxing in the shade. The hammer came down more viciously as his anger boiled to match the heat of the sun on his back.

"I ain' agonna wait much longer," he thought, as his eyes moved involuntarily to the corner of the house where the dynamite was hidden.

It was common knowledge that Harry's attentions to Hallie was causing friction between Ezra and him. The ever increasing animosity between Ezra and Harry had led to the conception of Milt's plan. He had plotted and schemed on it until he could think of nothing that would prevent it from working.

First, he had stolen several sticks of dynamite from the mine and had hidden them under the corner of the house. He had taken them one at a time so they wouldn't be missed. Next, he had confided in Lucille, who owned the general store, that he feared Ezra was planning to kill Harry. Lucille was the biggest gossip on Middle Fork, and he was confident that she could be counted on to spread the word to others.

Milt turned his head away from the smell of hot rubber as he pulled the tube from the tire and thought, "Yep, thar iz sartin benefits in bein' young, but not as dum' as people 'spect ya ta be. I got me a edjucashion rat under thar noses, evin if'n Ezra did keep me frum goin' ta school. Don' rekkin nobody evvir figgered out thet I wuz th' one whut stole thet big dictionary frum school. Nobody'd think it, but ya kin git a lotta larnin' frum them romantic true stories Maw neglects th' housework ta read. Yep, I'm gonna git rid of both of 'em at th' same time."

He glanced at Harry and Ezra lolling in the shade.

"Their cuffin' an' slappin' days iz about over," he thought as his sharp young mind once again went over his plan, seeking for a flaw.

He planned to plant the dynamite in the section of the mine where Harry was working and wait for a time when Ezra was near the mine alone. He would then set off the dynamite and purposely drop one of Ezra's truck driver's gloves which would later, no doubt, be used as evidence, because everyone knew Ezra didn't work in the mine.

Milt intended to hide in a small side tunnel until Ezra passed him on his way to check the unexpected explosion. He would then slip out of the mine behind him and go over the hill to Lucille's store. First, he would be hysterical; then he would go into shock. He knew all about shock. He had read a story in one of the magazines about a man who was suffering from shock.

Later, when the law came, he would make it a point to encounter Ezra, at which time he would scream and run from him. The vision of the sheriff taking a kicking, howling Ezra to jail made him smile.

"I'll bet he'll be a real runnin' nut in th' death house. In thet last split secont afore he dies, I hope th' cowardly bastard figgers out whut I dun to 'im."

As Milt finished patching the tube and prepared to replace it in the tire casing, he began to mentally compare the method with which he planned to eliminate his enemies with those that had been used by his real great-grandfather, Devil John Barron.

Not finding the comparison too favorable, he excused himself by rationalizing, "Times has changed. Now a man has to do things by 'is wits."

He stopped working on the tire to watch a fast-moving dust cloud coming up the Middle Fork. When the car came into sight he wondered who could be driving the big dust-streaked Chrysler. The car swerved from the road into the yard and stopped abruptly.

The car door opened and a man stepped out and looked intently at the raggedy youth standing straddle-legged over the truck tire. With no change of expression, he moved around the front of the car and walked toward the group of people in front of the house.

Milt stood for a second—transfixed.

"By God, 'e's come!"

Breaking out of his mental lapse, Milt moved quickly to the front of the house to hear what was going to be said. He had hoped and waited for this moment for years. Excitement welled up within him as he waited for the explosion that he knew wouldn't be long in coming. He was oblivious of the weight of the tire iron still in his hand.

Recognizing Clay, Ezra nearly upset his chair getting out of it. "Whadda ya want?" he growled as Clay stopped in front of him.

Harry had gotten up, too, and he stood sniffing the air like a weasel who couldn't decide whether to stand and fight or run.

Waving a hand in Milt's direction, Clay said, "I came to see the boy."

"Ya seed 'im. Now git!" Ezra's voice was rising.

"I want to talk to him now, and in private," Clay replied calmly.

Ezra was losing all control and he stormed, "Ya'll hav'ta go over me ta do it!"

"That's been done before," came the sardonic answer.

"Thet mighta bin true at one time," Ezra gritted, "but things has changed some around here since then. Th' man whut done it iz rottin' in 'is grave, an' this is another. . . ."

Clay's open hand cracked across his mouth. The sentence was never finished.

Triggered into action by the blow, Ezra charged Clay, swinging blindly. Clay jumped sideways, threw out his foot and chopped Ezra across the back of the neck as he lunged by. With his legs in the air like plow handles, his momentum carried him scooting across the dusty yard on his face.

As Ezra hit the ground, Harry saw his chance and leaped for the front steps to get the shotgun that sat just inside the front door. Halfway up the steps he found his way barred by a grinning Milt. There was no time to avoid the tire iron that struck him full in the face. He crumpled to his knees on the steps. Tilting over backwards, he slid down them and lay with his head in the dirt of the yard, with his feet still hanging onto the steps.

With the panther-like quickness of a mountain-bred savage, the boy sprang on the prostrate form and raised the tire iron for the blow that would expose the brains to the sun. The iron never descended, however. It was caught in a strong grip from behind and a soft voice reasoned, "Don't kill him now. That'll just complicate things. Later, if you want to, but not now."

Milt loosened his grip on the tire iron and watched Clay toss it away. Man and boy stood there looking straight into each other's eyes. Clay's face was unreadable; Milt's showed defiance.

"If there's anything here you want, go get it. I'm taking you with me," Clay said presently.

Turning toward the car, Milt answered, "All I wan' is ta git outta here."

Ezra was struggling to his feet, looking dazed and beaten, while Harry still lay unmoving. Clay had won the skirmish, but the real battle was facing him now in the form of an angry woman.

This was Hallie May, but if he hadn't seen her there, he wouldn't have recognized her. The once-proud breasts hung down now like a pair of enormous sow's ears. The red hair, formerly so luxuriant, was now frizzy from too many trips around the hair curlers. Small beads of perspiration stood out on her as-yet downy mustache.

Her pride in herself had been long gone. When pride is taken from a hill woman, there remains one of the laziest, dirtiest, most spineless pieces of human jelly found anywhere in the world. This same woman, if allowed to retain her pride, can be a bottomless pit of energy. Raising a garden, canning food, digging coal for the winter, chopping wood, working in the fields, taking care of a large family on limited funds is all done without a complaint.

Last, but not least, this woman is also capable of keeping her man home in bed on moonlit nights when the hounds are running the foxes, and lesser women's husbands are gambling and drinking whiskey around a fire under some overhanging cliff. The woman screaming and cursing now at Clay could have been such a woman, but she wasn't.

"You sons-a-bitchin' Barrons won' never change, will ya? Yore allers walkin' in somewhars an' takin' whutever suits ya. Ya don' never consider nobody else or how they might feel. Didn' ya cause me 'nuff grief, gittin' me knocked up in th' furst place? Whut right do ya think ya got ta th' boy? Now thet he's big 'nuff ta be some he'p ta me, I s'pose ya wanna take 'im away frum me. Wall, by Jesus, this time ya ain' agonna run over me. I'll law ya; thet's whut I'll do."

Ignoring the woman, Clay walked back to the car, took a checkbook from the glove compartment and began to write. Hallie had stopped her verbal assault on him, and now stood watching him suspiciously until he finished writing the check.

Turning back to her, Clay spoke quietly, but his words were audible to all. "Here's a check for fifteen thousand dollars for taking care of my son."

"Jest like thet, is it? Drive in 'ere in yer big car, sportin' a fat pocketbook an' all of a suddent he's yore son. Mebbe I don' wan' yer damn money; mebbe I wan' th' boy."

"Maybe you do," Clay conceded. "I could be wrong. It's your choice to make, and you'll only have one chance, so make up your mind. Which one do you want—the check or the boy?"

Ezra sidled up behind Hallie and whispered, "Good God, woman, take th' money. Fifteen thousand dollars! Thet's more'n we kin make in five years!"

Hallie stood at the crossroads of decision. At the end of one stood her own flesh and blood; at the other, the pot of gold. With lowered eyes, she plucked the check from Clay's hands and turned away.

Thirteen years was a long time to wait, but she still felt that there was something for her beyond these mountains. The greedy smile on Ezra's face would disappear as she rode the Gray Dog out of here with the money tomorrow morning.

As they drove down Middle Fork, Milt was sitting on the edge of the seat with his toes curled in the thick carpet in order to keep his balance and to prevent his dirty back from soiling the upholstery of the car.

"What made you so intent on killing that scarred up fella?" Clay asked, breaking the silence.

"He's had it acomin' fer a long time. I shoulda finished 'im off."

"Why?"

"Why not? I'm a Barron, ain' I?"

"What's that crack supposed to mean?" Clay asked.

"It means ever since I kin 'member I bin tol' least onct a day 'bout ma bad blood. They said I'd mos' likely end up a killer. Ezra allers said th' Barrons like ta kill better'n hogs like ta eat acorns. Rekkin I'm shore 'nuff a Barron, 'cause I shore did hanker to cave in thet Harry's head."

Clay drove for some time before he answered. "That's not true—about the bad blood, I mean. We aren't any different than other people, except that we believe in honoring our obligations to each other. What's wrong with that?"

"Ain' nothin' wrong with it, fur as I kin see," Milt answered. "Thet's th' way I wan' it ta be with me, too. Everbody said you'd be back ta kill ol' man Hook, but everbody sez thar's too many of 'em fer ya. You don' hafta worry none, though. After they kill ya, I'll take care a' th' rest of 'em. Thet's ma right now, ain' it?"

Glancing sideways at the boy, Clay realized that he meant what he said. His only answer could be, "Yes, it's your right."

"Good!" the boy shot back. "Afore I'm through, people's gonna fergit all 'bout Devil John Barron."

Surprised at this last statement, Clay asked, "What do you know about my grandad?"

"I've heerd all th' stories thar' is ta hear 'bout 'im. Onct I run off an' went up on thet mountain of your'n an' seen 'is grave. I stayed up thar two whole days afore I got so hungry I hadda come back down."

As they travelled on, Milt gradually seemed to relax. Finally he asked, "Whar we goin' to now?"

"We're going to stay with my aunt and uncle until I can get a house built on the mountain," Clay informed him.

"Rekkin as how all thet's gonna be mine someday when yer gone. Ain' thet right?"

Clay found himself amused at the gall of the boy. "Yes, someday it will be yours," he smiled. "But not too soon, I hope," he finished to himself.

After passing the school building, Clay drove up the dirt road until he reached the point where the path and road separated. He pulled the car off the road and parked it behind a clump of bushes, and they took the path that led to Big Pap's.

When they had crossed the fence and were standing on Big Pap's property, Clay turned to Milt and said, "Now that you're a Barron on Barron land, I'm going to tell you what it means to be one of us, and what will be expected of you. If, at any time, now or in the future, you find that you can't live up to these things, just keep in mind that these steps over this fence lead both ways, and you are free to go at any time."

Milt nodded and waited for Clay to continue.

"Years ago my grandpappy told me that the most important thing for a man to be in life is a real man; not just some male that walks around in pants and doesn't sqat to pee. Pride is a way of life with us. I would rather see you dead than have you bend your knee or beg to any man. No Barron is a thief. If there's something you want, go after it, but don't ever steal it. To this rule there is one exception. Women. We consider them the property of no one. If there's a woman you want, we believe the end justifies the means."

Clay paused and asked, "Do you follow me so far?"

Milt nodded again, and Clay went on.

"We always walk with our heads high and look every man in the eye. We are never insolent or domineering towards those who are less fortunate than us, but we never fawn over any man because of his wealth or position. In time of war, we are prepared to fight to the death for our government, if necessary, to keep them from taking away any of our constitutional freedoms. We constantly strive to be the best friend our friends have, and the most vicious enemy possible to our enemies. These things should never have to be repeated to you. If you remain with me, some day you will be teaching these same principles to your children, so learn them well."

Milt seemed to have grown taller while Clay was talking. Pride was gathering around him like a cloak.

"I wanna stay here," he said huskily. "I won' never disappoint ya."

"I'm sure you won't, Milt. And one other thing. Don't you concern yourself about any bad blood. What's bad blood to some is good mountain stock to others. Our blood runs red, the same as everyone else's. It's just a little harder to spill than most."

As they walked on towards Big Pap's, Clay pointed out several different spots and related incidents that had taken place there in the past.

Before reaching the house, Milt had smiled wryly and said, "Rekkin as how I won' be in no hurry ta make folks fergit 'bout Devil John. But," he added quickly, "I'll be as good as enny a' th' rest of 'em."

"I know you will," Clay answered solemnly.

"By th' way, whut am I s'posed ta call ya?" the boy asked.

"Why don't you start out calling me Clay, and we'll go from there. OK?"

"OK."

As they approached the house, Aunt Sarah came out to meet them. Clay introduced the two.

"Mammy, this is my son, Milt. If you don't mind, he will be living with us from now on."

"Glad ta meet cha, Milt," the old woman beamed. "I'm most pleased yer gonna be astayin' with us."

Standing on the porch behind her, Big Pap was glad, too. He thought, "With all these new responsibilities, Sarah'll be as happy as a cow loose in th' sweet corn."

Sarah took charge of Milt immediately. After giving him some of the clothes Clay had worn as a boy, she filled the big iron kettle in the smokehouse with water and instructed him to take a bath.

When he returned wearing the oversized clothing, Sarah offered to cut them down to fit him.

As he observed Milt Clay thought, "He probably never had anything new."

Aloud he said, "Mammy, if you don't mind, I'd like to keep my old clothes. You and Milt go to town tomorrow and buy whatever things you both need."

Later, as they ate supper, Sarah commented, "Milt, I hope ya larn ta love this mountain as we do. To other folks, it's jist a big ol' hill, but hit's bin another father ta us. It's pertected us, fed us, and with hit's beauty alone we bin rewarded fer lovin' it."

That night, for the first time in his life, Milt slept in a feather bed with clean sheets and quilts. He had been used to a hard pallet on the floor. Clay awoke during the night to hear him muttering in his sleep. In the dark he felt Milt's hand touch his shoulder, then dart away. Reassured, the boy was soon sleeping soundly again.

After breakfast, Milt and Clay relaxed on the front porch. The boy sucked in his breath and let it out in a slow whistle, saying, "Geeminy, it's shore purty 'round here. I ain' nivver seen no place so purty afore."

"Yes," Clay agreed, as he looked around. "This is the most beautiful place in the world. Not just this mountain, but the whole country around here. It's hard to appreciate it until you have been taken away from it. The things you take for granted, other people will travel hundreds of miles to see. Sometime soon the rest of the world will discover Kentucky, and then the money men will come, the spoilers. They'll dam up the valleys, build lodges, and bring in the hunters and fishermen. The quiet easy days we know now will be broken by the whine of motorboats and hysterical people who rush from place to place, frantically trying to have a good time before they return to the drudgery of another year of the prison that is city life."

"Maybe I'm selfish not to want to share this country with the outsiders, but not one in a thousand will take the time to just sit quietly on a stump and listen to the sounds of the land around them. People are so busy trying not to miss anything that they miss the most important thing in life—the feeling of belonging to the earth. My body and existence were formed here on this mountain, and I want to be returned to it when I die. That's why it's so important to keep the mountain all in one piece. As long as there's a Barron living who feels as we do, we'll never permit the commercial rape of this land."

Sometime later Clay harnessed the horse and hitched him to the buggy. As he watched Big Pap, Sarah and Milt excitingly prepare to leave for town, Clay recalled a Bible verse that Big Pap had often read to him.

"My cup runneth over."

To get away from the confusion inside, Clay wandered out to the wood yard. He had always loved the feel of a double-bitted ax in his hands. If a man were angry or had problems on his mind, there was no better way to relieve the pressure than with the ax. He was pecking away at a hickory pole when they came out of the house to leave.

"Haw! Haw!" laughed Big Pap. "Thar's one thing fer shore. Ya ain' done much log cuttin' since ya left. Ya swing thet ax like a ol' woman."

Clay smiled. "It does seem awkward, at that. Guess I'd better leave the wood chopping to you."

"Aw, no, Son. Don' pay no mind ta somethin' a senile ol' man sez. You'll make a fine wood chopper, mos' likely. Ya jist keep on gittin' more experience." As they drove away, Big Pap called over his shoulder, "Jist don' be athrowin my ax, now."

Clay smiled again. Big Pap had a way of bringing back happy memories of his childhood.

When Clay was approximately ten years old, he had read a story about a man who had lived in Canada who could throw a double-bitted ax with such accuracy that he had won a bet by killing a grizzly bear with it.

This fictional character from the pages of the book had become Clay's hero, and all the axes his family owned became the worse for it. He had dulled and gapped the blades and split the handles as he had practiced throwing them indiscriminately. Big Pap had returned from town one day with a new ax. As he handed it to Clay he said, "This is fer you. Throw the hell outta it if'n ya want to, but keep yore hands off'n mine frum now on!"

It had taken most of the summer, but Clay finally mastered the art of ax-throwing. The secret, he found, was in letting it loose in such a way that it turned over only once before striking the target at which it was thrown.

Clay hefted the ax now. There was no strain to his muscular arm as there had been when he was a youth. He walked a few steps towards the woods, drew the ax back over his head and threw it at a hickory tree. The blade made its arch in the air, but stuck face first on the edge of the tree and only skinned loose some of the bark. He retrieved the ax and tried again. Whoomp! The ax turned once in the air and the steel blade buried itself into the tree. Clay satisfied himself by throwing it several more times, then returned to the wood yard.

After carrying enough wood into the house to fill the wood box behind the kitchen stove, he picked up Devil John's pistol and two boxes of shells and started the long climb to the top of his mountain.

Approximately twenty-five yards behind the burned-out barn in the middle of what had once been the barn yard stood a huge, ugly beech tree. When Devil John Barron had been a small boy, he had been climbing this tree when a limb broke, causing him to fall. More frightened than hurt, he had flown into one of his later famous rages and threatened to cut down the tree. His mother had forbidden him to touch it, so he decided to kill it by shooting into it.

As the years passed and Devil John practiced with his gun, the big beech just swallowed the lead he shot into it, grew a new skin and kept right on living. Many years later Devil John still grumbled about being unable to kill the tree.

"Maw tol' me not ta touch thet tree, an' I won', but I musta put a ton a' lead in it. Guess thet's whut's holdin' it up."

Today another Barron set his target against the tree, and the long-barreled forty-five was once again blazing away at its favorite target. No man could ever shoot the big gun with the deadly accuracy with which Devil John had, but the man crouched behind it now was no amateur.

As he returned to the house he could see Milt unloading the buggy. He didn't look like the same boy he had picked up the day before. His hair had been cut and he was now dressed in Levi's, a checkered shirt and boots. The realization that Milt was already subconsciously beginning to pattern himself after him hit Clay. This was something he hadn't thought of or counted on. Setting an example for someone else is a fearful responsibility. In Clay's position, it was impossible.

"How did things go in town?" Clay asked, as he approached the boy.

"Hit couldna gone no better. You should'a seen ol' man Hutchinson's face when I walked in an' ordered all them things an' throwed thet hunnert at 'im. Thar was some others doin' some gawkin', too. I had a righ' smart buncha money left over, an' Aunt Sarah said ta give it back ta ya."

Not bothering to count it, Clay peeled off two bills and put the rest in his pocket.

"Here, Milt. It's always good for a man to have a little walking around money on him," Clay said as he pressed them into his hand.

Holding the bills uncertainly Milt said, "I dunno why, but it allers makes me feel funny whin somebody gives me somethin'. I dunno whut ta say. I'll say 'thanks,' anyhow."

"You're welcome, Milt."

After they had put the horse in the barn and returned to the house, Clay was shown the other purchases they had made. Big Pap and Sarah were as delighted as children. It took so little to please them. They had acquired little from life but each other. Clay vowed to himself that he would change this. He would make it possible for them to have everything they desired. Clay did not realize that these two people had the wealth the rest of the world searches for every day. They knew what it was to love and be loved.

Chapter Sixteen

Jubal Hook drove his lead-colored Olds 88 cautiously through the small mountain hamlet of Moses' Mills. Here in this little out-of-the-way community on the West Virginia border, the Hooks had one of their largest outlets for the "white lightening" that Jubal was hauling. The 88 was equipped with overload springs, but the weight of the whiskey still gave it an underslung look.

Everything was all right. The sign in the garage window said, "Honk Horn for Service." If it had said "Blow Horn for Service," he would have blown—not the horn, but out of the vicinity.

He pulled into the driveway and touched the horn. A face appeared at the glass in the side door, disappeared and quickly the overhead door rolled up. Jubal drove across the interior of the garage to the grease rack, straddled it and stopped.

Ruben Skaggs, the proprietor, came slinking alongside the car and whined, "Ya have enny trouble on th' way up?"

"No trouble," Jubal answered shortly. "How quick kin I git unloaded?"

"Ya gotta full load?"

"Don' I allers? Quit jawin' an' call th' man. I wanna git movin'."

"Somebody bin atailin' ya?" Ruben asked, suspiciously.

"No, goddammit, nobody's tailin' me. I ain' stupid 'nuff ta come here if'n they wuz. I'm in no humor fer bullcrappin' taday, so if'n ya wan' this load, call th' man."

"Holt onta yer pants. I'll call 'im," Ruben grumbled as he sauntered to the phone. "It really frosts ma balls th' way these beeg shots talk down ta a feller. Ol' Silas an' th' man didn' act like this whin they wuz atalkin' me inta lettin' th' garage be used as a drop."

As he told the operator the number he wanted he thought, "I may jist quit 'em!"

Waiting for the answer from the other end, however, he remembered what the man had threatened at the time the deal was made.

"Ya cross me up, Ruben," the man had said, "an' I'll shove a double-barreled shotgun up yer ass an' let loose with both barrels."

Ruben was unconsciously rubbing his ample rear as the phone clicked on the other end and a voice curtly answered, "Yes."

The conversation that followed made no sense to the everpresent eavesdroppers on the party line, but the message was delivered.

Presently, a radio-equipped pickup truck swung into the driveway and backed up to the door. Ruben opened the door, and after the truck was inside he lowered it again. The driver backed across the garage until the truck sat directly beneath Jubal's Olds, which had been raised on the lift.

The sign on the side of the truck read "Mt. States Construction Co." However, the toolboxes attached to the side of the truck held no tools. Each box was equipped with a two hundred-fifty gallon whiskey tank.

"Th' runner frum Harlan County's beat me agin taday," surmised Jubal, as he noticed the truck tilting slightly to the right.

Ruben climbed up on the bed of the truck and connected a hose from Jubal's tank to a spout on the truck's toolbox. The truck began to level itself as the whiskey flowed into the left tank.

A car, bearing the same lettering as the truck, pulled to a stop in front of the garage. The driver went inside and greeted Jubal. After turning over a bundle of greenbacks to him, the driver of the car departed saying, "Hit's a pleasure ta do business with ya."

Jubal knew that what he really meant was that they would need another load next Monday. None of the Hooks but Silas knew who "the man" was. This was a sore spot with Jubal, but today he had other things to think about. He impatiently waited for the drivers of the car and truck to go over their signals again. These two men had been reviewing these same signals once or twice a week for as long as he had been delivering to them. Their seemingly over-cautious planning had resulted in these two partners being among the most successful whiskey transporters in the country.

The car pulled out, but the truck waited until it had a good mile's head start before following. The car was used to detect law enforcement agents who might be lying in wait. In case of their appearance, he would simply radio the truck, whose driver would immediately leave the highway and follow a preplanned alternate route.

After Ruben lowered the hoist with Jubal's car on it, he kicked the dump drain to be sure the tank was empty.

"Rekkin thar's only one thing that'd make ya in sich a hurry, an' thet's a leetle split-tail awaitin' fer ya somewhars," he chided.

Without bothering to answer, Jubal got into the car and backed out of the garage. As he shot out of the driveway, Ruben spit on the floor and scowled, "Wal, screw you, too, Big Shot!"

Empty now, Jubal cast caution to the wind and stomped on the 88. The fox tail attached to the antenna began to whip about violently. He drove as if pursued by demons. Today was his day. He wouldn't have to worry about his old man showing up unsuspected, as he had a habit of doing. Old Silas wouldn't leave the house today. He would sit on the front porch and get drunk and cuss Clay Barron and damn the souls of all the other Barrons now deceased.

Silas always seemed to think and plan better when he was half drunk. He was running scared now and trying not to show it. Jubal was sure that before this day had passed, Silas would have a workable solution to get rid of Clay Barron, with the least danger to himself.

Sometime later, Jubal turned onto the Dry Fork Road and gunned the 88 down the graveled highway. He never let up on the accelerator until he had to slow down to turn unto the trash-littered yard of Lige Begley. When he stopped the car, the rocket hood emblem pointed right at the front door.

The house was a two-room ramshackle shack constructed of logs many years before, which were now covered with unpainted weather boarding. Jubal sat in the car until the dust he had stirred up had drifted by or settled on the house before he got out of the car.

Beulah came to the unscreened front door and idly swatted flies with a newspaper as she waited for him. Her stocky, or more truthfully, plumb body was covered by a cheap looking pinafore. A red scarf was tied around her head in "Aunt Jemima" fashion. Her uninteresting bland face showed neither surprise nor pleasure at his arrival.

"Howdy, Jubal," she said, not moving out of the doorway. "I waren' 'spectin' ya taday. Did kinder think ya mighta showed up yisterday."

"I didn' git back frum Memphis 'til late last night," he explained. "Paw's agonna hafta git somebody else fer thet long run. I'm gittin' tireda riskin' ma ass fer 'im fer nothin'."

"Whar is Silas? He comin' over taday?" she asked.

"No. Clay Barron's come home an' Paw is holed up at th' house gittin drunk. 'Fraid ta stick 'is ass out. 'Fraid he'll git it shot off."

"Frum whut Paw's sed, seems like this Barron's liable ta try," she answered. "Hit shore would be a shame if'n thet happent, but as th' ol' folks say, 'Hit's a ill wind thet don' blow some good fer somebody'."

"Whut da ya mean by thet crack?" Jubal questioned, half angered.

"Don' mean nothin' 'tall. Hit's jist thet, God ferbid, should somethin' happen ta Silas, thin I could move over thar with ya, an' you'd have th' still an' all. You could run off yer brothers, without too much trouble. With things th' way they iz now, I ain' too hepped up 'bout goin' over thar ta live with yer paw, cause I know I'd end up packin' an' totin' fer all of you'ins."

Jubal answered, "Ya don' havta go over thar with 'im anyway. I tole ya thet whin Paw first come asmellin' round ya. I shoulda gone right

ahead an' tol' 'im how things wuz between us right at th' start 'stead
alettin' ya talk me outta it. Whut you want with 'im, anyhow? I kin do
more fer ya than he kin."

"In some ways ya shore kin, an' thet's a fact. I love ya, too, an' thet
shore makes it hurt me ta have ta be made over by any other man, but
facts is facts. Yer paw hangs onta th' money strings in yer fam'ly like
ma daddy in thar' hangs onta a whiskey bottle. Jubal, much as I care
fer ya, I'm not about ta stay over here in this god-awful hole 'til I'm more
dried up'n thet creek bed out thar. I know hit would be a shame, an' I'd
shore feel sorry fer ya if'n somethin did happen ta Silas, but if'n he was
gone, we shore could begin ta live, an' thet's a fact."

"Ain' nothin' agonna ta happen ta Paw," he half grumbled. "He's too
ornery ta git hurt. Makes me madder'n hell th' way he sits 'round abraggin' 'bout th' way he makes ya squeal an' moan when he's cuttin' ya.
Does he make ya holler louder'n I do?"

He stood waiting fearfully for her answer. Every man needs to think
he can outdo his father in something.

She walked toward him until she was very close. "No, Jubal, I'm
atellin' ya th' truth. Thar' ain' nobody ever made me feel whut I do with
you. Seems like sometimes yer gonna jist rip me wide open. Ya need a
woman, Jubal; one ta sleep with ya ever night. Ya need a woman like
me ta take care of yer needs."

Rubbing against him now she continued, "I'd take care a' yer wants,
Jubal, like ya'd never believe I would take care a' 'em."

Jubal grasped her against him, and then pushed her back through
the door into the dim room. Her father lay on the broken-down couch,
snoring loudly, oblivious to the flies buzzing around his open mouth.

"Rekkin Paw got a leetle too much ta drink an' passed out."

She made no apology for him. Jubal dragged Beulah toward the
rumpled bed in the corner, ignoring the sleeping man.

Beulah had removed her sheer pink panties when she first heard
Jubal's car in the yard. Silas had bought them for her because he liked
to see her strut around in nothing but her red heels and pink panties
before making love to her. She knew that if anything happened to those
pink panties she would have a hard time explaining. Silas wasn't as
young or stupid as Jubal.

Jubal had about as much finesse as a boar hog when it came to sex.
Once before he had torn to shreds a pair of her panties in his haste to
get to her. At the edge of the bed he grabbed her and kissed her, ram-
ming his tongue into her mouth. He jerked away from her and spit on
the floor.

"Jeezchris', whut th' hell ya bin eatin'? Yer mouth tastes like hell."

"I jist bin achewin' on a few leetle ol' cracklins. I'm sorry hit both-
ers ya."

Shaking loose from her, he walked over and yanked the whiskey bottle from the hand of her sleeping father.

"Here, slush somea' this 'round in yer mouth."

She took the bottle, tipped it up and took a generous amount in her mouth and swished it around before swallowing it. Setting the bottle down beside the bed, she reached for Jubal again.

"Thet's better, Baby," he grunted, as he pushed her to the bed.

As soon as he had freed himself of his clothes, he threw himself on top of her, and tasted her lips once more. As always, she wriggled up against him and he lost all control. He kissed and bit at her lips, all the while pulling and squeezing her breasts. As usual, he made no effort to remove her clothes before satisfying himself.

As Beulah endured Jubal's lovemaking she thought, "Thar's one thing thet kin be said fer ol' Silas. He might only be good fer one a week, but he knows how ta take 'is time an' injoy it whin he does git it."

It might be, as she had heard someone say, that old people went after each one as if it might be their last. She thought it was a shame that young men, with their constantly hard bodies, didn't have the same worries.

Beulah was positioned facedown on the bed. Jubal liked it best that way. He rode her now as a rodeo rider would a mean bronc. All he needed to complete the picture was a pair of spurs and a ten-gallon hat.

She smiled against the sheet as he clutched her hips and began slamming against her harder and harder. It was time for her to go into her act. It seemed to give him pleasure to grunt and lunge at her as some animal would.

She began to twist and squirm beneath him, crying out in a pleading voice, "Not so hard, Jubal, honey. Oooh, oh, please, sweetheart, yore hertin' me!"

As her cries of apparent pain filled the room, they brought Jubal to the explosive state.

"Does this hert more'n Paw does?" he wheezed.

"Yes! Oh, God, stop! Yer killin' me!" she shrieked.

He made one more terrific lunge, then rolled off her, his lust completely satiated.

Pleased with herself, Beulah snuggled up against Jubal thinking, "I'll jist keep afoolin' 'round with both of 'em 'til I figger out which way ta jump. Th' ol' man's got all th' money, but he cain't git along without Jubal. Well, rekkin I'll jist hav'ta wait an' see."

Jubal was passing into the last throes of his passion when Lige awoke from his drunken stupor. He turned his head toward the unfamiliar noise and watched the mating pair with watery eyes.

"Thet Beulah shore ain' humpin' nothin' like her maw usta," he thought, impersonally. "Course, hit takes a man ta put a arch in a woman's back, goin' frum thet direction."

He perceived that Jubal wasn't much of a man, even though she was howling like a turpentined dog. His long years of drunken sex bouts with anyone who was available told him that the cries rang false.

"A woman who ain' made them squeals fer real ain' lived. Beulah hadn' orter be denied thet," he reasoned.

After Jubal had thrown his exhausted form off Beulah, Lige rolled off the couch shouting, "Jeezchris' on a crutch! Whut th' hell do ya think yer doin'?"

He wobbled and weaved across the room and stood looking down at the naked couple. They made no effort to move or cover themselves.

"Drunk as you are, ya orter know whut we're doin'," Jubal sneered.

"Ya tryin' ta git us both killed?" Lige shouted, undaunted. "Ya know thet Silas tol' me ta keep a eye on 'er an' keep everybody away frum 'er. I never heerd 'im make no 'ceptions fer you."

"I'll tell ya what, Pops," Jubal shot back sarcastically, "if'n ya don' tell 'im—I won'."

"Goddam you! Git outta here! Git righ' now or I'll take ma mule an' ride over ta yer paw's an' tell 'im ya bin over here amakin' a cuckold outta 'im."

Jubal reared up in bed, drew back his fist threateningly and said, "Ya ain' gonna tell nobody nothin'. All yer gonna git is a busted mouth fer yer trouble!"

Lige whirled around and headed for the door, shouting over his shoulder, "Wonder 'f ya'll be as smart with yer mouth after Silas finishes with ya."

Jubal leapt from the bed and grabbed Lige from behind by the collar. He spun him around, threw him down on the couch and hissed, "Ya tell Paw anythin' 'bout me bein' here an' I'll break yer scrawny neck!"

"Git out, then," the old man screamed, taking courage from the liquor he had previously consumed.

After dressing clumsily, Jubal still tried to bluff the old man. On his way out he put the flat of his hand against Lige's head and upended him on the couch.

He stalked out of the house, unable to meet Beulah's eyes that said, "Big man! Still afraid of his daddy!" She didn't understand why it was so important to all men to be able to surpass their fathers at some endeavor. It was just unfortunate that Jubal had chosen sex.

Without realizing it, Beulah's thoughts had just proven the old wives' tale wrong that said the way to a man's heart is through his stomach. Any damn fool should know that the shortest and easiest route is through the zipper in his pants.

As Jubal's Olds ripped up the front yard on his way out, Lige got up from the couch and skulked drunkenly across the room. He stood over Beulah, who hadn't bothered to get up during the argument.

"Ya orter had more sense'n ta do thet," he complained. "Ya wanna git us throwed outta this house an' us with no money 'er nowhars ta go?"

"Wouldn' thet be a hell of a thing ta happen," she answered hauntingly, "gittin' throwed outta this rat trap?"

"Don' you go givin' me no sass!" he said menacingly.

"An' don' you go givin' me none of this father-and-daughter crap. Yer more worried 'bout yer whiskey supply bein' cut off than how or whar' we live. You'd sell yer interest in hell fer 'nother drink. Frum now on, you look out fer yourself, 'cause that's jist whut I'm gonna do fer me! I'm shore I ain' gonna have no trouble findin' somewhars ta go, evin if'n I don' never see another Hook. While we're at it, thar's another thing I'm shore of. Whin I leave here, hit's gonna be alone. I ain' spendin' th' resta ma life with you hangin' 'round ma neck like a dead weight!"

"I'll tell ya whut ta do, an' don' you fergit it!"

His voice was loud, but it no longer held the authority she had always feared.

"Stop yellin' at me, ya ol' bastard! I don' hav'ta take yer abuse no more. I'll git up an' leave righ' now!"

She raised herself up, as if to get out of bed. Lige backhanded her across the face, knocking her back. She tried to crawl off the bed, but he grabbed the front of her dress and shoved her back.

The dress ripped open in his hand, exposing her oversized breasts. Lige's whiskey-fogged mind swirled as he looked at the cowering girl on the bed. All the fight had been knocked out of her. She was her father's daughter in that respect. She was a coward who would do anything rather than endure physical pain.

Pictures of the scene he had witnessed earlier ran through his wretched mind as he said, "If'n yer gonna give it away ta ever stray dog whut wonders in here, rekkin I migh' jist as well have some of it, too."

Realizing his intentions, she pleaded, "No, Paw! Please! You don' wanna do thet ta me! You don' know whut yer sayin'."

As Lige clambered into the bed, she tried to fend him off.

"Please let me be, Paw. I won' try ta leave 'er nothin'! I swear ta God I won'!"

He was not to be dissuaded, however, as drunken passion had doubled his strength. Slow, but steadily, he forced his way between her legs. Only the buzzing flies were witness as the drunken old bootlegger ravished his own daughter.

Chapter Seventeen

As Jubal drove toward the Sandy Valley, he was in an especially exultant mood. He was relaxed and stress-free as the result of his recent cuckolding of his father with Beulah. In spite of himself, his thoughts kept returning to what she had said about how things could be if his father were out of the picture.

As he flashed along the highway, his mind halted and dwelt on Silas' hidden money. He was certain that no one but him knew where it was buried. Jubal's brothers were too stupid to trust. Silas had never given them anything but a place to live and food to eat. The only thing that held them to him was fear.

Jubal thought, "Thar's one thing fer certin. Silas' gonna hav'ta git somebody else ta make thet run ta Memphis. I'm tired atakin' all them chances. I bin lucky so far, but sooner er later them feds is gonna catch up ta me. 'Sides, thar's no Beulahs with thar plump, warm little rears ta snuggle up to thar at th' federal pen."

Subsconsciously he now began to form plans that no longer included his father.

Jubal always derived a sense of power from the 88 he was driving. Many had tried, but no one had run him to the ground in this one. He pulled the wire that opened the cut-outs on the exhaust pipes and thrilled to the way they bellered and bawled as he gunned the Olds into the curves leading to the top of Brown Ridge.

Sometime later as he drove into Hookville, he observed the usual Saturday evening crowd beginning to gather on the street in front of the pool hall and movie theater. He waved casually at a couple of acquaintances, but would have driven on through if he hadn't heard his name called as he passed the pool hall. He stopped the car and waited as his brother, Wilson, ran toward him with the perpetual foolish grin fixed on his face.

"Ya goin' ta th' house now, Jubal?" he asked.

"Yep," Jubal answered, "I'm gonna go clean up a bit."

"Ya thinkin' 'bout comin' back later?" Wilson asked hopefully.

"Mos' likely I'll be comin' back. Why?"

"If'n yer comin' back ta town, I'll ride out with ya an' git somethin' ta eat. I'm hungry'ern hell, but Paw wouldn' give me no money afore I come in."

"Git in an' I'll bring ya back with me after we git somethin' ta eat."

Recalling some of his earlier thoughts, Jubal began initiating the first phase of his plan to transfer his brothers' loyalty from Silas to himself. When he gained control of the still he would need all of them to help.

He took a five dollar bill from his jeans and said as he handed it to Wilson, "Here. Hev yerself some fun tonight. I'll git a jug a' whiskey fer ya afore we come back in. A jug a whiskey an' a five dollar bill oughta make ol' Effie th' Coon screw th' pants off'n ya."

"Yeh! Yeh!" Wilson nodded his head excitedly.

This small act of kindness had completely won him over. He was incapable of wondering why, for the first time in years Jubal was being decent, when for years he wouldn't even give him the time of day. Wilson took out a plug of tobacco and offered his brother a chew. Continuing his new policy, Jubal accepted.

Jubal had the Olds streaking down the valley, running flat out. Wilson shrieked like a child in delight. He loved to go fast.

"She runs like th' haints is after 'er," he shouted above the wind screaming through the car.

Jubal laughed wildly as the telephone poles rushed by them. The love for speed was the only thing that he and his idiot brother had in common. At the last second he let off the gas enough to make the turn into the driveway at the side of the house. The geared-down car sent out balls of fire from the exhausts.

As they slid to a stop, Silas came out of the house and shouted angrily, "Yer gonna git yer ass picked up one a' these days over yer hell drivin' an' them pipes. Mebbe it'll take a stretch in th' pen ta convince ya hit's not too smart ta be ashowin' off in a tanker!"

"Ya still got frost on yer balls, I see," Jubal answered sarcastically.

It had always impressed his brothers the way Jubal talked back to the old man, but never before had there been any doubt between the two of them as to who was the bull moose of the family.

"I jist don' wan' no trouble now thet th' sheriff's watchin' us so clost," Silas snapped back.

"Piss on th' sheriff," Jubal muttered.

"Yeah, piss on th' sheriff. Thet's a good answer. Pissin' on' th' sheriff ain' gonna do me no good if'n thet son-of-a-bitchin' Barron sneaks over here an' kills me."

"Then I'd say we better git ta doin' somethin' 'bout 'im then. I don' care much fer th' 'idear asettin' 'roun' here waitin' fer 'im ta decide who's gonna be first. I'ze th' one whut started thet fight. Hit's mos' likely gonna be me."

Noticing that Wilson was still standing there listening to their conversation, Silas ordered him to go inside to eat supper.

As Wilson automatically obeyed, Silas lowered his voice and continued.

"Thet's whut I wanna talk ta ya 'bout. We ain' gonna wait. We gonna hit 'im first. I bin sittin' righ' thar on th' porch all afternoon amakin' up th' best way ta go 'bout it."

Jubal listened silently as Silas went on. "I'm gittin' too old fer this gunfightin' bullshit. I already throwed my share a' lead at th' Barrons, an' ta this day I'm still carryin' some of theirs. You boys iz agonna hav'ta step up an' take yer turn now. Ya cain't beat a combination of ol' brains an' young hands. Now don' ya fergit whut I jist said some day when yer gittin' 'long in years. Th' thinkin' is fer th' older folks an' th' fightin' is fer th' younguns. Now, since he's th' last of 'em, when we finish with 'im thar ain' gonna be no more ta worry 'bout."

"We, Paw? What'cha wan' me ta do?" Jubal asked suspiciously.

"I'm 'bout ta tall ya now, an' I wan' ya ta keep yer trap shut 'bout it after I'm finished. Now then, ya know thet fer some time we had a problem with Wilson—him not bein' right an' all."

Silas had never before admitted, even to himself, that Wilson had been mentally retarded since birth. It had been much more satisfying to him to pretend that Clay had caused his condition when he had hit him in the head with a rock.

"Here's whut I thought ta do," Silas said. "Since Wilson's th' one whut suffered th' mos' frum thet bastard, hit's only fair thet he git first crack at 'im. Cause th' sheriff sez he's gonna send anybody thet starts trouble ta th' pen, we gotta let someone else start it. Hit cain' be me 'er you. If'n it weren't fer me an' you, everthin' here would fall apart. Ya agree on this point, don' ya?"

Silas peered closely at Jubal.

"Yer right as rain, Paw."

Jubal was getting the picture now. Wilson was to be the sacrificial lamb.

"'Course," Silas went on, "if'n he should git lucky an' kill poor Wilson, then we got a right ta go fer 'im all out then. Hit won' be no different than whut th' whole county's sayin' now 'bout 'im havin' th' right ta come after me. On t'other hand, if'n Wilson does kill 'im, thar' ain' nothin' they kin do ta 'im 'ceptin' sen' 'im ta th' bug house. Hit wouldn' hurt Wilson none ta have some a' thet special schoolin' they give ta them thar anyhow."

When he had been younger, Jubal had held a certain amount of affection and respect for his father, but as he listened to him rationalizing his own flesh and blood into a grave or an institution, the last thread of feeling was severed, and he felt empty.

Too caught up in his own thoughts and plans to notice the change in Jubal's expression, Silas rambled on.

"With me retirin' soon an' yer Maw goin' away, hits gonna be best fer you however this turns out. Ain' no sense you bein' strapped with 'im. When yer runnin' things, you ain' gonna have time ta be alookin' out fer no addled brother."

Jubal decided that he wasn't going to make it easy for Silas.

"He ain' much trouble. I wouldn' mind lookin' after 'im."

"Don' keer whether ya mind 'er not," Silas continued, doggedly. "Ya ain' yer brother's keeper."

Jubal was now seeing his father as he really was; a man completely devoid of feeling.

He thought, "He'd sacrifice me as quick as he's agoin' to Wilson, if'n he thought it would save his own skin."

Jubal knew that Silas had no real intentions of retiring. He was too much like an old herd bull. When Clay Barron was disposed of, Silas would find some excuse to turn on him and break all the promises he was making now.

"Old man," Jubal thought to himself, "frum now on ya'd better keep pretty sharp, 'cause now hit's ever man for hisself."

"Ya gotta give th' wormy ol' bastard credit," Jubal thought as he listened to and agreed with the plan Silas laid out, which included scaring their cousins, the Rigsbys, into joining them.

He was unaware of how much he had become his father's son. Even as he gave lip service to Silas, he was planning to get rid of him.

"With all thet money, I'll bet I could git maself a better lookin' poontang than Beulah," he thought. "Hit shore wouldn' hurt none ta try."

"Hey, goddammit, you payin' attention ta whut I'm sayin' ta ya 'er not?" Silas' voice rose angrily.

"I heerd ya, Paw," Jubal answered, jerking his mind back to what Silas was saying. "I heerd all but th' last part."

"I said fer ya ta take Wilson back ta town with ya an' git 'im all het up at Barron afore ya drop 'im off. Thar' ain' no use draggin' this out. If'n he shows up tonight, Wilson might jist as well go fer 'im now. After ya git 'im all set, then I wan' ya to go over an' collar them no-count Rigsbys an' tell 'em thet Clay Barron's come back an' he's sayin' 'round thet he's gonna kill ever damn one of 'em fer burnin' down 'is house an' stealin' his stuff."

"How did ja know thet?" Jubal asked in surprise.

"I know 'cause I had 'em do it. Now, jist scare hell outta them an' mebbe they'll git off'n thar' lazy asses long 'nuff ta be of some benefit ta us. You got whut yer supposed ta do all straight in yer mind now?"

"Got it!"

"Good! I wanna git this all over with as quick as we can."

"So do I," Jubal agreed softly.

Their reasons, however, were quite different.

On their way back to town, Jubal cautioned Wilson to be on the lookout for Clay.

"Ya know he's swore ta kill ya on sight."

"I ain' ascared of 'im!" Wilson boasted.

"No sense takin' chances, though," Jubal said as he handed his brother an army .45. "Here, ya take this jist in case 'e should show up lookin' fer ya."

As Wilson got out of the car, Jubal warned, "Now, don' take no chances, Wilson. If'n ya see 'im, jist cut down on 'im right then an' keep ashootin' 'til th' gun's empty. Paw'll see thet nothin's done ta ya fer it."

"Don' worry none 'bout me. I ain' ascared of 'im," Wilson repeated.

He turned and shuffled down the street, his bib overalls sagging from the weight of the Mason jar filled with whiskey in his left pocket, and the .45 in the right.

As Jubal watched him walk away, a sudden tenderness came over him for the big dummy. The moment of feeling passed quickly, however, with the hard fact that it would be better for the dummy to go up against Clay Barron than for him to have to.

Jubal took the road out of Hookville that headed for Devil's Fork where the Rigsbys lived. There was quite a clan of them, but Jubal knew that there were only three that it would do any good to contact. After Devil John Barron had killed Jack and Tom Rigsby, the remaining clan had lost their will to continue the feud.

The three he wanted to see had been too young to remember much about the killings. Ernest and Brine were the two youngest sons of Tom Rigsby and Elmo was still unborn at the time Devil John had killed his father, Jack.

It had been three or four years since Jubal had seen them. Here in the hills there was class distinction the same as everywhere else. The three bachelor Rigsbys who lived together here on the Fork were well-known as petty thieves and shiftless fox hunters. In the past, Silas had always ignored them, as a poor relative is usually looking for a handout.

The road up the Devil's Fork was rutted and full of chuckholes from years of neglect. The county grader never got around to making a pass through here, mainly because the Rigsbys never got around to voting. In this county, if you wanted your road graded, it was wise to get out to vote, and imperative that the vote be for the Democrats.

Jubal's car was finally halted by a big gully in the road. He would have to walk from here. After leaving the car, he continued on until he came to a deep washout. As the beam from his flashlight played over the road, he found that it wasn't really a washout at all, but a trench made by someone who had been digging there. On closer inspection, he found that they had been following a strip of coal out of the creek and across the road.

Jubal chuckled to himself, "Jist like them no-count shiftless skunks ta dig up thar road, jist ta keep thar damn asses warm."

Presently he left the road and followed a winding path up the hollow until he came within sight of their house. The Rigsbys' pack of hounds, sensing his approach, began to raise a clamour that could wake the dead.

Ernest Rigsby came out on the porch of the ramshackle shack and called to the dogs, "Here, Bowser! Here, Gert! Git yer damn asses under thet porch and shet up. Git under thar now."

When the dogs ignored him, he ambled off the porch, picked up a rock and hurled it at them. One hound, yelping and hopping on three legs, headed under the porch and was followed by the rest of the pack. Another figure appeared in the doorway and stood slouched against the door jamb.

As Jubal materialized out of the shadows into the light from the kerosene lamp that sat inside the open door, Ernest called out, "Thet's you, ain' it, Jubal?"

"Hit's me all right, Ernest."

Jubal was close enough now to recognize Elmo on the porch.

"Jeez!" he thought, "He's th' creepiest bastard I ever seen."

Elmo was an albino; the only one that Jubal had ever seen. The Rigsbys all thought Elmo had been marked because his mother had been pregnant with him at the time she saw Devil John Barron kill her husband.

"Whut's fetchin' ya up here in th' dark like this, Jubal?" Ernest asked.

"Thar's somethin' you fellers better know 'bout, so I come on over soon's I heerd 'bout it. Is Brine around? I'll make one tellin do it."

"Brine's in thar drunk on th' bed. Don' worry 'bout tellin' 'im nothin. Jist tell me."

"Wal, hit seems thet some damn fool in Frankfert dropped th' charges agin' Clay Barron an' he's come home. Th' word's out he's home ta kill us Hooks."

"So whut's thet ta us? Hit ain' none a' our business whut comes off 'twixt you an' nobody else. I ain' never seen ya comin' roun' here with enny he'p fer enny of us'n."

"I ain' over here lookin' fer enny he'p from you people now. We don' need no he'p frum nobody if'n he comes 'round us. I jist come over ta do ya a favor. Hit seems thet somebody tol' Barron they seen you fellers burn down 'is house up thar on th' hill an' carry off 'is belongins'. One a' th' fellers thet wuz ahangin' roun' up to Upton's Restaurant heerd 'im say he wuz agonna hang all three a' you'ins up by th' feet alive over a open fire an' cook yer brains righ' inside yer heads."

The Rigsbys just stood there, neither denying nor confirming their guilt.

"Wal," Jubal said as he turned to leave, "I got dun whut I come over fer. I don' 'spect Barron's gonna be 'round much longer, but I thought you fellers oughta be put onto whut he's plannin'."

After relating to the awakened Brine what Jubal had said, Ernest continued without waiting for any comment.

"We gotta go over thar an' find thet Barron an' kill 'im. If'n we don', he'll hunt us down one at a time an' we won' never know whut hit us. We're gonna git 'im tonight. I ain' waitin'."

Elmo's pink eyes gleamed as he giggled, "I wanna do it! I wanna kill 'im!"

"Shore, ya do, ya warped-up pink-eyed bastard. Ya bin wantin' ta take yer spite out on somebody long's I kin 'member. Whin th' time comes, ya'll probably turn frum white ta yeller, an' I'll have ta do it maself."

Ernest hated Elmo. He had never tried to reason why. He just didn't like having the albino near him. He had talked to Brine once about knocking Elmo in the head and burying him where no one would ever find him. Only their laziness had saved him.

Sometimes, when they got tired of eating groundhog and greens, they would force Elmo to go out and do a day's work for money. He would grumble about it, but as long as they didn't ask him too often, he would work. Elmo had continued to live with his two cousins, unaware that the only thing that kept him alive was the small thread of ambition he possessed.

"How we gonna git over thar annyhow?" Brine questioned.

"We're gonna walk," Ernest answered, as he began to load a rusty pistol.

"Walk? Like hell I'm gonna walk all th' way over thar!" Brine complained. "Why didn' ja have Jubal wait, an' we coulda rid over with 'im?"

"I don' 'spect ya two morons ta be able ta understan' this, but I will take th' time ta 'splain if'n it'll git yer asses in gear. One reason I didn' have Jubal wait fer us is thet I didn' wan' 'im ta know nothin' 'bout us goin' over thar. I bin thinkin' 'bout th' way them Hooks bin usin' us ta do thar dirty work fer a long time. This time, we's gonna tarn th' tables. We'll do th' killin, but they's gonna take th' blame. Th' law's gonna think they done it. Th' reason we're gonna walk is 'cause on foot thar ain' nobody in this part of th' country could ketch us if'n somethin' wuz ta go wrong. Nobody knows these hills like us'n."

He handed the pistol he had finished loading to Brine, and as he loaded another for himself, he said to Elmo, "You bring yer rifle. We might git a chance fer a long shot. Now, let's git movin' Elmo, you lead out. You allers could see in th' dark jist like a big yeller-eyed cat. Make shore we stay on 'nuff rocks an' creek beds thet thar cain' be no way atrakin' us back."

"I think we orta think 'bout this some more," Brine cautioned.

"I don' keer a damn whut ya think," Ernest retorted. "I'm not sittin' here waitin' fer no bullet ta come through thet winder. You two's too young ta 'member how them Barrons fight, but I 'member. They won' give ya no chance a' tall. Now thet's jist whut he's gonna git frum us tanight. No chance a' tall."

Chapter Eighteen

Clay's thoughts were pleasant as he chose the clothes he would wear to dinner at Valarie's. After rifling through the clothes hanging from a wire stretched across the corner of his room, he finally chose a pair of powder-gray trousers. Then he pulled a burgundy broadcloth shirt from its hanger and searched through the dresser drawer until he found the pin-striped black and burgundy ascot. Expensive black alligator shoes and a gray cashmere blazer harmonized with the rest of his attire.

When he entered the living room Big Pap gasped, "I daclare! Sarah, will ya look at th' dude!"

Clay smiled good-naturedly.

"Clay, ya look purty as a pitchur. He's jist jealous 'cause he's too old ta be taggin' along," she answered.

"Big Pappy, maybe you had better sing me the song before I go," Clay laughed.

"Lord, how long's it been since I sung it?" he smiled.

"Too long, Pappy. Too long," Clay reminisced as he began to tap his foot.

"What song?" Milt broke in curiously.

"Bachelor's Hall," Sarah laughed. "Clay always wants ta hear Bachelor's Hall."

Sarah brought Big Pap his banjo and, smiling, he began to strum and sing in a beautiful deep voice.

> "How hard is the fortune of all woman kind.
> They're always controlled, they're always confined.
> Confined to their parents till they are made wives.
> Made slaves to some man for the rest of their lives.
> Washing and ironing they daily do,
> Darning and mending, I'll bring that in, too.
> Four little children they have to maintain.
> Oh, how they wish they were single again.

When young men go courting,
They dress up so fine.
They dress up and fix up and use a good line.
They tittle and tattle, and make fun and lie,
They keep the young girls up till they're most ready to die.
Then all the next day they stagger and reel.
Singing God bless those girls, how sleepy I feel.

If I was a young man, I'd court not at all,
I'd live my life single, keep Bachelor's Hall.
For I say it's the best,
Go home drunk or sober, lie down and take your rest.
No wife there to scold you, no children to squall,
Come all ye young men and join me at Bachelor's Hall."

Clay and Milt applauded loudly. There was much joking and bantering about the merits of bachlorhood. The Barrons never knew who wrote the song, but it had given them much pleasure for generations.

As Clay left the house he winked at Milt, who was smiling broadly at the couple as they began a friendly argument concerning the age when certain mountain men should no longer be concerned with courting.

Clay drove the big dust-streaked Chrysler up the winding street to Valarie's house which sat on the top of the hill overlooking the town. Pine trees marched in single file along each side of the driveway that ran from the street to the house. Set in the midst of a cluster of maple trees., the house was a two-story white brick colonial with forest green shutters, the doors and the roof to match. A second-story veranda ran the full length of the house.

A small white barn and a corral made of white board fence took up a good part of the five-acre estate. As Clay stepped out of the car, he heard a wild scream. With a Kentuckian's love for horses, he watched Valarie's black Arabian stallion race across the meadow and glide up to the fence.

The horse stood on his rear legs, flailing at the wind with his powerful front hoofs as he whistled and screamed his challenge. He whirled and spun like a ballet dancer, his nostrils flared, and his neck arched. He was a king, and he knew it.

"God, what a horse!" Clay thought. "I've never seen his equal."

Reluctantly, he turned away.

Clay's ringing of the doorbell was answered quickly by Valarie, who looked stunning in snug-fitting gold lame slacks. They were topped by a cowl-necked, long-sleeved blouse of the same material. Gold leather strap heels complemented her outfit. She wore a ridiculously frilly apron that could not possibly be of any potential value, but still gave the impression of a certain amount of domesticity.

Valarie took Clay's hand and led him through the marbled foyer into a richly decorated living room. She directed him to the massive black sofa, then went to the bar to mix their drinks. Her light chatter immediately put him at ease. Her smile dazzled and her lips intrigued him.

Like a beautiful doe in the forest, this magnificent creature was now secure in her own habitat, and felt completely confident that the evening would progress as she had planned. As she returned to the kitchen to put the finishing touches on the meal, he surveyed his surroundings.

Deep brocaded red wallpaper adorned the walls. Thick white carpeting blanketed the floor from wall to wall. He was impressed with the tasteful furnishings of the room, but decided the feature he liked best was the marble fireplace, above which hung a massive portrait of Valarie's father.

"Dinner is served, Mr. Barron," Valarie said seductively, as she stood in the doorway removing her apron.

He joined her and they walked hand-in-hand to the dining room. The only light in this area came from two candles that flanked a centerpiece of yellow daisies that brought out the color of the pale jonquil floor-length tablecloth adorning the oval mahogany table. The delicate lines of the silver and fine bone china were reflected in their glow.

After finshing dinner, Clay sincerely complimented her on the meal of juicy filet mignon, baked potatoes with sour cream, tossed salad and home-made biscuits. He had never tasted the pineapple concoction she served for dessert, but admitted that it added the perfect finish to a superb meal.

They returned to the living room and Clay prepared two bourbon and branch while Valarie chose records for the stereo.

She accepted her drink from Clay and raised her glass in a toast, saying, "To love and life."

Their glasses clinked softly and he repeated, "To love and life."

Beautiful and sophisticated women were no novelty to this man. In the past, he had changed women almost as often as he had changed shirts. He had always moved on before the relationship had time to develop into anything of a lasting nature.

Valarie set her drink on a table and beckoned Clay.

"Come dance with me."

He took her outstretched hand and he followed her to the marble hallway. She slipped into his arms and they danced slowly, each entranced with the other. The music stopped but Clay still held her to him until the next record started. They again danced. Opening her eyes, she looked up at him and thought, "Dear God, I've got to have him!"

The dancing feet stopped. One pair stood motionless. The high heels of the other pair left the floor. After a long pause they came back down and the feet danced on. As they moved to the music, her arms involuntarily tightened around him.

He could resist her no longer. One hand tenderly touched her uplifted face. With thumb and forefinger he framed her chin and his lips claimed hers. This wasn't like the first cautious, exploratory kiss. This was a kiss of awakening passion, which both thrilled and frightened at the same time. She pulled back somewhat, startled as she felt the tip of his tongue touch and run around the inside of her lips. As her mouth opened slightly his tongue darted in and out. Caution had been replaced by need. Her mouth opened wider. With a small moan, she ground her throbbing body to his. He was the first to pull away.

"We'd better have another drink."

After freshening their drinks, he returned to the couch where she joined him.

"What's wrong, Clay?" she asked hesitantly. "Don't you like me?"

"That could get to be the trouble, Val. I don't want to become involved with anyone right now, and I'm not going to lead you on. I don't believe in using anyone."

"I'm not a child, Clay," she answered. "I'm perfectly intelligent enough to know what I want and to make my own decisions. I invited you here because I want to be with you. I dressed the way I did to try to be attractive enough to make you want to make love to me. I've waited too many years and wanted you too long to play coy now."

"What if you find out later I'm not what you want? Things might not work out the way you want them. Where would you be then?"

"The same place millions of other women have been—lucky to have had the man they loved, even if it was only for a little while."

"Val, to be perfectly honest with you, I don't know if I'm capable of loving anyone now. You're one of the most beautiful and exciting women I've ever known, and I want you physically. It is a fortunate man who has the love of a woman like you, but I don't know if there's room inside me for hate and love, too. If you are willing to accept the fact that nothing is going to change my mind about what I have to do, we can go on to whatever the future has for us, but if you have any hopes of changing my mind, then I'd better walk out that door right now. I have few ethics or morals, but I swore an oath to my Paw, and no Barron goes back on his word."

"Clay, I'm scared to death something is going to happen to you, but I'm more frightened at the thought of losing you. I want you with me. I don't want you to leave me tonight."

Tears glistened in her blue eyes as she kissed him and clung to him. Her head turned slightly, until her lips were next to his ear.

"Clay."

"Yes, Val."

"Have you known a lot of women?"

"Yes. Why do you ask?"

"I just wondered what kind you liked best."

He chuckled slightly. "I never thought much about it before, but I guess that up to this point the thing that was always the most desirable about a woman to me was her availability."

"Clay, I'm serious," she pouted. "You're going to find out anyway, so I might as well tell you. I've never slept with a man before. I'm afraid you won't think I'm much of a woman, and I want to be the best woman you ever knew."

"Val," he said, pushing her back to where he could look at her. "Do you know what you're getting into?"

"Yes, I do!" she said emphatically. "I've been thinking about it all day. I want you to pick me up and carry me upstairs to my room, just as you would if we were married. This is going to be my wedding night, Clay. I don't think it really matters which comes first, the wedding or this night. If I can't make you think enough of me to marry me later, then I shall still have this."

She stood up suddenly, pulling Clay to his feet.

"Take me upstairs now and love me," she whispered.

He bent down and gathered her up in his arms, then kissed her as he headed for the stairs.

"First room on the right," she instructed, as she nibbled at his ear.

Effortlessly, he carried her toward the top of the stairs. As Clay crossed the threshold, she flipped on the light switch. He gently lowered her down to where her toes barely touched the light lavender shaggy goat's wool carpet and kissed her long and tenderly before releasing her.

She crossed over to the large oval bed and turned on a tiny bed lamp that sat on the stand beside it. Clay's eyes followed her, his emotions mixed as he watched her turn down the dotted swiss bedspread. She turned on a small radio and music seeped through the room.

"Would you please turn off the other light, Clay?"

He flipped the switch and walked slowly toward her. She trembled as he touched her, but met and matched his mounting passion as he covered her neck, lips and face with kisses. As she clung to him tightly, his hands searched for the buttons on the back of her blouse.

His head again bent over her as he whispered, "A kiss for each button."

His lips kept the promise as his fingers unbuttoned her blouse. As he loosened the last button, he pulled the blouse down over her shoulders toward him and let it slip to the floor between them. The loveliness of her milk-white shoulders addded fuel to the fire that was already beginning to run rampant inside him. With an easy, smooth motion, he unsnapped the bra and sent it on its way to join the blouse.

Clay drew in his breath raggedly as he looked at her framed in the faint glow of the room. He dropped to one knee and buried his face against the satin-smooth skin of her bosom. The small pink nipples sprang taut from contact with his face, as he pressed them gently against his cheeks.

Her hand went behind his head and she hugged him to her so hard he could hear her heart pounding furiously. Even on the threshold of paradise, the human body must have oxygen. He withdrew his face from between her exquisite breasts and kissed the full ripe curves again and again.

His lips moved on down her stomach, leaving a trail of tingling flesh behind them. His fingers found the zipper of her slacks and unzipped it. His lips continued to play havoc on her stomach as he slipped her slacks and underpanties down over her rounded hips simultaneously. As the clothes fell to the floor, he put his arms around her hips and held her tightly against him, nipping at her with his teeth.

Her fingernails bit into his shoulders as he gently pushed her down on the bed. As he kneeled beside the bed, his lips began a trip that was sweet for him, but tortuous for her. They journeyed down her thigh and over her knee, causing her to shudder involuntarily. His lips never lost contact with her as he removed her shoes and pulled the slacks over her feet.

She stood with eyes closed, her body undulating as she pleaded, "Hurry, Clay! Please hurry!"

His clothes fell to the floor like raindrops scattered by the wind. Gathering the delicate beauty once again in his arms, he held her for a second more to convince himself that this was not some dream from which he would awaken unfulfilled. He then placed her in the bed and slipped quickly in beside her.

She was stretched out straight in the bed, pressing against him from breasts to hips, their legs intertwined.

"Relax, darling," he breathed, as his fingertips ran lightly over her body.

She tilted her head back to allow him to kiss her throat. His lips moved slowly down over her shoulders until they reached her breasts. Using tongue and lips, he left a touch here, a kiss there.

The rigid pink nipples enticed him and his lips closed over one. She rolled and tossed against him, a series of soft cries escaping her, as his teeth imprisoned and his tongue made wild love to her nipple. It was now time. Clay shifted slightly so that he now covered her. His lips sealed hers as he took the path that led to God's gift to man.

"Oh, my God!" she cried. "Oh, my God!"

Through a fog of passion, Clay suddenly realized that he held a woman in his arms; a real woman. She was catching the rhythm now, and her passion was truly a thing of beauty. He had always thought that the most worthless thing on earth was a frigid woman. He felt sorry for all the men who had lived and died and never really knew what it was like to make love to a real woman, a woman such as the twisting, biting, scratching creature beneath him now.

Time slipped by unnoticed as Clay teased, then satisfied; teased, then satisfied. His ardor started its climb to the peak of emotion, where she was already waiting for him. He hooked his arms under her legs and his hands seized her hips. As he went into her completely, he was vaguely aware of the sting of her fingernails as she buried them into his back.

Her head thrashed from side to side and her body became rigid as spasm after spasm erupted from her. As he reached the point of no return, she collapsed beneath him. The time-immortal male cry of fulfillment that came from him fell on deaf ears.

It was sometime later before Clay forced his mind to return from the drowsy world that can only be reached by complete satisfaction and utter contentment. He lay for long moments, taking pleasure in the soft lips that kissed the hollow of his shoulder and the clean fragrance of her hair.

She held his face with her hands and tenderly kissed and nuzzled him. As his eyes opened she smiled, her teeth flashing white in the near darkness.

"Welcome back to the world, darling," she whispered.

As he reached for her, she pulled away and sat up in bed. Without shame or modesty, she asked, "Tell me the truth if I ask you something?"

"Of course, I will, Val."

"Was I any good?"

Clay chuckled, "I hope no one else ever finds out how good. I don't want to have to fight the rest of the world in order to keep you."

She bent down and clasped his head to her bosom and uttered softly, "I hope I can always please you."

"Val, if you pleased me any more, I wouldn't be able to take it. Everything is probably going to work out just as you want it to. Why don't you relax and stop trying so hard?"

The kisses and caresses that followed steadily increased in tempo until once again the room was witness to the violent storm of their lovemaking. Clay had given her the nectar from the flower of life, and her quivering lips and eyes bright with tears spoke eloquently of her joy.

Clay's eyes popped open.

What was it? He had heard something. Some foreign sound had awakened him. He carefully untangled himself from the arms of the sleeping girl and eased out of bed.

He dressed quickly as he thought, "What if her parents have come back for some reason? I don't give a damn what they think of me, but I don't want her to be embarrassed."

He moved quickly to the open French doors that led to the terrace and stepped outside. There was no sound now but the usual ones that go with any warm spring night. He surmised that he must have been dreaming.

As he turned to go back inside he was startled into immobility by the outline of someone moving about inside his car.

He looked around wildly as he thought, "The Hooks! They followed me here. It's a set-up to bushwack me. Goddammit, just like a sitting duck and me with no gun."

He quietly cursed himself for being without it, and mentally promised himself that he would never be so careless again.

The figure in the car moved again, but this time the moonlight permitted Clay to see the face.

"Why, it's not the Hooks. It's Milt! What's he doing here?"

Clay paused for a last look at Val before tiptoeing from the room. Downstairs he found his jacket in the darkness and left the house.

As he opened the car door, Milt jumped in surprise. Clay slipped in under the wheel and asked irritably, "What are you doing here?"

"I brung yer gun."

"Why did you do that? If I had wanted it, I would have brought it myself."

The boy explained, "Me an' Big Pap come ta town fer awhile after ya left. I went into th' restrant and one a' 'em Hook fellers was there. Th' one I mean is th' looney one. He wuz kinda drunk an' braggin' 'bout how he wuz gonna gun ya down as soon as he seen ya. He kep' mumblin' somethin' 'bout you hittin' 'im in th' haid with a rock. Big Pap knowed ya didn't have no gun on ya an' he was afeart ya'd go back up to town so we shook a leg righ' back home ta git it, an' he sent me over here with it."

The boy handed the gun to Clay and said, "Whin I seen th' house dark an' th' car still here, I thought I'd better wait here in th' car."

Clay's hand reached for the gun. A remarkable transformation had come over him. All the hours of tenderness and lovemaking were forgotten now. The beautiful body sleeping and waiting inside the house held no more appeal. Clearly defined, his faced showed stark hatred.

He removed his jacket and calmly slipped into the gun harness. After checking the gun and holstering it, he opened the glove compartment and took a handful of .45 shells from a box and dropped them into his jacket pocket.

"Whut ya gonna do now?" Milt asked hesitantly.

Clay didn't look at him as he started the car, but his answer sent a mixture of excitement and dread through the boy.

"What else? Kill a Hook!"

Clay drove the car down the hill no slower or faster than he would have if he weren't going to kill a man. He avoided the main street and parked in an alley about a half a block from the restaurant. He looked at his watch—11:45. He remembered that the sign in the window of the restaurant said "We Close at Midnight."

Clay thought, "He might be gone now. That would be too bad."

He knew he would have to kill the first Hook in front of witnesses and make sure it looked like self-defense in order to keep from going to jail. After that first one there would be little interference. He wasn't a kid anymore. There would be fewer people eager to take sides. Those who did needn't expect any more mercy than he intended to give the Hooks.

"You stay in the car until I get back!" he commanded Milt.

"No! I'm not staying here. I wanna go with ya," the boy protested.

"Dammit, don't argue with me! I don't want to have to worry about you. You stay here like I said!"

Clay got out of the car and walked up the alley toward the restaurant.

Chapter Nineteen

The shadows of evening were creeping across the countryside on Saturday when Larry Stein drove his three-year old Ford into Hookville. He had wanted to leave Cincinnati the day before, but there had been too many loose ends to tie up.

He entered the town with mixed emotions. He had been surprised that Clay Barron had remembered his promise after all this time. Larry knew there could be only one interpretation of the telegram he had received from Clay which said

ENDING OF THE STORY I PROMISED YOU NOW GOING TO PRESS.

He felt certain he would get a story, but was uncertain of what the ending would be.

He wasn't being conceited when he admitted to himself that there was no other newspaper man who knew the feudists as well as he did, nor could write about them or their feud as well as he could.

All his stories on the subject had been well written and widely read. People, safe in their own homes, seemed to get some sadistic delight from reading about the bloody mountain war. This, however, would be the final battle and the final story.

If Clay Barron were killed, there would be no one to step forward to take his place. If he lived, he would destroy all the remaining Hooks. He had sworn it. If a man remembered a promise he had made as a boy to a reporter, it was certain that he hadn't forgotten the one he had made to his father.

Yes, this would be his last trip, no matter who won. He was glad it was going to be finished. He was no longer the daring young reporter he had once been. The years had mellowed him, and although he sometimes grumbled about the monotonous routine of his job, he would gladly give up the story he was about to write if there were some way to stop the killing. It was, of course, too late for that.

Clay had been under the influence of the Barrons too long to be any different than they had been. Larry had stood in an open doorway and watched as the dying Devil John whispered something to the boy.

The love between the old man and his grandson had been so great that it was almost a tangible thing. Any chance that civilization and education might have had to end the trouble of the two families was lost when Silas Hook shot down Brack. The boy had been too old then to forget, and he hated too much now to forgive. Yes, his story would be written. It would be written in someone's blood.

Larry pulled his car to the curb and parked it in front of a faded sign that read "Huston's Rooming House." Hookville had no hotel, but the ancient rooming house was a familiar sight to him. He had always stayed here when he came to this town. The rooms were not fancy, but the home-cooked meals were unexcelled.

As he approached the house carrying his one piece of luggage, Harve Huston rushed to meet him, his long angular face creased in a smile of welcome.

Harve and his wife, Rachael, had operated the rooming house for years. Rachael had learned early in their marriage that Harve and hard work were going to remain strangers, so she had converted the big house into boarding rooms.

Most of the time Harve could be found downtown soaking up the local news and passing it on to anyone who would take the time to listen. The chuckles of his fellow loafers never seemed to faze Harve when his wife's sharp tongue would drive him home.

"Howdy, Mr. Stein," he said, as Larry set his bag down and shook the offered hand. "Whut brings ya back ta our necka' th' woods?"

"Oh, just thought I'd take a vacation and do some fishing in the Little Sandy."

"Now, Mr. Stein, don' go atryin' ta fool ol' Harve. I nivver could figger out how you fellers allers seems ta be able ta smell out somethin' afore it even happens. I took it on maself ta call ya an' tell ya thet Barron feller'd come home, but I knowed ya waren' thar whin they didn' take ma collect call. I jist come on back an' started gittin' yer room ready. Hit's th' same one ya had afore—th' one with th' winder thet looks out on th' streets."

Harve was obviously pleased with himself for guessing correctly that Larry had been on his way here.

"Harve, you missed your calling," Larry laughed. "You should have been either a newspaper man or a divorce detective."

Picking up Larry's bag to carry it upstairs, Harve nodded solemnly, not getting the jest.

"Yep, I'm like you thet way. I do like ta know whut's agoin' on."

As Larry settled himself in his room, Harve sat in a straight-backed chair in front of the window, and talked incessantly.

"Yep," he said, pointing down to the sidewalk, "I seen 'im walk right by here. Left thet big car righ' up town. Somebody sed th' sheriff's got th' keys. Carries a gun under 'is shirt, too, accordin' ta th' waitress up ta Upton's."

It took some effort for Larry to hide his amusement. Clay Barron hadn't been in town any time at all until everybody knew who had his car keys and that he had a gun under his shirt. This was something that never ceased to amaze him about these people. The smallest detail never escaped their sharp eyes. He had no doubt that they would have a complete biography on him by morning.

"Christ!" he thought. "If they find out about the leopard shorts I've become addicted to, I hope they don't spread it around."

Aloud he said, "When did Clay get here?"

"He come in Thursday," Harve answered. "Went righ' on over ta Newt's. You recollect 'im, I rekkin."

When Larry nodded, he went on. "He come back ta town yesterday. Went leggin' it by here lickety-split. Course, at th' time I din' know whar he wuz goin'. I know whar he went now, though."

"Where was he going?" Larry asked, knowing that the other man wouldn't go on until he did ask.

"Wal," Harve continued, "I didn' know 'til las' night whin I was up ta Upton's an' thet Ezra Fultz come in. Higher'n a kite he was, an' abraggin' about him havin' fifteen thousand dollars. Now, everybody knows Ezra ain' never had over a hunnert dollars at eny one time in his life afore. We wuz all sorta pokin' fun at 'im and nobody, maself included, wuz 'bout ta believe 'im. Ezra didn' take kinely ta th' ribbin', so he jist up an' tells everbody whar he'd got it."

Larry paused in his unpacking to ask, "Well, where did he get it?"

"Git this! Ezra said Clay Barron give it ta 'im fer raisin' th' youngster fer 'im."

"Whoa! You've lost me now, Harve," Larry said impatiently.

"Oh, thet's right," Harve leered. "You wouldn' know 'bout th' boy, would'ja? Wal, it seems thet Ezra's wife, Hallie, had a kid by Clay. Mos' people think hit happen't thet time whin Brack won 'er in a card game an' had Clay collect."

"Yes, I heard about that, but I wasn't aware that there was a child involved. Where is the boy now?"

"Thet's whut I'm tryin' ta tell ya. Thet Barron went over thar an' give Ezra fifteen thousan' dollars fer takin' carea' 'im an' he took 'im with 'im—over ta Newt's, I 'spect."

A voice from below shouted, "Harve, git down here an' he'p me an' quit apesterin' Mr. Stein!"

Harve shrugged his shoulders and left the room commenting, "Rachael's actin' like a sore-tailed cat taday. I rekkin I'd better git."

Larry took Harve's place in the chair at the window, as darkness crept into the room. He was oblivious to the people strolling leisurely along the street below. His mind was on Clay Barron.

"Wonder what kind of man he's become. No ordinary man would pay fifteen thousand dollars for a kid he had never seen before. Wonder where he got the money. It's not easy to save that kind of money on a salary. I should know. He must have made some money somehow. There might even be a story in there on where and what he's been doing since breaking jail."

Now came the hardest part of being a reporter—the waiting. The question wasn't in this case, "Would something happen?" but "Where and how soon?" He turned on a light and began to write the background of the feud from memory.

"At least I'll have this much done," he thought.

Later, after having dinner, he lit a cigar and retired to the front porch, where he smoked and relaxed. It was great to be away from the harried existence he led. There were no loud noisy presses, no ringing phones, no phony smiles. He would be content to sit and relax like this for a few days, but the peace and quiet would soon force him out of the rocker and back to his old haunts. His reverie was disturbed by Harve, who came huffing and puffing up onto the front porch.

"Better slow down, Harve," Larry drawled. "You could get a heart attack rushing around like that."

"I jist come frum Upton's," Harve said, breathlessly. "Thet Wilson Hook's asettin' up thar in th' res'trant gittin' drunker'n a skonk an' meaner'n hell. He's got jug of whiskey an' a gun, both layin' righ' out in plain sight on th' table in fronta' him. Sez he's gonna kill Clay Barron soon's he shows up."

Larry nonchalantly pulled himself out of the cane-bottomed rocker and stretched.

"Well," he said, "it'll probably be a waste of time, but I might as well be loafing uptown as here."

"I thought ya'd wanna know 'bout it," Harve said, barely able to contain his excitement. "I'll go back with ya. Two pairsa' eyes'll see more'n one kin."

Larry chose two empty stools at the restaurant counter, which were situated so that he could observe both Wilson Hook, who sat sullen and alone at the rear of the cafe, and anyone who came through the front door. He ordered coffee for both of them, then looked around at the roomful of people, who were conversing in low tones. Tension was apparent throughout the room.

Wilson Hook raised the Mason jar of whiskey to his mouth and took a big swallow. He wiped his dripping chin on his brawny arm and glared as he asked, "Enny you fellers here be a friend ta Clay Barron?"

When no one answered, he took another drink.

"Thet's too bad," he griped. "I'd kinda like ta git ma trigger finger warmed up a mite afore he shows up."

Still getting no answer, he set the jar down and continued to brood in silence.

As he looked around the room at his companions-in-waiting, Larry thought how much they all, himself included, resembled a group of buzzards and jackals. These men would quickly cheer the victor and ridicule the loser. Most of them didn't care at all how it turned out; they just wanted to be able to brag about seeing it happen.

"Look thar, Larry," Harve said as he nudged him. "Thet boy gettin' th' ice cream iz th' one I tol' ya 'bout. Thet's Clay's little bastard."

Seeing Milt at the counter, Wilson began cursing and shouting at him.

"Hey, ain' ya thet brat they say balongs ta Clay Barron? Why don' ya go fetch 'im over here if'n he ain' afeard ta come?"

The boy got his ice cream cone and paid for it before he turned to see who was speaking. He stared coldly across the room at Wilson and took a couple of deliberate licks off the cone. He then smiled at the fuming Wilson and swaggered out of the restaurant.

"Colder than hell," Larry thought. "Just like all the others."

"Hit won' be much longer now," Harve whispered.

As the minutes dragged into more than two hours, some of the thrill-seekers drifted out and were replaced by others. The most two relaxed men in the room were Wilson Hook, who continued to drink from his jar, and Larry Stein, who had learned long ago that it took time and patience to get a story.

The low hum of voices stilled suddenly. Larry's eyes shot towards the door. Clay Barron was there. He stood poised on the balls of his feet. His eyes flashed over the room and came to rest on Wilson, ignoring the others. He stood calmly with no word or facial expression to reveal the least bit of nervousness or anxiety. Smoke curled lazily through the air between the two men. Wilson now became aware of his presence. The only sound in the room was the click, click, click of a pinball machine that had been abandoned in the middle of a game.

Wilson set the half-empty whiskey jar on the table and got to his feet. His hands remained on the table top near his gun. He shook his shaggy blonde head, much as a bull who is about to charge. His maniacal laughter echoed throughout the room.

"Everbody here thinks I'm a dummy, but leastways I ain' standin' here like a fool without no gun about ta git maself killed, like Clay Barron is," he thought.

The mirthful expression left his face and he said to Clay, "You hit me in th' head with a rock onc't. Now I'm gonna kill ya fer it."

Temptation nagged at Clay. The temptation to start it, to gun down this hated enemy, raced through his brain like wildfire. He took control of his rage by forcing himself to think of Wilson as the man in the mirror. It would be just like practicing. All he had to do was beat the man in the mirror.

Giggling insanely, Wilson grabbed the pistol and fired.

When Wilson reached for the gun on the table, Clay dropped to one knee. His hand snaked in and out of his coat. As he squeezed off the first shot, he was aware that he had finally done it. He had beaten the man in the mirror.

The first bullet from Clay's gun struck Wilson in the center of the forehead. Wilson's pistol flew out of his hand and exploded as it hit the floor. The bullet went awry and lodged in the ceiling. The force of Clay's slug slammed Wilson back against the aquarium. Dead on his feet, Wilson began to topple forward, but was straightened up and spun completely around as Clay shot him again. He fell forward and his arms slid down into the deep aquarium, causing him to hang there.

Coldly and methodically Clay arose and stood over his extended gun. It roared again. The bullet made a plopping sound as it found its target and split the skull. Twice more the gun cracked in unison.

The spectators gasped as they squinted through the smoke-filled room. All five shots had hit Wilson in the head; the last three had caused it to bounce and bobble like a cork in the water. As his head stopped bobbing, it seemed to slip forward, stop and then slip again. Then it came apart. A hunk of hair and gristle hung suspended by a string of skin.

Everyone held his breath in disbelief. Then the skin tore loose, and the section of brains and skull slopped into the fish bowl. In terror, the fish darted back and forth, but there was no escape from the dark red blood that was enveloping them.

Clay faced the stunned crowd and waved his gun in a half circle. No one moved.

"You all saw it," he said unemotionally. "It was self-defense. I'll kill any man who says otherwise."

The only answer he got was silence, so he turned and walked placidly back into the night.

Chapter Twenty

After Clay left the restaurant, it came alive. Everyone began to talk and shout at once. Larry ignored them and scribbled in his notebook. Years ago he had been promised a story by a wild, bushy-haired mountain boy, and tonight the first installment had been delivered by a handsome, well-groomed composed killer.

Sheriff Billy Sutton rushed through the door, rubbing sleep from his eyes.

"What happened in here?" he demanded, as he made his way to the circle of men congregating at the back of the cafe.

The sight of the gory remains of Wilson shocked him wide awake.

"Who's thet?" he asked incredulously.

"Thet's whut's left a' Wilson Hook," Upton, the proprietor, answered.

"Clay Barron do this?"

"He shore'n hell did!" Harve broke in, unable to contain himself. "Look a thar! Thet's a big chunk a' 'is haid down thar' 'mongst th' feesh!"

"Yeah, I see," Billy said grimly. "Don' nobody leave this room 'til I git all yer names. Yer all witnesses."

After completing a list of those present, the sheriff dispatched a man to get the undertaker and another to take word to Silas. He then called Larry over to question him about what had taken place.

"I have it all down here just as it happened," Larry said, handing his notebook to the sheriff.

He read it slowly and carefully, then asked, "Are ya positive thet Wilson was intendin' ta shoot 'im?"

"There's no doubt about it. As a matter of fact, there's the hole just above your head where Wilson's bullet hit when his gun went off. Clay had no choice. He either had to kill Wilson or get killed himself. It was self-defense all the way."

"I haven' seen you 'round since Brack was killed. How'ja happen ta be here tonight?"

In answer, Larry handed the sheriff the telegram he had received from Clay.

Shaking his head in exasperation, he read it and handed it back to Larry.

The undertaker came in and rolled Wilson's body onto a stretcher and covered it with a blanket. Next, he reached down into the aquarium, fished around, retrieved the grisly piece of head and dropped it into a rubber bag.

"Take 'im on over ta th' funeral parlor an' wait fer Silas or some member of th' fam'ly," the sheriff instructed him. "When one of 'em shows up, you make it clear ta them thet I said I'd take no interference from anyone. The law's goin' ta take carea' this. Make shore thet they understan' thet I'm goin' ta pick up Clay Barron."

Larry followed the sheriff out of the restaurant.

"You going after him now, like you said?" he asked.

"Yes, I don' dare wait 'til mornin'. Silas ain' gonna pay no attention ta me. This is what he wanted—an excuse to go after Clay."

"Do you mind if I ride along?" Larry asked. "I'll make sure I stay out of your way."

"Don' rekkin it'll hurt anythin' if ya do," the sheriff answered absently. "I'll pick up th' jeep. We kin go all th' way ta th' house in it."

As they rode the bouncing jeep along the tree-bordered dirt road, Billy shook his head and muttered, "Dammit, I nivver wanted it ta come ta this. He knows I'll be along after 'im. Even if'n I do lean his way, I still gotta do ma job."

When they came near the house, the sheriff said in a half-hearted attempt at humor, "I hope you kin drive one a' these things in case I won' be makin' th' trip back with ya."

"Do you expect trouble?" Larry asked.

"Who knows?" he shrugged. "Thar's no way ta tell how a wolf'll act thet's jist tasted fresh blood. I don' kid maself 'bout bein' any match fer Clay with a gun, but if'n he don' wanna come, I'll hav'ta try an' bring 'im in anyway."

At that moment all pandemonium broke loose. A rifle went off, then a pistol, more shots came from both, and screams rent the night. The sheriff drove the jeep at full speed towards the sounds.

"Jeezchris', don' tell me th' Hooks beat me over here already."

As the jeep came out of the woods and screeched to a halt, they saw a shadowy figure running headlong down the path toward them. The fleeing man was being chased by Clay. As they ran through the wood yard, Clay yanked the double-bitted axe out of the chopping block.

As the pursued man ran into the beam of the headlights, the spinning steel blade of the axe flashed out of the darkness and buried itself in his back. His screech of terror turned into screams of agony as he thrashed around in a circle in front of the jeep. The sheriff and Larry still sat inside the vehicle, shocked into momentary immobility, as the stricken man's cries died to a gurgle in his throat. Finally, no sound came from him.

"God Almighty!" the sheriff breathed as he slowly left the jeep and walked toward the fallen man.

The dead man lay face down on the ground with both hands back over his shoulders. In death he seemed to be reaching to pull the axe out of his back.

Larry walked up behind the sheriff and asked, "Who is it?"

"Thet's Elmo Rigsby, one a' th' Hooks' cousins," he answered, looking down at the dead albino.

Clay came running towards them, carrying a limp figure in his arms. Big Pap, lugging a shotgun, and Sarah ran out of the house, still dressed in their nightclothes.

"Clay! Are ya all righ'?" he shouted.

"I'm all right, Pappy," Clay choked, "but Milt's been shot. He's bleeding badly."

Sarah took a quick look at Milt and said, "Git 'im in th' jeep an' in thar ta th' doctor jist as fast as ya kin! Ya gotta git 'is head ta stop bleedin'."

"Pappy," Clay shouted as he lifted the boy into the jeep. "There are two more back there between the chicken house and the barn."

"I'll sen' somebody back here jist as quick as I kin ta see to 'em," the sheriff told Big Pap as he ground the jeep into gear.

"Don' worry 'bout this carrion. I'll deliver it in ta ya," Big Pap answered.

From his seat in the rear of the jeep, Larry looked back and saw Big Pap jerk the axe out of the albino and toss it aside.

"Won't this damned thing go any faster?" Clay shouted.

"If'n it would, I'd be drivin' it faster," the sheriff retorted.

"How did the boy git hit?" Larry asked.

"The little devil jumped in front of me when one of those sons-of-bitches stepped out from behind the house and cut down on me."

The boy was losing blood fast.

"Milt, can you hear me?"

Clay tried to rouse the boy, but was unsuccessful.

When the sheriff brought the jeep to a stop in front of the clinic, Clay carried the boy to the front door and kicked at it. It was opened promptly by Dr. Jody.

Seeing the boy's condition, she said, "Bring him in here," and led the way to a small emergency room.

"What happened?" she asked, as Clay placed him on the operating table.

"He's been shot."

"Did you shoot him?"

"No, I didn't shoot him! How bad is it?"

She examined the wound in Milt's head and answered, "It isn't as bad as it looks. He's just been creased. He'll be coming to shortly."

"Are you sure he's going to be all right?"

"Look, Mister, I can't give you a written guarantee, but my professional opinion is that he's in no serious danger."

Clay took out a roll of bills, peeled off several and tossed them on the desk.

"You take care of him. If it's more than this and I don't get back, Big Pap will be in to pay you. Now, I've got to go."

"Hold it, Clay! Yore not goin' anywheres." The sheriff's voice came from behind him. The gun in his hand and the look on his face said he meant it.

"I'll hav'ta take ya in 'til thar's a hearin' on Wilson. Them others you don' hav'ta worry 'bout. They come over thar an' jumped ya on yer own property, but Wilson was killed in a public place. Thar has'ta be a hearin'."

"It was self defense. Ask him," Clay said, pointing to Larry.

"He's awready tol' me thet, but I still hav'ta hold ya."

"Uncle Billy, tonight's the time to end it once and for all," Clay argued. "They'll be out in force. Maybe I can get them all tonight."

"Thar's not gonna be no more killin' tonight. I'm stoppin' it here an' now," the sheriff said grimly.

"Please don't get in the way, Uncle Billy. Just stay out of it. I've got the feel now. No bullet can kill me!"

"Listen to him, Sheriff. This must be the Barron killer instinct I've heard so much about," Dr. Jody broke in.

She turned to Clay and added, "Mr. Barron, you disgust me!"

Clay glared at her and said sharply, "Shut up and take care of the boy. If I want anything out of you, I'll ask for it!"

"Now, Uncle Billy," he said, turning toward the sheriff, "I'm going to walk out of here. If you're going to stop me, you'll have to shoot me."

"I'll do it, too," the sheriff warned. "I'll bust both yer laigs if'n I have to, but yer not goin' nowhars tonight!"

Clay's face began to cloud up but as he stepped toward the determined sheriff, Milt moaned behind him, and he whirled and ran to him.

"Kee-rist! Ma haid feels like it's about ta crack apart!"

"You're going to be all right, Son," Clay assured him. "It's just a scratch."

"Whut happent after thet white-headed feller shot me?"

"They won't shoot anyone else," Clay answered.

"How many of 'em wuz thar?"

"Three."

"Did'ja git 'em all?"

"They're all dead, but right now I want to tell you something else. Don't ever jump in front of me again. You might have been killed."

"I tol' ya I wasn' afeard a' nobody."

"I know you aren't, so you don't have to get yourself killed to prove it."

Milt grinned up at him.

Clay's tone changed as he said, "Look, Boy, I've got to keep you around to look after Aunt Sarah and Big Pap in case something should happen to me. They will be here soon to stay with you, so just try to get some sleep now and don't worry about anything."

"Whar ya goin'?" the boy asked drowsily.

"I have some things to take care of. I'll be back soon."

"Yer goin' after 'im now, ain' ya, Clay?" Milt turned to rouse himself. "I wanna' go with ya. Hit's ma righ'. You said so."

As sleep dulled his senses, he muttered, "I'm a Barron, Barro. . . ."

Clay patted the boy's hand and turned back to the sheriff, but before he could speak, Dr. Jody interrupted.

"Look, you two. I'm not having a mess made in my office while you settle your differences. Mr. Barron, for the sake of law and order, why can't you wait until the hearing? I'd think your revenge, or whatever you choose to call it, would be all the sweeter for the wait."

"Look, lady, I appreciate what you're doing for my son, but why the hell are you needling me? I never saw you before in my life."

"Mr. Barron, I just don't like to see people take the law into their own hands. The day of the claw and fang is past."

Arrogantly he answered, "I'll make you a deal. I won't practice medicine, and don't you give me any opinions on how to run my life!"

Leaving her standing there, he walked out on the porch and waited for the sheriff to follow him.

The sheriff grinned at the frustrated doctor and joined Clay, then motioned to Larry to follow him.

Larry suddenly became nauseous. Four men had died violently this night, and his witnessing two of them personally was more than his normally strong stomach could stand. He leaned back against the porch railing and looked up at the moon that continued to shine on, undisturbed by his sickness, the dead, the dying, the soon to die.

"By damn," he thought, "the devil's had himself a harvest tonight."

Larry realized now that there was more than a newspaper story here in the mountains for him. He had a chance to record something that was the last of its kind. It was a big responsibility, but there was no one else who was close enough and qualified to do it. He would have to write the true story of the last mountain feud and the characters who fought it.

Clay Barron and the Hooks were the last of a dying breed. They would be the last of the true mountain feudists. Sure, there would be killings here, as in other places, but a feud takes half a century to make, and there were no others started. The law that was slowly gaining control in Kentucky would see that they did not start. The mountains were now bearing witness to the last of the family wars.

He had to somehow try to understand the feud and the men who perpetrated it. This was the end of an era of American history. It had to be recorded.

His thoughts were interrupted when Big Pap and Sarah drove up in the buggy. There were three blanket-covered forms in the back. Sarah rushed inside to be with Milt.

Big Pap, still carrying his shotgun, stopped on the porch and asked Clay, "Whar' do we go frum here?"

"I guess I'm going to jail, according to Uncle Billy."

"Seems I recollect ya goin ta jail onct afore an' things not workin' out too good. Rekkin if'n ya don' wanna go, ya don' haf'ta this time."

"Now, don' git hostile, Newt," the sheriff said nervously. "This here is whut's knowed as 'pertective custody'."

Big Pap looked disgusted. "Since whin did a Barron need 'is custody pertected?"

"Big Pappy, Uncle Billy's got a job to do, and I don't want to make it any harder for him. It doesn't matter whether it's today or tomorrow or the nexr day. Now that the blood's been spilled in the water, the sharks are all going to come to try for their pound of flesh."

Clay now turned to Larry and asked, "Well, Mr. Newspaperman, how's the story I promised you going? Is there enough action or would you like the script livened up?"

"Clay, why don't you let me see if I can work out some kind of an agreement with the Hooks to end this killing? I've seen four dead men tonight. It's a sight I don't care to see again."

"Then get the hell back to Cincinnati and mind your own business. If you think I invited you here because I like you or what you write, you're wrong. I asked you here because I promised you something when I was angry. If you don't have the guts to write it, that relieves me of my obligation. I don't like long-nosed writers coming in here and psychoanalyzing me or my family. You don't know anything about us, so when you finish the story, get out and stay out. You're lucky my grandpappy wasn't alive to read some of the things you wrote about him. He would have killed you."

In his line of work, Larry had learned to take abuse in stride, but he knew that in this case he would have to choose his answer carefully.

"I don't think he would have. Your grandfather and I were friends. I have a ledger full of notes I took from him. He told me once that it was his right to live however he chose, and since my occupation was writing, I had the right to express my opinions the way I chose. You may prove to be as vicious as your grandfather and possibly even as brave, but I doubt that you will ever attain his inner greatness. So if you're trying to frighten me by being another Devil John Barron, you have a long way to go and a lot to learn."

Doubling his fist, Clay slid off the railing where he had been sitting. This was the first time anyone had ever come out and said aloud the thing he had known since the day Devil John had died. He had been copying him; walking, talking and now killing like him. Subconsciously he had been a little boy all these years, still trying to communicate with a spirit.

"Let it drop, Clay," Big Pap said, as he pushed him back against the rail. "Ya got troubles 'nuff without cuffin' this word-slinger. Now, 'bout yer goin' ta jail."

He turned to the sheriff and patted his double-barreled saying, "If'n he goes, ya'd bes' know thet me an' Hannah here iz gonna be righ' in thar with 'im. Case ennybody shows up with any funny idears, ya better be alookin' fer some extry grave diggers."

"Fair 'nuff, Newt. I'll evin make it legal and depatize ya."

"Don' wan' no badge. I don' wanna be strapped by no promises ta uphold no law. I'm only gonna be thar fer one reason, an' thet's ta see that nobody don' git close ta Clay 'til he's turned loose."

Chapter Twenty-One

Clay awoke to find Valarie outside his cell, watching him through the bars. He swung himself out of the bunk and walked over to her.

"What are you doing here?" he asked.

As if she hadn't heard him, she questioned, "How could you, Clay? Last night of all nights! How could you?"

"I told you before—this is why I came home."

"I can accept that, Clay, but did it have to be last night?"

"I didn't choose last night. I only took advantage of the opportunity."

"But did you stop to think at all how I would feel to wake up to find that you had left my bed to kill a man?"

"No, Val, to be honest, I didn't. I don't want to think until the last one is down. I never said it would be pleasant. If you can't understand and not interfere, then I'll stay away from you."

"Is it easy to say something like this to me? Don't I mean anything more than that to you?"

"Val, I don't want to hurt you, but you must understand that I can't let you become involved in this problem of mine."

"I'll try to do what you want, Clay, but I don't want you to be hurt or killed. Last night you made me begin to live. You were the missing link that it took to make me know real happiness. Last night proved to me that all those years I had waited for you and kept myself for you weren't wasted. I can stand here with these bars between us, and just seeing you makes me weak. I could make love to you right now. Clay, I want to marry you. I want to do everything for you."

"Val, if you'll listen to me, we'll be alright. Let's just be happy when we're together. Let time take care of the rest."

"It's just that I'm so close to having everything I want out of life that it scares me. I can't imagine what I would do now if you went away again or something happened to you."

"I promise you I'm not going away again, and I have no intention of getting killed. What's wrong with having a little faith in me?"

"I'll try," she said weakly. "I guess I need to quit worrying about myself so much. I think I'll go down to the clinic and see how Milt is."

As she started to leave she had a sudden thought and turned back.

"Oh, by the way. Uncle Billy said you will have to stay in here until the hearing is held at 2:30 tomorrow afternoon. Is there anything I can do for you in the meantime?"

"No, nothing that I can think of. Big Pap is sitting out there like a guardian angel looking over me."

"Uncle Billy told me you won't have any trouble proving self-defense, so will I see you after the hearing?"

"There are some things I have to do first. It may be a day or two before I'll be able to see you."

The proceedings of the inquest were conducted swiftly and no charges were filed against Clay. Surprisingly, none of the Hooks were present at the hearing.

Later, in the sheriff's office, when he asked that his gun be returned, Uncle Billy said, "Clay, do ya know thar's a law in this here state 'bout carryin' concealed weapons?"

"Yes, I know there is. Arrest me, if you have to, and I'll post bond. By the time you get it to trial, there will be no need for me to wear one anymore."

"No, Clay, I'm not goin' ta arrest ya. Make no mistake 'bout it, yore gonna be needin' yer gun. Th' Hooks ain' gonna stop at nothin' now ta kill ya. You wuz lucky t'other night, but don' underestimate neither Silas or Jubal. They ain' as stupid as th' ones ya already went up agin, an' they's gonna be harder ta kill. Yer wide open now, Clay. Ain' nothin' I kin do fer ya, 'ceptin' ta give ya a word of advice. 'Member thet guts iz somethin' mighty fine ta have, but any bullet made'll tear the hell outta 'em. So go easy."

"I'll do that, Uncle Billy, and thanks for everything."

When Big Pap and Clay left the jail, they headed down the street toward the clinic. Big Pap was still lugging the shotgun.

On their arrival, Clay was pleasantly surprised that Dr. Jody greeted him civilly. He was encouraged to hear that Milt was recuperating satisfactorily. When Clay entered Milt's room he found him sitting up in bed with his head swathed in bandages.

"Hey! I'm glad yer' here. Th' doc sez I kin go home if'n I come back evver day an' have th' bandages changed."

"Will it be alright for him to leave this soon?" Clay asked her.

"Yes, but he's going to have some pain for a few days. However, you can probably give him more attention at home than I can here."

"Well, that solves one problem," Clay said to Milt. "If you're well enough to go home, you're well enough to travel."

"Travel? Whar we goin'?" Milt questioned eagerly.

"We aren't going anywhere. Just you, Aunt Sarah and Big Pap are going to take a little trip."

"Whut's this all 'bout?" Big Pap asked warily.

"Pappy, today when I was talking to that lawyer down here from Lexington, I told him to make hotel reservations in Lexington for the three of you. I want you to go there and stay until things work themselves out here."

"I ain' goin' no damn place 'ceptin' back over ta my own house," Big Pap growled.

Aunt Sarah, who had been sitting quietly broke in, "Yore not sendin' me off nowhars neither."

Clay cut in then saying "Pappy, you have to listen to me. I know that you're not afraid of anyone. I know that you would stand beside me, even if you knew it would get you killed, but now there's more than me and your pride to consider. There's Milt. He's almost gotten himself killed already. Besides that, your going will make things easier for me. I'll be able to move around more freely by not having to worry about your safety. I want to fight them on my own terms. You three people are the only way they could get an edge on me. Now, will you go?"

Big Pap answered for all of them. "If'n it'll really hep' ya, we'll do whut ya say. Ennyhow, I could take them up thar' an' git 'em settled an' then come back."

"No, Big Pappy, I want you to stay there with them so I can be a hundred percent sure that you'll all be alright."

"Hev' ya got inny plans in mind, Clay?"

"Yes, I want you to drive my car. I'm not going to be needing it here. From now on, this is going to be like a game of hide and seek. Alone and on foot in the hills, I'll stand a better chance than any other way."

"Hit don' seem righ' somehow," Aunt Sarah interrupted. "Seems ta me like yer fam'ly orta be standin' with ya like allers."

"I know how you feel, Mammy," Clay said as he put his arm around her shoulder, "but this is one fight I want to be all mine. Besides, if I do succeed in getting the others and something should happen to you in the meantime, I'd still be a loser. You're all I have left. You just take care of each other and I'll take care of the Hooks."

"If'n thet's really whut ya want, thin thet's whut we'll do," she agreed reluctantly.

"Mammy, give me a list of the things you will need to take with you and Pappy and I will go get them," Clay said.

"If'n I give you two a list, you wouldn' find halfa' whut I want. You stay here with Milt, an' I'll go with Newt ta fetch 'em."

"Okay, but do be careful. There could be trouble at any time now," Clay cautioned.

"Don' fret none," said Big Pap as he stroked the worn walnut stock of the shotgun. "If'n thar's ennybody ahangin' 'round over at th' house, whin I git done with 'em thar won' be no need fer us ta go nowhars!"

Clay smiled and handed the car keys to him.

After Big Pap and Sarah departed, Dr. Jody entered the room and handed Clay some money. "Here's your change from Saturday night," she said. "You gave me too much."

For the first time Clay looked directly into her eyes and said sincerely, "Thanks. I appreciate the way you have taken care of the boy for me."

"I'm just doing my job," she replied.

She was slightly startled when he reached out and caught her hand in his.

"I'm sorry I got sharp with you the other night. I'd been under quite a strain, but that's no excuse for being ill-mannered. Will you forgive me?" His voice was like a caress.

"There's nothing to forgive," she stammered. "It was as much my fault as yours. A doctor should practice medicine and not become personally involved with the patients."

"Then let's start over again," he said.

She nodded her head, fearing that her voice would crack if she spoke.

"Damn that man," she thought as he continued smiling down at her. What was it about him that made her so flustered? Why did her body call out for soft music and moonlight whenever he was near?

Extracting her fingers from his hand, she left the room and went into her office. She was trembling as she surveyed herself in the wall mirror.

"What in the world is wrong with you?" she questioned the image. "He's not the first man who ever touched you."

"Physical attraction," her scientific mind answered.

"But why one of these people? Why a hillbilly killer? Why someone who is everything I despise in a man?"

As she turned from the mirror she saw Clay standing in the doorway. She couldn't determine whether his half-smile was an attempt to be friendly, or whether he was amusing himself with her.

"Do you mind if I use your phone?" he asked.

"Of course not. Help yourself," she said, pointing to the phone on her desk.

After she had gone, he asked the operator for the number of the sheriff's office.

"Uncle Billy," he explained, "I'm sending the folks to Lexington to stay for a while. Get a pencil and I'll give you the phone number of my lawyer there. If anything should happen to me you can get in touch with Big Pap through him."

Milt had drifted off to sleep. Clay nervously thumbed through an obsolete magazine, waiting for him to wake up.

"Mr. Barron," Dr. Jody said softly as she came into the room, "if you'd like to have a drink, I have some bourbon in my office."

He followed her into her office and sank into the big leather chair in front of her desk. His face looked haggered.

"Just make it on the rocks," he said as she filled the glass with ice. "Won't you join me?"

"I think I'd better just have this Coke," she replied, and sat in the chair behind the desk.

After a few moments of silence she said, "Mr. Barron, I've heard so much about you and your family since I came here that I have to admit that I was eager to meet you. Now I find myself being curious about you. Judging from your appearance and speech, you seem to be an intelligent and educated person. Obviously, you have money. Would you mind telling me why a man with all these things going for him would come back here and engage in this useless bloodshed over ancient history?"

Clay answered her question by asking, "You aren't from around here originally, are you, Doctor?"

"No, I'm from Philadelphia."

"Then that somewhat explains your attitude toward me. Now, let me ask you something else. Is the memory of a man who worshipped me and died fighting for me to be pushed aside and forgotten? Is there any way to put a value on the years I have spent away from the place and the people I care for most? Is love 'ancient history?' I realize there is no way to replace these things, but I feel that I do have the right to collect the highest price possible for them. The thing man values most is his life. That's the price I intend for the Hooks to pay for killing my father."

"But then what?" she asked. "What do you do then? Even if you choose to disregard man's law, what about God's law? Have you forgotten the commandment 'Thou Shalt Not Kill'?"

"I never remember that part. I only remember the passage that says, 'An eye for an eye'."

She got up from her desk.

"I can see that trying to talk to you will get me nowhere so I will mind my own business. Just relax and have another drink if you like. I have patients waiting."

Her body felt stiff and clumsy as she left the room.

Clay became so completely relaxed that he dozed off. He was startled awake by a gasp behind him. He looked up to find the doctor standing in the doorway.

"Oh, God! I don't know how to tell you, Clay."

He sprang out of his chair and grasped her by her shoulders.

"Milt!" he shouted, and started toward the patient's room.

"No!" She held him by the arm, her face a mask of agony. "The sheriff just called. It's your car. It blew up, and your relatives were in it. He wants you to come right away!"

Chapter Twenty-Two

Clay ran as he had never run before. He ran up the street and down the road beyond the school yard. As he crossed the fence behind the school, his lungs were close to bursting, but he charged on. When he came into sight of where he had parked the car, he found it engulfed in flames.

Not unlike a drunken man, he staggered and weaved toward the scene of the tragedy. As the volunteer firemen poured water through the broken windows of the automobile, the black smoke boiled out and drifted upward and hung over them like a cloud of doom.

Clay stumbled up to where the sheriff's jeep was parked and collapsed across the hood, staring unbelievably at the sight before him. Uncle Billy came to him quickly and put his hand on Clay's arm.

"Clay, I jist cain' believe it! I don' know whut ta say."

"I do!" gasped Clay, his chest still heaving from his run. "I know what to say. I should have killed them Saturday night and didn't. If I had done what I knew I should have, this wouldn't have happened. There's no one to blame but myself!"

"It must have been wired up with dynamite," the sheriff reasoned, ignoring Clay's self-criticism. "Leastways, ya kin be glad they wen' quick."

Clay sneered. "Yeah, that's a big help to them. Everybody's dream; instant death and no suffering. Some aren't going to be so lucky."

His bleak eyes watched the fireman remove the twisted, charred bodies of the old couple from the still-smoking shell of the car. He walked around the jeep toward the car, but the wiry arm of the sheriff blocked his way.

"Don' go over thar, Clay. Thet ain' no sight fer ya ta see."

"I'm OK now, Uncle Billy," Clay said as he brushed by him and continued on to where the firemen were trying to get the bodies into a rubber sack.

One of them turned his head away from the odor of burning flesh; the other fled, vomiting. Clay retrieved the fireman's rubber gloves and carefully, tenderly, placed the blackened remains into the rubber bag.

The funeral director arrived and hurried toward the sheriff. Wringing his hands he asked, "Whut'll I do, Sheriff? I still got Wilson Hook's body back at ma parlor. He ain' agonna be buried 'til Tuesday. If'n I take these two in, an' th' Hooks an' this feller run inta each other, they're gonna end up tryin' ta kill each other righ' thar in ma place!"

Overhearing this conversation, Clay called to them, "Help me put them in the jeep. I'm taking them home!"

"Clay, ya cain' do thet. They gotta be prepared," the sheriff argued.

"I'll take care of them myself," Clay shouted impatiently. "If you want to help, find me a casket large enough to hold both of them."

"Ya gonna bury 'em tagether?" the funeral director asked incredulously.

"That's right!"

"I don' know if'n thet's legal," the sheriff said. "The state health department kinda got on us here in th' county 'bout not follerin' thar rules 'bout puttin' people away."

"Screw the health department! You just find me a casket or have one made tonight. Cost doesn't mean anything. Just have it ready tomorrow! I'll take care of digging the grave myself."

The rubber bag was placed on the bed in the room that the couple had shared for so long. After the sheriff departed, Clay stood staring at the mound that had such a short time before been two very alive people who had loved, worked and now died together. They would have wanted it to be this way. One would have been lost without the other.

Clay collapsed into a chair and sat holding his head in his hands. Uncle Billy had told him to look in the Barron graveyard and then decide whether or not it was worth it to start the killing again. The rubber sack on the bed was a mute reminder of the price he was paying for his revenge. He realized now that he had been a fool to think that there would be no sacrifice on his part. There was no white-hot anger in him now. There was only the numbness of the realization that he was indirectly responsible for their deaths.

Clay knew that if it had been he who had been killed, Big Pap would have gone alone against the Hooks, but with his sense of fair play, he would have been no match for them. Even though he had lived among the Barrons for years and their fights had been his fights, Big Pap had never possessed the killer instinct that was symbolic of this family. He would fight for the cause of love and honor, but his was not a vengeful nature.

Yes, Big Pap would have gone, and he would have died, and Aunt Sarah would have suffered. Perhaps this way was best.

Later when Clay heard the sheriff's jeep stop in front of the house, he walked to the door and stood waiting. The sheriff was accompanied by Valarie and Milt.

She flung her arms around Clay and sobbed, "Oh, I'm so sorry! I thought so much of both of them. This is the most horrible thing I ever heard of!"

He held her shaking shoulders in his hands and tried to comfort her with soft words and caresses.

Milt tried vainly not to cry when he saw the rubber bag laying on the bed. In the short time he had been with them, the old couple had shown him what a loving family could be like. He would never forget them. He suddenly realized that he was lucky not to be lying there with them. He touched his bandaged head and shuddered.

He looked at this strange man who was his father, knowing how much he loved the couple who had been killed, and he wondered what he would do now.

The sheriff touched Clay's shoulder and said, "I brung some tools frum town ta dig th' grave with. Don'cha think we better git on with it?"

"You'd better stay here with Valarie and Milt, Uncle Billy. I can make out all right."

Moving away from him she said, "Don't worry about us, Clay. We'll be all right, won't we, Milt?"

Milt nodded.

"I wanna he'p dig th' grave, Clay," the sheriff said. "Newt wuz ma friend fer more years than ya has lived."

"Very well. You go get the tools and I'll be right out."

Clay returned to the bedroom where the bodies were and came back out carrying a half-gallon sealing jar that was two-thirds full of Big Pap's homemade whiskey. He screwed off the top of the jar, took a long drink, and then went to join the sheriff.

The moon was rising as they started to mark off the oversized grave. Its brightness made it unnecessary for them to light the lantern they had brought along. Clay offered Uncle Billy a drink from the jug, and they commenced to dig. One would dig while the other sat on the edge of the hole and drank from the jug. When the digger tired, they changed places. As the grave became deeper, the diggers became drunker.

Both men were covered with soil and sweat. Clay's hands were blistered and bleeding from the rough handles of the mattock and shovel. Each time Clay took a drink, he would spit a little whiskey on his hands to prevent them from getting infected.

When they had finished digging, Clay reached down and pulled the sheriff out of the hole. They sat on the soft damp earth at the edge of the grave and finished off the whiskey. They were almost totally drunk now.

"This shore is one purty mountain ya got up here, Clay. Yep, shore is. Ain' none no purtier nowhars."

"That's the way I feel, too, Uncle Billy. I just want to live up here and have things the way they used to be."

"Things ain' never th' same, Clay. When ya leave somewhars an' then go back, things has changed. Mostly, you're whut's changed. Thet's why sometimes I think it's bes' nivver ta go back."

"I think you're right, but this doesn't apply to me. My mountain is just like I left it, and inside I'm no different. I'll never leave here again."

"Mebbe yore righ'. Anyhow, now ain' th' time ta think 'bout it."

They sat silently for a few moments, each engrossed in his own thoughts.

Presently the sheriff spoke. "Say, Clay, thar's somethin' Elviney and me been thinkin' 'bout, so I guess now's as gooda time ta bring it up as enny."

"Uncle Billy, if there's anything I have that you need or want, you're welcome to it. You know that."

"Whut I'm gonna ask fer is th' last thing we'll ever need. Since we ain' got no fam'ly buryin' groun', me an' Elviney would like ta be buried up here in your'n."

"Of course, you can. It makes me happy that you would want to be up here with the rest of us. Let's mark off your plot right now."

They got up and staggered around the cemetery and finally chose two plots in the corner some distance from the Barrons. They were laughing and joking as they gathered stones to mark the site. The liquor had taken complete control of their minds.

Clay set the empty jug on a fence post and called to the sheriff. "Can't leave a dead Indian around here. See if you can hit it from there."

"Hit's awful dark," the sheriff answered as Clay joined him. "Why don' you try?"

"If you miss, I'll blast it," Clay laughed.

The sheriff cocked his gun, aimed uncertainly, fired and missed. Clay howled gleefully as he drew his gun. His shot also missed its mark. The sheriff cackled and fired again. Clay shot. Their guns roared simultaneously and the jar jumped into the air and disintegrated.

The jug was empty and broken. The game was over. The reason for being at this place was forced back on them. Clay turned and moved as if in a trance towards the freshly dug grave.

When the sheriff came up to him, they stood together somberly for some time before leaving.

Valarie rushed to meet them when they reached the house, her face white as a sheet.

"Was that gunfire I heard?" she asked.

Clay laughed. "Nothing to get excited about. We were just having target practice."

She realized then that they were drunk. She thought of criticizing their actions, but changed her mind and said nothing. She had learned from observation that hill people drank to hide their grief, but meant nothing disrespectful.

She made a pot of coffee, but before she could persuade the sheriff to drink any, he had passed out. Clay made an attempt to put him in bed with Milt. His drunken condition prevented him from carrying him, but he did succeed in dragging him across the floor and unceremoniously dumping him into bed.

He returned to the living room, sat down beside Valarie on the sofa and promptly went to sleep with his head in her lap.

"Whut's happen't ta them?" Milt asked sleepily from the doorway of the bedroom.

"They're just drunk," she answered truthfully.

"Oh," he said, and disappeared back into the bedroom.

She blew out the light and sat in the dark thinking about the man whose head she held in her lap. All her thoughts were not pleasant. She had almost dozed off when she saw the shadow of someone moving across the room. When it neared the window she could see that it was Milt.

The moon glinted off the steel revolver in his hand. He had evidently taken the sheriff's gun and was now standing guard at the window. He had found his place; he was a Barron.

It was midmorning the next day when a preacher from Hookville led a small procession of people into the front yard. Milt and Clay were standing on the front porch beside the casket containing the bodies of their relatives.

Eight men voluntarily stepped from the crowd, lifted the casket in unison, and began the difficult journey up the mountain to the Barron cemetery. The pallbearers were replaced several times, but there was never a pause in the steady climb.

Clay was glad that Valarie had engaged a preacher for the ceremony. Big Pap and Sarah would have wanted one, but he wouldn't have thought of it.

Upon completing the difficult journey, the men set the casket at the edge of the grave. After the preacher had delivered a short eulogy, the bodies were lowered into the ground. As was the custom, Clay, the nearest relative, stepped forward and tossed the first shovelful of earth onto the casket. He then passed the shovel to Milt.

As Clay left the gravesite, he thanked the preacher for conducting the services. He knew that he would be insulted if he had offered him money.

As Clay walked away he thought, "Big Pap and Mammy began their life together here on this mountain, and here they would remain for whatever awaits everyone after death."

Chapter Twenty-Three

The crowd left the cemetery in straggling groups and returned to Big Pap's cabin where they gossiped and speculated about the future in hushed tones. Some were long-time friends of the deceased couple, but most were just the curious and had come to get a look at the infamous Clay. When they returned to their homes and jobs they wanted to associate themselves with him. Not even the notorious Devil John had cut down four men in one night. The curious wanted to be able to say they knew him in case he was the next to fall and be returned to the clay from which he was named.

Like blowflies they were drawn to the smell of death. Clay curbed his impatience and observed the rules of hospitality that forbade him from asking them to leave.

Dr. Jody disengaged herself from the crowd and came to Clay to offer her condolences. She could think of nothing to say but a sincere "I'm sorry."

"I appreciate your coming here," Clay answered, as he pulled her aside. "Doctor, I'd like to ask you a favor."

"Of course," she answered, "I'll do anything I can."

"Could you keep Milt at the clinic for awhile? I don't want him near me until this is over."

"Of course he can stay. He's too bright to be wasted on this senseless carnage. I hope you live long enough to finish this stupidity so Milt doesn't grow up with nothing to look forward to."

Turning abruptly, she walked away, not giving Clay a chance to answer.

After the last of the stragglers had gone, the sheriff turned to Valarie and asked if she would like a ride back to town.

Valarie gave a questioning glance to Clay, and he told her, "You ride on back in with him."

"I thought I would stay here for awhile and go home after I fixed you some dinner," she answered hopefully.

Clay shook his head. "No, you go on back with Uncle Billy."

She was not going to be dismissed that easily.

"Don't you want me here with you, Clay?"

"That's not the point," he answered impatiently.

There was a determined tilt to her chin as she asked, "What are you going to do now?"

"Why?" His impatience was obvious.

Her anger was rising. "Why can't this stop right now?"

"I buried two more reasons today," he snapped back.

"Clay," she continued stubbornly, "I don't like to talk to you like this, but have you stopped to think that if you hadn't started the killing all over again those wonderful old people would be sitting here now laughing and joking and enjoying life like they deserved? Their deaths are as much your fault as the Hooks. No one bothered them while you were gone."

Clay whirled away from her and walked to the end of the porch and stood looking off into the woods.

She followed him and continued, "I just can't take it any more. If you care anything in the world for me, leave with me now."

The sheriff interjected softly, "There is some truth ta whut she's asayin', Clay. Why don' ya take Valarie an' Milt an' go away somewhars an' have a decent life?"

"I made my father a promise and I'll keep it," he answered grimly.

The sheriff was not to be dissuaded. "Thet promise wuz ta a dead man. Brack wouldn' hol' ya to it. He loved ya. He would wan' ya ta stay alive an' be happy. He wouldn' wan' ya to be up thar in th' groun' beside 'im afore yer time."

Clay's slumped shoulders straightened as he turned toward them. "You're wrong! My father can have no peace until they are all dead. I know what he would want!"

All the tenderness was gone from him now. He didn't want any more of this conversation. He was anxious for them to leave. The young rosebud of love that was so close to opening for him and Valarie was beginning to wither and die because the dark cloud of his hate kept the sunlight of desire from nourishing it. He wanted no thought of love to clutter his mind.

The sheriff put his hand on Clay's arm. "Ya know I cain't hep'. This iz all fam'ly now. Be careful. Fight smart. Don' underestimate Silas Hook, an' stay alive."

He then took the sobbing Valarie by the hand and led her to the jeep. Clay stood silently, watching them go. His heart was heavy. Valarie was a woman of great pride. She would not be put second to anyone or anything.

As the sheriff's jeep disappeared from sight, the numbness that had held him together through the funeral began to melt away like butter in a hot skillet. His mind became inflamed with the merciless hunger for retribution.

He changed quickly into the clothes he had worn home. Devil John's gun was lying on the dresser. Clay picked it up and spun the cylinder. A full load. He was ready.

It was nearly dark now. Clay sat with his back against one of the twin beeches. He divided his time between watching the ants scurrying about and watching the Hook's house. The house seemed deserted. There was no light on. He jumped to attention as a car turned off the Valley Pike and stopped in the front yard. A man got out and went inside. Clay waited and watched until it got dark, but saw no evidence of anyone else moving about. There was light in the Hook's house now, but the blinds had been pulled.

"No matter," he thought, as he moved down the hill. "One of them is there. I'll take him."

He straddled the wire fence and began picking his way down the brushy hillside, cursing the green briars that tugged at his legs. At the bottom of the hill Clay crossed another fence and walked across a permanent pasture of bluegrass. He had angled his descent so as not to pass too closely to old man Waggoner's house.

As Clay neared the trees along the river bank, he was started by the loud snort of a mule. Out of the shadows the magnificent animal came running. Bay and tall, he raced with tremendous speed in circles around Clay. With tail held high, he galloped across the meadow to the barn. A faint smile crossed Clay's hard visage.

Clay picked his way carefully through the trees until he reached the path that followed the river's edge. The moon filtered through the leaves in irregular shafts of light. He continued to follow the worn trail until it came to a huge sycamore that stood on the riverbank opposite the Hooks' house. All the soil had been washed away from the roots of the tree, leaving it looking like a giant octopus about to spring into the river.

He remained in the shadow of the tree, watching the house. A ghostly calmness seemed to come over the land. Nothing moved. There was no breeze to stir the trees, nor insects to break the brooding silence. It seemed that everything waited and watched—as did Clay.

The shadowy figure tensed. The door to the house across the river opened. A man came out and headed for the hills, carrying a lantern. Clay moved quickly down the riverbank until he came to the footbridge, a bridge that was made of long poplar logs hewn smooth on one side and cabled together and anchored to trees on both sides of the river. His nostrils flared like a scenting fox as he cautiously crossed over.

Clay circled wide around the house so as not to disturb any dogs the Hooks might have. Once again he took the trail, following the bobbing lantern. The night shadows were confusing and deceptive. The moon was playing hide-and-seek with an enormous cloud, unconcerned with the drama being enacted below. Man hunting man. To the ageless moon, there was nothing new about that.

The light ahead turned sharply and was lost from Clay's sight. He followed, moving cautiously now. As he peered around an outcropping of rock he froze. Ahead of him was Silas' moonshine still. It was under a gigantic overhanging cliff, whose "ceiling" was black from the smoke of a thousand fires. Water gurgled out of a steel pipe that had been driven into a water vein that seeped out of the rock wall.

Silas' greed had sent one of his sons up here to tend the still. He didn't know which one of them it was stoking the fire. He didn't care.

The big pistol rose and lined up with the working man's back, then tilted down. Clay wanted him to see it coming. He must have made some sound, or maybe it was the sixth sense of the hunted because the man by the fire whirled, his teeth flashing in the firelight like a wolf at bay. He sprang for the shotgun that was leaning against the mash barrel. Clay waited for his hands to touch the gun before he let loose the .45. The heavy slugs tore indiscriminately through the man's body, tearing the life out of him. Isom Hook was hard to kill. He gathered himself up for one superhuman valiant effort to take this hated nemesis with him. His last conscious thought on earth was of his failure. His mind was willing, but the shotgun was slipping from his lifeless hands. He lay on the ground quivering and dying, listening to the echoes fade away.

Clay calmly punched out the spent cartridges and reloaded the gun. He then methodically shot up the still. Boom! Boom! Boom! The .45 bucked and roared. As he turned away, the sour mash was squirting out of the barrels and splashing onto the sightless eyes of the dead man.

The dark cloud tired of its game with the moon and moved on.

Clay stood in the shadow of the Hooks' barn, watching the house. He had waited on the trail, hoping one of the others would come to investigate. He waited in vain. The blinds were up and the lights were on. He could see a woman moving about. As he watched her through the window he felt a pang of regret. He felt no regret for the dead man on the hill, or for the ones he still had to kill; his regret was for the worn-out creature inside.

After recrossing the Little Sandy, he took a roundabout way to the top of his mountain. He wondered where the other Hooks were holed up. It would be just like old Silas to offer him one of his sons as bait, and then be waiting for him to return to Big Pap's and ambush him. Tonight, if they waited, it would be for nothing. Tonight he would sleep in the cellar on Rainbow Mountain.

Upon reaching the ruins of the burned-out house, he dragged a piece of the heat-twisted metal roofing to the edge of the entrance to the cellar. He dropped down inside, and standing on the stove, reached up and pulled the tin over the opening. It would be impossible for anyone to get to him without awakening him first.

Expecting to spend an uncomfortable night, he still laid down and tried to sleep, but the stuffy air closed around him. He felt himself in the lonely grasp of the mountain. The killing fever had subsided. He now felt the weight of his loss: Devil John, his father, Big Pap, Sarah, and now, Valarie. He pulled out Devil John's gun and held it against his face. The gunpowder smell filled his nostrils; the cold steel reassured him.

Finally, he slept.

Chapter Twenty-Four

As the sheriff drove slowly back to town, Valarie sat ramrod straight beside him. She had stopped crying.

He turned to her and said, "I've knowed you since you was borned, an' it hurts me ta see you so tore up, but Clay has not lied to ya. You've knowed from th' beginnin' whut he come home fer."

She bit her lip, trying to hold back the tears. "I know that, but Big Pap and Aunt Sarah. My God, they're dead! I'll never see them again."

The flood broke and the tears came again. The sheriff stopped the jeep and held her tenderly in his arms until she cried herself out. After she regained her composure, he continued talking to her in a reassuring tone.

When she entered the house, her father came forward to comfort her. She broke down again.

"What am I going to do, Papa? I love him so much, but I hate him for what he's done to those old people. I hate him for what he's doing to me."

Clyde held her as she succumbed to her grief. Suddenly she pulled out of his arms and her tears began to dry up. Her eyes flashed angrily bright.

"Damn him! There are more people than him involved here. What's going to happen to Milt if he's killed? What the hell am I supposed to do—dry up and blow away? I've spent a good part of my life waiting for him. Goddamn him! If I'm not worth more than this senseless stupidity, then he can go to hell!"

Clyde wanted to hold and console her, but kept his distance as she strode around the room, cursing and kicking the furniture. He had observed her temper only rarely, but felt sorry for all those who crossed her when she was on a rampage. He became hard pressed not to show his amusement as this normally classy, proper lady continued to curse and rant like a drunken sailor.

Her mother came and demanded, "Stop it. That kind of language isn't going to help. The question is—what are you going to do about your situation?"

Valarie strode into the middle of the room. Hands on her hips, she threw her head back.

"At the risk of sounding like a conceited bitch, I'm telling you I don't have to kiss any man's ass. There has to be a decent man out there somewhere who would want what I have to offer and love me for giving it to him."

She glared at her father, as if hoping he would argue with her. Clyde knew she would be alright now. Anger had replaced grief. He knew his daughter; she would solve her problems.

Valarie turned to her mother. "Do you still want to go to Europe?"

"Of course she does." Clyde jumped on it immediately. He wanted his family out of here while these people were killing each other.

"I guess so," Izetta answered, taking her lead from Clyde.

"It's settled then. Mom and I are leaving for New York tomorrow morning. We're going shopping, and I may spend twenty thousand dollars. I'm not going to Europe looking like some milk maid from Kentucky. I'm going to flaunt my ass all over the continent. I may marry one of those washed-out English counts or dukes or whatever and stay over there. At least they are civilized."

"I'll make all the arrangements, and I don't care if it costs me a farm," Clyde approved. "It will give you time to get your mind straightened out."

"There's nothing wrong with my mind," she retorted. "It's other people who are crazy—not me!"

When they were settled into a motel in New York, Valarie began shopping with a passion. She had left all her conventional upbringing at home. She bought the latest fashions—ultramodern revealing clothes. Her mother was in a state of shock. She couldn't believe that Valarie would choose clothes that were so revealing. However, she soon got caught up in her own shopping frenzy and purchased more clothes for herself than she ever had, including a couple of daring numbers. They laughed like a couple of school girls as they returned to the hotel.

It was entirely possible to buy a farm in Kentucky for what they had spent.

As the cruise ship pulled out of the harbor, Valarie was already making the rounds.

"I want to see where the action is and what the prospects are," she told her excited mother.

Then it began. She strutted around the deck or pool area and lay in the sun in the skimpiest bathing suit on board. Men were drawn to her like bears to a honey tree. She smiled at them, batted her enormous blue eyes, tossed her inky black hair and played the role of the senseless beauty to perfection as she went through the men, one at a time. Izetta loved watching her manipulate them.

She was looking for something very special in a man, and as soon as she was convinced he didn't have it, she would ditch him and move on to the next one so smoothly that the man would be left standing stripped naked by failure and not knowing what he had done wrong.

At night she wore her long gowns and danced the night away, captivating every man with whom she came in contact. She collected the scalp of Rich Braden, the captain, and was asked to dine at his table every night. She drank champagne and became giggly and heady, but she always returned alone to her cabin to join her mother each night.

Two days before reaching London, she abruptly stopped leaving her cabin. She had all her meals sent in, took no calls and left word that she was not to be disturbed by anyone.

"What's wrong with you, Valarie?" her mother questioned. "I thought you were having such a good time."

"It's the men," Valarie answered disgustedly. They're all a bunch of candy-assed weaklings. If I were a man and a woman teased me like I have them, I'd throw her ass down and rape her. None of them had the balls to do it, so to hell with them!"

Izetta could only shake her head in exasperation and say, "Valarie, stop being so crude."

In London they saw all the shows and did all the touristy things. Valarie flirted shamelessly. In short order she informed her mother that she wanted to go to Paris.

"I'm looking for a man and all I'm finding here are gentlemen. I can teach him to be polite and have manners, but you have to be born a man."

In Paris she seemed to come alive again, again doing the theaters and clubs. Valarie drank, danced and left men scattered like bowling pins behind her. She radiated sex, power, money and danger. The sheer force of her personality was intimidating to the normally aggressive Frenchmen. One of them pinched her rear in an elevator. She turned to him and said sweetly, "If you want it, take it like a man; don't scratch for it like a dog!"

She laughed when he scurried out of the elevator.

Becoming bored with the monotony of the lifestyle in which they had become engulfed, she decided that she wanted to return to London.

"I'm tired of men who dance with their noses between my boobs," she announced to her mother.

Back in the London airport, Valarie caught her mother's arm as they passed a magazine rack. There on the cover of the magazine was the leering smile of Silas Hook. She opened it up. She could not believe that halfway around the world there were people fascinated by a family war in a backwoods Kentucky county. She saw no romance in the killings.

The Brits were actually making bets on who would survive. She dropped the magazine back into the rack and leaned against the wall.

Tears welled in her eyes. Gone was the arrogant, cocky, cursing, flirty, teasing woman.

"Mamma," she whispered, "there's only one Clay Barron. I have to go home now."

Izetta took her in her arms, held her close and patted her shoulder.

"I know, Baby, I know. As soon as we can get a plane."

Valarie had found out something about herself. She found herself looking for the same qualities in other men that she had rejected in Clay.

Chapter Twenty-Five

The lazy days passed into the heat of summer. Still the Hooks did not come. It was as if the mountains had swallowed them, leaving no trace. Like an angry wolf Clay prowled the hills and valleys searching for them. He spied on all their relatives, without catching so much as a glimpse of them.

Clay's appearance had undergone a drastic change. His face was gaunt and haggard from constant tension and lack of sleep. His hair had grown down over his collar and forehead in an unkempt mass. The Hooks were waiting him out. From some place near they were waiting and watching. One mistake was all he would get to make.

At last Clay ran out of food and had to go to town. He knocked on the back door of the clinic and smiled wryly at Dr. Jody's startled look.

Quickly regaining her composure she invited him in. As he stepped inside she moved to pull the shades.

"You look terrible," she commented matter-of-factly.

"Yes, I do," he admitted.

"Do you want to see Milt?" she asked.

"Yes, please. I want to give him a list of things I need from the store."

"He's in the room at the end of the hall. Take all the time you want. He misses you," she added.

In a matter of minutes Clay came back into the room.

"Doctor, I thank you for your kindness. I've told Milt where to leave the things I ordered. I won't take the chance of coming here again. I shouldn't have this time, but there wasn't anyone else I could trust."

He caught her hand and squeezed it lightly, switched off the light and slipped quickly back into the night.

Dr. Jody sat in her office trying to sort out her thoughts and feelings after Clay left. Why did this man so appeal to her? At twenty-eight, he was nine years her junior. She had never been attracted to younger men; her husband had been fourteen years older than she. Clay was educated and an obvious man of the world, but not educated

in the sense she was—he was not a professional. He was such a frus-
trating man. He had, in effect, purchased Milt and it was obvious that
he was beginning to care for the boy. She dealt with life and death constantly, yet she was appalled at how cheaply he held human life. She
had seen the body of Isom Hook. He hadn't been just shot and killed—
he had been brutally butchered.

In the weeks that had passed since she brought Milt to the clinic
she had grown fond of him. He was so grown up in some ways and yet
so naive in others. Many times each day he would walk out on the porch
and look at the mountains. He wanted to be up there with his father.
She allowed herself to speculate what life would be like up there with
Milt and Clay.

There had always been in the back of her mind the thought that
sometime when she was emotionally healed that she would go back to
Philadelphia and pick up her life. Now, she wasn't sure what she
wanted to do.

She had heard that Valarie had given up on Clay and had gone to
Europe with her mother. She hated to admit it, but she had been jealous of the way Valarie had given the appearance of owning him. She realized that she was drawn to him by an animal magnetism, and she was
aware that certain men just seem to give a scent that only women detect and respond to. Just as in the animal world, these men always have
their choice of the available females. She knew by instinct that he would
be a great lover. High-strung, aggressive men have always won the wars
and the hearts.

Dr. Jody walked outside and looked at the shadowy mountain. Her
body was in torment.

"I have to know," she finally admitted to herself.

Knowing she had finished her last call of the day, she decided to
drive her jeep back to Big Pap's cabin to see Clay. At this point, she had
no idea what she wanted to do or say. She knew that she was taking the
chance of making a fool of herself. She parked the jeep in the front yard
and knocked on the door. Getting no response, she walked around back
calling out to Clay. There was no answer.

The place was deserted. It had an eerie atmosphere about it. Weeds
had taken over the yard and garden. If it sat here empty much longer,
she knew the local people would begin to say that the place was
haunted. Then only the bravest of the young boys would come about the
place to prove their mettle.

Since he wasn't here, she decided to climb to the top. The heavy
rain clouds concerned her, but she dismissed them. As she was nearing
the summit she stopped with a jolt as Clay stepped into the path in
front of her.

"So here you are," she said breathlessly from the long climb.

"Is the boy all right?" he asked anxiously.

"Yes, he's fine. I just thought I'd stop to check on you. Milt's been worried about you."

"I'm OK."

The man's eyes were pools of blackness in his bony face. He had suffered, and it showed. These mountain people were always closer to their family groups than people of other places. Jody found herself lately wondering what it would be like to belong to a group like this one. What would it be like to be so close and so loved that you would actually take a human life if your group was threatened?

"I thought you would be living at the cabin," she said.

"I do sometimes. I move around a lot. Someday they will get tired of hiding and when they do, they will come here and I don't want to be trapped in a house. That's why I stay up here most of the time."

"Did you know the sheriff has been over here looking for you?" she asked.

"Yes, I saw him," he answered.

"Do you know what he wants to ask you about?"

"Yes, I know."

He then casually admitted killing Isom Hook. Five men had now died from his gun, and the purpose that had brought him here had not lessened. He would suffer his grief in silence and he would continue to kill or be killed.

Jody didn't want to leave just yet, but stood silently just looking at him. Her mind raced frantically for a reason not to leave.

"Since I'm this far up, I think I'll have a drink of water before I head back down. I've heard the sheriff say that you have the coldest and the sweetest water here that he ever drank."

"Yes," he answered, "the water is very good."

When they reached the well he dropped the bucket and pulled it back up with the chain pulley.

"You'll have to drink out of the bucket. I don't have any cups."

"That's fine; I've drunk out of buckets before. Mmmmm, this surely is good," she said appreciatively. "How does water get up here so high?"

"I never thought about it—it's just always been here."

As he poured the remainder of the water out of the bucket, the dark clouds opened up and the rain fell in big fat drops. At first they spattered like the freckles on the face of a child, and then without warning, turned into a downpour. Clay grabbed Jody by the hand and ran for the cellar. She had no idea where they were going, but she was soaked to the skin. Clay grabbed the tin roofing, yanked it aside and told her to swing down until her feet touched the stove. He instructed her to stand on it until he could get down beside her, and then holding her hand he swung her down into the darkness.

Her hand was wet and slippery from the pelting rain, but his strong grip on her never slipped. Reaching up over his head, he pulled a piece of log near the entrance and propped one side of the tin roofing on it so the rain would run off.

"Just stand still and I'll light the lantern," he said as he moved off in the darkness.

She heard the scratch of a match on the wall as he lit the kerosene lantern. She looked around the cellar. In one corner was a featherbed spread on the earthen floor. The shelves were full of canned goods that he had obviously carried from the cabin below.

"This isn't the Ritz, but it would be much harder to find me here than down there in the cabin."

"Is this all you have been eating?" she asked as she pointed to the canned food.

"No. I go down to the cabin and cook myself a hot meal every so often. Say, you're soaked! You might catch a cold if you stay in those wet clothes. I have some extra things here. They won't look too good on you, but at least they will be dry."

"If you don't mind, I would like to borrow them."

She blushed in the near darkness at the thought of undressing in the close quarters with him. If he noticed that she was going through any discomfort he never let on. He tossed her a pair of trousers and a shirt and then moved to the other side of the stove and leaned against it with his back to her.

She quickly peeled off the wet clothes. For only a second she hesitated with the underclothes, and finding them too uncomfortable to keep on, she removed them. As she pulled on the trousers she looked at the still figure with his back to her. Looking beyond him, she stifled a gasp. Her shadow was right in front of him. Her heavy breasts swung like twin pendulums as she grabbed the shirt and quickly buttoned it over her nakedness. Without waiting for her to say she was dressed, he turned toward her. This dispelled any notion that he hadn't noticed.

She felt mounting apprehension as he walked forward and stopped directly in front of her. The smokey eyes looked down at her.

"I'm sorry," he said. "I didn't mean to look, but when I noticed I guess I didn't have the character to close my eyes."

She laughed nervously. "No harm done. It's only a body. Nothing to be ashamed of."

"That's very true in your case, Doctor," he smiled.

"Since we're marooned here in this cellar for the duration of the rainstorm, can't we dispense with 'Doctor'? My name is Jody."

"OK, Jody. And now, if I might, I would like to ask you what you are doing here in the hills when class and culture stick out all over you? Why did you come here to punish yourself?"

"I came here to get as far away from Philadelphia and all the memories of my husband as I could. I came here to forget."

"What did he do—run off with another woman?" he asked sardonically.

"No, he didn't do that," she answered evenly. "He died."

The hard face softened. "I'm sorry, Jody. I had no reason to say something like that to you. I don't know what's wrong with me. I always seem to be hurting the people I like. I'm sure he was a fine man and loved you very much."

"Yes, he was a fine man, and he did love me as I did him."

"What happened to him?" Clay asked.

"He had a brain tumor. We were both neurosurgeons, and he insisted that I operate on him. He didn't make it."

"So you blamed yourself and came here to the hills to hide."

"Something like that," she answered. "I lost my nerve. I couldn't perform surgery anymore, so I came here. I only wanted to practice medicine and be left alone. Then one day a man got caught in the mine and I had to amputate his leg to save his life. After that, I wasn't afraid anymore."

"Why didn't you go back then?"

"I thought about it, but these people accepted me when I needed them. I don't think I could run out on them now. There's a great need for a doctor here. Someday, when I'm completely healed and ready, I'll go back. What about you, Clay? When your private war is over, if you're still alive, what are you going to do?"

"I'm going to build me a house right out there over us. Then I'm going to buy as much land in every direction around this mountain as I have money. I don't want Milt or my grandkids to have to look out and see strangers all around us. I'm going to fish in the Little Sandy and hunt squirrels on the mountains and be happy."

"What about a woman? Who is going to be mistress of all this?"

"I don't think there's going to be a mistress—at least, it doesn't seem so."

"That's too bad," she answered. "I had heard that there was a thing between you and Valarie, but I knew it must have been wrong when she left for Europe. I was sorry to hear about that. I think Valarie's such a nice person and she seemed so attached to Milt. I had hoped, for his sake, that it was true."

She watched him closely, but there was no change in his expression. If he had known she was gone, or if he cared, it was impossible to tell.

"Yes, she was good to Milt. As a matter of fact, Valarie was always good to everyone. That's a fine trait, if you can afford it." he answered.

After this exchange of words there was a long silence. The rain continued hammering on the roofing overhead.

"I hope this lets up soon—it'll be dark before long."

"That's something you can never tell about these summer rains here on the mountain. It might go on all night."

"Well, I hope not."

"Don't worry, Jody. No one knows you are here, do they?"

"No, except that Milt's at home alone. But I guess he's old enough to take care of himself," she said.

"Well, then, you're perfectly safe. I won't tell anyone that you got stuck in a cellar with that 'no account Clay Barron'."

"I don't worry about what anyone thinks about me. I'm over twenty-one. I don't have to answer for my actions to anyone," she retorted.

"My sentiments exactly," he smiled. "Well, look, we can't stand here in the middle of the room all night. I'm sorry there aren't any chairs to sit on and I know how embarrassing this must be for you, but why don't you sit there on the bed and I'll fix you one of my favorite drinks?"

Without waiting to see if she complied he turned away and took down a Mason jar of home-canned peaches and a jar of white lightening. As he poured some of the fiery liquor into a tin cup he said, "This is the last of Big Pappy's squeezin's."

He then poured some of the peach juice over the whiskey. Taking one of the spoons out of a tin pan, he stirred the two together and handed it to her.

She sat cross-legged in the middle of the bed, her back against the wall. She tasted the drink and smiled up at him.

"Well, now, that's not half bad. Where is yours?"

"I only have one cup; I wasn't actually expecting company for cocktails."

"Then you will have to share mine," she replied as she handed the cup up to him.

He took the cup and dropped down on the side of the bed. The whiskey was warming Jody's insides. The closeness of this man was as intoxicating as the drink.

As time passed and he returned again to fill the cup, the restraint left the pair and they talked and laughed. Finally, Clay took the jar of peaches, poured the remaining contents of the whiskey into the jar and shook up the two. They laughed as they fished for and ate the whiskey-soaked peaches. As Clay brought out the last one, he held the peach half between his teeth and leaned toward her. She leaned forward and took the peach between her teeth.

The whiskey had begun to affect her and the whole situation seemed quite unreal. Sitting on a featherbed in a cellar eating peaches from the mouth of Clay Barron—it struck her as amusing. She thought no one would believe it; she didn't even believe it, and she was here.

As she pulled back and tore the peach in half, she felt the pressure of his lips for just a fraction of a second. That second was enough. She swallowed the peach and looked directly at Clay. He set the jar down beside the bed, took the cup from her hand and put it aside. He leaned forward and touched her with his hands, pressed his lips to hers, ever so lightly, ever so tenderly. His lips nibbled at her mouth. Her lips parted, taking him in. Her arms reached out for him and then he came at her, all fire and passion. There was no thought of resistance in her now. His lips were raping her mind. This was what she had wanted from the first time she had seen him on the bridge.

She had fought it, trying to dislike him. She finally admitted the physical attraction, but had convinced herself that she had nothing in common with this half-wild man from the hills. At the moment, the differences were gone. He pulled her arched body down beside him. She felt him tremble as his hands moved to unsnap his shirt. She tugged at the gun harness; Clay pulled away, removed it with the shirt and laid it aside.

As he turned back he found that she had also removed her shirt. She could see the excitement and approval her body was bringing to him. It was a look like the one on Clay's face now that made it worthwhile for women who carried around breasts like the ones she bared for him. He bent to her again and this time his lips had become tender again. This only heightened her passion. As his mouth crisscrossed its way down her neck and back and forth across her breasts, she wriggled out of the pants. His fingertips played hop-scotch down across her stomach, bringing forth a small involuntary cry.

Gone was the efficient, intelligent doctor; now she was a woman who would demand from a man and give everything. As Clay removed his trousers, she clung to him, her hands exploring his body.

"Oh, my God, Clay! Take me now. Take me like you never had another woman in your life."

Clay went after her and found himself with an equal. Their lovemaking was like the pounding surf trying to ravish the seashore. His hands became entangled in her hair. Her hair fell out of the bun and laid in a golden mass about her white shoulders. Unselfishly, equally, they gave and took. Her needs equaled his. He maneuvered her until he found her area of vulnerability and then he drove her to the pinnacle of passion. He toyed with it, teased it and used it to completely possess her. She moved as only an adult passionate woman who understands her body and its needs can. No man could ever make love *to* this woman—he would make love *with* her.

Clay began to lose control, but he realized that it no longer mattered. She was with him—all the way through she had been with him—giving as much as she took; a woman the equal of any woman. As her arms moved up and locked behind his neck, her body throbbing and jerking to his, she was conscious of his breath quickening in her ear and this heightened her own passion as they collapsed against each other in total mutual satisfaction.

Clay lay there, his face buried in her hair, feeling her breasts still heaving against his chest, her hands still holding his head. When their breathing had returned to normal, Clay raised up and looked down at her. Her lips were trembling. Tears were welling out of her eyes and running down her cheeks. No sound came from her, but the tears continued to flow.

Clay felt strange. He wanted to do or say something to make her feel better.

"This is the first time since you lost him, isn't it?" he asked.

She nodded. Clay continued looking at her, not knowing what to say. Suddenly she took a deep breath and sat up and wiped the tears from her face.

"Well, I guess I really needed that!" she said without embarrassment or shame. "It has been so long I had almost forgotten what a wonderful gift nature has blessed us humans with."

He tilted her face up and kissed her tenderly and snuggled closer to her.

As she caressed his shoulder she said, "Clay, you don't owe me anything because of what happened here. I came up here like a bitch in heat, so don't blame yourself."

Snuggling closer to her he whispered, "Why don't you shut up?"

"OK," she murmured, as she burrowed even deeper into his arms.

They lay for hours, talking and getting to know each other.

"Clay, do you really want me here now?" she asked.

"Just you try leaving." He squeezed her tighter.

"Good! My husband always said you could tell if a man cared for you if he didn't want to leave after having made love to you."

"I never thought about it, but I guess he was right," Clay answered.

"Does it bother you for me to speak about him?" she asked.

"No, of course not. We all have a past."

Her lips stopped him from going on. They came together again, and this time the raw passion was gone, replaced by tenderness and the slow seeking of pleasure. This time was even more fulfilling. She was a true artist at making love. She pleased him as only a true woman of the world can.

It was nearly midnight when she finally stirred beside him. He had been sleeping for sometime with his cheek against hers.

"My magnificent male animal," she thought, as she roused him.

"Clay, I have to go. Everyone will be worried about me."

"I know you do, but I wish you could stay here."

"My God!"

She sat up suddenly, shoving him away.

"I just thought of something!"

"What?" he asked anxiously.

"Oh, no!" She slapped her head and said, "A doctor should know better."

"What are you talking about?"

"You may not want to hear this, but what if I get pregnant?"

Chapter Twenty-Six

Clay awoke to fine daylight filtering through the nail holes and cracks in the metal that covered the entrance. He stretched and sat up in bed, with his mind full of thoughts of the night before. He hadn't realized how strong his need had been for a woman. His thoughts turned to Valarie and he experienced exasperating confusion.

"Oh, hell," he said to himself. "I don't want to think about it; I'll probably end up dead anyway."

He noticed that the air in the cellar was becoming warm and stuffy. He got dressed, climbed up on the stove and shoved the tin aside to pull himself out. He reached down to replace the tin cover. This move saved his life.

The bullet struck him simultaneously with the sound of the exploding gun. His sudden move downward had caused the slug that had been so carefully aimed at his heart to hit him in the upper left shoulder. The impact from behind drove him head first back down into the cellar. He belly flopped off the stove and onto the dirt floor, where he lay stunned for several seconds.

When his mind cleared, he scrambled across the room and leaned against the wall. He jerked open his shirt and probed with his fingers to find where the bullet went in and came out. When he removed his hand it was dripping with blood. He took out his handkerchief and stuffed it into the puckered wound as best he could. While doing so, he kept glancing up at the opening above him.

Clay drew and cocked the .45. Whoever had shot him would want to make sure he was dead. It would be next to impossible for anyone to see anything by looking down into the dark cellar.

"He's only going to get one little peek anyway," Clay promised himself.

"Hey, Barron!" came a drunken raucous voice from above. "You dead or jist playin' possum?"

Clay remained motionless and silent, hoping that the intruder would look over the edge, giving him a clean shot.

"Don' think yer gonna trick me inta stickin ma haid over thet hole 'cause I ain't gonna do it."

After a short pause the voice went on, "I ain' takin' nairy a chance with ya. OK, OK, Mister. Mebbe a live Barron don' answer. Thar's more'n one way ta git a skunk outta 'is hole. 'Course, if yer playin' a little possum, I rekkin yer gonna come a hot-footin' 'hit outta thar."

Still getting no answer from the cellar, he went on, irritation showing in his voice. "Git out here 'rat now or I'm gonna burn ya up—alive or dead."

Clay recognized the voice now. It wasn't one of the Hooks who had shot him; it was the damned stupid Ezra Fultz.

"Who the hell had put him up to this?" Clay wondered.

The first batch of half-charred pieces of timber came hurtling through the entrance and fell on the stove and floor around it. Clay knew he had to do something, and decided to try to talk or scare him out of it. Maybe if he didn't know how badly he was shot he might be able to frighten him off.

"Ezra!" Clay called out. "What the hell got into you anyway?" His voice was steady and controlled. "I know there's no love lost between us, but what brought this on?"

"So ya *are* alive, ya sneakin' bastard," Ezra screeched gleefully. "How da ya like it? How da ya like bein' trapped down thar like a rat? Hit ain't no fun bein' trapped, is it? 'Member whin you sons-a-bitches locked me in th' smokehouse—do ya 'member thet?" he shrieked madly.

"Look, Ezra, I've had about enough of your bullshit. Either get out of here and stay away from me, or I'm going to crawl out of here and kick your brains out!"

"Ya do jist thet. Come on out righ' now. I still got five a' these little lead pills left ta give ya."

"Ezra," Clay said, still speaking casually, trying to bluff his way out, "what's come over you? What brought this on?"

"Whut brung this on! Whut brung this on!" Ezra mimicked from above. "Ya know goddamn well whut brung this on. Ya already had it made up with Hallie, givin' her all thet money an' lettin' me brag 'bout it an' make a fool outta maself. Well, don' worry 'bout hit. Now I know whut you wuz up to. She cashed th' check an' took off, but I know ya got 'er stashed somewhars. Ya thought thet would be th' easy way ta git her an' Milt both an' make a ass outta me ta boot. Well, ya ain' gonna be asleepin' with ma wife or enjoyin' thet money 'cause I'm gonna kill ya right here."

"Who fed you all this bullshit, anyway?" Clay asked angrily. The very ignorance of the whole situation enraged him.

"Nobody ain' feedin' me nothin'. Silas Hook tol' me whut ya done ta me, so I jist sneaked on over here an' I'm gonna fix yer plow righ' now. I didn't 'spect ta find ya holed up like a damn ground hog."

"So that's it! Ezra, don't you see what Silas is trying to do? He's trying to get you to do his killing for him. He lied to you. All I wanted from you was the boy, and I paid well for him. Your troubles with your wife and her whereabouts are your problem—not mine."

"Then where th' hell did she go?"

"I can't answer that, or I would. I have no idea."

"I don' believe you!" Ezra' voice was shrill with anger. "I'm gonna roast ya like a pig on a spit. I'm gonna set righ' here an' listen ta ya squall an' holler whin ya start fryin', or I'm gonna shoot yer ass off whin ya crawl out. I don' give a fiddler's damn which way ya git it, neither."

Clay struggled to his feet. He wasn't about to stay here and burn. Perhaps he could stand on the stove and wait for the next bunch of fuel to be thrown down, and then climb out. He would then have a chance to escape while Ezra was looking for other things to burn. He felt light-headed as he climbed up onto the stove. The loss of blood was taking its toll. He stood on one side of the stove and waited. Through the opening came a bunch of sticks and leaves.

Clay had been looking up, hoping that Ezra would get close enough for him to get a shot at him, but Ezra had pushed the stuff over the edge with a long pole. Clay waited to the count of three and then reached up and grabbed the edge to pull himself out. That was as far as he got. Something smashed down on his fingers, breaking his grip and plunging him back to the cellar floor.

"Ha! Ha! Ha!" roared Ezra. "Though' ya'd sneak out on me, didn' ya? Well, changed ma mind. Decided I wanna hear ya beller a little whin it gits hot. So I'm gonna keep whackin' ya on th' head whenivver ya try ta git out."

Down through the opening came a flaming torch of dead grass. It landed on the leaves and sticks and began to burn. Clay struggled to his feet and rushed forward, trying to kick out the flames, but he was knocked down as Ezra threw a half-burned-out section of the old foundation log down on top of him. As he rolled out of the flames, swatting at his clothes with scorched hands, he knew that it would do no good to try to put out the fire now. It had too good a start. The flames now completely barred the entrance, and Ezra was still throwing more fuel down on the fire.

A memory from the past flashed into Clay's frantic mind, as he recalled playing in this same cellar on a rainy day long ago. He remembered finding a loose stone in the wall, prying it out and finding a tunnel that led to the well. The tunnel had been dug at the same time as the well, and it was to be used as a refuge for women and children in case of an Indian attack. After being gathered inside they would put the stone in the entrance behind them. Even if the house burned, they would be safe for there was enough air from the well for them to survive until the attack was over.

Clay's hands raced across the stone wall, jerking and pulling at the larger stones. Finally, he felt one give slightly, but could not pull it out as it had been mortared in with blue clay. He staggered across the room to the shelf holding the canned goods and grabbed the rusty old knife and the broken muzzle-loading gun.

At this time Ezra pushed the piece of tin roof over the cellar entrance. With no place to go, the smoke began to spread out and fill the room. Clay dug frantically into the mortar at one side of the stone. Soon he had an opening large enough to push the barrel of the gun through. He began to cough as his lungs started to fill with smoke. Each cough sent excruciating pain through his shoulder, causing tears to stream from his eyes. Putting every ounce of strength he could muster into one mighty heave, he pried the stone out of the wall with the gun.

Clay quickly scrambled into the entrance. The air was foul, but his oxygen-starved lungs consumed it in great gulps. As he plunged ahead into the pitch black darkness, his mind refused to consider the possibility that the log ceiling that had been supported all these years on rock walls might have rotted and collapsed.

As he crawled on hands and knees, the blood ran down his arm and left a sticky trail behind him. Cobwebs clutched at his face, but he ignored them, and continued crawling, dragging and pulling himself on through the darkness. When he had nearly reached the end of his endurance he received renewed energy from the sight of a shaft of light ahead.

He was at the end of the tunnel now. The damp air of the well was a welcome relief to his scorched lungs. He collapsed in the tunnel exit, sucking in great gulps of air. As his breathing stabilized, he began to worry about the loss of blood he was sustaining. Twisting sideways, he replaced the handkerchief over the wound and pressed it to him. His injury was jarred from his mind as the smoke drifted over his head and out into the well. The smoke had filled the cellar and then, like Clay, had sought escape through the tunnel.

He tried to plug up the exit with his body, but it was no use; he wasn't large enough. He knew that the well would soon fill with smoke and then it would work its way out the top. He had to beat the smoke out of the well. If he stayed here he would suffocate or Ezra would see the smoke and figure out where he was and find a way to kill him.

To this point he had been desperately trying just to survive. Now a reckless abandonment came over him. His foggy mind became incensed with his predicament.

"Ezra, you rotten son-of-a-bitch," he whispered aloud to himself. "I'm going to crawl out of this goddamned hole and blow you to hell!"

He reached across the well and grabbed a metal spike that had been driven between the stone in the well wall and began to pull his tortured body out of the tunnel. The spikes went all the way from the top of the well to the bottom, and had only been used for cleaning it. Still cursing and muttering under his breath, he was now straddling the well. Standing on and holding onto the spikes, he climbed. One foot, rest; one hand, rest; one foot, rest; one hand, rest. He counted as he worked his way up the damp, slick, mossy wall.

His head struck something. It wasn't a hard blow, but in his weakened condition it almost made him lose his grip, which would have dropped him into the water. The well shaft rocked and rolled beneath him. It seemed that it was trying to tilt up and pour him out. He closed his eyes and clung to the spikes with a death grip until the rocking of his senses subsided.

Slowly he looked up. His head had struck the well bucket. It sat on a frame over the center of the well and worked on a chain pulley to keep it from hanging up on the spikes when being drawn up. He would have to be careful not to touch it again. The bucket, if jarred too much, would cause the rusty pulley to rattle and give him away. He leaned sideways as far as possible and inched his way up past the bucket and chain.

"Just don't go getting thirsty, Ezra," he kept muttering to himself.

At last his hand reached the flat stone that was set at the top of the well wall. There was a space of about a foot between the wall and the wooden well box. Standing on the top spike, Clay could see through a crack between the rotting board. Ezra was standing with his back to the well, and was holding the piece of tin that had covered the cellar entrance. Angrily, Ezra hurled a piece of wood down the cellar entrance and took a pint bottle of whiskey out of his pocket and drank from it.

"Your last drink, you bushwacking crud," Clay gritted.

He took a firm grip on the top stone with his left hand and eased the .45 out of his waistband with his right. He worked the barrel through the crack between the rotting boards of the box and lined the long barrel up with the middle of Ezra's back. His thumb drew the hammer back to full cock. There was no thought of mercy.

Had he wanted to give Ezra a chance to live, he didn't have the strength to take that risk now. Slowly and carefully, so as not to move the front sight from the target, he squeezed the trigger.

The .45 shattered the stillness of the well chamber and Ezra seemed to be slammed in the back by a giant invisible fist. His hands and feet touched together behind him as he was raised into the air and came down on the edge of the same tin that still half covered the cellar entrance. Ezra and the twisted, blackened piece of roofing both slipped from sight beneath the ground.

Clay switched the gun around in his hand until he could use the butt as a hammer and knocked the boards off the well box. He crawled outside and lay on his back, the world tossing and pitching beneath him. As the ground steadied itself, he struggled to his feet and weaved across to the cellar entrance. Dropping to his knees, he tried to look down, but there was new smoke coming out, and the smell wasn't timber. At the cellar's edge he found Ezra's bottle of whiskey.

"Now then, Ezra," Clay grinned wolfishly as he unscrewed the cap. "It sure was nice of you not to take this bottle to hell with you."

He raised the bottle in a half-salute to the smoke pouring out of the ground, and drank. He then poured some on the wound in front that still had a small, steady stream of blood seeping from it. He poured a little more over his shoulder so it would run down into the bullet hole on his back, and then drank the rest.

Tossing the bottle into the cellar, he laughed crazily. "Hellfire and an empty whiskey bottle, you poor old dumb bastard."

As Brack Barron had done once so long ago, Clay spit at the cellar entrance and turned away.

Clay now tried to get back down the hill to the cabin, resting often and moving slowly. Then he tripped and rolled, tumbled into a hollow where he was brought to a jarring stop by slamming into a tree. He tried unsuccessfully several times to get to his feet. Finally he gave up and began to crawl. He crawled, cursed, laughed, cursed, and crawled some more. He was delirious and sometimes hysterical, wandering between self-pity and rage.

At last, bruised and scratched, covered with blood, he realized that he wasn't going to make it. Like a wounded animal he dragged himself out of the path and hid behind a mushy, rotten old log. Clay Barron had reached his limit. His head dropped to the ground. This time the earth rocked him off the edge into unconsciousness.

Chapter Twenty-Seven

Milt slipped quietly out of bed and dressed quickly. He raised the window and dropped soundlessly to the ground outside. It was early dawn.

"Ma place is up on th' mountain an' that's whar I'm agoin'," he thought.

Dr. Jody had told him about Clay's living in the basement of the burned-out house.

"I'm goin' up thar' an' I'm stayin', whether he likes it or not," he promised himself.

By the time he reached Big Pap's cabin the sun had drunk the dew from the greenness around him. He gave the bobwhite call and when he got no answer he entered the house. It had a strange and somewhat frightening feel to it. This house that had known so much love and grief was just gathering dust.

Finding the house unoccupied, he returned to the outside and began the long climb up the mountain. As he left the trees and walked across the grassy field toward the burned-out house, he saw smoke curling. Clay was nowhere in sight. As he got closer to the smoke, his lungs began to fill with the sweet-sickening smell of burning flesh. Feeling somewhat nauseous, he wondered what kind of meat Clay could be cooking.

Apprehensively he approached the entrance and yelled, "Clay, ya down thar?"

No answer came. As he peered down, a shaft of sunlight let him see the smoking body of a man on the cellar floor. Gagging and coughing, his eyes smarting from the smoke, Milt grabbed the cellar roof, swung down and dropped.

He ricocheted off the stove and landed on the smoking corpse. Scrambling off the smouldering body, he slapped at the sparks that were trying to catch his clothes on fire. He grabbed the body by a leg and drug it out of the fire. He sobbed with relief when he saw it wasn't Clay. He took a second to glare at the smoking form of Ezra.

"Damn ya! Ya finally got whut ya deserved," he hissed.

Holding his hand over his mouth, Milt searched the cellar. He found the hole where Clay had escaped. Not knowing if Clay was still in there, he struggled through to the well. His heart was pounding; his lungs felt like they were on fire; his eyes were so filled with smoke that he couldn't tell if there was anyone in the well. He went down the wall of the well until he reached the water. After feeling around, he was convinced there was no one there, and fairly tore up the side of the well to the daylight above.

When he reached the top he hung his head through the hole from which Clay had escaped and took in quick gulps of fresh air.

"Thank God, he got out!" he rejoiced, unaware that this was the first time in his life he had called on his Maker for anything.

Still coughing the smoke from his lungs, he raced around the ruins of the house like a person possessed as he searched for Clay. Then he saw it—the big pistol lying there by the tin roofing. Clay had to be hurt, or he wouldn't have left the gun there. On closer inspection he saw the bloodstains on the ground. He knew that if Clay were in his right mind he would head off the mountain for help. He would have to be somewhere between here and town. Milt started out at a trot, checking both sides of the path carefully. The huge, heavy pistol swung forgotten in his hand.

As he came to the uprooted tree that had fallen over the path he caught a glimpse of movement on the path ahead. Thinking it was Clay, he hurried around the dirt-filled roots and stumbled to a stop. It was his Uncle Harry. His scarred face was pressing against the walnut stock of his shotgun. He was pointing it at something beyond Milt's vision. Without thought, Milt whipped up the pistol and fired. The thunder of the big gun shook the woods, and a limb two feet above Harry's head was ripped loose from the parent tree.

Milt began running towards Harry, screaming and firing wildly. The sudden onslaught so unnerved Harry that he dropped the shotgun and fled in a panic. Milt stopped firing when the pistol clicked on empty. He grabbed Harry's shotgun and fired it at him in blind fury. Such was his rage that it gave him little pleasure to hear Harry squeal as the pellets penetrated his skin.

Milt found Clay leaning against a mushy, rotten log. He had regained consciousness and had tried to move, but was unable to do so. Harry must have noticed him as he was going to the top to check on what had happened to Ezra.

Clay smiled weakly as he whispered, "Boy, I sure am going to have to teach you to shoot."

"I ain' much with th' pistol, but I shore busted 'is ass with th' shotgun."

"You did alright, Boy. If you hadn't shown up when you did, that lead would have been in me by now."

"How bad are ya?" Milt asked.

"I don't think there's any permanent damage. I've just lost so much blood and I'm so weak I can't move."

"I'll help you."

Milt tried to lift Clay to his feet, but was unable to do so. The exertion knocked Clay out again. As the blood started spurting again, Milt took off his shirt, tore it in strips and bound Clay's wound as tightly as possible. He laid Clay down behind the log again, fished around inside his pockets, found some shells and reloaded the gun. Clay's breathing was labored. Milt would have to hurry if his father was to survive. For the first time he was thinking of Clay as his father.

Milt jerked off his boots and bolted down the hillside, running as only a barefoot mountain boy can. He was running for his life, as well as Clay's. He was running to save the life that he hoped to have here on this mountain. He went through the woods, taking all the shortcuts. The callouses on his bare feet gave up the fight to hold back the blood, and his feet became raw meat. The hanging limbs and grapevines clutched and beat at him, but he ran on.

People stopped on the street to stare at the blood-soaked, exhausted boy who stumbled doggedly on. He was at the point of total fatigue when he collapsed on the porch of the clinic.

Dr. Jody rushed outside and picked him up in her arms.

"Where have you been?"

"Clay's been shot!" he gasped. "I think he's dying."

"Where is he?"

She was the doctor now; she would be the woman later, but now there was no time for that.

"He's on th' sidea' th' hill behind th' cabin next to a big uprooted tree."

Jody grabbed her bag and told the nurse to call the sheriff and tell him to follow her. When she got to the jeep, Milt was already there.

People were standing in small groups now watching the activity. They knew that something was going on. When they saw the jeep heading up the road toward Rainbow Mountain, they speculated that Clay Barron was either badly hurt or dead. They were more convinced when shortly they saw a grim-faced sheriff speeding by in his jeep.

Harve phoned Larry Stein, who had returned to Cincinnati, to inform him that things were popping again.

"I know ya wouldn' wanna miss whut's comin' down," he said excitedly.

"I'm on my way," Larry answered quickly, and hung up.

When Jody reached Clay, he was still unconscious. The sheriff came huffing and puffing up the hill as Jody was finishing her preliminary examination.

Sternly she said to the sheriff, "He's got to be moved to the cabin where I can get hot water, and I'll have to have some supplies from my clinic."

The three of them began half-carrying, half-dragging Clay to the cabin. The pain brought Clay back to consciousness. He tried to speak, but was too weak, and collapsed again.

Once inside, the doctor worked frantically. She took a sample of his blood and sent it with the sheriff to be typed, and ordered plasma to be sent back. After she had done all she could do until the sheriff's return, she could only sit there and watch the man who had caused her so much frustration fight for his life. The odds were good if she got the blood back in time.

Walking the floor, she said to herself, "When this is over, a lot of people are going to catch hell. There is no reason for any place in this country to have to endure the primitive medical facilities that are here. It's no wonder so many people die from illnesses that are minor problems elsewhere. There's going to be a hospital built here if I have to embarrass every politician in the state to get it."

It was hours before the sheriff drove the jeep into the yard. He rushed inside with the cooler of blood.

"Sorry I took so long. I dun th' best I could. I had th' state police take th' blood sample ta th' university hospital in Lexington, an' they jist got back."

Dr. Jody resumed tending Clay. Now only time would tell. They took turns watching over him throughout the night.

The next morning Jody dozed off in the chair sitting beside his bed. Her head had slipped down beside him and when she awoke he was watching her. He smiled weakly. She tried unsuccessfully to hold back her tears. The doctor had done her job, and now Jody was a woman. She sobbed quietly as he gently stroked her hair.

That evening Larry Stein made his appearance at the cabin.

"Well, Clay," he said, "you seem to be a pretty lucky fellow. Lucky to have the son, doctor and friends you have."

"Yes, I am lucky to have all of them," Clay agreed.

"Clay, may I ask you a few questions about what took place up there on the mountain yesterday? They have taken Ezra to town, and I would like to get your story."

"He tried to kill me," Clay answered grimly, "and didn't. I killed him."

"That's enough talk for now," Jody said as she entered the room. "I want you to rest."

"Are you going to post a guard on him, Sheriff?" Larry asked.

"No, I'm gonna stay with 'im maself."

"I'll be here, too," Milt broke in. "Ennybody comes 'round here iz gonna git 'iz ass shot off."

"Milt, I told you to stop using that kind of language," Jody said firmly.

"Yea—I fergot," he shot back.

Larry wrote this unexpected chapter on Ezra in his continuing coverage of the war in the county and phoned it in to his editor.

He had no way of knowing that his story would rapidly bring the last of the Hook wolf pack. They would come like snarling wolves after a crippled animal. No mercy would be given. They would kill with no thought of honor. To the Hooks, the end always justified the means.

Chapter Twenty-Eight

Moe Carrio entered the room and took his seat at the head of the table, as he had done for some thirty-five years.

He was a swarthy, squat, powerfully built man. His massive, hairy arms and hands drew people's attention. He was a man of tremendous physical strength. His face showed the scars of his early years. His grey hair was thick and curly. His hooded eyes concealed his quick mind.

Although he never married, he usually had a favorite mistress that he kept at different hotels around town. He always had access to the most beautiful hookers, and used them as needed.

Once he had been heard to say that the only difference between a good woman and a hangman's noose was that the noose strangled one faster. His obsession had been the pursuit of money. Single-mindedly he had put his fortune together. Like the pieces of a puzzle known only to himself, he had taken his money from the rackets and invested in legitimate businesses all over the world.

He realized that it was time for him to step aside. The young bulls were getting restless. Had Boots had the desire to succeed him, he would have continued, but without him there was no incentive. Boots had gone to war, and Moe was eager to join him.

"Good evening, gentlemen," he greeted the hard-eyed men at the table. He knew they were on pins and needles. Rumors had been flying around town ever since Boots had disappeared. They knew they had been called here tonight for something important. Each man was concerned about how it would affect him.

"Cracker" Jones came in and poured coffee or hot tea for each man, set pots around the table and then departed. There would be no alcohol served until the meeting was over.

Moe began to speak. "As I look around this table tonight I see men who I have known since you were children. I have known most of your fathers and some of your grandfathers. You have made my life full and worthwhile. Tonight I have brought you together to reward you for your affection and loyalty. Tonight I am retiring."

He held up his hand and the murmuring ceased.

"For some time I know you have been concerned that I planned to bring Boots into the business above you. My friends, Boots has his own priorities and you shall have it all. I've worked everything out with my attorneys. You're about 75 percent legal now. I'm not going to tell you how to run your business, but my advice is to keep getting as legal as possible. The man with the gold badge is coming, and don't ever forget it."

"The old days are coming to an end. Educate your children and fade into the populace. I have survived by keeping a low profile. All the big-time operators and high-profile dummies are either in jail or dead."

"Tonight I will leave the city for good. Boots has gone to Kentucky, and I will be joining him. I know there has been a lot of speculation about what's going on, so I am going to share a story with you so you will understand."

"During the first World War, I was in France and got all shot to hell. I was lying out in the woods alone, surrounded by Germans, and I was dying. This big strong hillbilly came along and carried me on his back until we reached our lines. I couldn't even guess how many Germans he killed along the way. I lived, and he was awarded the French De Guerre in addition to his U.S. medals. Friends, that man was the famous Kentucky feudist, Devil John Barron."

Moe laughed out loud.

"Yes, he was a devil with a gun, but was also a very good friend. He visited me often in the hospital. Before I came home, I gave him my vow of friendship for him and his family forever. Boots is Devil John's grandson. His real name is Clay Barron."

The room began to buzz; everyone began talking at once. Moe held up his hand.

"Yes, the man in the news is Boots. He's gone to war with his family's enemies. I asked him to let us go down and take out the whole damn bunch, but he wouldn't hear of it. He wants the blood personal. However, if they kill him, I will finish this thing," Moe continued. "Boots came to me after his father had been killed and I took him in. He has become a son to me. I'm going to Kentucky to watch over my son."

After an extended period of questions and answers, Moe arose and went to the door and summoned his secretary, Nora Fletcher; his cook and housekeeper, Dino Garamenoi; and his driver, "Cracker" Jones.

"Friends, I want you to witness these gifts. I want you to always remember these three. If they ever need help, be there for them. They are to be given all your respect."

"Nora, for over thirty years you have worked with me shoulder-to-shoulder. The ten-unit apartment house on Martin Street is yours. Dino, all the men in this room have been pleasured by your cooking for years, and I don't want to deprive them of your services now. You are the new owner of The Italian Spoon restaurant on Broadway. Cracker, you are now the owner of the Town and Country Limousine Service. The people in this room have lots of weddings, lots of babies baptized, lots of confirmations and a few funerals. I'm sure you will all be successful."

All three employees were overcome at Moe's generosity. He hugged them affectionately. Dino and Cracker brought in the food and wine, served everyone quickly and left. Moe was going to miss the camaraderie he shared with his friends, but the string was cut, and he was anxious to start his new life. After the wine, cigars, hugs and tears, they parted for the last time.

After the last man had departed, Moe sat at the table alone with his wine and cigar. He was remembering his life and how it had led to this night. He thought back to his poor beginnings, the Army, Devil John Barron, his business and then Clay.

He recalled the first time he had seen Clay in the waiting room of his office. He sat there looking dirty and hungry, but with defiant black eyes and squared shoulders.

Nora spoke to Moe as she pointed to Clay. "This young man has been waiting all day to talk with you."

Moe had been in a bad humor all day.

"Get in here, kid, and make it quick."

Clay got to his feet and Moe saw that he was wearing hobnail boots.

"You always tear up people's carpet?" Moe grumbled as he closed the door behind them and took his seat behind the desk.

"No," was the answer, without explanation.

The boy stood in front of Moe's desk, opened his fist and dropped the French De Guerre medal in front of him. Moe picked it up and studied it intently.

"This is supposed to mean something to me?" he questioned.

"Ma Granddaddy said it would," he answered quietly.

Looking at him closely Moe asked, "Who is your granddaddy?"

Proudly the boy said, "Devil John Barron of Kentucky. Granddaddy said if I wuz ever in trouble an' had no fam'ly ta turn to, I wuz ta come ta you an' show ya this medal and you would he'p me."

"What kind of trouble you in, Son?" Moe's face was unreadable.

"Shot a man in Kentucky," the boy answered, matter-of-factly.

"Kill him?" Moe asked.

"No, but I will nex' time," he stated with total conviction.

"Where is the rest of your family?" Moe questioned.

"All dead but ma great-aunt and uncle, an' th' law iz watchin' them."

"What's your name, Boy?" Moe questioned, not unkindly.

"Blue Clay Barron. I go by Clay," he answered.

Moe stood up and stared straight into Clay's eyes as he spoke. "John Barron's blood is my blood; his family is my family; your fight is my fight. You are welcome here. I will have my driver take you to my house while I figure out some things."

In the ensuing years Clay had been taken care of by the big, black, ex-pugilist Cracker Jones. He had been responsible for giving Clay the Boots nickname.

Moe solved Clay's identity problem by having legal papers forged to identify him as Clay Carrio. He hired private tutors to prevent Clay from having to attend public school.

As the years passed, Clay spent all his time with adults and was quite advanced for his age. He became Moe's right hand. As he went around the city doing business in Moe's name, Cracker was there to back him up. It was Cracker who spent long hours in the gym teaching him the art of self-defense. Clay would go to the shooting range several times a week to practice with his guns.

As Clay matured, Moe sensed that he was eager to return to his home.

Finally the word came from Moe's lawyers that they had been successful in getting the charges against Clay in Kentucky dismissed. Without ceremony, Moe gave him this news.

"Now by God! Now I can go back. Thank you! Thank you!"

It was the first time he had ever said "Thank You" to Moe. No words of affection had ever passed between them, but it was there for all to see.

Only once had Moe witnessed in Boots the killing side of the Barrons. A cocky young hood name Von Maglie had challenged Moe's authority in front of a group of his subordinates. In the dead silence that followed, the only sound in the room was the click of a cocking gun.

His face scarlet with fury, Boots stalked toward Maglie. He jammed the barrel of the pistol between the terrified man's eyes. Moe's big hand pushed the barrel of the gun aside.

"No, Boots, he has the right to his opinion."

Boots glared at Maglie saying, "If it weren't for Moe Carrio, you would be eating crow somewhere instead of the pheasant you are used to."

Maglie apologized, "I was out of line. It won't happen again."

Moe patted him on the shoulder saying, "No harm."

He had learned long ago to give a man a way out. He knew there wasn't a man in the room who would challenge him again.

Moe finished his wine and put out his cigar. He walked out of the house, got into the new station wagon and drove away without looking back.

As he passed through the city, he determined it would be forever. He had put together a fortune here that he estimated at ten million. The public thought he was a crude, uneducated gangster. It had been to his advantage to cultivate that image. Now he could abandon this role forever.

The wagon turned south on the interstate. His new life in Kentucky was at the end of the road.

Chapter Twenty-Nine

Silas Hook sat brooding on the edge of the rumpled bed in Lige Begley's cabin. In spite of all his careful planning and scheming, things hadn't gone as he had planned. All he had to show for his finagling were two dead sons, three dead cousins, a ruined business and disrespect from everyone he knew.

Clay Barron hadn't been blown up in the car as he had hoped. He hadn't reacted like Silas thought he would. Silas had laid an ambush for Clay, but he hadn't come charging out of the hills and into their guns as he had anticipated. He had waited until after the funeral, then gone like a thief in the night, killed and faded away.

Silas and the two boys had to go to talk to the man about not being able to deliver his whiskey for a while. He had told Isom to stay in the house and not go outside. Isom hadn't listened and he had died.

Not wanted to take a chance at being picked off one at a time, he had taken Jubal and Everett and gone to Lige's until he could decide what to do.

Ezra Fultz had come to Lige's to buy whiskey, and Silas had gotten him drunk and filled his mind with hate for Clay. Before he left, Silas had convinced him that Clay had his wife hid somewhere just to make a fool of him.

"Whut wuz th' idea of all that crap ya was feedin' thet big stupe?" Jubal asked.

"Oh, it didn' cost nothin' but a little booze an' a few worthless words. Nivver kin tell whut ya will reap 'less ya plant a few seeds now an' then. Remember thet, Boy."

Jubal laughed.

"Whut's so funny?" Silas asked.

"He ain' gonna do it. He ain' got th' guts. He's jist like us. He don' have th' guts ta go up thar on thet mountain an' kill thet son-of-a-bitch any mor'n we do," Jubal said.

His words cut Silas to the quick. Something had to be done, but he just couldn't face the thought of doing anything until he had the odds stacked in his favor. He told himself that this was only being smart, but the knot in his guts made him wonder if being smart was a reason or an excuse. At least Clay had done one thing for him.

He had forced him into close and constant contact with Ruby, and now he knew that he wouldn't worry anymore about whether she stayed with him. He had become disenchanted with her shortly after arriving here. She was a pig about herself and the house. The thing that really was getting on his nerves was her whining, child-like voice. When he had first met her he had been excited by it, but now she only irritated him more each passing day.

Since moving in, he had made Lige and the boys sleep in the barn so that he could have privacy. They didn't like it, especially Lige.

"Thar's somethin' botherin' 'im," Silas thought, but he didn't have time to worry about some drunk's troubles. He had problems of his own.

Ruby had gone the half mile down the road to the general store and post office to get the mail. Silas had been careful not to let them buy any more groceries than they normally did. He had been sending Jubal to out-of-the-way places at night to buy food. He had to have his newspaper, so every day Ruby had to go get it for him. It came by mail and was a day old.

She came in now and handed it to him. He opened it and read Larry Stein's account of Ezra's trying to kill Clay. Clay's being wounded made this a whole new ballgame.

"I'll be goddamned," he muttered.

"Whut did ya say?" Ruby asked.

"Nothin'," he answered. "Nothin' 'tall."

Ruby couldn't read, so none of the others knew about this latest development yet. He put the paper in the stove, burned it, then called to the men outside.

"Hey, evverbody, come in here a minute."

They obeyed his command, sweating and swatting flies on their way in.

"Set down! Set down!" Silas said, in high spirits.

"Wal, boys, let's have a drink."

He picked the jug off the table and passed it around, noticing that Lige drank unusually long from it. Today, he didn't care; let him drink.

"Whut's th' occasion?" Jubal asked suspiciously.

"Th' occasion iz thet taday we're gonna kill Clay Barron, thet's whut."

"How ya plan on doin' thet?"

"We're goin' up thar on thet mountain an' blow 'is head off like we shoulda did th' first day he wuz home."

"Yeah, we'll run righ' up thar an' do thet," Jubal said sarcastically.

Lige sat on the lumpy, filth-encrusted couch scratching the bottoms of his equally filthy feet. The pig-like eyes in his whiskey-bloated face never left Silas'. They were unfathomable.

As usual, Everett said nothing.

Silas ignored Jubal's sarcasm and said, "Okay, ya all had yer drink. Now, boys, I wan' ya ta go check out th' Olds an' make shore she's ready ta roll. An' Lige, you jist get th' hell out of here an' get lost somewhere. This ol' boar hog wants ta git a little. Nothin' like a few drinksa whiskey an' a romp in th' hay on a hot day ta git a man in shape fer a good fight. Settles th' nerves, I allers heard."

He pulled Ruby down on his lap and was squeezing her breasts as they filed out of the room. When he reached the door, Lige looked back, but Silas was paying him no heed. He shuffled on toward the barn, digging his toes into the sandy yard with anger and jealousy.

Silas was roughly fondling Ruby now as he thought, "This one las' time I'll take th' heat from her plump young rump, and then I don' care if I nivver see her again."

Ruby was struggling to get off his lap, her lower lip protruding in a pout.

"I ain' doin' it! Hit's too hot!"

"Don' give me no lip," Silas said irritably. "Git in th' bed."

"No, I ain' gonna. I tol ya hit's too hot an' I ain' gittin' all messed up this early in th' day."

Silas shoved her off his lap and towered over her. "Git in th' bed now."

"No!"

His hand cracked across her face, upending her into the bed. She screamed in pain. He walked to the front door and as he closed it he could see Lige standing in the doorway of the barn. Ruby was out of the bed again as he turned. He grabbed her by the front of her dress and ripped it off and cast it aside. As he started to remove his clothes she made a break for the door. He grabbed her and ignoring her struggles, removed his clothes with one hand. It was clumsy, but he was becoming very excited by her resistance. As he slung her once again onto the bed and leaped in behind her, she jumped out the other side. Like a rooster chasing after a hen, he ran her around the room until he caught her. Once more he slung her onto the bed, this time not letting her loose.

Her obstinant stubborness was driving him mad. However, it saved his life. As she was thrashing around he turned his face toward the door just as it was opening, and Lige came through. He was holding high a long, machete-like corn knife. Like a naked scorpion, Silas scrambled off the bed, trying to escape the slashing knife.

"Kill 'im, Paw!" Ruby screamed. "Cut 'is goddamn head off."

Round the room he went, slinging the table and then upsetting a chair in front of Lige. Finally he made it to the couch and grabbed the gun he had hid under the end cushion. Lige was almost on him when Silas whirled and shot him in the chest. The bullet drove him back over the upset table and left him hanging, arms and legs spread like a giant turkey buzzard on the upturned rockers of the chair. Silas shot him again.

His body shook from the impact of the slug, but still hung where he was, with blood pouring out of his open mouth. Ruby screamed again, not in anger this time, but in sheer terror—and with good reason.

Silas, in his rage, had grabbed up the corn knife and was now going after her. She leaped off the bed and headed toward the door. He sprang forward before she could reach out, and slashed down with the knife. She was laid open from the point of her shoulder down and across her hanging breast.

She shrieked in terror as he continued to hack at her. Each flash of the bloody blade brought another blood-curdling scream. Finally the blade drove her to the floor. He raised the knife a final time and then there were no more screams—only complete silence.

That was how Jubal and Everett found him; standing there with the bloody corn knife in his hand, his naked body covered with the splattered blood of the gory creature that had once been a woman.

"Whut th' hell's goin' on here?" Jubal screeched as he burst through the door.

"Jist a couplea' people gettin' th' final lesson on whut th' penalty is ta cross Silas Hook," he gritted.

Silas threw the corn knife onto the floor, walked over and poured a bucket of water over his head. As the water ran down over his nude body, he pulled the dirty sheet off the bed and wiped the blood off himself.

"Everett," he said as he was getting dressed, "look in the wall over there behind Lige an' in th' floor beneath 'im ta see if'n ya kin find th' two slugs. They shoulda gone through 'im. Dig 'em out—I want 'em."

"Jubal, take th' corn knife, wipe it off good—an' I mean good—an' put it back in th' barn. Gather up all th' bedclothes or anything else ya might have used in th' barn and bring 'em back in here."

After getting dressed he took the lamp and dumped the kerosene it contained all around the room, as well as over the dead couple. Jubal came back inside and dumped the bedclothes on the floor as Everett handed Silas the flattened hunks of lead he had dug out of the wall and floor.

"Jubal, git th' car an' bring it 'round front. Everett, you foller 'im an' make shore thar ain' no tire prints left whar we bin parkin' it."

In a short time they returned.

"Thar' ain' nothin' left," Everett reported. "Th' ground thar is covered with so many pine needles thar's no tracks atall."

"Good."

Silas turned back to the room, lit a kitchen match and tossed it down onto the bed. He displayed no regret or remorse as he walked to the Olds. There was renewed respect on the faces of his sons as he sat in the back seat alone. It gave him a feeling of power and importance to ride in this position.

He was the leader. He was the herd bull again. He'd gotten off track for a while, but he guessed that every strong man messed things up once in a while. The main thing was to overcome whatever the problem is. Today he would overcome Clay Barron, and tomorrow he would begin to overcome anyone else who crossed him. He wasn't so old. Maybe he had settled for too little. There probably wasn't any reason he couldn't take over two or three counties. He might just kill The Man and take over his action, too. Then he could live in Memphis.

"Bet thar's a lot of hot little fat-assed gals in Memphis, if'n a man's got th' money ta buy 'em purties."

The thought of his knowing that Clay had already been seriously wounded and was perhaps helpless right now never occurred to Silas as the reason for his newfound courage. He enjoyed having his sons' confidence in him again. He knew now that if he showed no fear they would follow him anywhere.

"Men are just like animals," he thought. "They can smell fear or take courage from a leader. Wal, frum now on ol' Silas is goin' ta smell strong as hell."

But first things first—Clay Barron. None of these other things would be possible as long as he lived.

Belle was standing on the front porch when the Olds pulled in. She made no comment to them about their weeks of absence. They ignored her as they went about arming themselves with extra pistols and a high-powered rifle.

"Git a shotgun, too, Everett, and some .00 buckshot," Silas ordered as he stuffed .45 slugs in his pocket.

How many times had she seen the Hooks repeat this as they went out to fight the Barrons? Sometimes they came home laughing and bragging, and other times they came back shaking with fear, carrying their dead and wounded.

She wondered what had happened to give Silas the courage to go after Clay. He was strutting along in front of Jubal and Everett as they crossed the road and the footlog over the river.

"Well, jist strut on, you low-life, son-of-a-bitch," she snarled as she took down the old rusty pistol and loaded it. She then slipped it into her apron and headed for the barn.

She took the hoe and scraped the manure from off the moneybox and removed it. She got a piece of baling wire and fastened one end to the box. Carrying it to the river, she lowered it into the water under the bridge. She fastened the other end to one of the steel cables.

"I'll leave 'is money in th' river with ma cat. If'n I ain' around ta spend it maself, I don' wan 'im ta have it."

This done, she returned to the front porch and ran the hound dog off the chair to sit down and wait. The old pistol covered by her apron in her lap reassured her.

One way or another, she was going to get out of the kind of life she had lived. If Clay Barron killed Silas, she would probably mourn him and then get the money out of the creek and go on a buying spree that would make up for thirty-five years of doing without.

If Clay failed, she would kill Silas herself when he returned. She leaned back with pictures of Speed Queens, Frigidaires, electric lights and new curtains running through her mind.

Chapter Thirty

It was the morning of the second day before Clay came fully awake. After the blood transfusion and sleep he was feeling much stronger. The cabin was an active place. Dr. Jody hovered over him. Her affection was unmasked for the others to see. Milt was constantly on the move from room to room, from window to window. They would not be surprised. When he was alone he would point the big long-barreled .45 at imaginary targets outside. This mountain boy would shoot on sight. He kept his vigil until late in the afternoon.

The sheriff came in and stood looking at Clay.

"They'll be acomin' soon," he stated. They're bound ta know by now thet you have been hurt. I'm agonna stay here with ya. I'm agonna sen' th' doctor and Milt back ta town an' I'm sendin' ma badge an' letter of resignation with 'er. We will fight 'em together."

Clay was pulling on his pants and boots as he answered, "Uncle Billy, you are my true friend and I love you, but this is something I don't want to share with anyone. This I have to do alone. My guts have been in a knot for almost half my life, and here and now I'm going to finish it. I'll be ready when they get here."

"OK, Clay, if'n thet's whut ya want, I'll tell th' others an' we'll start back afore dark so's you kin git prepared."

Milt put up a howl, but Clay stilled him by saying, "I got my father killed trying to protect me. I don't want to worry about anyone but myself."

Milt was vainly trying to still his trembling chin as Clay continued, "If I fail, they belong to you."

Clay put his arm around Milt, turned to Dr. Jody and said, "I want you to put a bandage on me that is tight enough to stop the bleeding for a few hours. I also want something strong for the pain, but nothing that will dull my mind."

As Dr. Jody bandaged his upper body, she was beginning to understand what it was about these people that made them the way they

211

were. She cared for this man, and his enemies were beginning to become her enemies. She had never had a violent thought towards any human being before. She was angry now.

She finished, stepped back and said, "Kill them; get it over with."

She stepped forward, stood on tip-toe and kissed him quickly on the lips. She gathered up her things and after giving him a long, loving look, left the house and went to the jeep. The sheriff shook Clay's hand saying, "Don' underestimate 'em. They's all tough an' clever. They'll not give ya a chance in hell, so if'n ya git a chance at 'em, don' hesitate; shoot 'em down."

Milt was the last to go. His chin was quivering again as he said huskily, "I'm glad yer ma father."

He turned on his heel and walked away.

As some of the most important people in his life drove away, he stood for a long moment looking after them. He shook his mind free and let it return to the business at hand. They could be on their way here now. The adrenaline began to flow as he checked his guns. Both were forty-fives. He dropped a handful of bullets into his pocket. He spun the cylinder of the snub nose and put it into his back pocket. He put Devil John's gun in his belt. The bandages made it impossible to wear the gun harness.

The final chapter was about to begin. His mind was locking in on Silas Hook—the image was again searing his mind. The killing fever was beginning to rise.

"Satan, this harvest is for you," he mumbled as he prepared to leave the house. Wanting the Hooks to think he was still in the house, he lit the lamp and pulled the blinds.

He slipped outside into the gathering dusk, crossed the footbridge over the swollen stream and hurried to the barn. As he entered the barn he could hear scattered raindrops on the metal roof. He picked up a pitchfork and set it beside the door. A silent weapon could come in handy. As time passed, a major storm developed. He waited patiently.

So much time had passed since his world had been turned upside down. Such wasted years—both his father's and his. He was here to collect the ultimate price for those years of pain. He watched the house as total darkness fell.

There—he saw a shadow come between the lamp and the blind. They were here; they were in the house. As the lightning flashed, he caught a glimpse of someone on the front porch. The next flash showed a man sneaking across the footbridge on his way to the barn. Clay ran his hand along the wall until his hand closed around the pitchfork. With both hands he raised it above this head and waited there in the dark. He had to kill the first one quickly to cut down the odds.

Clay waited with bated breath as the figure bolted through the door and stepped to the side toward him. After several moments he flicked his lighter and held it out in front of him. That second of blindness cost Everett Hook his life. With all his strength, Clay drove the pitchfork into the back of his neck.

Everett dropped his gun, grabbed the tines of the fork with both hands, but failed to pull the pitchfork out. With a piercing cry he ran from the barn as the fork handle waved like a dog's tail behind him. His heart was pumping the life out of him, as the blood gushed through his fingers.

The end came for Everett Hook when he reached the footbridge. He collapsed and died there. His blood was running off the bridge into the stream that flowed into the Little Sandy River. Clay's promise to the river had been kept.

From the front door of the house Silas yelled, "Enny signs in th' barn, Everett?"

All he got was silence. His voice was rising as he called several more times.

"Jubal!" he roared. "Th' bastard musta got Everett in th' barn."

From the woodshed Jubal called back, "Set fire ta th' house so's we kin have sum light."

Silas ran back inside and threw the lamp onto the floor. The flames shot up instantly. With the snub-nosed .45 Clay shot at Silas' silhouette and took pleasure from the yelp it brought. As Silas ran from the house, Clay shot at his shadowy figure twice more, with no apparent success.

Inside the woodshed Jubal told Silas his plan. He was going to circle around the barn and go in from the rear. Silas was to cover the front door.

He said to Silas, "Give me five minutes, then empty th' rifle inta th' barn and then stop shootin'. Thet should give me time ta git inside while 'e's still thinkin' 'bout dodgin' bullets."

Jubal wanted to be the one to kill Clay Barron. He didn't want Silas to get the credit. He was never going to play second fiddle again. Jubal was the bravest of all the Hooks, and he had been chafing at the bit all summer.

With a gun in each hand he said to Silas, "Le's kill 'im!"

After the five minute wait, Silas opened fire on the barn, and the splinters flew like confetti. Clay had nothing to fear, because he had left the barn and was now in the total darkness of the rear barnyard. He preferred to fight out in the open. He was hunkered down behind a large water tank, with his back against the fence. If anyone came at him from the back, he could feel it when they crossed the fence. He could see the light from the burning house through the cracks of the barn. He would see their shadows if they came at him from the front.

Clay was having a bad time. The rain was giving him chills and his shoulder was beginning to bleed again. He forgot his pain as he felt the fence against his arm move ever so slightly. Someone was crossing very cautiously. Clay cocked his gun.

When the lightning flashed again, Clay could see Jubal straddling the fence. He had one of his guns holding down the wire, and the other extended in front of him.

Jubal saw Clay at the same time. Clay dove behind the corner of the tank as the bullets from Jubal's gun ricocheted off the rocks. A sliver of rock cut Clay's cheek to the bone. He emptied the snub-nose in the direction of Jubal, and heard a loud grunt as one of the bullets hit flesh.

At the next flash of lightning he could see Jubal hanging upside down in the fence. The force of Clay's slug had knocked him off his feet. However, Jubal wasn't finished. He was firing with both guns, and the bullets whizzed and pinged off the tank.

Clay pulled out the long-barreled .45 and started shooting at the flashes of Jubal's guns. Five times the big gun roared. When lightning struck again, Clay could see Jubal still struggling in the fence. He lay the big gun on top of the water tank and quickly reloaded the snub-nose. He hadn't counted Jubal's shots, so he waited for the next lightning flash. It came and he was ready. He shot Jubal to pieces in the fence.

He ran forward and waited for another bolt, and when it came he pumped another slug into Jubal's heart. He had to make sure. Devil John's rule.

Hanging upside down in a barbed wire fence, Jubal Hook's visions of grandeur had ended.

From the darkness across the stream came Silas' plaintive voice. "Jubal, you alright?"

There was no answer.

Clay's physical condition was rapidly deteriorating. His shoulder and face were bleeding, and he was chilled to the bone. As he reentered the barn he knew he didn't have much time. He was becoming somewhat delirious as he reloaded his guns. Chuckling insanely he removed his shirt and spread it out on the barn floor. He then proceeded to scrape horse manure on to it. Holding the sleeves and tail, he now had a sack of horse manure.

"Jubal," Silas' voice probed through the rain hopefully, "are ya' alright?"

It was here now; the long-awaited moment. Clay licked his bloody lips. Forgotten were his aching wounds. The shivering ceased.

"Barron, ya still 'live?" Silas voice was flat and emotionless.

"I'm still alive."

"Jubal's dead, I rekkin." Silas' voice sounded as if he already knew the answer.

"Yes, he's dead," Clay answered. "Everyone's dead except you and me."

There was no fear in Silas Hook now. He had manipulated everyone, as was his way, and now they were all dead. Now he would fight. He experienced a strange kinship with the man in the barn he was going to try to kill. Of course this changed nothing, and he hated Clay none the less. He would fight like the cagey fox he considered himself to be. He would have to move swiftly. The burning house could be seen for miles, and would soon bring people. He knew Clay had to be in bad shape.

To cut down his own risk, he had to get Clay out of the barn into the firelight.

Forcing a harsh laugh, Silas shouted to Clay. "Wish yer chicken-hearted daddy wuz here ta see me peel th' hide offn' yer ass. 'Course, 'e ain' gonna make it. He's up thar on thet hill rottin' in 'is grave whar I put 'im. 'Member how he held 'is hand out to ya an' ya didn' do nothin'?"

From the barn there came a wail of anguish and rage. The wily old fox had opened bare the festering sore of Clay's soul. A crack of lightning and a loud clap of thunder drowned out the second cry. Clay went through the open barn door at a dead run. In his left hand was the shirt filled with horse manure, and in his right the snub-nosed Colt.

A gun cracked from the shadows across the stream. Clay was knocked off his feet and went sliding down into the water. He had taken a bullet in the left rib cage. The natural thing for him to have done would be to go downstream toward the darkness and away from the light of the burning house. Instead, he fought his way upstream to the footbridge. He ducked under the bridge and grabbed onto the log on the upper side.

Clay could feel the warm blood running down his stomach from his new wound. His spinning mind told him that his time was running out. He had to take Silas now, or he wouldn't have the strength to do it. From behind the footbridge he peered over the top of Everett's body.

Trying to conceal himself, Silas was at the corner of the woodshed trying to peek down into the water to see if Clay's body was there.

Clay rested his gun on Everett's body and shot Silas, who was bowled over backwards. Like a wounded bear he struggled to his feet. Seeing Clay behind Everett's body, he charged him, firing his gun furiously. The bullets were severing his dead son's body, but left Clay unscathed.

Silas threw down his now-empty gun. Clay's gun roared again and Silas went down on his back, skidding in the muddy yard. He rolled over and started crawling toward the burning house. He had a concealed second gun, but he had to lead Clay to the light before he could make use of it.

Leaving the snub-nosed gun on the bridge, Clay pulled out Devil John's .45, dragged himself out of the water and crawled up into the yard. Silas pulled his second gun and fired. The slugs were tearing up the mud, seeking Clay. Rolling, Clay took a hit in the thigh. Blood soaked and nearly incoherent, he turned over and turned the big gun loose.

Silas tried repeatedly to raise his gun as Clay crawled through the mud, firing at him. The rain was coming down in torrents and the lightning and thunder added to the eeriness of the dancing flames and the crackling of the burning wood.

Clay continued to creep laboriously toward him, shooting as he came. The big gun clicked on empty. Silas' mind was still functioning, but it had no control over his expiring body.

Clay continued on doggedly, trailing the manure-filled shirt behind him. As Clay straddled Silas' dying body, the burning house collapsed, showering sparks and debris on the pair.

Held up only by seething hate, Clay opened the shirt, grabbed Silas by the hair and held the horse manure above his face.

"Horse shit, Silas," he choked into the dying man's face.

"Look at it, " he commanded.

"My father died for horse shit. Your sons died for horse shit. You're going to die for horse shit."

He shoved the manure into Silas' greying face, slammed the pistol repeatedly into his skull until it was a mass of bloody bone and brains. The last descendant of the founders of Hookville slipped away with no one left to mourn him.

Clay leaned back and raised his face to the sky. The light from the fire was pregnant with heat. He hoisted Devil John's gun above his head and chortled incoherently.

"Hey, Barron!"

Clay tried to focus on the man moving toward him. He seemed to be stepping out of the fire. Before him was the frightful countenance of Harry Balls. Clay brought the gun down and pulled the trigger.

Click. The gun was empty. In his rage, he had ignored Devil John's rule.

Harry sneered contemptuously. "Yer gun's empty. I counted them shots. How duz it feel, purty boy—you with all th' wimmen an' money. How duz it feel ta know yer gonna git yers from ol' scar-faced Harry? You an' th' goddamn Hooks lordin' it over evverybody. It ends here an' now fer th' whole passel a' you bastards."

Harry raised his gun.

Chapter Thirty-One

Clyde Vansant was not surprised when Valarie and her mother returned early from Europe. He knew his daughter. She had needed time to cool down. He trusted her to make the right decisions concerning her life. One way or the other, it was going to be very interesting.

On her return, Valarie wasted no time going to see the sheriff, who filled her in on the latest happenings. She asked him to take her to see Clay. He looked uncomfortable and avoided her eyes.

"I really don' know whar he is."

"Uncle Billy, I've known you too long for you to fool me. What is it you don't want me to know?"

With lowered eyes he said, "Valarie, it's Clay and the doctor. Thar's rumors thar's somethin' goin' on between 'em. Accordin' ta' June Brickey. . ."

He didn't get to finish. Her gasp raised his eyes. The stricken look on her face touched his heart. He didn't want to tell her, but he didn't want her to make a fool of herself. Without another word she turned and fled his office.

For two weeks she never left the house except to care for Bones. Her mind was in turmoil. Another woman. That was something she had never considered or been prepared for. What had happened to her? Now faced with competition, she sat in her room and pouted. She was not bothered by the women in Clay's life before he came back, but then she didn't know any of them. She vacillated between rage and jealousy. The picture of the luscious body of the doctor's in Clay's arms incensed her. She had no idea she was capable of such jealousy. She wanted to blame Clay, but she knew she was the one who had run out. As the days passed her frustrations mounted.

At dusk one evening her father came hurrying into the house and interrupted her thoughts.

"Valarie, I have to talk to you. Something has happened."

"He's dead!" she gasped.

"No, but he has been shot. I just talked to the sheriff. Ezra Fultz waylaid him and shot him up pretty badly. Clay killed Ezra."

"Where's Clay now?" she half whispered.

"He's at Big Pap's cabin. He ran off the doctor and the sheriff and said he didn't want anyone else there. It was in the paper today, so you can bet the Hooks have heard. The sheriff says everyone else is to stay out of it. It's come down to family."

"Can't you help him, Papa?" she asked plaintively.

"Valarie, you know I can't mix in this. Honey, it's family. Family has to settle it. That's how things are done here."

Valarie went slowly up the stairs to her room. Her father was powerless to help. She stood at her window looking up at Rainbow Mountain. How does a woman justify the stupidity of men? Are they born to fight—war and prey on each other? It's not just here in the mountains, but all over the world. Someone wants to be free. Someone wants to enslave someone. People professing to love the same God kill each other because of their different forms of worship. Men kill for greed and possessions. They kill in the name of love. They prey on each other's wives, then kill when they get caught.

Here in the mountains the men kill most often for revenge. A slight or an insult equals a dead man; then the family honor has to be taken care of at all cost back and forth over the years without end. The mothers, wives and children suffer the most.

Valarie remembered hearing a preacher once say that God had turned his face away from the Appalachian Mountains, and until the insanity stopped he would never smile on them again.

Valarie's eyes traveled down to the Sandy Valley.

"Damn you Hook bastards," she gritted. "You're not going to ruin my life. I'm going to stop this right now."

She whirled from the window, went to her closet and took out her riding clothes. Dressing quickly, she went quietly down the back stairs and left the house through the door that led to the barn.

She opened a stall door and gave a low whistle. She heard a nicker, and a shadowy figure came out of the darkness, snorting, dancing and flinging his head. With her emotions in tumult she still took time to love this magnificent animal. She put her arm around his neck and leaned her head against him as she led him out of the stall. In the artificial light of the barn he was the color of ink.

Valarie had first seen him cross-tied in a cattle truck parked in front of the bank. He was skin and bones, and his ribs and hips protruded. Drawing closer and peering through the slats of the truck she could see that he was covered with welts and blood. It was the great dark eyes that drew her to him. They flashed defiance and hatred. His mouth was snapping like an angry dog. He was physically wrecked and abused, but it was obvious that the spirit had not been broken. Even in his present condition she admired the chiseled, dished head, which was a sculptor's dream, and she knew she was going to own him.

A shabby-looking man had walked up behind her and said, "Don't get too close, Missy. He's a real rogue—a killer. Last man to own him tried to starve him and break him. I'm not going to waste my time on him. He's dog food."

Brutally he shoved a cattle prod through the slats and gave the horse a shock. The horse came up on his back legs as far as the rope would allow and fought viciously to be free. Valarie had grabbed the cattle shock from the man and cut him across the face with it. Hookville got a glimpse of her temper for the first time. She was whipping the man about the head and shoulders when her father grabbed her from behind, lifted her off the ground and held her until she calmed down.

Finally back on her feet she demanded of the man, "What do you want for that horse?"

The wily horse trader rubbed the welts that Valarie had bestowed on him, but they were soon forgotten as he concentrated on turning a profit.

"Thousand dollars," he said hopefully.

"That bag of bones isn't worth a thousand dollars," Clyde argued.

"He's registered," the trader countered.

"Pay him!" Valarie hissed.

Clyde was shocked. "Valarie, that horse isn't worth fifty dollars."

"I don't give a damn. I want him!" she spat out.

"Where are you going to put him? You don't even have a barn," Clyde said in exasperation.

"I want him tied between the two hickory trees in the back yard, and I don't want him hurt anymore," she answered as she stalked away, her high heels clicking furiously on the sidewalk.

The crowd of onlookers made no effort to conceal their glee as their conservative banker shelled out a thousand dollars for a horse that they would not have taken as a gift.

As the trader put Clyde's check in his big trucker's wallet Clyde muttered to the crowd, "He's registered. I'll need some help to get him unloaded."

With the horse tied between the two trees, Valarie began the month-long chore of winning his trust. Without talking about it, Clyde brought in carpenters and built a small barn and corral behind his mansion. It was worth it to him to see Valarie so happy. The horse had become the focal point of her life. He had recommended that she have him gelded, but she refused to do so.

The horse was a purebred Arabian with an unpronounceable name, so she called him Bones. He responded to love, affection, carrots and sugar cubes. Eventually he allowed her to mount him. As his body filled out, his quality came through. Horsemen in the county vied with each other to let their mares run with him. Purebred mares were trucked in from as far as California to be bred to him.

Clyde loved to brag how much he was collecting in stud fees. It was important for the banker to know what he was doing at all times, or at least give the impression to the public that he knew. Bones had been a good investment. He would suffer Clyde to feed him, but no man could handle him.

Valarie's thoughts were mixed as she saddled up. She led Bones as quietly as possible past the house. He was eager to go. Once mounted she took the back way around town. She thrilled to the sound of his steel hooves on the Little Sandy Bridge. She took the gravel street that was the beginning of her ride to Rainbow Mountain.

She was having her hands full with him. He wanted to run. She could feel the power in the arched neck. As she talked softly to him, trying to calm him down, it began to rain. She reached the top of the street and looked back. She experienced a moment of doubt about going on. When she turned back toward the mountain she saw in the far distance a great yellow glow in the sky.

"Fire!" she cried aloud. "Oh, no! No!"

For the first time since she had owned him the stallion felt the sting of spurs. Shocked and surprised, he bolted forward.

"Go, Bones!" she cried as she bent forward over his neck, riding like a jockey.

The spurs raked his flanks again and instantly his stride lengthened. People sitting on their porches were getting up to stare as the horse thundered by. Valarie slowed him slightly as they made the turn off the gravel road onto the dirt road that went to the mountain. They left the street lights behind and were running now in near darkness.

The rain was coming down harder. As the lightning cracked, Bones responded with new effort. The road was becoming muddy and slick, but the racing stallion under her was sure footed and his speed never slackened. His long flowing mane was whipping her in the face. She lay closer to his neck. The fence posts were blurs, and the road flashed by beneath his flying feet. Her mood matched his savage running. She was drinking now from the cup of wildness.

Her man—her love was in danger—perhaps dead, but she gloried in this ride. This war horse of the desert was out of the past. He was running to the battle as his ancestors from the past had run. He would hold back nothing, but would run until he dropped. He had caught the excitement of the ride and responded with each powerful stride.

Steam began to rise from his body, and flecks of lather peppered Valarie's face. She could see the glow in the sky become even brighter now. She guided the horse off the public road and onto the private road. It now became nothing more than wagon tracks.

She put Bones between the tracks and his powerful back legs drove him up the steady grade. As the road leveled off and followed the side of the mountain he gained momentum. The driving wind was robbing her of her breath. Each tremendous stride was jarring her in the saddle. Air was beginning to scream through the stallion's extended nostrils. On and on he ran. He labored through the mud of Blue Bank and such was his speed as he made the curve at the twin beeches that he ran wide and his powerful back feet woke the ant colony as he tore their hill apart. At this speed a misstep or a stumble could be disastrous to both horse and rider.

As they pounded along the wooded trail, Valarie thought she heard the faint sound of gunfire. However, with all the thundering and lightning she could not be sure. The rain and wind had increased to a howling gale. She had given him his head, and so clung to the stallion's mane with every ounce of her strength. There it came again—the unmistakable sound of gunfire. She spurred Bones again, but got no response. He was giving her all he had. The gunfire was louder now.

As the plunging stallion came out of the darkness into the light of the fire, he was a fearsome sight; wild-eyed, mud-covered, nostrils screaming for air. He was a war horse in all his powerful, violent glory.

Harry Balls was so engrossed on his intention to kill Clay that he didn't see the horse until he was halfway across the yard. Clay's spinning senses reveled in the courage of the woman who was running the horse into the barrel of the gun. Valarie screamed as she spurred the muddy animal straight at him. Harry got off one shot before the horse hit him. Harry was knocked sprawling into the muddy yard. Valarie pulled with all her might as Bones slid to the edge of the stream. She spun him and screamed as she drove home the spurs.

Harry was scrambling across the yard like a crippled bird, trying to retrieve the gun he had lost from the impact. As he recovered the gun, Valarie came after him again. She lay on Bones' neck, shrieking and spurring him on towards the crawling figure.

Harry was on his knees, firing point-blank at the on-rushing horse. As the hated man tried to rise, Bones' steel hooves caught him in the chest, and he lay there stunned. Harry had no chance. Valarie was now spinning the insane horse in circles on top of him, until his broken body was driven into the mud by the slashing hooves.

Clay exalted in this wild woman. This was a woman to replace all other women. Here tonight in the muddy, blood-soaked yard he had seen his mirror image. Mesmerized, he watched her leap from the horse and run to him. He saw the stallion turn from Harry's mutilated body, stagger and fall to his knees. Bones tried valiantly to get up, but with a sigh he rolled over on his side. His body was heaving. Blood was gushing from the wounds in his chest. He began to cough and choke on his own blood. His powerful body collapsed, and he stretched out in the mud.

Valarie was on her knees beside Clay, crying hysterically.

"Don't worry about me," Clay whispered. "Help the horse."

Rushing back to Bones, Valarie knelt and picked up his head. He looked up at her with his big soft eyes, shuddered violently and stopped breathing. Bones had run his last race. The war horse was dead.

Valarie placed Bones' head gently on the ground and returned quickly to Clay. She rolled him into her lap with superhuman strength and sat rocking back and forth. She had nothing else to give.

This was the way they were found when the sheriff's jeep slid into the yard. The sheriff and Larry Stein carried Clay to the jeep and Valarie jumped in to hold him.

"I'll be back to get you and take care of this mess!" the sheriff shouted to the newspaperman as he spun the jeep out of the yard.

Larry Stein stayed behind until help came. Then, with flashlights and camera, he got his story. He wandered among the bodies, recording everything on film. He had never seen such carnage. Once he had told Clay that he would never be the equal of Devil John Barron, but he had been wrong. No Barron had ever killed with the cold-blooded ferociousness this one had.

Larry would write his book, but he still did not understand. What he did realize was that you had to be born to these people to feel what they feel. He would do his best.

It was the end of an era. The last mountain war was over.

The Devil had reaped his harvest.

Epilogue

The guns were silent now. Peace and tranquility had returned to the mountains and valleys. The dead had been buried, and the living resumed their lives.

Against all odds Clay had lived. Sensing that her future was not here in the hills with Clay, Dr. Jody hired her successor and returned to Philadelphia. She was now emotionally healed. She hid her disappointment concerning Clay, but looked forward with anticipation to resuming her previous lifestyle in the city.

Larry Stein completed his book, and its success was phenomenal. His account of the final family war had made him wealthy and had made Clay a folk hero. The autographed copy he sent to Clay contained the inscription, "To Clay Barron, the only man tough enough to walk in Devil John's shoes."

Belle Hook was barely recognizable. She made a trip to the beauty salon every Friday, purchased a set of new dentures and ordered hundreds of dollars worth of clothes from the Sears Roebuck catalogue. She took driving lessons and went to a Cadillac agency in Lexington. The slick salesman was flabbergasted when she pulled cash from a brown paper bag and paid the full amount for the sedan.

After having her house wired for electricity, she bought all new appliances and furniture. Her pride and joy was the elegant inside toilet. Her new tomcat, whom she named Silas, was the king of his domain.

No one in Hookville questioned her paying cash for all this. What they did wonder about was what transpired between her and Clay that Saturday afternoon when she stopped him on the street and whispered in his ear. Clay hugged her and whispered something back. She then kissed him on the cheek. What had passed between them stayed between them.

Moe Carrio moved to Hookville and caused quite a stir. When he made his initial deposit at Clyde Vansant's bank, he gained instant celebrity status. There are no secrets in small Kentucky communities.

When Clyde saw the size of his money transfer, he almost lost his composure. When Moe stated that this was only the first transfer, the banker could barely get his breath.

After acquiring the Huston's boarding house, he had it remodeled and moved into the lower level. He retained them to maintain it and prepare his meals. He loved to sit on his porch and chat with all his new friends.

Since Moe was the only Italian or Catholic in the county, Clay built a beautiful log chapel on the former site of Big Pap's house. Because there was no Catholic church in the vicinity, Clay wanted him to have his own private place to worship. Moe was overcome with emotion when Clay brought in a bishop to bless it.

Izetta Vansant was content to return to her mundane routine after touring Europe with Valarie. Clyde, however, felt like he was twenty-one years old again. He could barely wait to get up in the mornings. When Moe Carrio came to town, he filled a void in Clyde's life. He now had someone with whom he could talk big money and big deals.

He did not have to be concerned about Valarie any longer. He had given her and Clay the most elaborate wedding ever seen in the county. Everyone, rich or poor, was invited. They ate and drank and honored the family of the bride with their presence.

Milt Barron. How he loved the name. A name change wasn't all that happened to him. He went back to school and worked at the bank part time as a teller. He had the ear of the two richest men in the county. Clyde introduced him as his grandson, and treated him like one.

Milt had developed a deep affection for Moe, and would sit for hours listening to him talking about acquiring wealth. He read volumes on business and management. He knew Clay was disappointed that he did not spend more time with him up on the mountain, but there was just so much action here with Clyde and Moe. The two of them had bought a coal company and since he knew about coal, they let him in for ten percent. He was proud when they asked him for his advice.

Clay had worked himself back into good health. He bought a bull-dozer, backhoe and a dump truck and built his own gravel road up to Rainbow Mountain. He had a crew come in and cut and build a massive log house over the burned-out basement. He added a log barn and a split rail fence.

All the violence had left him, and he was now a laughing, joking, happy man. He was where he wanted to be—on his beloved mountain.

Valarie was completely happy. She had the man she loved. She had had a fairy tale wedding. Clay's kindness and tenderness had grown daily. His plans for the mountain excited her. She loved to take him by the hand and walk among her horses at sunset. She was so glad she had waited for him.

Bones had been buried where he fell. A large granite stone stood in front of Moe's chapel with the lettering that simply said Bones. Valarie and Clay never drove by that they didn't speak to him. His sacrifice had made all the rest of their lives possible.

It certainly seemed that God had once again turned his face to the mountains.